The Risk of Darkness

The Risk of Darkness

A Simon Serrailler Mystery

Susan Hill

THE OVERLOOK PRESS
New York

First published in hardcover in the United States in 2009 by
The Overlook Press, Peter Mayer Publishers, Inc.

NEW YORK:
141 Wooster Street
New York, NY 10012
.

Cataloging-in-Publication Data is available from the Library of Congress

Manufactured in the United States of America
ISBN-13 978-1-59020-290-6
1 3 5 7 9 8 6 4 2

To
The Never Forgotten Ones

Acknowledgements

I am most grateful to RAF 202 Squadron Search and Rescue for their help and information and for talking me through a typical, and typically dangerous, air-sea rescue. Their website www.202squadron.com is a reminder of what a debt we owe to these brave crews.

I would like to thank consultant forensic psychiatrist Dr Jane Ewbank for many stimulating and helpful conversations about the criminal mind and I am grateful to her husband, consultant gastro-enterologist Dr Sean Weaver, for suggesting Variant CJD.

One

There was no fly and there should have been a fly. It was that sort of room. Grey linoleum. Putty walls. Chairs and tables with tubular metal legs. But in these places there was always a fly too, zizzing slowly up and down a window pane. Up and down. Up and down. Up.

The wall at the far end was covered in whiteboards and pinboards. Names. Dates. Places. Then came:

Witnesses (which was blank).

Suspects. (Blank.)

Forensics. (Blank.)

In each case.

There were five people in the conference room of the North Riding Police HQ, and they had been staring at the boards for over an hour. DCI Simon Serrailler felt as if he had spent half his life staring at one of the photographs. The bright fresh face. The protruding ears. The school tie. The newly cut hair. The expression. Interested. Alert.

David Angus. It was eight months since he had vanished from outside the gate of his own house at ten past eight one morning.

David Angus.

Simon wished there was a fly to mesmerise him, instead of the small boy's face.

*

The call from DS Jim Chapman had come a couple of days earlier, in the middle of a glorious Sunday afternoon.

Simon had been sitting on the bench, padded up and waiting to bat for Lafferton Police against Bevham Hospital 2nd Eleven. The score was 228 for 5, the medics' bowling was flaccid, and Simon thought his team might declare before he himself got in. He wasn't sure whether he would mind or not. He enjoyed playing though he was only an average cricketer. But on such an afternoon, on such a fine ground, he was happy whether he went in to bat or not.

The swifts soared and screamed high above the pavilion and swallows skimmed the boundary. He had been low-spirited and restless during the past few months, for no particular reason and then again, for a host of them but his mood lightened now with the pleasure of the game and the prospect of a good pavilion tea. He was having supper with his sister and her family later. He remembered what his nephew Sam had said suddenly the previous week, when he and Simon had been swimming together; he had stopped mid-length, leaping up out of the water with: 'Today is a GOOD day!'

Simon smiled to himself. It didn't take much.

'Howzzzzzaaaattt?'

But the cry faded away. The batsman was safe and going for his hundred.

'Uncle Simon, hey!'

'Hi, Sam.'

His nephew came running up to the bench. He was holding the mobile, which Simon had given him to look after if he went in to bat.

'Call for you. It's DCS Chapman from the North Riding CID.' Sam's face was shadowed with anxiety. 'Only, I thought I should ask who it was . . .'

'No, that's quite right. Good work, Sam.'

Simon got up and walked round the corner of the pavilion. 'Serrailler.'

'Jim Chapman. New recruit, was it?'

'Nephew. I'm padded up, next in to bat.'

'Good man. Sorry to break into your Sunday afternoon.

Any chance of you coming up here in the next couple of days?'

'The missing child?'

'Been three weeks and not a thing.'

'I could drive up tomorrow early evening and give you Tuesday and Wednesday, if you need me that long – once I've cleared it.'

'I just did that. Your Chief thinks a lot of you.'

There was a mighty cheer from the spectators and applause broke.

'We're a man out, Jim. Got to go.'

Sam was waiting, keen as mustard, holding out his hand for the mobile.

'What do I do if it rings when you're batting?'

'Take the name and number and say I'll call back.'

'Right, guv.'

Simon bent over and tightened the buckle on his pad to hide a smile.

But as he walked out to bat, a thin fog of misery clouded around his head, blocking out the brightness of the day, souring his pleasure. The child abduction case was always there, a stain on the recesses of the mind. It was not only the fact that it was still a blank, unsolved and unresolved, but that the boy's abductor was free to strike again. No one liked an open case, let alone one so distressing. The phone call from Jim Chapman had pulled Simon back to the Angus case, to the force, to work . . . and from there, to how he had started to feel about his job in the past few months. And why.

Facing the tricky spin-bowling of a cardiac registrar gave him something else to concentrate on for the moment. Simon hooked the first ball and ran.

The pony neighing from the paddock woke Cat Deerbon from a sleep of less than two hours. She lay, cramped and uncomfortable, wondering where she was. She had been called out to an elderly patient who had fallen downstairs and fractured his femur and on her return home had let the door bang and had woken her youngest child. Felix had been hungry, thirsty and cross, and in the end Cat had fallen asleep next to his cot.

Now, she sat up stiffly but his warm little body did not stir. The sun was coming through a slit in the curtains on to his face.

It was only ten past six.

The grey pony was standing by the fence grazing, but whinnied again, seeing Cat coming towards it, carrot in hand.

How could I leave all this? she thought, feeling its nuzzling mouth. How could either of us bear to leave this farmhouse, these fields, this village?

The air smelled sweet and a mist lay in the hollow. A woodpecker yaffled, swooping towards one of the oak trees on the far side of the fence.

Chris, her husband, was restless again, unhappy in general practice, furious at the burden of administration which took him from his patients, irritated by the mountain of new targets, checks and balances. He had spoken several times in the past month of going to Australia for five years – which might as well be for ever, Cat thought, knowing he had only put a time limit on it as a sop to her. She had been there once to see her triplet brother, Ivo, and hated it – the only person, Chris said, who ever had.

She wiped her hand, slimy from the pony's mouth, on her dressing gown. The animal, satisfied, trotted quietly away across the paddock.

They were so close to Lafferton and the practice, close to her parents and Simon, to the cathedral which meant so much to her. They were also in the heart of the country, with a working farm across the lane where the children saw lambs and calves and helped feed chickens; they loved their schools, they had friends nearby.

No, she thought, feeling the sun growing warm on her back. No.

From the house Felix roared. But Sam would go to him, Sam, his brother and worshipper, rather than Hannah, who

4

preferred her pony and had become jealous of the baby as he had grown through his first year.

Cat wandered round the edge of the paddock, knowing that she would feel tired later in the day but not resenting her broken night – seeing patients at their most vulnerable, especially when they were elderly and frightened, had always been one of the best parts of working in general practice for her, and she had no intention of handing over night work to some agency when the new contract came into force. Chris disagreed. They had locked horns about it too often and now simply avoided the subject.

One of the old apple trees had a swathe of the white rose Wedding Day running through its gnarled branches and the scent drifted to her as she passed.

No, she thought again.

There had been too many bad days during the past couple of years, too much fear and tension; but now, apart from her usual anxiety about her brother, nothing was wrong – nothing except Chris's discontentment and irritability, nothing but his desire to change things, move them away, spoil . . . Her bare feet were wet with dew.

'Mummmeeeee. Tellyphoooooonnne . . .'

Hannah was leaning too far out of an upstairs window.

Cat ran.

It was a morning people remembered, for the silver-blue clear sky and the early-morning sunshine and the fact that everything was fresh. They relaxed and felt suddenly untroubled and strangers spoke to one another, passing in the street.

Natalie Coombs would remember it too.

'I can hear Ed's car.'

'No you can't, it's Mr Hardisty's, and get downstairs, we'll be late.'

'I want to wave to Ed.'

'You can wave to Ed from here.'

'No, I –'

'Get DOWNSTAIRS.'

Kyra's hair was all over her face, tangled after sleep. She was barefoot.

'Shit, Kyra, can't you do anything for your bloody self? . . . Where's your hairbrush, where's your shoes?'

But Kyra had gone to the front room to peer out of the window, waiting.

Natalie poured Chocolate Frosties into a blue bowl. She had eleven minutes – get Kyra ready, finish off her own face, find her stuff, make sure the bloody guinea pig had food and water, go. What had she been thinking. *I want to keep this baby*?

'There's Ed, there's Ed . . .'

She knew better than to interrupt Kyra. It was a morning thing.

'Bye, Ed . . . Ed . . .' Kyra was banging on the window.

Ed had turned from locking the front door. Kyra waved. Ed waved.

'Bye, Kyra . . .'

'Can I come and see you tonight, Ed?'

But the car had started. Kyra was shouting to herself.

'Stop being a pest.'

'Ed doesn't mind.'

'You heard. Eat your cereal.'

But Kyra was still waving, waving and waving as Ed's car turned the corner and out of sight. What the hell was it about bloody Ed? Natalie wondered. Still, it might give her a half-hour to herself tonight, if Kyra could wangle her way next door, to help with the plant-watering or eat a Mars bar in front of Ed's telly.

'Don't slosh the milk out like that, Kyra, now look . . .'

Kyra sighed.

For a six-year-old, Natalie thought, she had a diva's line in sighs.

The sun shone. People called out to one another, getting into their cars.

'Look, look,' Kyra said, dragging on Natalie's arm. 'Look in Ed's window, the rainbow thing is going round, look, it's all pretty colours moving.'

Natalie slammed the car door, opened it again, slammed

it for the second time, which was what she always had to do, otherwise it didn't stay closed.

'Can we have one of them rainbow-making things in our window? They're like fairyland.'

'Shit.' Natalie screeched to a halt at the junction. 'Watch where you're going, dickhead.'

Kyra sighed and thought about Ed, who never shouted and never swore. She thought she would go round tonight and ask if they could make pancakes.

It was the sun, brilliant on the white wall, that woke Max Jameson, a sheet of light through the glass. He had bought the loft because of the light – even on a dull day the space was full of it. When he had first brought Lizzie here she had gazed around her in delight.

'The Old Ribbon Factory,' she had said. 'Why?'

'Because they made ribbons. Lafferton ribbons were famous.'

Lizzie had walked a few steps before doing a little dance in the middle of the room.

That was the loft – one room plus an open-tread staircase to the bedroom and bathroom. One vast room.

'It's like a ship,' she had said.

Max closed his eyes, seeing her there, head back, dark hair hanging down.

There was a wall of glass. No blind, no curtain. At night the lamps glowed in the narrow street below. There was nothing beyond the Old Ribbon Factory except the towpath and then the canal. The second time, he had brought Lizzie here at night. She had gone straight to the window.

'It's Victorian England.'

'Phoney.'

'No. No, it really is. It feels right.'

On the wall at the far end of the room was her picture. He had taken the shot of Lizzie, alone beside the lake in her wedding dress, her head back in that same way, hair down but this time threaded with white flowers. She was looking up and she was laughing. The picture was blown up twelve feet high and ten feet wide on the white wall. When Lizzie had first seen it, she had been neither startled nor embarrassed, only thoughtful.

'It's the best memory,' she had said at last.

Max opened his eyes again and the sunlight burned into them. He heard her.

'Lizzie?' He flung the clothes off the bed in panic at her absence. 'Lizzie . . . ?'

She was halfway down the staircase, vomiting.

He tried to help her, to lead her back to safety, but her unsteadiness made it difficult, and he was afraid they would both fall. Then she stared into his face, her eyes wide and terrified, and screamed at him.

'Lizzie, it's OK, I'm here, it's me. I won't hurt you, I won't hurt you. Lizzie . . .'

Somehow he struggled with her to the bed and got her to lie down. She curled away from him making small angry sounds inside her throat like a cat growling. Max ran to the bathroom and sluiced cold water over his head and neck, scrubbed his teeth, keeping the door open. He could see the bed through the medicine cabinet mirror. She had not stirred again. He pulled on jeans and a shirt, ran down into the brilliant room and switched on the kettle. He was breathing hard, tense with panic, his hands sweating. Like a bitter taste, the fear was in his mouth and throat all the time now.

The crash came. He swung round in time to see Lizzie sliding in terrible slow motion from the top of the stairs to the foot, lying with one leg under her body, arms outstretched, roaring in pain and fright like a furious child.

The kettle gushed out steam and the sunlight caught the glass door of the wall cupboard like fire.

Max felt tears running down his face. The kettle was too full and splashed as he poured it, the water scalding his hand.

At the foot of the stairs, Lizzie lay still and the sound that came from her was the bellow of some animal, not any noise that she would make, not Lizzie, not his wife.

*

8

Cat Deerbon heard it, holding the telephone.

'Max, you'll have to speak more slowly . . . what's happened?'

But all she could make out, apart from the noise in the background, were a few incoherent, drowned words.

'Max, hold on . . . I'm coming now. Hold on . . .'

Felix was crawling along the landing towards the stairgate, smelling of dirty nappy. Cat scooped him up and into the bathroom, where Chris was shaving.

'That was Max Jameson,' she said. 'Lizzie . . . I've got to go. Make Hannah help you.'

She ran, zipping up her skirt as she went, avoiding his look.

Outside, the air smelled of hay and the grey pony was cantering round the paddock, tail swishing with pleasure. Cat was out of the drive and fast down the lane, planning what had to be done, how she could make Max Jameson understand, finally, that he could not keep Lizzie at home to die.

Two

Serrailler was in the room without a fly. With him were the senior members of the CID team investigating the child-abduction case.

DCS Jim Chapman was the SIO. Not far from retirement, amiable, experienced and shrewd, he had been a policeman in the north of England all his working life, and in different parts of Yorkshire for most of it. The rest were considerably younger. DS Sally Nelmes was small, neat, serious and a high-flyer. DC Marion Coopey, very much in the same mould, had been newly transferred from the Thames Valley. During the session she had spoken least, but what she had said had been sharp and to the point. The other Yorkshireman, Lester Hicks, was a long-term colleague of Jim Chapman and also his son-in-law.

They had been welcoming to a member of an outside force when they might have been suspicious or resentful. They were focused and energetic, and Serrailler had been impressed, but at the same time he recognised the incipient signs of frustration and discouragement he had known in the Lafferton team working under him on the David Angus case. He understood it absolutely but he could not let his sympathy create any sense of impotence, let alone defeatism.

A child had gone missing from the town of Herwick. He was eight and a half. At three o'clock on the first Monday after schools had broken up for the summer holiday, Scott

Merriman had been walking from his own house to that of his cousin, Lewis Tyler, half a mile away. He had carried a sports bag containing swimming things – Lewis's father was taking them to a new Water Dome half an hour's drive away.

Scott had never arrived at the Tyler house. After waiting twenty minutes, Ian Tyler had telephoned the Merrimans' number and Scott's own mobile. Scott's eleven-year-old sister Lauren had told him Scott had left 'ages ago'. His mobile was switched off.

The road down which he had walked was mainly a residential one, but it also took traffic on one of the busiest routes out of the town.

No one had come forward to report that they had seen the boy. No body had been found, nor any sports bag.

There was a school photograph of Scott Merriman on the conference-room wall, a foot away from that of David Angus. They were not alike but there was a similar freshness about them, an eagerness of expression which struck Simon Serrailler to the heart. Scott was grinning, showing a gap between his teeth.

A DC came into the room with a tray of tea. Serrailler started to make a calculation of how many plastic cups of beverage he had drunk since joining the police force. Then Chapman was on his feet again. There was something about his expression, something new. He was a measured, steady man but now he seemed to be sharpened up, shot through with a fresh energy. In response to it, Simon sat up and was aware that the others had done the same, straightened their backs, drawn themselves from a slump.

'There is one thing I haven't done in this inquiry. I'm thinking it's mebbe time I did. Simon, did Lafferton use forensic psychologists in the David Angus case?'

'As profilers? No. It was discussed but I vetoed it because I thought they simply wouldn't have enough to work on. All they would be able to give us was the general picture about child abduction – and we know that.'

'I agree. Still, I think we ought to turn this thing on its head. Let's play profiling. Speculate about the sort of person

11

who may have taken one, or both, of these children – and others for all we know. Do any of you think it would be a useful exercise?'

Sally Nelmes tapped her front teeth with her pen.

'Yes?' Chapman missed nothing.

'We've no more to go on ourselves than a profiler would have, is what I was thinking.'

'No, we haven't.'

'I think we need to get out there, not sit weaving stories.'

'Uniform and CID are still out there. All of us have been out there, and we will be again. This session, with DCI Serrailler's input, is about the core team taking time out to think . . . think round, think through, think.' He paused. 'THINK,' he said again, louder this time. 'Think what has happened. Two young boys have been taken from their homes, their families, their familiar surroundings, and have been terrified, probably subjected to abuse and then almost certainly murdered. Two families have been broken into pieces, have suffered, are suffering, anguish and dread, they're distraught, their imaginations are working overtime, they don't sleep, or eat, or function normally, they aren't relating fully to anyone or anything and they can never go back, nothing will ever return to normal for them. You know all this as well as I do, but you need me to remind you. If we get nowhere and all our thinking and talking produces nothing fresh for us to work on, then I intend to bring in an outside expert.'

He sat down and swung his chair round. They formed a rough semicircle.

'Think,' he said, 'about what kind of a person did these things.'

There was a moment's charged silence. Serrailler looked at the DCS with renewed respect. Then the words, the suggestions, the descriptions came, one after the other, snap, snap, snap, from the semicircle, like cards put down on a table in a fast-moving game.

'Paedophile.'

'Loner.'

'Male . . . strong male.'

'Young . . .'

'Not a teenager.'

'Driver . . . well, obviously.'

'Works on his own.'

'Lorry driver . . . van man, that sort . . .'

'Repressed . . . sexually inadequate . . .'

'Unmarried.'

'Not necessarily . . . why do you say that?'

'Can't make relationships . . .'

'Abused as a child . . .'

'Been humiliated . . .'

'It's a power thing, isn't it?'

'Low intelligence . . . class C or below . . .'

'Dirty . . . no self-esteem . . . scruffy . . .'

'Cunning.'

'No – reckless.'

'Daring, anyway. Big idea of himself.'

'No, no, dead opposite of that. Insecure. Very insecure.'

'Secretive. Good at lying. Covering up . . .'

On and on they went, the cards snapping down faster and faster. Chapman did not speak, only looked from face to face, following the pattern. Serrailler, too, said nothing, merely watched like the DCS, and with a growing sense of unease. Something was wrong but he could not put his finger on what or why.

Gradually the comments petered out. They had no more cards to snap down. They were slumping back in their chairs again. DS Sally Nelmes kept snatching glances at Serrailler – not especially friendly glances.

'We know what we're looking for well enough,' she said now.

'But *do* we?' Marion Coopey bent forward to retrieve a sheet of paper by her feet.

'Well, it's a pretty familiar type . . .'

For a second the two women seemed to confront one another. Serrailler hesitated, waiting for the DCS, but Jim Chapman said nothing.

'If I may . . .'

'Simon?'

'I think I know what DC Coopey means. While everyone was throwing their ideas into the ring I started to feel uneasy . . . and the trouble is . . . it's just a familiar "type" . . . put everything together and it paints a picture of what you all suppose is your typical child abductor.'

'And isn't it?' Sally Nelmes challenged.

'Maybe. Some of it will fit, no doubt . . . I'm just concerned – and this is what always concerns me with profiling when it's swallowed whole – that we'll make an identikit and then look for the person who fits it. Great when we really are dealing with identikit and it's of someone several people may have actually seen. But not here. I wouldn't want us to become fixated on this "familiar type" and start excluding everyone who doesn't fit.'

'You've got more to go on in Lafferton then?'

He wondered whether DS Nelmes had a chip on her shoulder or had simply taken a dislike to him, but he dealt with it in the way he always did, and which was almost always successful. He turned to her and smiled, an intimate, friendly smile, with eye contact, a smile between themselves.

'Oh, Sally, I wish . . .' he said.

Out of the corner of his eye he saw that Jim Chapman had registered every nuance of the exchange.

Sally Nelmes shifted slightly, and the trace of a smile lifted the corners of her mouth.

They broke for lunch, after which Serrailler and Jim Chapman took a walk out of the flat-roofed, 1970s HQ block and down an uninteresting road leading towards the town. In Yorkshire there was no sun and apparently no summer. The sky was curdled grey, the air oddly chemical.

'I'm not being much help,' Simon said.

'I needed to be sure we weren't missing something.'

'It's a bugger. Your lot are as frustrated as we've been.'

'Just not for so long.'

'These are the ones that get to you.'

14

They reached the junction with the arterial road and turned back.

'My wife's expecting you for dinner, by the way.'

Simon's spirits lifted. He liked Chapman, but it was more than that; he knew no one else up here and the town and its environs were both unfamiliar and unattractive and the hotel into which he had been booked was built in the same style as the police HQ with as much soul. He had half wondered whether to drive back to Lafferton at the end of the day's work rather than stay there, eating a bad meal alone, but the invitation to the Chapmans' home cheered him.

'I want to take you over to Herwick. I don't know about you but I generally get a feel about a place by mooching about it. We've no evidence, there's nothing . . . but I want to get your reaction.'

Serrailler and Chapman went to Herwick with Lester Hicks in the back. Hicks was a taciturn Yorkshireman, small and chunkily built with a shaved head and the chauvinist attitude which Simon had encountered before in Northern men. Although apparently without imagination, he came across as sane and level-headed.

Herwick was a town on the fringes of the York plain and seemed to have spread haphazardly. The outskirts were a ribbon of industrial units, DIY warehouses and multiplexes, the town centre full of charity shops and cheap takeaways.

'What's the work here?'

'Not enough . . . chicken packing factory, several big call centres but they're cutting back – all that work's going abroad, it's cheaper. Big cement works . . . otherwise, unemployment. Right, here we go. This is the Painsley Road . . . there's a link road to the motorway a couple of miles further on.' They continued slowly and then took a left turn. 'This is where the Tyler house is . . . number 202 . . .'

It was a road without feature. Semis and a few run-down detached houses; a couple of shopping rows – newsagent, fish-and-chip shop, bookmaker, launderette; an undertaker's with lace-curtained windows and a flat-roofed building at the back.

15

The Tyler house was two doors away from it. Bright red herringbone bricks were newly laid where a front garden had been. The fence was gone too.

They slowed.

'Scott should have approached the house from this end . . . he would have come from the junction.'

No one took any notice of the car crawling along the kerb. A woman pushed a pram, an old man drove along the pavement in an invalid buggy. Two dogs mated by the side of the road.

'What kind of people?' Serrailler asked.

'Tylers? He's a plumber, the wife works as a shrink-wrapper in the chicken factory. Decent sort. Kids seem fine.'

'How have they been?'

'Father doesn't say much but he's blaming himself for not fetching the boy by car.'

'Scott's parents?'

'On the verge of killing one another . . . but I think they always have been. His sister seems to carry the weight of the family on her shoulders.'

'And she's . . .'

'Thirteen going on thirty. Here's where Scott would have turned the corner . . . this road leads to his own house. It's in a small close a couple of hundred yards down, set off the main road.'

'No sighting of him along here?'

'No sighting, period.'

Another bleak road, with the houses set behind fences or scruffy privet hedges. Three large blocks of flats. A disused Baptist chapel with wooden bars across the doors and windows. Traffic was steady but not heavy.

'It's hard to believe nobody saw the boy.'

'Oh they'll have seen him . . . just didn't register.'

'It must have looked normal then, there can't have been any sort of struggle, just as there can't have been any when David Angus was taken. No one misses the sight of a child being forcibly dragged into a car.'

'Someone they both knew?'

16

'Both boys can't have known the same person, that's way off being likely. So, we've got two different kidnappers. Each one well enough known to the child to . . .' Simon trailed off. They all knew it was not worth his finishing the sentence.

'This is Richmond Grove. It's number 7 . . . bottom right.'

The houses were crammed on to a skimpy plot. Simon could guess how much noise came through thin dividing walls, how small the area of garden at the back of each one.

Chapman turned off the car engine. 'Want to get out?'

Serrailler nodded. 'Will you wait here?'

He walked slowly round. The curtains of number 7 were drawn. There was no car, no sign of life. He looked at the house for a long time, trying to picture the gap-toothed boy coming out of the door, swimming bag over his shoulder, walking up towards the road . . . turning left . . . marching along, cheerful. He turned. A bus went past but there seemed to be no bus stop for some way ahead. Simon looked along the grey road. How far had Scott gone? Who had stopped beside him? What had they said that had persuaded the boy to go with them?

He made his way back to the car.

'Give me an idea of the boy . . . Shy? Forward? Old or young for his age?'

'Cheeky. Teachers said that. But OK. They liked him. Not a problem. Lots of friends. Well liked. Bit of a ringleader. Football supporter, the local team. They call them the Haggies. Had their logo on his swim bag, all the strip.'

'The sort of kid who would chat to a stranger, maybe someone asking for directions?'

'Very likely.'

Whereas David Angus was altogether more reserved but one who would have spoken to the same sort of stranger because it was the polite thing to do.

Hicks's phone rang. Three minutes later, they were racing back to police HQ. Hicks's wife, and Chapman's daughter, had gone into labour a fortnight early with their first child.

*

Serrailler spent the rest of the afternoon alone going through the files on the Scott Merriman case. At one point he found the canteen for a mug of tea. At half past six, he drove over to the hotel.

His room was beige with gilt fittings and smelled of old cigarette smoke, the bath big enough for a ten-year-old. Jim Chapman had left with hurried apologies, saying he would 'catch up later'. It was a toss-up as to which would be worse . . . lying on the bed in his room brooding, sitting alone in the bar brooding, or making the long drive back to Lafferton down overcrowded motorways. Heavy rain had set in. Simon did not fancy the drive.

He showered and put on a clean shirt.

The bar was empty apart from a businessman working at a laptop in the corner. The furniture was lacquer red. There was a cocktail menu on every table. Simon got a beer.

He was always content in his own company but the ugliness of these surroundings and the isolation from everything he knew and loved seemed to be draining the life out of him. In a couple of months he would be thirty-seven. He felt older. He had always loved being a policeman but something about the life was beginning to frustrate him. There were too many restrictions, too many political-correctness boxes to be ticked before getting on with a job. Was he making any difference to anyone? Had a single life improved, even marginally, because of what he did? He thought of the difference his sister Cat made, as a conscientious and caring doctor, of what his parents had done in their time to change lives. Perhaps they had been right all along, perhaps he should have gone into medicine and made his father happy.

He slumped against the shiny red banquette. The barman had switched on starlights around the bar but it did not lift the atmosphere.

What he missed, Simon thought suddenly, was excitement, the adrenalin rush, such as he had had pursuing the serial killer on his own patch two years previously, and which had almost always been there in the early days of his police career. His Chief Constable had hinted more than once that he should get on to the next rung of the ladder but if he rose to Superintendent and beyond he would spend even less time out on the job, even more in his office, and that he did not want. It was the old story . . . don't become a Head if you love teaching, don't take a senior medical role if you enjoy looking after patients. If you want the thrill of the chase, stay in uniform or as a DC. But he had not and there was no going back. Should he get out altogether? He knew what he would do if he left the force. Some of his drawings were to be exhibited in a London gallery; the show was opening in November. He would travel and draw full time, give them the attention and concentration they deserved. He would get by. Money was not his motive. But he wondered as usual whether he would gain as much satisfaction and pleasure from art if he had to live by it. Perhaps everything staled after a time.

Perhaps.

He got up to go to the bar for another beer, but as he did so, heard his name called.

DC Coopey looked very different in a floating black dress with her hair piled up and long earrings. For a second, Simon stared at her without recognition. But she walked confidently towards him, smiling.

'This is sad,' she said. 'Really . . . a lonely drink in a dump like this. We can do better for you.' She looked around. 'Where are you sitting?'

Simon hesitated, then pointed to his table.

'Good. I'll have a vodka and tonic please and then I suggest I take you to somewhere halfway decent. It's called the Sailmaker.' She sashayed across the room and sat down.

He was furious. He felt cornered and judged. Suddenly, the charm of this quiet bar and of his own company revealed themselves. But good manners were instinctive when Simon was irritated; he bought her drink and took it over.

'Aren't you having another?'

'No. I've got to make an early start tomorrow.'

Marion Coopey drank her vodka, looking at him over the glass. She had a pleasant enough face, he thought, neither plain nor pretty, though she wore too much make-up. He could not reconcile this person with the DC who had spoken such careful sense in the conference room. He had had her down as career-orientated, up for the next promotion.

'But you'll come and eat with me – it's not a restaurant, it's a club, but they do very good food. I'm surprised you haven't heard of the Sailmaker.'

'This is my first time up here.'

'I know, but the word about gay joints is out there on the grapevine.'

He felt a shock run through him at what she had said, at her confident tone and the assumption behind it. The blood rose to his face.

But Marion Coopey laughed. 'Oh, come on, Simon, I'm gay, so are you. So what? That's why I thought we could enjoy an evening together. Problem?'

'Just your complete and total mistake. And I have to go and make some calls.' He stood.

'I don't believe this . . . how old-fashioned can you be? It's really OK now, you know. LEGPO and all.'

'DC Coopey . . .' He saw her open her mouth to say 'Marion', but she checked herself at his tone '. . . I'm not going to discuss my private life with you, except to repeat that your assumption is wrong. I –'

His mobile rang in his jacket pocket. Jim Chapman's number was on the screen.

'Jim? Good news?'

'From home. Stephanie had a girl at four o'clock. All fine.'

'That's excellent. Congra –'

'The rest isn't good.'

'What?'

'We've another.'

Simon closed his eyes. 'Go on . . .'

'This afternoon. Girl aged six. Went to get an ice cream from a van . . . someone snatched her. Only this time, there's a witness – time, place, car description –'

'Car number?'

'Part . . . it's more than we've ever had.'

'Where did this happen?' He glanced at Marion Coopey. Her expression had changed.

'Village called Gathering Bridge, up on the North York moors.'

'Can I be any use?'

'Wouldn't say no.'

Simon put his phone away. Marion was standing.

'Another child. I'm going over to your HQ.'

He walked across the room and she followed him quickly. At the door, she stopped him. 'I'd better apologise,' she said.

He was still angry but the job had taken over now and he merely shook his head. 'It's hardly important.' He headed for his car, outstriding her.

Police HQ was buzzing. Simon made for the incident room.

'The DCS has gone off to the scene, sir. He said to fill you in.'

The wall boards were being posted with information and half a dozen CID were at computers.

Serrailler went across to where a photograph of a silver Ford Mondeo was being pinned up.

'*XTD or XTO 4 . . .*' was written beside it.

'Do we have the press on board?'

'The DCS is giving them a briefing up at the scene.'

'What do we know?'

'Gathering Bridge is a big village . . . old centre, new housing around . . . it's grown in the last ten years. Pretty place. Child is just six . . . Amy Sudden . . . lives with her parents and younger sister in a cul-de-sac of cottages. Went to get an ice cream from the van parked just beyond there, on the corner of the main street. She was the last child at the van – the bloke was all set to go when Amy came running up. She got her ice cream and turned to walk back towards the cul-de-sac, the van started up and was just moving off when a car came down the main road and pulled up beside the girl . . . driver leaned or half got out and pulled the kid in. Happened like lightning apparently and he was off and shutting the door at the same time . . . the ice-cream van

21

driver stopped and jumped out but the Mondeo was away
. . . he got the beginning of the number . . . not the rest. Van
man ran down the street shouting . . . someone came out of
a house . . . we got the call.'

'Where's the Mondeo now?'

The DC finished chalking up some names on the board.
'Vanished into thin air. No sighting since.'

'Much traffic?'

'Not in the village, but a couple of miles off you get one
of the main roads leading to the coast. Busy there.'

'And the number?'

'They're running checks . . .'

'But you haven't got enough?'

'No, computers'll throw up a few thousand.'

Simon went down to the canteen, bought tea and a toasted
sandwich and took them over to a corner table. He wanted
to think. He pictured the silver Mondeo, driver speeding in
a panic towards a motorway with the child, desperate to get
away from the area, heart pounding, not able to think straight.
This one had gone wrong. It had been done on impulse, like
the others, and in daylight, but this time his luck had run
out. He'd been spotted. For all the abductor knew his car
number had been taken in full and he himself had been seen
at close quarters. His description would have gone out to all
police forces. The instinct would be to move, far and fast.

In the end luck did run out. Usually. Sometimes.

All the same, Simon had to think of the other possibility –
that this abductor was someone different and if found would
turn out to have nothing to do with the disappearance of the
two young boys, almost a year apart. But he trusted his
instincts and his gut reaction was: This is the one, this is him.

He felt a surge of excitement. If they could get a lead on
the Mondeo they had a chance. This was not only Jim
Chapman's chase, it was his too.

He went to the counter to get a refill of tea and almost
knocked into Marion Coopey, wearing jeans, a jacket and no
earrings. She gave him a wary look. He nodded and went
back to his seat, not wanting to have to speak to her. He had

not minded her arriving at his hotel in a bid to get him to spend the evening with her; it might have been a friendly enough move after all, trying to entertain a visiting colleague on his own in a strange town. He might have responded in kind. It had been her assumption that had angered him. He had been taken for gay before now and been unbothered. Tonight, though, he had felt both angry and defensive. He was a private person, wanting to keep his work life separate from the rest.

How bloody dare she? summed up his feelings.

But he was good at setting things to one side and he did it now. It was trivial. It didn't signify. What signified was what had happened to a six-year-old girl in a Yorkshire village a few hours earlier.

He drained his tea and made for the incident room, going up the concrete stairs two at a time.

Three

'Kyra, stop bloody jumping about, will you?'

Kyra went on jumping. If she went on for long enough her mother would sling her out and she could go next door.

'I'll sling you out, you carry on like that. Go and watch the telly. Go and do a puzzle. Go and put my make-up on – no, don't do that. Just stop bloody jumping.'

Natalie was trying out a new recipe. She did it all the time. Cooking was the only thing she enjoyed so much she forgot where she was and that she was on her own with Kyra, jump-jump-bloody jump. In her head, she had her own restaurant, or maybe a catering business doing dinners and weddings. No, not weddings, she didn't want to do Chicken à la King for a hundred, she wanted to do this Barbados Baked Fish with Stuffed Peppers for four. Or six. It was fiddly and the fish wasn't the right sort, she could only get haddock, but she liked trying out things she'd never heard of to see how they came up. Then it would go down in her book, the book she was going to use for showing people what she could do. For when she started up her own business. Super Suppers.

She started coring the green peppers.

Kyra jumped until the timer fell off the shelf.

'KYRA . . .'

Kyra seized her moment and ran.

*

Next door on one side, Bob Mitchell was cleaning his car. He saw Kyra and turned the hose slowly, slowly towards her but she knew he wouldn't really soak her. She stuck out her tongue. Mel was shutting the gate of the house opposite.

'Hello, Mel.'

'Hi, Kyra.'

'You look ever so nice.'

'Thanks, babe.'

'I got a new hair scrunchy, Mel.'

'Cool. OK then, babe, see ya.'

'See ya, Mel.'

Mel was sixteen and looked like a model. Kyra's mother had said she'd kill for Mel's legs.

Ed's car wasn't in the drive. Kyra wandered up the front path, hesitated, then went round the back. Maybe . . .

But Ed wasn't in. She'd known really.

She tapped on the back door and waited just in case, but there wasn't any point. She wandered back. Bob Mitchell had gone in. There was nobody. Not even a cat.

Natalie put the foil-wrapped fish into the oven and washed her hands. Kyra slipped in through the door like grease.

'Told you,' Natalie said. She picked up the apple-shaped timer from the floor and turned it to thirty-five minutes, before going to watch the news.

Four

'You have to understand,' Cat Deerbon said.

'Lizzie isn't going anywhere. I'm fine, I can manage.'

'Then why did you call me?'

Max Jameson stood at the far end of the long room, looking up at the floor-to-ceiling photograph of his wife. Lizzie herself was curled on the sofa under a blanket, sleeping after Cat had given her a sedative.

'I know how hard this is, Max, believe me. You feel you've failed.'

'No, I don't. I haven't failed.'

'All right, you feel that by letting her go into the hospice you *will* have failed. But this is bad and it is going to get worse.'

'So you've told me.'

'If this were an easier place to live in . . .'

'It's the place she loves. She's happy here, she's never been so happy.'

'Do you think she still is? Can't you see how frightening it is for her? This huge space, those stairs, the height when she looks down from the bedroom . . . the slippery floors, the way the chrome shines in the kitchen, in the bathroom. Brightness is painful to her now, it actually hurts her.'

'So they'd keep her in the dark, would they? At this hospice? It would be like going into prison.'

Cat was silent. She had been with Max Jameson for forty minutes. When she had arrived, he had wept on her shoulder. Lizzie had been sick again and was sitting in the middle of the floor, where she had fallen, her leg bent under her. Amazingly, she was only shocked, not seriously hurt.

'But how long before she falls down those stairs head first? Is that the way you want her life to end?'

'Do you know . . .' Max turned to Cat and smiled. He was a tall man and had been handsome but now he was haggard with anxiety and fear. His face had sunken inwards and his shaved head had a blue sheen. '. . . I don't actually want her life to end at all.'

'Of course you don't.'

He walked slowly towards Cat, but then veered away again to return to the wall with the photograph.

'You think she's gaga, don't you?'

'I would never, ever use that expression about anyone.'

'OK, what would you say she was?' He was angry.

'The illness has reached her brain now and she is very confused, though there may be flashes of awareness. She is also very frightened for most of the time – fear is a symptom of variant CJD at this stage. I want Lizzie to be in a place of safety so that she has as little to frighten her as possible. She also needs physical care. Her bodily functions are no longer under her control. The ataxia will increase so she will fall over all the time, she has no motor . . .'

Max Jameson screamed, a terrible howl of pain and rage, his hands pressed to his head.

Lizzie woke and began to cry like a baby, struggling to sit up. He went on bellowing, an animal sound.

'Max, stop that,' Cat said quietly. She went to Lizzie and took her hand, encouraging her to lie down under the blanket again. The young woman's eyes were wide with fear and also with the blankness of someone who has no sense of their surroundings, of other people or even of their own selves. All was a terrifying confusion.

27

The room was quiet. In the street below someone went by whistling.

'Let me make the call,' Cat said.

After a long pause, Max nodded.

It had been less than three months since Lizzie Jameson had come to the surgery. She had been walking too carefully, as if afraid she might lose her balance, and her speech had seemed slow. Cat only remembered seeing her once before, on a birth-control matter, but had been struck then by her vibrant beauty and her laugh; she had scarcely recognised the unhappy young woman coming into her room.

It was not difficult to diagnose severe depression but neither Cat nor Lizzie herself could find a cause. She was very happy, Lizzie said, no, there was nothing wrong with her marriage, nor with anything else. Work had been going well – she was a graphic designer – she loved the apartment in the Old Ribbon Factory, loved Lafferton, had had no shocks or illness.

'Every day I wake up it's blacker. It's like sliding down a pit.' She had stared at Cat hollow-eyed but there had been no tears.

Cat had prescribed an antidepressant and asked to see her weekly for the next six weeks to follow her progress.

Nothing had changed for over a month. The tablets had barely touched the surface of her misery. But on the fourth visit, Lizzie had presented with a badly bruised arm, and a dislocated finger where she had tried to stop herself falling. She had just lost her balance, she said.

'Has this happened before?'

'It keeps happening. I suppose it might be the tablets.'

'Hm. Possibly. They can cause mild dizziness but it usually passes within a few days.'

Cat had got her an appointment with the neurologist at Bevham General. That night she had talked to Chris.

'Brain tumour,' he had said at once. 'The MRI will show more clearly.'

'Yes. Could be very deep.'

28

'Parkinson's?'

'That crossed my mind.'

'Or maybe the two things are unconnected . . . look at the depression and the lack of balance separately.'

They had gone on to talk of something else, but the following morning Chris had crossed the corridor from his own consulting room to Cat's.

'Lizzie Jameson . . .'

'Idea?'

'How was her gait?'

'Unsteady.'

'I just looked up variant CJD.'

Cat had stared at him. 'It's very rare,' she'd said finally.

'Yes. I've never seen it.'

'Nor have I.'

'But it checks out.'

After her last patient left Cat had put in a call to the Bevham neurologist.

Max Jameson had been widowed five years before meeting Lizzie. His first wife had died of breast cancer. There had been no children.

'I was mad,' he had said to Cat. 'I was crazy. I wanted to be dead. I *was* dead, I was the walking dead. It was just a question of getting through the days and wondering why I bothered.'

Friends had invited him to things but he would never turn up. 'I wasn't going to go to this dinner party, only someone was detailed to fetch me – they practically had to haul me out physically. When I walked into that room I was thinking of a way I could walk right out again, find some excuse to turn round and run. Then I saw Lizzie standing by the fireplace . . . actually I saw two Lizzies – she was in front of a mirror.'

'So you didn't turn and run.'

He had smiled at her, his face blazing up with sudden recollected joy. Then he remembered what Cat was now trying to tell him. 'Lizzie has *mad cow disease*?'

'That's a hideous term. I won't use it. Variant CJD.'

'Oh, don't hide behind words. Jesus Christ.'

There was no way of discovering how long the disease had been lying dormant in her.

'And it comes from eating meat?'

'Infected beef, yes, but when, we can have no idea. Years ago probably.'

'What will happen?' Max had stood up and leaned across her desk. 'Plain words. What Will Happen? How and When? I need to know this.'

'Yes,' Cat had said, 'you do.' And had told him.

The illness had run its terrible course very quickly. From depression to ataxia, with other mental symptoms that were harder for Max to bear – violent mood swings, increasing aggression, paranoia and suspicion, panic attacks and then hours of sustained fear. Lizzie had fallen over, lost her sense of taste and smell, become incontinent, been repeatedly sick. Max had stayed with her, nursed and cared for her, twenty-four hours a day. Her mother had come from Somerset twice but was not able to stay in the loft flat because of a recent hip replacement. Max's mother had flown from Canada, taken one look at the situation and flown back home. He was on his own. 'It's fine,' Max said, 'I don't need anyone. It's fine.'

Cat went out of the apartment and down the strange, brick-lined stairwell, which still had the feel of a factory entrance, to the street, where she could get a signal on her phone and leave Max to be quiet with Lizzie.

The Lafferton hospice, Imogen House, had a bed, and Cat made the necessary arrangements. The street was empty. At the end of it, there was the curious blackness which indicated the presence of water, even though there was nothing of the canal to be seen.

The clock chimed on the cathedral tower, a short distance away.

'Oh God, You make it very difficult sometimes,' Cat said aloud. But then prayed a fierce prayer, for the man in the apartment above, and the woman being taken away from it, to die.

Five

The bleep of a mobile interrupted the orderly calm of the cathedral chapter meeting.

The Dean paused. 'If that's important, do take it outside and answer it.'

The Reverend Jane Fitzroy flushed scarlet. She had arrived in Lafferton a week earlier and this was her first full chapter meeting.

'No, it can wait. I do apologise.'

She pressed the off button and the Dean moved the agenda smoothly forwards.

It was over an hour later before she could check the caller display. The last number was her mother's, but when she rang back the answerphone was on.

'Mum, sorry, I was in a chapter meeting. Hope you're OK. Call me when you get this.'

She spent the next couple of hours at Imogen House, to which she was now Chaplain, as well as being the Cathedral Liaison Officer at Bevham General hospital. The work would take her out into the community but bring her back to her base at the cathedral, where she would take a full share in the worship and ministry.

At the moment, the most important part of her job was to get to know people, and let them size her up in turn, to listen and learn. It was an absorbing afternoon, at the end of which she sat with a man a few weeks off his hundredth birthday and determined, as he said, 'to go for the telegram'. He was like a bird, a fledgling of skin and bone, tiny in the bed, his skin the colour of a tallow candle, but his eyes bright.

'I'll get there, young Reverend,' Wilfred Armer said, squeezing Jane's hand. 'I'll be blowing out all those candles, you'll see.'

Jane doubted if he would live through the next twenty-four hours. He wanted her to stay with him, to listen as he wheezed out story after story about his boyhood, of fishing in Lafferton's canal and swimming in the river.

As she left the building, she switched on her mobile again. It beeped a message. 'Jane?' Magda Fitzroy's voice sounded distant and strange. 'Are you there? Jane?'

She pressed 'call'. There was no reply and this time the answerphone did not come on. She sat under a tree, wondering what to do. There was only one of her mother's Hampstead neighbours whose number Jane knew and he was in America for three months. The house on the other side belonged to a foreign businessman who seemed never to be there. The police? The hospitals? She hesitated because it seemed too dramatic to involve them when she was not even sure if anything was wrong.

The clinic. That number was on her phone. Other numbers might be somewhere among her things which were still in boxes in the garden cottage of the Precentor's house.

A boy bounced past her on a bicycle doing wheelies over the cobbles. Jane smiled at him. He did not respond but when he had gone by, turned and stared over his shoulder. She was used to it. Here she was, a girl, wearing jeans, and a dog collar. People were still surprised.

'Heathside Clinic.'

'It's Jane Fitzroy. Is my mother there by any chance?'

Magda Fitzroy still saw a few patients at her former work-place, though she had officially retired the year before and was now working with a fellow child psychiatrist on an academic textbook. She missed the clinic, Jane knew, missed the people and her own role there.

'Sorry to keep you. No one's seen Dr Fitzroy today, but she wasn't expected. She hasn't any appointments here at all this week.'

Jane tried her mother's number several times during the course of the next hour. Nothing. Still no reply and still no answer machine.

Then she went across to the deanery. Geoffrey Peach was out and she left a message. By the time she was away from Lafferton heading towards the motorway it was early afternoon.

The London traffic was dense and she sat on Haverstock Hill for twenty minutes without moving. From time to time, she dialled her mother's number. There was never a reply and she turned the corner into Heath Place wishing she had called the police after all.

As she drew up outside the Georgian cottage she saw that the front door was ajar.

For a second Jane thought the hall seemed as usual; then she realised that the lamp usually on the walnut table was lying broken on the floor. The table itself had gone.

'Mother?'

Magda spent much of her time in the study overlooking the garden. It was a room Jane loved, with its purple walls and squashy, plum-covered sofa, her mother's papers and books flowing from desk to chairs to floor. The room had a particular smell, partly because the windows were almost always open, even in winter, so that the garden scents drifted in, and also because her mother sometimes smoked small cigars, whose smoke had melded into the fabric of the room over the years.

The study had been taken apart. The walls had been stripped of their pictures, the shelves of every piece of old china, and both the desk and a small table had had the drawers pulled out and overturned. There was an unmistakable smell of urine.

It was only as Jane stood looking round in shock, trying to take everything in, that she heard a slight sound from the kitchen.

Magda was lying on the floor beside the stove. One leg was buckled beneath her and there was dried blood on her head, matted into her hair and crusted down the side of her face. She was grey, her mouth pinched in.

Jane knelt and took her hand. It was cold and her mother's pulse was weak, but she was conscious.

'Jane . . . ?'

'How long have you been here? Who did this to you? Oh God, you rang me and I didn't realise.'

'I, I think . . . this morning? Someone rang the doorbell and . . . just . . . I couldn't manage to get up again to the phone . . . I . . . thought you might . . .'

'Darling, I'm going to call the ambulance and the police. I'll get a blanket but I won't move you, they'd better do that . . . hold on a moment.'

Every room that she glanced into as she ran upstairs had been ransacked and overturned. She felt sick.

'This will keep you warm. They'll be here soon.'

'I am not going to hospital –'

But Jane was already calling the emergency services.

'I'll die if I go to hospital.'

'Much more likely to die if you don't.'

Jane sat on the floor and took her mother's hand. She was .a tall, strong woman, with grey hair usually coiled up into an idiosyncratic bun. Now, it was down and anyhow; her features, so full of character, so well defined, with the beaky nose and high cheekbones and forehead, seemed to have sunk in, so that she looked closer to eighty than the sixty-eight she was. In a few hours, old age and vulnerability had come upon her, changing her terribly.

'Are you in pain?'

'It's . . . hard to tell . . . I feel numb . . .'

'What kind of man was it? How did it happen for goodness' sake?'

'Two . . . youths . . . I heard a car . . . It's difficult to remember.'

'Don't worry. I'm just angry with myself that I didn't come sooner.'

It was only then that the old look crossed her mother's face, the one which Jane had come to know so well over the past few years. Magda's eyes fell, briefly, on her collar and there it was, even now, after everything that had happened – the look of scorn and of disbelief.

Magda Fitzroy was an atheist of the old school. Atheist, socialist, psychiatrist, rationalist, formed in the classic Hampstead mould. Where her daughter's Christianity, let alone her desire to be ordained a priest, had come from was to her both a mystery and a matter for ridicule. And then the look was gone. Her mother lay, hurt and afraid, in shock and Jane felt for her; she let the paramedics in and told them the little she knew.

One of them examined the cuts on Magda's head. 'I'm Larry,' he said, 'and this is Al. What's your name, my love?'

'I am Dr Magda Fitzroy and I am not your love.'

'Aw, pity about that, Magda.'

'Dr Fitzroy.'

He glanced up at Jane. 'She always like this?'

'Oh yes. Ignore her at your peril.'

'You all right?'

Jane had sat down suddenly, hit by the realisation that her mother had been robbed and attacked in her home one quiet weekday morning while the world went about its business, and that she might well have been dead. She began to cry.

Six

The Holly Bush was like something out of a Hammer Horror film, Ed thought, driving up the steep slope to the fore-court. It stood above the fast main road, ugly, turreted and, at night, lit with neon and strings of fairy lights. At Christmas, an illuminated Santa with sleigh and reindeer leered out at the passing traffic, outlined in lights that chased each other endlessly round. Enough to give you a bloody migraine if you stared at them long enough. Only no one did. They shot past, or they were up the slope and in through the door.

It smelled the way that kind of place always smelled, and in the day it looked frowsty and peeling. At least at night the lights gave it a bit of glamour. Not that Ed had been there more than a couple of times at night. Work and pleasure, such pleasure as there was coming to drink in the Holly Bush, didn't mix.

'Brian?'

Someone was whistling at the back. There had been one vehicle in the car park. It wasn't a time of year for the sort of people who stopped overnight at the Holly Bush, the reps and lower-pond-life businessmen. The hotel had five bedrooms, which Ed had never seen, three bars, a restaurant and a games room. The cloakrooms, which were all Ed really knew, were jazzed up with horrendous wallpaper, fat blue roses and vivid green vines.

'BRIAN?'

Keep your nerve, that was the thing. Business as usual. Act normal.

At first, that had been scary but it had sorted everything out the year before.

'Bri . . .'

'All right, I'm bloody here – Oh. It's you. Do you have to bloody shout the place down?'

'Thought you was in the cellar. OK, what'd you need?'

'How the hell should I know? Your job to go and find out.'

'Yeah, yeah, I'll get to the cloakrooms. I meant what else?'

'What you got?'

All the stock had been in the boot earlier, before it had happened, but now Ed had put the boxes on the back seat, covered with an old dog rug.

'Marlboro, Silk Cut, B & H. Oh and a few Hamlets.'

'How much?'

'Same as last time.'

'How many?'

'I can let you have five hundred.'

'Ay, go on then. You get t' cloakrooms sorted, I'll get your money.'

The door behind Ed opened and a couple of men came in. They'd walked past the car then, they . . . No. They hadn't. The car was closed and locked, everything covered up, looking like any other car.

'You do coffees?'

'Just the filter.'

'Right, two filters.'

'Owt for you, Ed?'

Yes, be best to hang about a bit, chat, not seem too bothered about rushing off.

'White, one sugar. Thanks.'

The cloakroom machines were easily sorted. Two of condoms needed, one of tampons, still plenty of tights in there, not much call for those at the Holly Bush. The profits weren't that great, even if the goods came at knock-off

37

prices. It was the cigarettes that fetched the money. They went into a cardboard box labelled Tomato Soup, all sealed up.

One of the men came in. Had a quick look. Ed went on filling up the tower of packets inside the machine, head bent. The man laughed.

'Helping to keep the birth rate down?'

In the bar, the coffee was on the counter, next to a flat tin. Ed glanced around but the other man was deep in the *Racing Post*, didn't even look up. The coffee was all right, though, and Brian had gone into the back so there was no need to chat.

'See you,' Ed shouted. There was a grunt from somewhere.

The stuff on the seat had to be covered up again. Later, it could go back into the boot. Later.

The thought of what was in the car boot now sent the old, longed-for surge of electricity up through Ed's body. When it came, there was nothing, nothing like it, no other excitement to touch it, nothing so utterly satisfying. Where did it come from, this urge that was like no other, this craving that, when answered, brought the deepest of pleasures? To other people, a child was a son or a daughter, a pretty little kid passing in the street, or a wailing nuisance, something to be taught the alphabet and dressed up, something smelly, snotty or cute, whatever. To Ed, a child was all of those things. But, every so often came the craving. When it did, a child was an opportunity.

The car turned out of the Holly Bush and accelerated on to the dual carriageway, just as the petrol warning light flashed amber.

'Bugger.' There was a service station at Kitby. Don't chance it, don't risk running out. Jesus, the thought was enough. OK, slow down, eke it out, don't burn up the bloody fuel.

Kitby petrol station was a lifetime coming.

Seven

Simon Serrailler sat with Jim Chapman in his office. They were both silent, both thinking. Simon had not gone back to Lafferton. Because he hoped the action was going to be here, and to end here, a result for him as well as for the North Riding force. And because his mood had lifted and he was enjoying his involvement.

Chapman sat, fingers tip to tip in front of his nose, looking down on his desk. The visit to the village where the abducted child lived had been as agonising as they had expected. Serrailler had had David Angus's parents at the front of his mind, but they had been controlled by comparison with the Suddens. He had never witnessed such raw, open grief, such anger and anguish and storms of tears. The mother had torn at her own face and pulled strands of her hair until they came out, screaming at the police liaison officer with her. People had stood staring, wild-eyed and hostile, at the police, at the same time as they showed their furious need of them.

Both men had come away shaken.

Now, Jim Chapman reached for the phone. His every movement seemed planned, every word measured. Simon watched him.

'I want,' he said, 'every silver-coloured Mondeo sighted anywhere on the roads in our area followed and the registration checked. Any details tallying with the first three, repeat, three letters, that car is to be stopped, the driver questioned

39

and the car searched. And I want every silver Mondeo registered in our area and having those initial letters traced and
the owner visited. Repeat, every silver Mondeo.'

He put the receiver down and looked at Serrailler. 'What?'
Simon shook his head. 'Your call.'

'It takes what it takes. Men. Overtime. Whatever.' He got
up. 'I'd like to nip up to the hospital again, see my daughter.
Are you still with us, Simon?'

'Am I still welcome?'

Jim Chapman raised his eyebrows at him as he left the
room.

'He'll go to Real Madrid.'

'Real wouldn't want him.'

'Crap, of course they'd want him. He's genius.'

'Well, they can't all go to Real. I reckon it'll be AC Milan.'

PC Dave Hennessy drained the can of Coke and scrunched
it up to the size of a chicken nugget. It was one of the things
he did.

'Here, Karl reckons he's gonna pop the question come
Friday.'

'Wondered what the fat grin was for. That'll sort him. No
more evenings pumping iron.' ———

'Naw, he's going for the nationals, he's gotta keep that up.
You can't afford to miss a day, that level of weightlifting.'

'Read my lips: "That'll sort him." You met Linda?'

'Seen her.'

'Yeah, well, I went to school with her. She's bloody terrifying. It'll be under the thumb.'

Nick Paterson laughed, thinking about it. They were sitting
up on the lay-by in the shade. He shifted his legs and slipped
down a bit in the seat. Might be time for ten minutes.

'You see that notice this morning? CID woman pinned it
up apparently.'

'Nope.'

'Gay march through York. Wear your uniform with pride.'

Nick snorted in derision. 'That's wrong. It's in the police
rules. You don't join political marches, you don't become an

activist . . . They want to go on perv marches they should get a different job.'

'You can't say that.'

'Pervs is what I said and pervs is what I meant.'

'Here!' Nick sat up. 'You see that?'

'I got my eyes shut.'

'Silver Mondeo.'

'Hundreds of them.'

'See the driver? Man, dark jacket, dark hair.' Nick let the clutch in and roared down the slip road on to the dual carriageway. 'Find out that number again.'

But Dave was already on to it.

Two miles on and doing eighty, they shot by the service station.

'Fuck it. He's in there,' Dave shouted.

'Stop at the Conway roundabout, wait for him.'

'There's four routes he could take. We can't cover them all.'

'Call for back-up.'

'Be halfway to Scotland by then.'

'Might not have been him anyway.'

They slowed to fifty. Ahead, in the east, the clouds were banking up, storm grey and darkening.

'I don't know though,' Nick said after a moment. 'I had a feeling about that one.'

It was difficult, not having any official role here. Simon couldn't stay for ever. If today ended in a blank, he would have to return to Lafferton tomorrow morning.

He wandered down the corridor towards the CID room. What did they think of him here? Were they all watching him, speculating? Stations were gossip shops, but it was unusual for the gossip to spread about an outsider. He was irritated.

The atmosphere was quiet but the tension was there, the sense that this time, maybe, perhaps, something would break, there would be a lead, it might be coming to the boil. At the far end of the room, the faces of the children, three of them now, looked out.

'Sir?'

A DC was beckoning him over. Simon took the phone he was holding out. 'Serrailler.'

'I'm heading back,' Jim Chapman said. 'Pick you up on my way.'

'Where are we going?'

'Main road towards Scarborough. Silver Mondeo speeding. Patrol car intercepted. Driver put his foot down. Registration tallies. Get down to the forecourt, I'll not be stopping.'

Simon dropped the phone and ran.

In the car, which barely drew up to let him scramble in, Chapman explained.

'They spotted him, then lost him. Picked him up again at a roundabout, flagged him down but he wouldn't stop.'

Chapman's driver was picking up speed.

'Description?'

'Tallies – driver has dark hair, wearing a dark jacket, has noticeably pale skin apparently, which the ice-cream van chap remarked on . . . no passengers. We've got cars coming in to cover routes off.'

They were on the dual carriageway now, and Chapman was in touch with the patrol immediately behind the Mondeo. Simon felt the old clench in the pit of his stomach, as the adrenalin rushed in. He had the sense that this might be it. Their car was doing over a hundred now, scenery flashing by. A face at a vehicle window, a driver alarmed at their speed, then another, gone. A lorry, pulling in to let them pass. A blur of red. A tanker. Blare of a horn. Gone. It was raining, the sky ahead was sulphurous.

A hundred and five, steady.

Then, just in front, the blue light of a patrol car.

'Storm's coming in from the sea,' Chapman said. 'You ever been over this way?'

'I've a photograph of myself on a donkey at Scarborough.' Serrailler glanced out of the rear window and spotted a second patrol car.

Chapman was on the phone again. The Mondeo was still moving, still heading east.

They hit a wall of rain and tore a way through it.

Eight

Crap way to earn a living. Crap way to live. Filling vending machines with condoms and tampons, selling illegal fags. What was it about? There ought to be more.

There *was* more.

The car could move when it had to, eating up the shining wet road.

What would he have said? Or she for that matter? *We expected better of you. We wanted more for you.* The whining pasty faces, his watery blue eyes. Pathetic.

Weak. Never be.

There was the dark space. Hole. No one knew. That was the end of it and didn't signify. It was the beginning that signified. The moment of waking. The faintest shadow of a shadow.

The needle of excited dread.

The rain was streaming down the window and bouncing off the bonnet. How far from home? Too far. No happy evening with Kyra then. Kyra's face shone out of the rainstorm, bright-eyed. Kyra. Different. Funny that. Kyra was safe as houses. No harm would ever come to Kyra. It was good to know, good to be confident. Kyra enjoyed coming round, getting away from her own home, the lack of interest or attention, the endless shouting and chivvying and swearing. Kyra deserved more, deserved someone listening, playing, having fun, thinking up things to do. Kyra.

Why was Kyra different?

It puzzled Ed.

They were there. They had been left a long way back but now they were there again, white streaking up, blue flashing. Fuck it. The road was straight and fast but the rain didn't help. It was good to know exactly what was ahead though, not be driving blindly anywhere, in the desperation to shake them off, get away.

The last time Kyra had been round she had looked at the box of photographs and there were half a dozen of Scarborough. She'd loved it. The donkeys. The castle. Then Ed on a donkey. Ed with a bucket and spade. Then a post-card of the foreshore with the fairy lights on.

'I wish I could go there. One day, will you and me go there? Will you take me to Scarborough, Ed?'

Why not? Natalie would probably jump at it, give her a break. There would be the donkeys and the glass of ice cream with cochineal sauce at the Harbour bar and the game of Whack a Croc at the funfair, the candyfloss-maker to watch, hot sweetness in their mouths, melting into a pool; then the rock stall; the sand, soft as silk in great heaps by the railings, but harder, flat and dark as honey towards the water's edge. Crazy golf. The maze. The cliff paths winding down and down.

The cliffs. The caves. Rock pools. Crabs and starfish. Kyra would love it all. A child to show the magic to, a child to laugh with. Kyra's face, curious, interested, hopeful. Kyra would be safe. Kyra was safe. Kyra would never lie bound in the boot of the car, eyes closed, breath still.

Rock pools. Now it was the reflection in them that shone through the windscreen and the rain, the clear water, with the creatures deep down stirring the sand about.

Pools.

Cliffs.

Caves.

Cliff.

Cave.

Pool.

Places to hide.

44

Nine

'I dreamed your father was back. He was sitting at the piano playing Scott Joplin. How silly.'

'Well, he used to play Scott Joplin.'

'Of course, but why should I dream he was doing it now?'

Magda Fitzroy shifted irritably about on her pillows. She looked bleached, and her eyes had sunk in, the bruises and cut on her forehead standing out crusted and dark as dried meat.

The ward had six beds and Magda was beside a window, but the view was of thin skeins of cloud and the side of another building.

'It was remarkable, you know, he played all that without reading music, just by ear.'

'Have you been thinking about him a lot?'

'No. Why do you ask?'

It was conversations like this, roundabout, argumentative conversations, which tried Jane's patience, reminding her why she had had to move away from London, breathe different air, psychologically rather than literally. Magda enjoyed argument and bouts of disagreeable confrontation. It had driven her patient husband mad.

Jane's best way was to snip off the thread of discussion sharply. But when she had done so, she had to unwind another. 'You can't go back home to be on your own after what's happened. Maybe we should talk about things.'

Her mother turned her head to look away. On the other side of the room, an old woman snored, lying humped sideways under the bedcovers, her head back. Magda drew in her breath in irritation. Jane waited. But her mother was good at ignoring a topic she did not wish to discuss.

A trolley came, trailing the smell of urn tea.

'Here you go, Violet, up you come, darling.'

Jane went to the trolley. 'Can I give you a hand?'

The woman had a long grey ponytail and a sour mouth.

'My mother doesn't have milk or sugar.'

'What, all black? I couldn't stomach that.'

'Nor could I.' Jane smiled. She got no smile in return.

'So you'll come back with me then?' she said, setting the cup and saucer on the locker. Dear God, she thought, help me find a way round this. She is old. You have to love her, you have to try. But it was hard to ignore all the years of gritty dislike, and the recent ones of bitter words and derision.

Magda looked at her. 'You couldn't stand it any longer than I could. I want to be in my own home. They won't come back, they've got what they wanted.'

'You can't be sure of that.'

'I'd better be.'

'I've phoned an alarm company, they're going to survey the house tomorrow morning. At least that will give you some security.'

'Of course it won't. There are damned alarms going off every night, people are probably having their throats slit but no one minds, the police certainly don't come. So don't waste my money.'

'Mother, I can't just go back and leave you, I'll –'

'What? You'll do whatever you do. Sing and pray.'

'And worry about you.'

'I thought you were supposed to have done with that. Trust the Lord and so forth.'

'At least come to Lafferton for a few days . . . see the place, it's beautiful. See where I live.'

'Like the fairies.'

'What?'

'At the bottom of someone's garden, isn't it? Seems quite fitting.'

One day, I may hit her. One day, I may kill her. One day . . . But she had gone past all that, years before, coming in from school at the end of every day, shaking with pent-up anger if her mother was at home, only calm when she was at the clinic, or lecturing, or, wonderfully, on some trip abroad. Sometimes, it had been Jane and her father for weeks at a time. They had looked at one another across the dining table and never said it aloud but caught each other counting off the days of freedom and peace that were left, seeing it all in one another's eyes.

But Magda was weak now, Jane thought, weak and frightened and confused. And when it happened, she rang me. Didn't that mean something?

'I've got a paper to write for the next *Journal*, and Elspeth is expecting me to have looked at our last chapter. I need to finish it, Jane. I still have a lot to do before I die.' She spoke matter-of-factly. She meant it.

'I know. You've plenty more to give.'

'Sentimental.'

'No. Truth.'

'Do you remember Charlie Gold? Maurice Gold's son?'

'Good Lord . . . yes, I do . . . I quite fancied him at one time. Why?'

'There's an invitation to his wedding in the house somewhere. Sunday week, I think. I'd like to go.'

'Charlie Gold.' She saw him, dark hair, olive skin, thick eyebrows. Goodness.

'Who is he marrying?'

Her mother shrugged. 'I hate the synagogue. I haven't been since your father died. But I wouldn't mind dying at a Jewish wedding.'

'I bet quite a few people do . . . all that eating, dancing as if they were still twenty . . . then pop.'

Jane remembered the arguments she had listened to from her room, the volleys of accusation, the despair in her father's voice. He had suffered for marrying not only a non-Jew but an unbeliever, a rationalist, a Marxist, a woman who had laughed in his face when he had suggested they go occasionally to the Friday-night meal with his parents.

When Magda was away, Jane had gone with him instead. The memory of the ceremony, the food, the prayers, the closeness of the atmosphere was precious. She had never told her mother, and when her grandparents died within six months of one another, it was as though everything had stopped, the whole of her connection with her Jewishness had been severed. Then her father had died. It had almost gone from her memory, until news like this, of someone she had once known, brought it back like the waft from a censer, swinging its perfume towards her.

'Do you suppose those youths knew me?' her mother asked. Just for a second, her eyes flickered with anxiety.

'No . . . they just liked the look of the house and thought there'd be rich pickings. They expected it to be empty but you were in, so they lost their heads. How would they know you? You didn't recognise them.'

'Might they have been watching?'

'Unlikely. There are plenty of swankier houses in Hampstead.'

'That is true. Oh, go on, get back to your cathedral. I'm sure they need you more than I do.'

'Not just at present. Anyway, I have to see the police. They've checked the house but they want a statement from me.'

'How can that be of use? You weren't even there. Tell them to see me. You don't know anything about it. I am going to discharge myself in the morning and I am then going home. And I don't want you to be there fussing about.'

Jane got up. Humour, she had decided long ago, humour works. Occasionally. But nothing remotely funny came to her.

It was dusk by the time she left London. The sky was feathered with blackberry cloud as she headed west. Scott Joplin came from the CD player. She had seen the police, sorted out the house as best she could, bought groceries and some sweet-scented stocks to bring fresh life to a house that felt tainted. She turned her mind away from thoughts of her mother alone again there, working as usual in her garden study among a drift of papers and cigar ash. She would be fine. She was a strong woman. It was astonishing that any burglar had got the better of her. Her mother . . .

But her mother, for the first time in Jane's life, had become vulnerable and the idea left her confused and anxious, half afraid, half irritated. How dare she? she thought, moving into the centre lane and picking up speed. How dare she do this to me?

The piano plinked out its jazz, faultless, confident. The memory of her father blinded her with unexpected tears.

Ten

'Can she see me?'

The nurse hesitated.

'Can she hear me?'

'She may . . . hearing is the . . . yes, she may.'

'Hearing is the what? *What?*'

Alarm flickered on her face.

Max Jameson had shouted. He was angry. He had spoken as if it was the nurse's fault and it was not, but he could not apologise. 'What? Please don't pretend to me.'

'Hearing is the last sense to go, that was all I was going to say. So she may hear you . . . always assume that she can. That's the best way.'

But when he looked at Lizzie, who might hear him or might not, he could think of nothing to say.

Lizzie. Already this was not Lizzie.

He saw that the nurse was looking at him with such sweetness, such concern, that he wanted to lay his head on her breast, take her comfort. She wiped Lizzie's forehead with a cloth dipped in cool water.

'Can she feel that?'

'I don't know.'

'I have to go outside. Can I go into the garden?'

'Of course. It's lovely there. Peaceful.'

'I don't want peace.'

He stood in the hot little dying room trying to speak, but only breath came. He stumbled to the door.

It had been three days and three nights and terrible to watch and still his wife would not die. Lizzie.

He sat on a bench. He wished he smoked. That would have been a good excuse. 'I need to get out for a cigarette', not 'I need to get away from her dying'.

There was no one else outside. On the right, the new extension building was being finished, the windows still glassless, like eye sockets.

'Can she see?'

It occurred to Max that if he could have known the future, when her illness had begun, he would have killed her then, that it would have been kinder to have killed. His love for her was so great that he could have done it.

The air smelled sweet, of earth and cooling grass, but the next moment, of cigarette smoke. A man had come to sit next to him on the bench. He proffered the packet.

'No, thanks,' Max said.

'No. Well, I didn't. Gave it up years back. Only you reach for it, you know, first thing you need.'

Don't talk to me, Max thought, don't ask and don't tell.

'Hardest bit, this, isn't it? Waiting. You feel guilty, like . . . wishing it was over, dreading it.'

Something flooded through him . . . Relief? Fear?

'It's not right. You've done everything for them then suddenly you can't do a bloody thing.'

'Yes.'

'Your mother or what?'

Max stared at the dark ground beneath his feet. His lips felt thick and numb. 'Wife,' he heard himself say. 'My wife. Lizzie.'

'Fuck it.'

'Right.'

'Daughter, me. Two smashing kids, everything to live for. I'd get into that bed and die for her if I could.'

'Yes,' Max said.

'Cancer?'

'No.'

'Right. Generally is, that's all.'

'Yes.'

The man put his hand briefly on to Max's shoulder as he stood up. Said nothing. Went.

It would have been better if he had never met Lizzie, never loved her, never been happy.

Better.

He knew he ought to go back to her.

He sat on alone in the dark garden.

Eleven

Cat Deerbon switched on her torch. The block had a concrete staircase but several of the lights had failed and it was the same along the walkway outside the flats. It was some time since she had been called out here at night. Televisions and sound systems blared through windows, there were raised voices and then patches of silence and blackness, as though people were hunkered down hiding from a storm.

Number 188 was like that. No light from the kitchen window, at the front, or through the glass door panel. A train went by in the distance.

Cat rattled the letter box, waited, and then banged on the glass. A dog began to bark from further along, booming, menacing. She knew the sort of dog it would be.

No one came to the door.

The call had come from an elderly man. He had sounded breathless and distressed, and over the phone she had heard the harsh whistling in his bronchial tubes. She rattled the letter box again, shouted, and then tried the handle, but the door was locked. She moved along the walkway to stand under one of the lights and took out her mobile. As she did so, she heard a slight scuffle, the scrape of a shoe sole, nothing more, and then someone's arm was round her neck from behind, her wrist was bent backwards and the phone was wrenched out of her hand. Cat swore and kicked out hard, but as she tried to pull away, felt a blow in her lower back which sent her, face down, on to the concrete. Footsteps, soft, sure footsteps, raced away and down the stairs.

The dog's barking had risen to a fury.

She did not know how long it took her to sit cautiously, checking herself for pain as she moved; but she was no more than bruised and shaken and stood up, reaching out to the ledge for support.

Footsteps up the stairs again, but these were the sharp, confident taps of high heels.

Cat called out.

Ten minutes later, she was sitting on a leather sofa beside a blazing gas fire, her hand shaking as she tried to drink from a mug of tea. Police and ambulance were on their way.

'You shouldn't be doing calls out here by yourself at night, Doctor, you was lucky it was just your phone. Bloody louts.'

Cat did not know the woman with burgundy fingernails who had been coming home off the late shift at the super-market, but she was near to tears with gratitude.

'Who was it you was going to see?'

'He lives at 188 . . . Mr Sumner.'

'Got a hearing aid?'

'I've no idea. I don't think I've ever seen him.'

'No, well, I wouldn't know his name or anything, you don't here. Well, some of the young ones do, the mothers with little ones, they all seem to get together, but the rest of us just come and go. Like that now, isn't it? You sure you're warm enough, you can get cold having a shock, I read that.'

Cat couldn't have said that she was too hot and the tea was so sweet she could barely drink it. It didn't matter. How could it?

The police and paramedics arrived together, boots crunching outside, sending the dog and others in the flats around into a frenzy.

The woman followed Cat and waited as the door of 188 was forced open. The flat was in darkness and smelled acrid. One of the paramedics almost slipped on a patch of vomit.

54

They found Cat's patient, Arthur Sumner, lying dead in the lavatory.

'Give you a lift home, Doc?'

'I'm fine.'

Fine, she thought, thanking the woman with the burgundy nails, thanking the crews, walking down the concrete staircase and across to her car. Fine. She sat for a moment, head down on the wheel. She would ring Chris, tell him what had happened. Then she remembered that her mobile had been taken, that she had to go into the station tomorrow and make a report, get a new phone, do the paperwork on Arthur Sumner. 'Got a hearing aid?' She had not even known.

Home. Now. She started the engine and reversed the car. As she turned, she saw a couple of youths peering at her, laughing, fingers raised obscenely. Just don't ever get ill when I'm around, she thought, don't call me, don't have an accident, don't . . .

Let it go. She was driving too fast.

The road away from the Dulcie estate took her on to the bypass, after which she skirted a grid of avenues leading to the Hill. Revulsion she had not felt for months, and fear too, rose up in her and seemed to fill her mouth with a bitter taste. She did not want to go near the Hill, where women had been attacked and so swiftly, expertly murdered. There was a stain over the place that would never be erased from Lafferton's consciousness. Someone had written a book about the case, someone else was making a television documentary, keeping it all alive, keeping the wounds open.

She took a detour round Tenbury Walk. The hospice was at the bottom of here. The lights shone softly behind drawn blinds; a couple of cars were parked at the front. Cat turned into the entrance and pulled up beside them.

Twelve

'Chapman.'

'Call just came in, guv. Natalie Coombs, aged twenty-six, lives in Fimmingham. Reports her next-door neighbour has a silver Mondeo registration XT . . . something. She suddenly panicked because her six-year-old daughter spends quite a bit of time round there apparently.'

'Has the child said anything?'

'Not as far as I know.'

'Neighbour's name?'

'Ed Sleightholme.'

'Get someone round there. Now.'

'Guv.'

The driver murmured urgently, and Chapman glanced up. 'Bugger.'

'They're turning off, sir.'

The patrol car in front had veered left, leaving the dual carriageway, and was following the Mondeo on to a B-road.

'He's not going to Scarborough.'

'Where then?'

'Not sure . . .' The rain had lessened slightly but the clouds were still dark, banking up as they ran towards the sea, and the narrower road was treacherous.

'OK, Katie, let's not cause a pile-up.'

'Sir.' The driver eased off but ahead of them, the patrol car streaked after the Mondeo, sending up sheets of spray behind it.

'Funny, isn't it,' Chapman said, leaning back in his seat, relaxed and calm. 'Give them a rope and they'll often hang themselves . . . If he hadn't panicked when the boys stepped after him, he'd not have roused any more interest. Now look at him.'

'Have you got enough to arrest him?' asked Simon.

'Just about enough to bring him in for questioning.'

'Jesus.' Simon closed his eyes. He opened them on an empty road ahead. The cars had peeled off on to yet another B-road. Lightning cracked across the sky, out to sea. The Mondeo drove towards it.

It took them twenty minutes to reach the coast, and a stretch of open, scrubby ground off the road.

They jumped out. The patrol car had stopped. The Mondeo was slewed round a few yards away from them and the driver was out and running fast towards the cliff edge.

'Bloody hell.'

'He's going to kill himself,' Chapman muttered.

'Not if I have anything to do with it he's bloody not.'

Something made Serrailler run, something that had been building up inside him like the storm and now hit him in the stomach as a burst of fury. The uniformed officers were making across the grass but they were slow, one of them a heavy man, the other seemingly in trouble with his boot. Simon passed them, confident, running easily. What gave him speed was his certainty, cast iron and unwavering, that he was following the murderer of David Angus, Scott Merriman, Amy Sudden . . . He had to catch the man before he reached the cliff edge and hurtled himself through the air on to the rocks far below.

But as he drew nearer, Serrailler realised that there was a path. He did not look back to see if the others were following. He was on his own now, this was his chase and his arrest.

The man vanished.

Simon reached the cliff edge and hesitated, looking down. The path was narrow and precipitous, cut into the cliff, without any handrail or holding place, but clearly the man knew exactly where to go and what to do after he plunged over the edge.

Simon did not hesitate.

It was the wind which shocked him and almost threw him off balance; rain was driven hard into his face. The sky was livid, lightning forking across it, though still a way off. He calculated that they had some time before the storm posed any threat and by then he intended them to be back up the path and into the cars.

He slithered, caught his breath and tried to grab an outcrop of rock, but the stones slipped out of his hand and rumbled down the cliff, gaining speed. Ahead of him, the man was like a monkey, agile, sure-footed, clambering and scrabbling down. Below them, far below, a narrow ribbon of dark sand, strewn with rocks. Ahead of that, the sea, roaring up, swollen and gathering height. Simon looked back. He had come further than he'd realised. The figures peering down at him from the clifftop seemed miles away. But heights had never bothered him and he was sure-footed now, though the rain was washing debris down the path behind him, and his hand slipped on the rock as he tried to gain a hold. The lower part of the cliff was the hardest to negotiate – the rocks here were jagged, full of crevices and slippery with lime green seaweed. Several times he almost fell and once, in saving himself, gashed his palm on a piece of outcrop. Then they were down and he was in pursuit, the flat sand sucking at his feet. The man was trying to run but they were both slowed now. The wind was full in their faces and the storm was being swept inshore; the lightning streaked down the sky followed within seconds by thunder. But it was not the storm which troubled Simon. It was the tide which was gathering speed and boiling in fast towards them.

They were in a small curved bay, separated from the others by long breakwaters of rocks that stretched out into the sea like the narrowing tails of prehistoric monsters; as he raced and leapt his way along the narrow belt of sand, the bones of the tails were being submerged one by one.

Ahead of him, the man leapt on to a high rock and clambered towards the cliff.

Simon was close now.

Then he saw the cave mouth, a toothless maw in the base of the cliff and guarded by a Cerberus of rocks. Seconds later, he was on to them. The cave smelled of long-dead fish and salt water.

For a moment, he wondered if it might be the entrance to some place of safety out of the tide, set deep in the cliff, but as he bent to get inside, he saw that it did not go far back and that the rock above was so low he would scarcely be able to stand upright. There was no light. He had no torch. Behind, the sea was roaring at one with the thunder.

'Get out of here, you idiot, come back out, the tide's going to pour in at any minute.'

Nothing. Then a voice that shocked him into complete stillness.

'God. Oh God, it's the wrong cave. You've got to get out. You're blocking me. Move.'

The voice rose to a hysterical pitch.

'Get out!' the woman screamed.

Serrailler began to back away slowly, holding on to the rocks, the sides of the cave . . . As he emerged into the greenish light of the storm, he saw that there was one way of escape, a ledge perhaps a dozen feet up against the cliff face, just reachable in three or four carefully placed strides. The tide was swirling a yard away.

'Come out and climb after me . . . can you do that?'

He looked round. The woman was coming out of the cave. Short dark hair. A dark jacket. Black jeans. White, horrified face. Dark sunken eyes.

Forget who it is, concentrate, focus.

'Come on . . . take one step at a time, do everything I do. Do as you're told, right?'

'OK . . . Jesus, help . . .'

'We can get up there. Don't panic. Take a deep breath. Right, I'm going up. Follow me exactly.'

His own voice sounded confident, he thought, authoritative.

She would believe he knew exactly what he was doing. He reached for the first handhold in the cliff, grasped it and swung himself up, scrabbling carefully with his feet to find a firm base.

Below him, he heard the woman's fast, whimpering breaths.

'It's fine. Wait. Now the next.'

It took a hundred years. It took two minutes. Once, some of the rock pulled away in his hand, almost taking him down with it, but he slid sideways and grasped another outcrop which stayed firm.

Simon reached the ledge, hauled himself carefully on to it, and then lay down on his stomach and reached out his hand to pull the woman up.

The sea had come racing on to the strip of sand, over the low rocks, into the mouth of the cave. The sky was a sullen, sulphurous grey, but for now the lightning had ceased.

'Press back against the cliff. You won't get blown away like that.'

She managed it, weeping with fear, her hands bleeding, face ashen.

Simon waited until she was next to him, back against the cliff, pressing herself into it as if she could make it open up to admit her body.

He looked at her.

Ordinary. Neither attractive nor plain, neither tall nor short, fat nor thin. An average smallish woman with cropped hair. *Ordinary.*

'I'm DCI Simon Serrailler from Lafferton Police. Your name?'

She gaped at him as if he had spoken in another language.

'What's your name?' He raised his voice above the crash and boom of a wave below.

It came out at last, her mouth moving queerly, pushed sideways as if she had had a stroke.

'Ed.'

'What kind of a name is that?'

'Edwina. Edwina Sleightholme.'

She looked at him. 'What will happen?'

'You'll be taken in for questioning in connection with the abduction of Amy Sudden.'

'*Now*, for Christ's sake, now, what's going to happen here, *now*?'

She crouched and bent her head. He heard her sobs of fear.

He could not see what was happening above them, nor turn to look up. Once, he thought he heard a shout, but it was swept away by the noise of the sea.

He was strangely calm. He was alone here, with the woman. But on the clifftop he had back-up, and they would have called for assistance; he had no idea how long it would take to come. When would the tide turn?

Ed Sleightholme moved suddenly, edging her body forward.

'Don't be so bloody stupid.'

'I might as well, I might as well.'

'Why?'

Her body was shaking.

Simon waited, then said, 'Nasty way to die.'

'Who'd care?'

'Haven't the faintest idea. Are you married?'

A slight shake of her head.

'Parents alive?'

Silence. Then the slightest movement again, an inch further forward.

'Friends?'

It sickened him to imagine it. But the family and friends wouldn't know. They never did. She might have taken and murdered these children and half a dozen more and still have had good friends, lovers, people who cared about her, simply because *they did not know.*

She said something.

'What?'

Again.

'I can't hear you.'

He had thought the storm had eased and drifted inland, but now there was a bolt of lightning so close to them Simon thought it had struck the cliff only a few feet away. The thunder made him duck his head. She cowered back, pressing into the cliff again, and grabbed his arm with such strength he thought she would pull him over the cliff with her.

'It's OK,' he said, keeping his voice calm. 'We're OK. It can't touch us, the rocks will conduct any lightning downwards.'

He had no idea if it were true but he knew that he had sounded convincing when she loosened her grip on him.

'I didn't . . . know that . . .'

'So long as we keep our backs in contact with the cliff. Just don't move away from that contact for a second.'

He looked sideways and saw that she had believed him and was pressing her body backwards as if her life depended on it. She had her eyes tight shut.

Simon forced himself to look away from her and to turn his mind to other places, other things . . . He imagined his nephew Sam at the wicket, face upturned eagerly to the bowler. The sun sifted between the poplar trees at the edge of the cricket field. There was the taste of home-brewed beer in his mouth. He went on painting the picture, animating it, making the film run, the cricket game continue. Anything to keep himself from remembering who was next to him, inches away on the narrow ledge and why and what she had almost certainly done. If he thought of that, he knew he might make a single movement to send her over the edge of the cliff.

He had seen Sam raise his bat to acknowledge the applause for his half-century, when there was a sudden noise which, after a moment, he recognised as the beep of his mobile, buried in his inside pocket.

'Simon? What the hell are you doing?' The line crackled, the voice breaking up.

Simon told Jim Chapman in half a sentence. As he spoke, he saw the woman's back stiffen.

'Bloody lucky you're alive.'

'Yes.'

'Right, coastguard's been alerted and he's just come back to say RAF 202 Squadron have scrambled a rescue helicopter. On its way.'

'Thank God for that.'

'Any injuries?'

'Nothing much . . . I'm restraining myself.'

'Right, well, you go on doing that, we want this one whole.'

'Too right. Anything up there?'

A fraction of a pause. Then Chapman said quickly, 'You'll get a full briefing later,' and cut off.

Simon had been close to violent criminals often enough, close to murderers and wife-beaters, handcuffed to them, his own flesh touching theirs, making his skin crawl. But this was different. He had complete authority and complete power over Edwina Sleightholme, barring the fact that she might still make a sudden bid to leap off the ledge to her death. But he did not think she would do that now. Fear was paralysing her.

He wondered how long they would be here before the helicopter arrived, and whether he could summon up the will to have a conversation with her. If it was a question of minutes, he had no need to, but if they were to be here for hours, he would have to talk, keep her going, keep her awake.

He looked at her legs, in the black jeans, her cap of dark hair falling forwards over the knees. Had she taken those children and killed them? How could this be? The profile was all wrong. This was not a woman's crime. This should have been a man.

If she was innocent, why had she failed to stop for the patrol car, why had she tried to break her neck, and theirs, racing for this coast? What else would have made her dive down the precipitous cliff path to get away from them, except guilt and fear of arrest?

The ledge was cold and his back ached. His arms were stiff and his cut hand throbbed.

The storm was grumbling away inland now and the sky had lightened to a paler grey over the sea. It began to rain again, at first lightly, blown into their faces with the sea spray, but then hard pins of rain lashing them to the cliff. But Simon was conscious of something inside himself that he had missed, something he had once known and almost lost touch with.

His tension and excitement were under control, the buzz was helping him not blurring his focus.

'I'm going to be sick.'

'Don't lean over, lean back. Close your eyes.'

'Makes it worse.'

'Look down at the bit of rock in front of you.'

'I'm scared shitless.'

He could have pounced then, asked her how she liked it, whether she realised this was how the children had felt, but worse, a thousand times worse. He wanted to put her through it, describe them to her as he had seen them on the conference-room wall, the pictures of three bright, cheerful, hopeful young faces, to tell her how it had been for the parents, to . . .

He said nothing.

His phone rang again.

'RAF helicopter ETA fifteen minutes. Can you hold on?'

'Yes.'

'Want the good news?'

'What?'

'The kid's alive.'

'Where?'

'Tied up in the car boot.'

Simon did not look at Edwina Sleightholme. He might have kicked her over the edge on to the rocks below.

'The chopper'll take you to Scarborough hospital. We'll get over there as soon as we have it in sight. Hang on to him.'

'Oh, don't you worry.'

'We'll make the arrest once the docs have discharged him.'

'Shame.'

'You'll get your chance.'

'One thing though.'

'What?'

'Ed stands for Edwina.'

He heard a long intake of breath.

Simon glanced sideways at her shoe, a black flat slip-on with a small bit of gold chain across the front. Not a man's shoe, just as the hands clutching her head were not man's hands, they were slim, soft, nicely shaped hands with neatly trimmed oval, unpainted nails. The hair he could see between her fingers was shining with rain, dark as a seal's back.

He had often looked at killers and understood what made them tick, seen violence pent up in their bodies, seen eyes wild with rage in deranged faces. Once or twice he had been puzzled. The Lafferton serial killer had been a psychopath, unable to feel empathy or emotion, self-absorbed, with a hidden agenda of his own. But this time, next to a young woman, terrified, sick, hunched down into a small slight figure against the wind and rain, this time, he was completely bewildered, lost for any explanation, any link between her and the abduction, torture, murder of young children. He could get no hold on it at all.

They heard the noise long before they could see the yellow bird emerge out of the grey mass of cloud and water. The blades churned up the air, seeming to chop it about and hurl it at them like clods of wet earth.

Sleightholme stood up suddenly.

'Get down. Stay absolutely still.'

'I'm not going in that fuckin' thing, I'll jump off here before that.' Her face was streaming with water, but her mouth was set, her eyes looking wildly about.

'Stay STILL.'

She lunged out without warning and grabbed at Serrailler's shoulder and he rocked, desperately trying to steady them both. Above them, the noise of the helicopter seemed to have broken through his eardrums into his skull. She jabbed out a hand again, fingers clasped open like a claw. He caught it and wrenched her wrist back so that he saw her mouth open in pain. He needed handcuffs and had none.

Then the helicopter began to retreat, the noise muffled in the cloud bank again.

'What the fuck is going on?' he shouted.

Seconds later his phone rang. He was holding on to the woman and his hand was slippery, so that he all but dropped it.

'Yes?'

'They've backed off because they need to know whether there is any chance she'd be a threat to safety if she's winched on board. Any weapon or potential weapon?'

'How do I bloody know?'

'Well, ask, dammit. Cigarette lighter, pen even . . .'

'Better assume so then.'

'OK. They saw a struggle . . . We've no view of you from up here. Is that correct?'

'Nothing serious. Just tell them to get us off this bloody ledge.'

'They won't take someone who is a risk to the safety of the crew and the chopper. Can you vouch that the woman is not?'

Serrailler hesitated. He could not. Ed was a woman, small and slight, easily overpowered, but she was also furious and terrified, and without much to lose. He knew he ought not to guarantee anything, but if he didn't, then what? There was no other way they could be brought to safety. It would be some hours yet before the tide had receded enough for them to be able to clamber down to the sand.

He clicked off his phone and turned to the woman.

'Listen. I have to guarantee that you have no weapon, and that you will not behave in a manner calculated to jeopardise anyone's safety – mine and that of the helicopter crew. I must be bloody mad to ask for your word on that.'

'And if you don't? If I don't?' She looked at him and he saw a flash of malice in her eyes. It had not been there before.

'If you refuse to cooperate?'

She nodded.

'I'll knock you out.'

She blinked.

'Or else they'll take me and leave you.'

'They wouldn't bloody dare.'

'Oh yes they would. That's what the call was about. So?'

He saw her thinking furiously. Looking down over the cliff. Thinking. Looking at him. Thinking.

'OK.'

66

'What?'

'OK, I said.'

He hesitated. He had to go with it. Trust her. Jesus. He called Chapman.

'Can you get the pilot to talk to me?'

'Disconnect. I'll ask.'

The rain came in a squall, battering at the side of the cliff and drenching them.

It was several minutes before the phone rang.

'Flight Sergeant Cuff, RAF 202 Squadron.'

'DCI Serrailler. I understand your concerns, Sergeant. It'll be fine.'

'Do you take full responsibility? It's your call, Chief Inspector.'

'Yes.'

'You don't see any threat to my crew?'

'No.'

A split second. Then, 'OK, we're coming back in. The winchman will be on his way down. But I can't get closer than fifteen feet in to the cliff and conditions are difficult. It may take some time. He will come on to the ledge and you will be strapped together – we can't risk taking the prisoner separately. Any injuries?'

'Minor.'

'OK. Hang on.'

Serrailler had known it before. Once a rescue was under way, once safety was almost his, the tension increased rather than slackened. The time it took for the chopper to get close enough to the cliff to send down the winchman seemed to be far greater than the time they had already been stranded on the ledge. The helicopter hovered above, driving cold air on to them, then pulled up and away, before coming in again at a different angle, swerved, backed off. Now Serrailler and the woman were crouching and he had hold of her wrist. Her arm was limp, her expression flat and tired. The rain had plastered her short hair to her head like a cap.

'They can't get us, can they?'

'They'll get us.'

The helicopter came in again slightly lower, and swung round against the wind. It hovered. Steadied. Then the door slid open. The winchman stepped on to the ledge and raised his arm as he swung. The winch went slack. He bent forward and gestured. The wind blew in a wild gust and almost knocked him off his feet, and it was several more minutes before he had reached Serrailler and Sleightholme and lashed them securely together.

Minutes later, they were being hauled over the ledge into the body of the chopper. Simon remembered how large the RAF rescue helicopters were inside, with room enough for a dozen stretcher cases as well as paramedics and crew. It was noisy, and the tilting and swaying unnerving.

Edwina Sleightholme slumped, head down, staring at the floor.

The winchman was back and the doors were closed and secured.

'We're taking you to the hospital. You'll meet up with DCS Chapman there. ETA four minutes.'

'Thanks. God, I mean it.'

'No probs. Wondered if we'd get close enough for a minute. Let's see your hand.'

'I'm fine.'

They both looked at the woman, sitting hunched forwards. Simon shook his head, then, in a moment of revulsion, turned away from Sleightholme, to stare out of the helicopter window at the churning sea and sky.

Thirteen

'I'm fine,' Cat Deerbon said, 'I'm fine. I ought to be able to see off a young thug like that . . .'

Sister Noakes took the cup of tea from her before Cat's shaking hand sent it on to the floor.

Something had happened as she had stepped through the doors of Imogen House into the night-time quietness. The muscles and bones inside her legs felt as if they had dissolved, and she had been saved by one of the nurses as she had started to crumple. Now, she sat in Penny Noakes's room, feeling a fool.

'What's wrong with me for goodness' sake? I've coped with a hell of a lot worse than that.'

'Funny thing, shock.'

'I'm tough.'

'Aren't we all? Then out of the blue, we're felled by something small. Happens to me. Death after death, all the difficult ones, young people, pain we can't control, someone's fear . . . and I'm very calm. I get home and there's a dead mouse on the mat and I'm in tears. Try this tea again.'

Cat's hand was steadier.

'What did the police say?'

Cat shrugged. One random youth on the Dulcie estate who had snatched her mobile, kicked out at her and run? She could hear Simon's patient sigh.

'How's Lizzie Jameson?' she said, setting down her cup.

Sister Noakes looked up. The desk lamp cast a shadow on to her face, but Cat was swift to catch the fleeting expression.

'It's a bugger,' Cat said. 'I'll go along and see her in a moment. Is Max there?'

'He is. He goes into the garden a lot . . . walks around . . . sits on the bench. He'll need a lot of support when it's over, Cat.'

'And he isn't an easy man to help. Very stubborn, very proud.'

'He's angry.'

'So am I. This is the first case I've seen, and I'm angry because it was preventable. Every case of variant CJD was preventable, they came about because of greed . . . greedy bloody farmers.'

'The farmers weren't to know.'

'Don't be so forgiving, I can't handle forgiveness at the moment.' She got up. 'I don't know what I'm going to say to Max either.'

'Come on, you always know. It's your best thing.'

'Hm.'

In the corridor, Cat felt the extraordinary atmosphere of the hospice, the tremendous, packed stillness, the feeling of being out of time. It was never like this in any hospital, there was always clatter, voices and footsteps, a sense of urgency. Here, that was absent. Here, nothing mattered except the individual patients being nursed, kept pain-free and comfortable, what they wanted to say listened to carefully. *'At the still point of the turning world,'* Cat always thought when she came here.

She opened the door of Lizzie's room.

And in that split second, time stopped. Max Jameson was standing beside the bed, holding his wife's hand between both his own, staring down, his face stark with disbelief and a sort of horror. The nurse on the opposite side of Lizzie glanced up at Cat and everything was clear from the expression in her eyes. There was the most profound silence and stillness. The room was a tableau, the people motionless, the dead woman's eyes still open, staring blankly at the ceiling.

70

Then the picture fractured and splintered into a thousand pieces whose sharp edges cut the silence as Max Jameson let out a sound Cat had heard only a few times in her life, a howl that mingled pain and grief, rage and fear. And then he hurled himself past Cat, pushing her as he ran, out of the room, down the corridor towards the hall, his cry trailing behind him like blood spilling out on to the floor.

Cat went to the bed, and drew her hand gently down over Lizzie Jameson's eyes. Already there was the look she knew so well, the strange, deep and distant look of the dead, sleeping with an absorption that took them far beyond reach. But, freed from the struggles and the fear, Lizzie was beautiful again and already years younger; it was as if, at the moment of death, time began counting backwards.

'Poor girl.'

'Hard for them both.'

'It was cruel.'

'I fear for him, Dr Deerbon. I've been watching him today. He's been like a hot spring boiling up inside, just about keeping the lid on for her.'

'I'll go and see him.' Cat lifted Lizzie's hands and folded them gently on top of each other. 'But not tonight.' She turned towards the door. 'I'm bushed.'

It was all she could do to stay focused enough to drive safely, and she opened the car windows and switched on the late-night news.

'Police in North Yorkshire have arrested a thirty-eight-year-old woman in connection with the abduction of a six-year-old girl, Amy Sudden, from near her home in the village of Gathering Bridge. The woman was taken to Scarborough hospital from where the detective in charge of the case, DCS Jim Chapman of the North Riding force, spoke to reporters.'

Cat turned on to the bypass. There was very little traffic, and she could slow down without causing annoyance.

The strong Yorkshire voice came over, speaking in the usual, robotic official way. 'I would like to confirm that, this afternoon, officers from the North Riding force pursued a car trav-

71

elling towards the coast and that a six-year-old girl was discovered in the boot of that car, when it came to a halt on scrubland above the cliffs some miles north of Scarborough. The girl was taken by ambulance to Scarborough hospital where she has undergone a medical examination. Although suffering from shock and dehydration, she has no serious injuries and should be allowed home in a couple of days. I can also confirm that police pursued and subsequently arrested the driver of the car and that tonight a thirty-eight-year-old woman has been taken into custody. That is all I can say for the moment.'

'Superintendent, can you comment on reports that charges may also be brought in connection with the disappearance of two young boys, one in the North Riding force area, and one from the south of England?'

'I'm sorry, I can't say any more for the time being.'

'Can you confirm that a senior officer from another force is with you in connection with these other two cases of presumed abduction?'

'I can't, no.'

Cat switched off the radio, and headed for home.

Lights were still on in the farmhouse but the kitchen was empty. From upstairs came her elder son's voice wailing loudly.

'I didn't know it would, I'm sorry, Daddy, I didn't know . . .'

Cat dropped her bag and headed up.

'What's going on?'

Chris, Sam and Felix were in the bathroom. Felix was in the bath.

'Mummy, it wasn't my fault, it wasn't, I didn't know it –'

'Sam, shut up. Stop whining. The more you go on the crosser it makes me, so shut up.'

It was rare for Chris to speak so sharply to the children.

'What happened?'

'Sam thought marker pen made good tattoos on Felix and I can't get the bloody stuff off.'

Cat sat on the laundry bin and began to laugh.

72

'The funny side of it escapes me. Felix, stop squirming.'

'You'll get nowhere scrubbing like that, Chris, it'll just have to wear off. Sam, you should know better. Gosh, is it that late? Where's Hannah?'

'Asleep. This is boys' trouble.'

Chris looked at Cat for the first time. 'Hey.'

'Hey. Glass of wine would be nice.'

'Christ, what a pack of mongrels in here.'

'Whereas outside it's more your baying wolves.'

'What happened?'

'Tell you later.'

Cat scooped her younger son out of the bath.

'His fingers have gone wrinkly,' Sam said. 'Like aliens'.'

'How do you know?'

'I know everything about aliens.'

'Maybe because you are one.'

He let out a gleeful shriek.

Twenty minutes later, children asleep, Cat went in search of the glass of wine that had never materialised. Chris was lying on the kitchen sofa.

'Asleep?'

'Yes.' She nudged him. 'Move your legs.'

Chris opened his eyes. 'It can't go on,' he said. 'And I want a whisky.'

Cat knew better than to take umbrage. Moods like this had become quite common. She thought she knew how to handle them.

'I'm absolutely pissed off.'

'Sam just didn't think. It's not the end of the world.'

'Not Sam, though he's too old to be so stupid, he should start thinking occasionally. But not that, bloody everything. I had a pig of a day, I had three emergencies, I had a mountain of paperwork, I had that meeting with the Primary Health Care Trust which you should have been at, I come home expecting you to be back within the hour and you're gone half the night. Anyway, I've told the PHCT neither of us will be joining the night-call rota and that goes for half the GPs

73

in our area, more than half, they can pay through the nose for agency doctors, serve them right.'

'You did *what*? Chris, you may not be prepared to go on doing nights now the new contract is on us – that's up to you – but I think you're wrong. Why should our patients suffer, so you and your chums can score political points?'

'Patients are not going to suffer.'

'Well, I'm going to carry on doing nights on call the same as I always have.'

'Anyway, where were you?'

'Don't *do* that to me, just ignoring what I say and changing the subject, it's so bloody arrogant. I'll make it clear to the PHCT tomorrow that whatever you said applies to you, not to me.'

'Thus slicing the practice down the middle. How supportive.'

'Oh, don't be childish.' She got up. The wine, which she had drunk too quickly, had hit her like a hammer, making her sway with exhaustion. 'I need to sleep.'

'You still haven't said where you were.'

'I was having my mobile nicked and being knocked to the ground in a passageway on the Dulcie estate, after which the paramedics found the patient I'd gone to see dead in his lavatory. Then I went to the hospice where Lizzie Jameson had just died and Max went roaring off into the night. Then I came home. On the way I heard that North Riding Police have arrested someone – a *woman* for God's sake. She'd abducted a little girl, and she might be the David Angus person as well . . . too much for one night.'

Upstairs, she sat down on the edge of the bed and began to sob. Seconds later, Chris was beside her.

'God, I am so sorry . . . I'm a pig.'

'Yes.'

'We don't need this.' He put his arms round her. 'Neither of us needs this. Just think if we didn't have to.'

'Please,' Cat said, 'please don't start about Australia. I really, really couldn't take it.'

74

'Well, something has to happen, Cat. A big change.'

'Oh God.'

'Listen, get a babysitter for Saturday. I want us to go out. I want to talk properly. Can you?'

'I don't want to spoil a nice dinner talking about Australia,' Cat mumbled. 'I'm too tired to get undressed.'

'Yes, look at you . . . look at us. You come in from being mugged on some poxy housing estate, I've been fighting bureaucracy instead of treating patients, then fighting my children because I'm tired and frustrated . . . What is this? What are we doing here?'

She had been on the brink of falling asleep in her clothes. Now Cat sat up, her brain and body charged and electric. 'Why are you shouting at me? We don't do this, Chris, we don't shout.'

'Exactly. *Exactly.*'

'This can't wait until we're sitting across some random restaurant table. I won't sleep now until it's sorted. It's not just about being on call at night.'

'No. It's a whole lot more. I've been trying to get to grips with it in my head . . .'

'Without talking about it to me?'

'We're never together long enough.'

'That's rubbish.'

She felt as if she was being attacked on all sides by hideous things which danced round her in an evil, gloating dance. And then it occurred to her, sickeningly, that this was what had happened to Karin McCafferty – one moment, rushing home to tell her husband that her scans were clear, her cancer gone, the next being confronted by a man who was leaving her to live with another woman in New York.

'It wasn't even a younger woman,' she said aloud. 'I don't know why that would have made it better but it would. Only she was older. An older woman for Christ's sake.'

Chris was staring at her blankly.

'Karin,' she said dully. 'When Mike left her.'

'What's that got to do with anything?'

'Hasn't it?'

There was a pause, then Chris closed his eyes. 'Oh dear God.' He took hold of her hands. 'What this has to do with is that I am sick and tired and I am almost burned out. It is about me not wanting to do this any more. I do not want to be what I am.'

'Which is? Husband? Father?'

'Of course not husband and father. A GP. I don't want to be a GP.'

'But you're a doctor through and through, you're –'

'I didn't say "doctor", I said GP. That's what I've had enough of. You still love it. I am beginning to hate it and when I don't hate it I resent it. The job has changed, the bureaucracy gets to me . . . but it isn't just that . . . I don't want to do it any longer. If I carry on I'll become a bad doctor.'

'We need a holiday, that's all.'

'No. It isn't all. We had a holiday and I didn't feel any better. Look, I didn't mean to start on this huge thing in the middle of the night when we're both shattered.'

'What do you really want to do?'

'Retrain . . . well, partly. I want to go back into psychiatry.'

'I think I might cry. Or be sick.'

'Shock?'

'Relief. Not Australia, not another woman.'

'I've given up on Australia and what other woman would have me?' He wandered into the bathroom. '*What* was that about a woman being arrested?'

76

Fourteen

'Father in Heaven, grant them comfort in their suffering. When afraid, give them courage, when afflicted grant them patience, when dejected afford them hope; and when alone assure them of the prayerful support of your holy people, through Jesus Christ Our Lord.'

The candle flames barely glimmered and the lamps made a glowing cave of the Chapel of Christ the Healer. The great cathedral spaces behind Jane Fitzroy were hollowed out of darkness. She knelt alone before the small altar on which stood a striking modern gold cross.

She loved to say the last office of the day alone here. Tonight she had come in to pray for the two patients who had died in Imogen House, and for another who would probably die in a few hours. The cathedral's night silence seemed not hollow or empty but crammed with centuries of prayer. She could understand how people gave themselves to the monastic life.

She bent her head for another moment to commend herself to God but, as she did so, a sound made her hesitate. She thought she had heard a door brush against the stone floor as it opened. She waited. Nothing. Silence again.

She bent her head.

Footsteps came down the side aisle, someone in soft-soled shoes.

The main doors would have been closed and locked but

the side door was open for her to secure when she left for the night.

She stood up. 'Is someone there?'

The footsteps stopped.

'Hello?' The candle flames were steady but her own voice wavered slightly. 'Can I help you?'

Nothing. She wondered whether to move forward confidently or wait. The footsteps came nearer.

'The cathedral is closed really, but if you've come in to pray please stay a few moments, there are things I can do before I have to leave.'

A man stood at the open gate of the chapel. He did not come in. He had a two-day stubble on both jaw and head, wore a navy reefer jacket and a red scarf. She sighed. Not a madman, not a thief, not drunk, not – she smiled as the word came to her – not *unrespectable*.

'Max,' she said.

He looked bewildered, as if he were not certain where he was or why. Then he said, 'Lizzie.'

'Max, I am so sorry.' Jane got up and went to him, put out a hand to touch his arm. He stared at it as if an alien creature had alighted there. 'I've been saying the evening prayers. Do you want to sit quietly for a minute?'

'Why?'

'You look exhausted.'

'I've been walking about. I can't go home. I can't go back there.'

'It's very hard.'

He took a few steps into the chapel. Jane waited. She and Max Jameson had met only once, when she had been to see Lizzie at Imogen House and he had been curt with her, telling her that she was not needed. She had left, understanding, but returned after he had gone, to give the then sleeping Lizzie a blessing.

'I hate this place.'

'The cathedral?'

He gestured around him. 'She made me bring her here. Early on. I would have taken her anywhere. I'd have carried her on my back . . . It was called a service of healing.' He laughed, a small, cold laugh. 'I knelt down there. I prayed as well. It might have worked, I'd have tried whatever she wanted. She believed it helped. She said so.'

'Would you like me to say a prayer now . . . or to pray with you?'

'No. There's no point.'

'I think there is.'

'Of course you do.'

'I'll pray. You just sit.'

'Why did Lizzie die?'

'I don't know.'

'You wouldn't put an animal through that. Who would? What is this joke?'

'Come on . . . why don't you come back to my house and I'll make some coffee . . . you can talk if you want to, not if you don't. You shouldn't be wandering the streets, you need company.'

'I need Lizzie.'

'I know, Max. If I could give her to you I would. I do know she is with you all the time now in spirit.'

'That doesn't make any sense.'

'Perhaps it will soon.'

Then he said, 'You look like her.'

'No.' Jane smiled. 'Lizzie had that wonderful long hair . . . straight and smooth . . .' Her own was dark red and sprang out from her head, impossible to tame.

'You are young, beautiful . . . you're like she was.'

'Come on, Max . . . come with me.'

'You are alive, though, that's the difference, and Lizzie is dead. Why isn't everyone else dead? Why aren't you?'

Jane took him by the arm and he allowed her to lead him, out of the chapel and down through the side aisle of the empty cathedral. He seemed bewildered, unsure of where to put his feet. She felt afraid for him, his grief and pain were so overwhelming, racking him physically as well as emotionally.

'How long is it since you ate anything?' she asked as they walked down the quiet close.

'I don't know.'

'I can make you something . . . It's up to you. Do you have any family coming for Lizzie's funeral?'

'I don't want any funeral. A funeral means the end of Lizzie, it means Lizzie is dead. Don't you see that?'

'Yes. But Lizzie *is* dead. Her body is dead,' she said gently.

'No.'

'We go in through this side gate. The security lights will come on in a second.' She took Max's hand like that of a child, and led him through the garden of the Precentor's house, along the path which had a trellis to one side, to her small bungalow. Somewhere in the bushes, there was the rustle of a cat or a fox, eyes gleaming momentarily out of the blackness.

The tiny hall was still in a state of disarray. Jane put lamps on in her study, and the gas fire, and held out her hands to take Max's jacket.

'I don't know what to do,' he said.

'Sit down there. I'll make coffee . . . or tea? And I'll do some sandwiches . . . I haven't had anything myself yet. Just you rest, Max.'

He looked around the room, at Jane's books, her desk, the crucifix and two candles on the small table. She drew the curtains against the night, left him there and went into the kitchen. The light on her answerphone was flashing.

'Jane? They're sending me home tomorrow morning. A district nurse is supposed to come but I shan't need her. I'll telephone you . . . I might catch you between church matters. Goodbye.'

She smiled to herself, recognising that nothing was going to change her mother now and refusing to worry about it. The thought of her returning to the house ransacked by the burglars and muggers was troubling, but she had done what she could and Magda would call on whoever she needed. She was good at that. She put the kettle on, and took out a loaf from the tin.

As she went to the fridge there was the sound of a step,

and an arm came round her throat from behind, not choking her, but making it impossible for her to move.

'Max . . .' she managed to say. 'What . . . ?'

'How can you be here? How can *you* be here, making tea, cutting bread when Lizzie is there lying dead? What did Lizzie do? Why did your God kill Lizzie? You shouldn't be alive, I can't let you live, not now, not after what happened. You're too like her. You shouldn't be alive.' He spoke in a strange, soft voice as if he were reciting what he said, had learned it by heart for just this time, this place.

'Max, please loosen your arm.'

To her surprise, he did so. He let her go then pushed her towards the study. When they were inside, he closed the door.

Suddenly, now, Jane felt afraid. Max was out of his mind with distress and people in his state could behave irrationally and wildly. He was angry. She did not know how his anger might explode.

Help me, she prayed, help me. There were no other words, except: Help him.

'Sit down,' Max said.

She did so. It seemed better for the moment, not to argue, not to plead. Stay calm.

'What do you want, Max?'

'Oh, a cosmic question? Let's ask a simple one. Simple answer. You're supposed to have those, aren't you?'

'Not really. I ask a lot of questions too. All the time.'

'You're not paid for that.'

She smiled.

'I *must* have answers.'

'It's hard, I know –'

He lunged at her, so that she shrank back in the chair.

'How dare you tell me that? How dare you say you know it's hard. How do you know? Has this happened to you?'

'No,' Jane said. 'If you mean, has a person I was in love with or was married to, died, no.'

'Then don't patronise me.'

'And please don't you threaten me.'

81

'Do you believe in it? Really believe in it? Would you die for it?'

'For my Christianity? I believe in it, yes. Whether I'd die for it . . . I wonder how brave I am. But plenty of people have died for their faith. They still do.'

'You believe Christ was raised from the dead?'

'Yes.'

'And prayer?'

'I don't believe prayer is a magic trick. We always get an answer but maybe not the one we wanted.'

'Good cop-out.'

'Is that what it sounds like? I just don't think it's like a note to Father Christmas . . . I want, please can I have?'

'Why did Lizzie die? Can you answer that?'

'No. I don't know . . . it seems cruel and horrible and point-less . . . the world often does. Is. I know we can come to terms with things in time and I know that when appalling things happen God is with us in the middle of it all.'

'Sorry, I failed to notice. How stupid.'

'Let me make that drink, then I'll drive you home.'

'No.'

'Give yourself a break, Max.'

'I'm not going anywhere. Nor are you. Not until your God brings Lizzie back to life.'

'He won't. There is no point in having this talk now, you're not fit.'

'Until you can explain to me why my wife died and unless your prayers can bring her back to me, woman priest, you are here and I am here. Maybe for tonight, tomorrow . . . maybe till we die.'

'What do you mean?'

'Nothing.'

'Let me drive you home. If you want to say anything to me, let off your feelings, whatever, that's fine, but not tonight. You're distraught, I'm exhausted. Come and talk tomorrow.'

'I want you to lock the door . . . is there only one door?'

Jane hesitated.

'TELL ME.'

'Yes. One door.'

'Go and lock it. I'll watch you.'

'Max . . .'

'I'll watch you.'

'Please calm down.'

He stood very still, scarcely seeming to breathe, very tense, focused.

She got up.

He took her arm and moved her towards the door with a strength she could not have fought. She turned the key. The door was solid, without glass, the lock an old-fashioned, heavy one. There was also a second, drop-down latch. Max waited. Slowly, she turned the brass knob.

'Where's your phone?'

'In the study, and there's an extension in my bedroom.'

'Pull them out of the wall sockets. Give me your mobile first.'

It was in the pocket of her cassock. She wondered how she might somehow dial as she reached to take it out. Before she could, Max grabbed her wrist and held it while with his other hand he found the pocket and the mobile phone, took it out and switched it off.

'Now the others.'

They went into the study, then to the socket beside her bed.

'Are there locks on the windows?'

'Security locks. Yes.'

'Are they locked?'

'Yes.'

'I'd like to have the tea now please. And something to eat. You promised that.'

'OK, Max, but please, this isn't going to achieve anything, it . . .'

He stood silently, waiting. She went ahead of him into the kitchen. Max followed, shut the door and put a chair up against it. He sat on the chair. She remembered what had happened to her mother, how they had taken everything and then beaten her about the head. She looked at Max Jameson.

No, it wasn't like that. This was about something else.

'I need to tell you something.' She heard her own voice, hoarse as if she had an obstruction in her throat. The obstruction was fear. 'I had to go to London urgently . . . I had a call from my mother . . . she's a child psychiatrist, she lives on her own. When I got there, I found the house turned upside down, a lot of things taken . . . and my mother on the floor in her own blood. She'd surprised them. They thought the house was empty. It was very, very frightening. I . . . I can't get it out of my head. Now you. It's –'

'I'm not a burglar. There's nothing here I want.'

'I don't understand what you *do* want.'

'Answers.'

'I have no easy ones, Max.'

'Miracles.'

'If I could bring Lizzie back to you I would . . . I can't. It doesn't work like that. God doesn't. It's complicated.'

She wondered what she was saying. She had always felt that, on the contrary, everything was not complicated but simple. Not easy, never, but gloriously simple. Now, she knew nothing. Her mind was a jumble.

Say nothing. Say nothing. Just do.

Yes.

She lit the gas, set the kettle on, opened a cupboard to take out the china, the fridge for milk. Think nothing. Say nothing. Just do.

Max sat in silence, hunched down into the wooden chair, watching her.

A strange sense of calm came over her and a sense of unreality, as if she were sleepwalking, but untouchable, unreachable. She cut bread, sliced tomatoes and cheese, found a fruit cake left for her by someone the day she had moved in. The kettle boiled.

When he had eaten and drunk the tea, he would come to, Jane thought, realise where he was, and then things would fall back into place. She would drive him home and make sure he was safe. It was like looking after a child.

'Please come and eat,' she said.

She waited for him to do so. Waited for everything to shift back again to normal. Waited.

Watched. Max watched.

She was like Lizzie. Her hands, cutting the bread, gripping the handle of the kettle. Her eyes. Lizzie.

He knew that she was not Lizzie but he was too exhausted to sort out the confusion that seemed to sway him now one way, then the other, Lizzie, not Lizzie, Lizzie alive, Lizzie dead. Lizzie/Jane, Jane/Lizzie.

He looked around every few moments and wondered why he was in this unfamiliar house, rooms smaller than the one he knew, darker, with more objects, books, furniture and strange pictures. Then he remembered. His mind cleared and it felt as if he had been rinsed through with ice-cold water and his purpose was firm-edged and obvious.

But he felt so tired he wanted to lie on the floor and sleep. Sleep for ever. He could not be with Lizzie any other way. Then he saw her, as he had seen her the last time, her eyes wide and blank, her expression inscrutable, vanishing away from him as he looked down into some other, dark, empty, silent world.

When Nina had died, he had not been there. She had been in hospital, hidden under masks and tubes, attached to machines, yellow and thin and ugly, a hundred years old, the pain dragging her life and looks from her. He had been asleep, unable to remain by the bed to watch, terrified of the moment of her death. By the time he had gone to see her, she had become someone else, waxen and still, in a chapel that smelled odd, of sickly artificial flowers, masking the antiseptic of hospital death.

He had not expected to have to watch another wife die, a wife who had come to him like a miracle and been loved greedily, desperately.

He looked up. There was a teapot on the table, a plate with food.

Inside him was a simmering anger and hatred which terrified him, a strength of emotion he had never known before.

It was pure, uncontaminated by anything other than the need for retribution.

She was wiping her hands on a towel. Her red hair was like a halo round her face, her robe topped by the ludicrous white collar, a symbol of everything that he had to destroy. He did not believe any of the things she believed, and yet they had a dreadful power.

'Who do you have?' he asked. She started at the sound of his voice.

He was pleased that he had frightened her.

'You have a mother . . . who else? Brother, sister, lover?'

'I'm an only child. My father died ten years ago.'

'And did he suffer?'

'I . . . I'm not sure. He had a stroke . . . Why?'

'I want you to have felt it. Why shouldn't you?'

'What makes you think I haven't? There are people suffering like Lizzie every day, people left behind feeling as you're feeling.'

Max got up and went towards her. He saw her creamy skin and the red hair, her slim throat beneath the white collar, and raised his hands. Up.

She said: 'I know what you want to do to me. But, would Lizzie want me to be dead?'

'Don't talk about Lizzie.'

'Why not? This is all about her. I can't believe she would be happy that, because she died, you killed me.' She moved. 'Let me pass.'

He hesitated. He wanted to kill her for something other than hatred now, he wanted to know how it would feel. How it would feel to hold his hands round her throat. He had always been a man quick to anger, had terrified people with his sudden, violent rages – Nina had always fled the house. Only Lizzie had not cared. Lizzie had simply laughed. But he had never been angry with her, only with things around her, things to do with himself. And her laughter had been enough.

He let Jane Fitzroy pass him. He did not touch her. She sat down at the kitchen table. She looked small and very young, he thought. A child. Only a child would be so naive. What could she possibly know?

'I'd like a cup of tea,' he said.

She reached for the pot. 'Then home?'

'No.'

Abruptly, she began to cry.

Fifteen

Edwina Sleightholme had said nothing when charged with the abduction of Amy Sudden. She had not spoken apart from confirming her name.

Once they had left the helicopter, Serrailler had barely set eyes on her. He wanted to. He wanted to interview her, to drag the truth out of her about David Angus. He was not allowed to speak to her, of course. This wasn't his patch or his case. All he could do was put in the formal request to interview her at a later date, when the Yorkshire cases were under way.

'Wish you'd stay another night,' Jim Chapman said. They were eating bacon sandwiches, brought up to his room by a willing DC. The entire HQ was on a high, amazed at what had happened, buzzing about the arrest of a woman.

Simon shook his head, mumbling through his bacon. 'I'm fine. Hospital said so.'

'Sufficiently fine to drive two hundred miles?'

'Yep.'

'Great, isn't it?'

They looked at one another in understanding.

'Nothing to beat it,' Serrailler said, 'even on a ledge halfway up a cliff face in a storm. But I have to get back. I want my hands on the David Angus file again.'

'It's her.' Jim Chapman took a huge mouthful. The whole room smelled savoury.

'I know. Got to prove it though. She's not going to co-operate.'

Chapman wiped his mouth and took a swig of tea. 'It'll have the shrinks on the hop.'

'I can't get my own head round it. It goes against every-thing we know.'

'Not quite. Remember Rose West. Remember Myra Hindley.'

'Hindley wasn't on her own, she was drawn into it by Ian Brady. OK, she was corruptible, but would she have done it alone? I doubt it. Same goes for West.'

'What makes them tick? Dear God. I was thinking about my grandson on the way back . . . kept seeing his face. Defies belief. What kind of woman is this, Simon?'

When he got home just after midnight, the light was flashing on his answerphone. One message was from the dry cleaner to say his suit was ready – otherwise three callers had not left any message.

He stood in the darkness in his long, cool drawing room. Beyond the windows there was a new moon with the evening star, reminding him of the genius Samuel Palmer, the artist he most revered.

Then he thought of Diana Mason. She had haunted him with silent calls the previous year but he had neither seen nor spoken to her for months. In all likelihood she had a new man and another life and he had been erased from her mind. Simon hoped so.

He went to bed exhausted, but his sleep was invaded by the sound of the sea crashing against the rocks and the zip of his car tyres down the motorway, and filled with visions of Edwina Sleightholme's thin, secretive face and defiant eyes and of the yellow rescue helicopter, veering towards them and away, towards them and away, swaying nauseously through his dreams.

He heard the cathedral clock chime every hour until five, when he turned over to sleep heavily until after eight o'clock.

*

'Guv . . . we heard. You got a result?'

DS Nathan Coates was waiting for him.

'The Angus file's on your desk. I thought –'

'I bet you did. Get some coffees from round the corner and I'll have a bacon-and-egg bap.'

He went to his desk, which was heaped with papers. Nathan turned reluctantly and headed off to the nearby Greek Cypriot café, which had transformed the lives of Lafferton CID and earned the eternal wrath of the station canteen.

Serrailler flipped through his papers, opened up his computer and, by the time Nathan returned, had zipped through a couple of dozen emails. He lifted the lid of his espresso and sniffed the pungent, fresh coffee. He had brought himself quickly up to speed on the David Angus file. Nathan waited, bursting with suppressed questions and enthusiasm. Serrailler looked at him.

'I take it the place is a hive of rumour and speculation?'

'Yeah, too right. Only, before we get down to it, there's something else, guv.' Nathan flushed.

'Nathan?'

Simon dreaded his DS telling him he was leaving Lafferton, had promotion to a DI in another force, would be gone by next week. Nathan was enthusiastic, ambitious and hard-working. He would rise fast. The DCI was loath to let him go but knew that he must. He waited.

'Thing is, I ent told anybody here . . . not yet. We wanted you to be the first.'

Where? The north? The Met?

'Me and Em's having a sprog.'

Nathan was a brighter shade of tomato. Simon let out a cry of both relief and delight.

Just before lunch, Serrailler called in the core team who had worked on the Angus case.

'It's not going to be easy,' he warned, looking around. He had to hit the right note – to dampen any over-optimism at the same time as indicating that he felt fairly certain they had got the person responsible. 'Sleightholme won't confess – she's barely said a word. They'll nail her up north, of course, because Amy Sudden was in the boot of her car. But both forces are going to have to get good evidence for the two boys. It'll take everything we can throw at it. We're looking at hard slog. I'm pretty confident we'll get there.'

'You could be wrong, guv . . . the woman might crumble and give us everything on a plate.'

'You haven't met her.'

'Word is out that you're a hero, guv . . . did a bit of SAS stuff.' A small cheer went up.

'Thanks, guys, that'll be all. Now let's get on with it.'

Sixteen

He had let her rest. She took a blanket and pillow and lay on the sofa in the sitting room, cramped and afraid but so exhausted that she managed twenty minutes of sleep a couple of times. When her eyes were closed, she turned away from Max and prayed for them both. Several times she had asked him what he wanted from her, what he hoped to achieve by keeping her here but his replies had made no sense.

If Max had slept himself, he had not let her see him do so. Every time she had looked at him, he had been sitting in an upright chair, eyes open, sometimes staring at her, sometimes blankly into space.

As dawn rose, she had made them breakfast from what little food was left in the kitchen. He went to the bathroom but locked her in the kitchen beforehand. When she used the lavatory, he stood outside the door. The window was a narrow slit high up in the wall; she did not even bother to try to reach it.

She now asked him if she could read and answer some letters, and he had agreed, but she was unable to concentrate. In the end, she made coffee with the last of the milk and simply sat, like him, doing nothing and not speaking.

She lost all sense of time, but at what felt like late in the morning she realised that Max was asleep, slumped slightly on to the side of the chair. He had not meant to sleep, she knew; exhaustion had simply overtaken him. She waited.

Watched. He slept on. There were dark stains below his eyes. She felt a pang of sorrow for him, an affinity with his misery, which had driven him mad and driven him to this. But she had to resolve things now.

After another ten minutes, very slowly she began to move. She stood up. He slept on. Step by careful step, she went across the sitting room to the door. She was afraid the handle would make a sound or the lock a click as she inched it open. She looked round. Max had not stirred.

She got to the hall. Hesitated. The only thing to do now was make one swift move to the front door, unlock it and run. She calculated how many steps she would have to take, how the key turned. She was shaking now, her heart squeezing in her chest. But she would get out. She had to.

She moved.

He had not been asleep at all. Or else the emptiness in the room had somehow conveyed itself to him. Or the slightest sound had woken him.

As Jane took a step, he had her round the throat from behind and grappled her to the ground.

She screamed, and screamed again, as she had never screamed before.

'Stop that. Shut up. *Shut up.*'

His hand was over her mouth now and his weight was on top of her. She was terrified that in his pent-up rage, exhaustion and frustration, out of grief and hatred, Max was going to rape her. It was the one nightmare she had always had. She lifted her leg to try to kick or put a knee into his groin but he was a big man and rage was making him like a bull, terrifying her.

'You're not leaving here,' he shouted deep into her ear. 'Don't do this again. You are not leaving me.'

His hand left her mouth for long enough to let her scream again, one agonised, animal scream.

Seventeen

'Guv?'

'Come in, Nathan.'

'Got a call a few minutes ago . . . bungalow in the Cathedral Close . . . gardener reported hearing screams. Uniform went down and they think someone's being held.'

'What, as in hostage? Doesn't sound very likely.'

'That's what I thought. Only, I'm off down there. It's your patch, I wondered if you'd got any info.'

'No. We don't get many hostage situations in our nice, quiet neck of the woods. You sure they're not wasting your time?'

'No, but . . .'

'No, but you fancied a breath of fresh air away from the paperwork.'

'Whatever gave you that idea?'

'Take Jenny Lyle.'

'Yeah, between us two we'll scare anybody into giving themselves up . . . my face, her –'

'Get out,' Serrailler said cheerfully. The image of the vast backside and washerwoman's arms of DC Lyle was more than he wanted to conjure up. He hauled out another file. He had put in a call to Jim Chapman to say he was ready to interview Edwina Sleightholme whenever they would let him. He couldn't wait.

*

Nathan found himself crushed into his driving seat by the bulk of Jenny Lyle, but he liked her and she was a good detective, with a natural nose for something not quite right. Besides, she was someone else to tell his news to.

She laughed. 'Who's the Daddy!'

'It's just great.' Nathan banged the steering wheel.

'All planned out, is it?'

'Yeah, only we won't be able to stop in our flat.'

'Babies aren't very big.'

'Have you seen all the gear they come with? Em's sister had one last year, you could hardly get in the door, prams, pushchairs, carrying things, baskets, cots, travelling cots, great bales of nappies. Yikes. I've changed my mind.'

They spun into the Cathedral Close.

'Be funny, living here,' Jenny said, heaving herself out of the small car.

'DCI does.'

'Like another world . . . different century.'

'Nice though.'

'Clock'd drive me nuts.'

It struck the half-hour as they walked along the row of houses. The patrol car was parked a few yards off.

'Here you go. The Precentor's house.'

'What's he do then? What's precenting?'

'Dunno.'

A uniform came out of the side gate and hailed them. They followed him, skirting the large Georgian house by a path beside a trellis up which honeysuckle and roses twined in swags.

'OK . . . gardener says one of the clergy lives in what they call the garden flat, only it's more a stone bungalow, down the end. She's not been moved in long, a Reverend Jane Fitzroy . . . Gardener was working in the borders near the house, but he had to take a barrowload of compost down to the bin and it was then he heard this scream . . . proper, terrified scream, he said, frightened him to death. He went to the bungalow and banged, but there was nothing else except maybe someone grunting in their throat. He couldn't tell, it

95

panicked him . . . he banged again, then ran and got his phone and called us. Kelly Strong and me were by the canal, got here in five, we went down there – nothing, silent. Only when we started knocking and shouting there was a man's voice, he yelled out at us. I called through the letter box . . . couldn't see anything – there's one of those felt strips on the other side – but he was in the hall. He said to get the hell out.'

'Who is he?'

'Won't say.'

'Bloody hell. What's he want?'

'Won't say.'

'Gotta be high on drugs then, burglary gone wrong . . . What's he sound like?'

'Nice sort of speaking voice – educated.'

Nathan gazed at the bungalow. Neat. Quiet. Prettily placed. He wouldn't mind living at the bottom of a garden like this, in a bit of a flowery wilderness. Think of a baby growing up here.

The place looked empty and dead, curtains drawn, no movement. Only inside, something had happened, or was happening. There could be the body of someone murdered.

'Wait there. I'm going up to the door.'

The two uniforms and Jenny Lyle stood, as he told them. Nathan crept up the path. There was a silence so deep it terrified him. He pictured Freya Graffham, lying on the floor of her sitting room. He lifted the knocker and set it down, once, twice, not loudly, but as any visitor might knock. Silence. He knocked again and lifted the letter box and pressed his ear to it, desperate to hear some sound, anything living. Nothing.

He knocked again and was turning away when a man's voice close up to the door on the other side said, 'Go away.'

'This is DS Nathan Coates, Lafferton Police.'

'Go away.'

'I'd like a few words, sir, if I can just come in.'

'Please.'

'Just to reassure myself everything is OK.'

Silence.

'We had a report of unusual sounds. I'm sure it's nothing.

Only if you'd just open the door.'

'GO AWAY. If you knock again, or do anything else, I'll
kill her, do you understand that? Tell me you've heard what
I said, please.'

Silence.

'I . . . heard.'

'So tell me you understand.'

'I understand.'

'I said, I would kill her. I have a knife, a very large, very
sharp kitchen knife, and I will slit her throat. If you do not
GO AWAY.'

Nathan backed off from the door, turned and sprinted up
the garden to where the others were standing.

'We need to get out of earshot, come on.'

They followed him to the front of the main house.

'He has a knife . . . and someone, a woman, with him.'

'You sure, Sarge?'

'Yes, and even if I weren't 100 per cent, it isn't something
to mess with. We need back-up.'

He jabbed the buttons on his mobile.

Fifteen minutes later, the close was lined with police cars. The
Lafferton Acting Superintendent was in command, Simon
Serrailler preparing to negotiate. Everyone else was standing
by.

'I want this kept low-key,' the CO said, 'and hopefully we
can resolve it quickly. We have no idea what this man wants
or hopes to achieve, whether he's sane or under the
influence of drugs or alcohol. So far as we know he has no
firearm. We know he is holding a woman but we don't know
if there are any others. We don't need any two-way devices
or to wire anything up at this stage. We'll stay back and stay
quiet. Simon? Let's hope we can get this all over before it's
begun.'

Simon went quietly towards the bungalow. It was a calm,
warm, sunlit afternoon. There were bees droning about the
honeysuckle and roses, a butterfly on the trellis. The contrast
between now and the stormy, lowering Yorkshire afternoon

overhanging the sea was absolute, but he had the same sensation of being back in the thick of the action and in a heightened state of alert. He had trained as a negotiator and found the week's intensive course fascinating; ever since, he had wished he would be called in to a major hostage situation to test his skills. This afternoon's exercise seemed routine and domestic, by comparison.

The bungalow was silent in the sun, the curtains drawn. Nothing moved. Nothing could be seen. He had a sense of foreboding. No house with people in it should be so still. The team waited, looking towards him. Someone leaned out of the window of the big house next door. He could hear the distorted voices from a walkie-talkie.

He stood at the front door and knocked, suddenly and loudly so that whoever was inside would be startled.

He thought he heard a slight scraping sound, but then a blackbird started up from a bush beside him and flew across the garden, making its warning cry and blotting out any noise that might have come from the house. He lifted the letter box. There was a flap of fabric on the other side, so he could see nothing.

'Police. If you are inside there and able to hear me, would you please call out? I would like to talk to you.'

He waited. Silence.

'I would like to speak with you. Please tell me who you are.'

The silence was so dense, so absolute, that he almost turned and beckoned to the team to come down and bring the rammer to break down the door. If anyone was inside this bungalow he was surely no longer alive.

The blackbird sang from the lilac tree.

'What do you want?'

The voice was low and came from inches away on the other side of the letter flap.

'I'm DCI Simon Serrailler. I would like to know who is in there, please. Would you open the door so that I can check things are all right?'

'No.'

'In that case, perhaps you'd just tell me your name. If there is anything wrong, I'd like to try and help.'

'There's nothing.'

'Will you tell me your name?'

There was a pause. Then, 'Do you have to shout?'

'If you can hear me, no, I don't.'

'Come to the window.'

'Which one?'

'At the front. She's asleep.'

'Who is asleep? Can you tell me who you are and who else is in the house with you? The usual occupant is the Reverend Jane Fitzroy. Can you tell me if she's in there with you?'

Now, there were footsteps, quietly receding. Serrailler waited. Then, signalling to the team that he had made contact, he walked to the front window. The curtains were drawn and, for a moment, there was no sound, no movement. Then one of the windows was pushed slightly ajar.

'Don't try and break in.'

'I won't.'

'Stay where you are.'

'I'm staying here, outside the window. I'm not going to try to enter the house. I'd just like to speak to you. It would be really helpful to know who I'm talking to.'

A pause.

'What did you say your name was?'

'DCI Simon Serrailler.'

'Who got you here?'

'Someone called us to say they had heard screams.'

'She's fine. I told you. She's asleep.'

'Who is asleep? Can you just tell me that?'

'She's OK.'

'And you?'

'Not. Not OK.'

'What's wrong?'

'Lizzie.'

'Is that Lizzie you have with you?'

'Lizzie is dead.'

'I see. Can you tell me who is with you?'

99

'Why?'

'I need to know if they're all right. Is it Miss Fitzroy? Is she all right?'

'She's all right.'

'Why won't you tell me your name? I'm Simon, you –'

'I'm not a bloody imbecile, you told me your name once, don't bloody talk to me like that.'

'I'm trying to get you to tell me your name, that's all.'

'OK, OK. Max. Max, Max, Max, Max, Max, Max, Max . . . Shit. MAX.'

'Thanks. Max.'

'Max Jameson.'

He sounded weary for a second. Weary enough to give in? He might have had enough.

'All right, Max . . . is there any reason why you won't let me inside there?'

'She's asleep.'

'Who is?'

'She is. I don't want to disturb her.'

'Fine. We needn't. So long as I can make sure she's all right – you're both all right – we can let her sleep.'

'She's fine. Lizzie isn't, Lizzie's dead, but she's fine.'

'Tell me about Lizzie, Max.'

'Lizzie.'

He said the name as if it were strange to him. Experimentally.

'Lizzie,' he said again.

'Yes. Tell me about her. Will you?'

'She's dead. What's to tell? She died.'

'Max, I'm sorry.'

'Of course you're not, you didn't know her, how could you be?'

'Because you sound distressed.'

'Distressed.'

'Yes.'

He laughed again, a short, dry, hard little laugh. 'Fuck it, you don't know.'

'So tell me.'

100

But then the man's hand reached out briefly to close the window. The curtain had scarcely parted.

Serrailler waited. The bungalow was again wrapped in the same, dreadful pall of silence. He stood for ten minutes but there was not the slightest further sound or movement.

He went to the letter box, pushed it open and called out Max Jameson's name, asked him to reply, to come back and talk. Silence.

He went back up the path through the shrubs and fruit trees.

'Guv?'

He shook his head.

It was going to take a long time. He had assessed the situation incorrectly. He headed into the close. They had thrown a cordon round the area and, outside it, people were gathering to watch, drawn as always and as if by some magic force to a scene of potential calamity.

He spoke to the Super. Was the situation in hand? More or less. Was it likely to escalate? Hard to tell. He still had no idea why the man was holding whoever it was inside the house, or what he wanted or hoped to achieve. How dangerous was he? Hard to tell.

It was all nebulous, the most frustrating and yet, curiously, potentially the most interesting sort of situation and one which Simon was gripped by and determined to resolve. Who was this man? Who was with him? Who was Lizzie? Was Lizzie dead in there? Did 'asleep' mean 'dead'? He would tease the truth out, little by little, moving carefully and tactfully. He wanted to know. This was not some crude criminal act of violence, the stupid game of an idiot off his head on crack. It was not so obvious.

It was not obvious at all.

'I think it may take some time but there's no threat beyond the bungalow, so far as I can tell. He's isolated himself there, it's easily surrounded and easily contained.'

'We'll stay back out of the way then.'

'Yes. I'd like to know if there have been any sudden or violent deaths in the last few weeks with a victim called

Lizzie, possibly Lizzie Jameson but I'm not certain, RTAs, suicides . . . And where is the Reverend Jane Fitzroy? Has she been to work? Anyone seen her?'

'Anything else?'

'Not yet.'

'Has he asked for anything?'

'No. We haven't got that far . . . not sure if we will. I'm not sure of anything much but I'm going back down there now. He's had a few minutes to think.'

How strange, Serrailler thought, this garden, half wild towards the bottom, everything flowering in the sun, birds, insects, sweet smells. How strange. In the middle of it all, there is this small silent stone bungalow and inside . . .

What?

'Max?' he called quietly. Then he lifted the letter box and raised his voice. 'Max? Will you answer me?'

The sun shone on his back as he crouched there, warming him.

Eighteen

She had slept again. How could she have slept? To sleep you have to feel safe and she thought she had never felt less safe in her life. Perhaps, in some strange way, she trusted Max not to harm her simply because he was beside himself with grief and confusion but no longer full of rage.

He had put a blanket over her. She stretched her legs and arms to ease her cramped muscles, then turned. The curtains were still drawn but the sun was behind them, filling the room with a blotted, honey light. And the sun caught something, making it shine. Jane sat up.

There were three knives laid out neatly on the coffee table, two large kitchen knives, and one small new paring knife which she had bought a couple of days before. The sun flashed against the metal.

Max was sitting in a chair beside the window, watching her. 'Don't touch them,' he said.

She felt a lurch of sickness. She had slept, innocently, trustingly, for how long? While he had laid out three knives beside her.

'What . . . ?' Her throat was dry with fear. 'What is happening? Why have you . . . what are the knives doing there?'

He got up and she shrank back into the blanket but he did not come near her, only turned to lift the corner of the curtain very slightly and peer out.

103

It was only when he turned back that she realised she would have had time to snatch one of the knives.

'Someone was there just now,' he said, his voice normal, pleasantly conversational, 'but they seem to have gone.'

'Who?'

He shrugged.

'Max, people will know I'm missing . . . they'll be coming down here to look for me. I had a meeting at the hospital, I should have been to sort something out in the Dean's office . . . people will . . .'

'It seems they already have. Don't worry, they won't come back.'

'Did you speak to someone?'

'Yes.'

'Who?'

He shrugged again.

'I don't understand what you want. Please, please just tell me what this is about.'

'You know.'

'Lizzie . . . yes, I do know that, but I don't see why keeping me here will help you. It can't bring Lizzie back, you have to accept that. Whatever you do to me can't change what has happened. I have to say this. Even if you . . . stab me with one of those, it won't change what has happened.'

'No.'

'Then what are you doing?'

'Getting even with God.'

'Do you believe in God?'

'No. But you do.'

'That doesn't make sense.'

'None of it makes sense. Death doesn't. Lizzie being dead doesn't.'

'So by holding me here you somehow think . . . what? I'm trying to get to wherever you are but it's quite hard.'

'You never will. You can't.'

'How do you feel?'

'What?'

104

'You're angry and distressed, I know, but how else? Does your mind feel . . . are you thinking clearly?'

'Oh yes.'

'Because I don't see that.'

'No.'

She fell silent. He looked grey and dishevelled, his eyes were dull. There seemed to be a weariness rather than any craziness or rage about him.

God, give me the right words.

But no words came to her. Her mind was a white, shining, empty space.

'What kind of God is yours, Jane?'

Her throat tightened. She did not know.

'The gentle Jesus? The healer? The merciful one? When we went to the service in the chapel and they prayed over Lizzie, they talked about mercy and healing and comfort and grace and she said it helped her but I don't understand that. How could it have helped her? She got worse and she died. She died a dreadful death, you know. We all have to die. I don't understand that.'

Do I? Jane thought. Now the space was black and swirling and dangerous, not a peaceful, beautiful emptiness. 'I don't know. I don't pretend to have all the answers to life and death.'

'Why not?'

'You are too intelligent for this, you must know I can't pretend to, all I can do is believe. Faith. It's about faith. And trust.'

'Lizzie trusted.'

'How do you know her trust was misplaced? You don't know. There are many sorts of healing.'

'Such as?'

'Max, listen . . . I'm exhausted. I need a shower and something to eat and some fresh air and so do you. We need normality. I can't think straight. I can't have this sort of conversation under threat . . . how can I? I'll talk to you, I'll pray with you . . . anything . . . but not like this.'

'It was the police.'

'Sorry?'

'A policeman. He talked and then he went away.'

'If the police are here then you've got to stop this. You've done nothing wrong and I wouldn't dream of pressing charges against you but you have to let me open the door and walk out.'

'No.'

'They can break in.'

'They've gone.'

'No. Maybe they've retreated but they won't have gone. Of course they won't.'

'No one will break in. I won't let that happen.'

'You can't stop it happening. Come on . . . think.'

He smiled then and his smile chilled her because it did not lighten his face or reach his eyes. Perhaps, she thought suddenly, this is not only about Lizzie. Perhaps he is not simply mad because of her death. Perhaps he *is* mad. And dangerous. And desperate. Perhaps . . .

There was a sound at the window. Max leapt out of the chair and went swiftly across to it but did not lift the curtain. He stood listening intently, but when Jane made a movement he turned round so quickly that she froze. He looked at the knives, then at her.

'Max?' A man's voice from outside. 'Please come and speak to me. Are you all right?'

Everything went still and silent for a long time. The sun crept over the small desk, catching the frame of her father's photograph. A butterfly was spread out in a corner of the white wall, a red admiral, rich and quivering in the warmth.

'Max?'

Please. Please . . .

'I'm here.'

'Will you open the window?'

He hesitated, then pushed the handle forward a little.

'Thank you. Can you open the curtain?'

'Why?'

'It makes it easier to talk to someone you can see.'

'I can talk.'

106

A pause.

'Is Jane there?'

Max did not answer.

'Can I speak to Jane?'

'No.'

'Is she all right?'

'Why?'

'Come on, Max, reassure me about her, please. You can see why.'

'Jane's here.'

'Will you let her come to the window?'

'No.'

'OK. Will you just show me your face?'

'No.'

'How long do you plan on staying there, Max? We don't even know why . . . if you tell me what it is you want, maybe I can help you sort it out.'

'Are you God?'

'No.'

'My wife's dead. Can you sort that out?'

'You know I can't. I understand your distress, I know what –'

'Do you? What do you bloody know?'

There was a slight pause. Then the man said, 'Because I know what it is like when someone you love dies. I'm a human being and I have had that happen to me and I know.'

'Your wife?'

'No, but that needn't make a difference, need it?'

Max turned to look at Jane.

'No,' she said.

'She says –'

'What was that? I can't hear you very well, can you come a bit nearer the window?'

'No. She says.'

'Who? Jane?'

Max waited.

'Do you want to talk to anyone?'

'I thought I was.'

'I can get a counsellor, if it's –'

Max laughed.

'OK, then just tell me, if you know, why you are in there and why you are keeping Jane there? Can you tell me? There has to be a reason. Intelligent people don't do this sort of thing at random. What is it you want? Max, we will help you as much as we can but none of us can bring your wife back to life. Not Jane. Not me. No one. You know that really, don't you?'

'God can.'

'Do you believe that?'

'No.'

'Who does? Does Jane?'

'I don't know . . . no. No. Ought she to?'

'I doubt it. Have you had any sleep?'

'No. I don't know.'

'You can't think clearly if you're exhausted. Why don't you come out and we can get you home to sleep . . . things are going to seem a whole lot worse the longer you stay there.'

'Nothing could be worse.'

'I think you realise that you are making them worse, don't you?'

'I don't know.'

'Let me look at you.'

'Why?'

'Helps me to talk to you. Might help you to talk to me if we saw one another.' Max did not make any move.

'Do you have enough to eat?'

'We ate something.'

'Is there food in the house? Milk, tea . . . all of that?'

'I don't know.'

'I can get anything brought down to you if you tell me why you're there. Help me out here, Max . . . I can't understand what's going on. Just help me.'

Max closed the window.

Jane was sitting hunched up on the sofa, her eyes down. He stared at her. He had thought that she was like Lizzie but now he saw that she was not. She was younger. Smaller. Hair and eyes differently coloured, skin paler. Different. She wore clothes Lizzie would not have worn. She was not like Lizzie. Not Lizzie. He sat down beside her on the sofa and she shrank back from him.

'Lizzie,' he said.

'No.'

'I want to tell you.'

'What?' She sounded tired. Her voice was flat. She didn't want to listen to him.

'That I have no reason at all to live. That Lizzie was everything and now there is nothing. No point. No reason. Everything I had was Lizzie, everything I did. For Lizzie. About Lizzie. Me. I was about Lizzie. So what is there?'

'Everything. Everything else in the world out there . . . What would Lizzie want you to do?'

'I hate it when people assume things about the dead. "It's what she would have wanted . . ." How do they fucking know? Unless it's something they talked about, they don't know. It's a way of them doing what they want to do with a clear conscience.'

'Sometimes. Yes. Oh yes. We don't want to cancel the party so we say –'

'"– It's what she would have wanted,"' they said together. Max smiled.

'I didn't know Lizzie. If it had been her . . . if you had died, would she have turned her back on life?'

'God, no. Lizzie was life. Until . . . life and Lizzie were interchangeable.'

'So?'

'I'm not Lizzie. I never much cared for life, you know. Then there was Lizzie. I cared for her. Not much else.'

'What a waste.'

'Lizzie's death is a waste.'

'If that is true – and I don't know if it is or not – it doesn't give you the right to throw the rest of life, your life, away. There is everything else . . . surely you owe it to her to take it with both hands.'

'It fits you, doesn't it, that bloody collar?'

'Max, I need to go to the bathroom.'

'OK.' He got up.

'I'm very, very tired. Can't you just stop this, can't you just go? Please. Just go. No one's going to do anything to you.'

'Go to the bathroom.'

Her legs were aching, her head felt light. She could no longer think in any sort of logical order. Random ideas came and went. She wanted to cry. She wanted to scream.

She went into the bathroom and locked the door. She rinsed her face and held her hands under the cold tap. Prayed, though she was past doing more than committing herself to God. And Max. She remembered to pray for Max.

At least she was being held in her own home. She could eat, drink, pass water like this, wash, sleep. She was unharmed. If she still felt like this, how must it be for people held in terrible surroundings – in the dark, in the cold, under threat, without food, in their own excrement, for days, weeks, months? How must that be?

She rinsed her face again, drank some water. Ran her hands over her hair. Came out.

Max grabbed her and span her round, his arm across her throat. Outside she could hear voices. He dragged her into the sitting room and across to the window, pulled back the curtain with one arm while holding her with the other. Jane caught a glimpse of a man's face on the other side. Then she realised that Max had one of the knives and was holding it near to her face. It caught the sunlight. She closed her eyes and prayed in desperation, sweat running down the back of her neck.

'Look,' he was shouting, 'see? I told you what would happen if you tried to get in. Look.'

But there were only seconds in which the man on the other side of the window and the others some way behind him could see them both, before Max dropped the curtain again. A moment later, he took his arm from her neck and threw the knife into the hearth.

Jane's legs buckled and she half fell on to the sofa. Max

was kneeling on the floor, his face buried in the seat of the upright chair, sobbing.

If she had not been so paralysed with fear and shock that she could not speak, she might have taken the chance to get up and make a dash for the door to get out before he could reach her. But she could do nothing. She just sat, shaking, the breath hurting her chest as she tried to take it in, her heart hammering, the sound of it pulsing through her ears, her head.

They stayed like that for a long time, then the room quietened and the two of them seemed to be in a strange state of suspension and of calm, as if they were sharing something intangible, unutterable, but acutely real and of importance.

After a while, they heard the voice again.

'Max? Can you hear me? Just let me know you can, then tell me you are both all right.'

Max lifted his head slowly. 'Tell him,' he said, as if he had run a marathon and could barely catch his breath. 'Get up, go to the window.'

Jane hesitated.

'I won't touch you, Jane.'

Trust, she thought, this is about trust, and I think I have lost mine.

She moved. Stood. Max did not look at her. She walked unsteadily to the window and pulled the curtain back. Outside, a tall man with very fair hair was looking at her.

She nodded.

'Good,' the man said. 'OK?'

She did not know.

'Max?' the man called.

But Max sat, looking at the floor, his breathing strange, rasping as if he were asthmatic.

'Jane, can you come to the front door?'

Max still did not look at her.

'Or else, I can come in there. Max, which do you want? Jane to come out here or me to come inside?'

Max shook his head from side to side. Did not speak. Did

not look up. He was trapped in his own tight, terrified circle, far out of their reach.

Jane went over to the door. Waited. Into the hall. There, she stopped. She felt as if she should rescue him but to do that she would have to bring Lizzie back to life. There was no way out.

'Jane?'

'The door is locked. He took the key.'

'Wait there.'

She waited. Max stayed in the sitting room, still and silent, head bent forward.

It took a couple of minutes. There was such quietness that she could hear the blackbird in the bush outside. Then footsteps running down the path and the heavy crash of cracking, splintering wood.

The man with the fair hair came through the broken door towards her.

A couple of hours later, she had been discharged from hospital, shaken but unhurt. She did not see Max Jameson.

'Where are you taking me?' she asked, in the police car driving through Lafferton streets, so calm, so normal in the late-afternoon sun. 'I'd like to go home. I have to see people . . . see to the door, I . . .'

'We'll get that secured, love. You've got to make a statement, get him charged.'

'No.'

There were two policemen, one in uniform, driving, a detective beside him. Ginger hair. Cheerful. Ugly.

'I don't want to charge him. There's nothing to charge him with.'

'Aw, come on, Reverend, he took you by force and kept you under duress, threatened to slit your throat . . . course there is. There's stuff a yard long to put on the sheet. It's assault, it's . . .'

'I don't want to do that.'

'Listen, you can't take it in yet —'

'I can take it in. I have. Thanks. He is out of his mind with

112

grief. His wife died. He doesn't know what to do or where to turn, he is angry . . . There's nothing to charge him with. I was just . . . a focus for it all. He didn't hurt me.'

'Right, tell me he didn't terrify you and all.' He smiled.

'Yes,' she said. 'But all the same.'

The DS shook his head. 'If it'd been my wife he'd taken I'd have bloody slaughtered him.'

'But he needs help. Someone to talk to. Not a cell and a charge of assault.'

'Tell you what, no offence, but there's such a thing as being too forgiving, you know, too Christian. I reckon there is.'

Jane leaned back. She was exhausted. She felt hollow inside, as if there were no blood running through her veins or bones holding her together. She did not go on arguing. She hadn't the energy.

As the car pulled up in the close, Rhona Dow, the Precentor's wife, came out of her door.

'Jane, my dear girl. I'm so relieved to see you. What an appalling thing to happen. Now, you're staying with us, of course.'

It was all Jane could do not to sit down on the path and cry.

Nineteen

The windows of the farmhouse were open and every so often the sound of the Deerbon children's laughter came out, as if someone were blowing little bubbles of it from a clay pipe. They had spent the afternoon in the paddling pool or under the garden hose, and were now having their baths.

Cat and Simon had two deckchairs, and a bottle of champagne between them on the plastic table. Chris was in and out of the kitchen, making supper.

It was Cat and Simon's birthday.

'Ivo's as well,' Cat had said early that morning.

'Happy birthday, Ivo.'

But they were unlikely to hear from the other Serrailler triplet, who ignored birthdays, as he ignored most of the usual markers of normal life.

The early-evening sun was still hot.

'Did you put on sunscreen?'

Simon's white-blond hair went with a skin that was burned readily.

He waved his hand.

'Well, don't come running to me in the middle of the night when your face is on fire.'

'OK, I'll wake Chris.'

It was good, he thought. His favourite place in the world. Dinner being prepared. No need to watch how many glasses of wine he drank, as he would sleep here.

In the field opposite, the ghost-grey pony pressed itself up against the high hawthorn hedge for shade. One end of the paddock had been fenced off for a chicken run, a wooden coop; a dozen ruddy brown hens were pecking about on the grass.

Cat was looking across at them now. 'Dear God.'

'You'll love it. All those good fresh eggs.'

'All that mucking out and the carnage when the fox gets in after I've forgotten to shut them up.'

The chickens were her birthday present from Sam, Hannah and Felix, kept a gleeful secret, until six that morning when they had led her, blindfold, into the field.

'A hen-run indicates permanence. You can't take chickens to Australia.'

'No, there is that to thank God for.'

'You couldn't leave here. How could you?' Simon reached for the bottle and topped up their glasses. 'Here's to the end of quite a week.'

'God, I still can't get my head round that. It's a man's crime. She's a man.'

'Sort of, yes. Looked like a boy. We thought it was a bloke in the car the whole time.'

'What is she like? *What?* I keep thinking about David Angus.'

'Oh so did I. On that ledge next to her, I was supposed to save her life and I thought about David Angus. And Scott Merriman. And Amy Sudden. And God knows, maybe others. I looked at her hair and her hands and her feet, and that is what I thought about. Those children.'

'You'll get a commendation.'

'Like hell.'

'Are you going up there to charge her?'

'Interview. No evidence for us to charge yet. North Riding have got it open and shut on the little girl but there's a long way to go on the rest. We'll get her as well though, and when we do I want to be there. I want to nail her to the bloody floor.'

Cat looked across at him. She had rarely heard him sound

115

so angry. There was something in him that was new, a bitterness, an edge he had either only recently acquired, or managed to conceal until now. She had always thought she knew him as well as she knew herself – certainly better than she knew Chris, who was still capable of startling and wrong-footing her.

Simon caught her eye. 'It got to you too,' he said. 'Don't pretend.'

'Yes. David Angus – that got to me. Every time I looked at Sam. It never left me, all day, every day. And it still hasn't quite sunk in that the person who abducted and murdered these children – children like Sam – is a woman. I'm a woman. I have no take on it at all. I'd have said it would never happen.'

'Most people would agree with you.'

'I wonder if we're changing. Women. Girls are behaving like boys. They have male aggressions and male attitudes, they are drinking like men, they even fight as readily as men, sometimes more so.'

'Every Saturday night in Bevham city centre.'

'I've been trying to teach Hannah to be feisty, to have opinions and stand up for them, to think independently . . . maybe I'm doing the wrong thing altogether.'

'I wouldn't worry. She's got a very girly pink bedroom.'

'When I was training, I was one of three women among seventeen men in my year. If Hannah went into medicine, she would find it the other way round.'

'Would that be a problem?'

'No, of course not. But it demands a big change in attitude. Men's attitude, principally.'

'I'm not sure Ed Sleightholme fits your new pattern . . . she's thirty-eight. A loner. I don't know what makes her tick but I doubt if it has anything to do with the new social order.'

'What has it to do with?'

'You tell me.'

'I'm not a shrink.'

'Don't have to be. Think back . . . not long ago, you got to know a psychopath quite well . . . saw how he operated.'

116

Cat shook her head. 'Don't.' She would not have that dark shadow fall across the sunlit afternoon.

'OK, but the point is, a psychopathic killer is a psychopathic killer . . . a loner, without the ability to form normal relationships, a fantasist, someone without a conscience, someone whose guiding principle is self-gratification, at any cost. I think it's a strangely sexless condition.'

'Can't be. There'd be equal numbers of men and women psychopathic killers and there aren't. I couldn't name half a dozen women who have killed in that way.'

Simon was silent, twisting the stem of his glass round and round between his fingers. 'What about a woman taking someone hostage . . . or holding them under threat?' he asked after a moment.

'It's been done . . . guerrillas . . . women soldiers. You get female religious militants, female suicide bombers.'

He shook his head. 'I don't mean in war.'

'I can see it in some extreme domestic situation . . . marital crisis. Someone pushed to the edge. It's very unusual though, isn't it?'

'Uniform see a bit of it. Introduce booze and drugs and it escalates.'

'What made you bring up domestic hostages?'

'Yesterday.'

'Yes. I heard on the church grapevine. You don't expect stray lunatics to wander into English cathedrals.'

'Not sure he is a lunatic. His wife died. He wanted revenge on God, and Jane Fitzroy was the next best thing. She's too Christian by half. Not pressing charges out of some sort of misplaced charitableness.'

'Well, if he's in distress –'

'So are a lot of people.'

'Not sure I like the new tough-talking DCI.'

'Get used to him.'

Cat looked sideways at her brother. Then she laughed. 'Presumably your chap's being referred?'

'No one to refer. He disappeared. We'd no reason to hold him.'

117

'I wonder if Jane's registered with us. Wonder if he is, come to that. Local?'

'Yep. Those yuppie conversions near the canal.'

'Max Jameson! Oh my God, I should have realised. His wife died . . . Lizzie. Beautiful, lovely Lizzie Jameson. She had variant CJD. First case I've had and I hope it's the last. I need to see him.'

'Why?'

'I'm his doctor, Si . . . what's eating you?'

'You're too conscientious, that's what. If he needs you he'll make an appointment.'

Cat snorted. 'Finish the bottle,' she said, making for the house. 'Might have a mellowing effect.'

Twenty

The metal grille slid back. The eyes gleamed through. She shrank back but they saw her. They saw her wherever she was in the cell. She had tried lying flat on the floor. They saw her. They came every fifteen minutes. Grille open. Eyes. The eyes swivelled. Focused. Saw her. Stared for twenty seconds. The grille closed again.

She knew what they were waiting for. Hoping for? Make their life easier, wouldn't it? Only she wasn't a quitter and killing yourself was quitting. Besides, there wasn't any way. No sheets. Nothing sharp. Nothing to swallow. The window was right up near to the ceiling. Bars on that too. She couldn't tell if it was day or night.

She thought a lot about Kyra. They used to make pancakes. Buns. Paper dolls in a row cut out of an old gas bill. She'd never touch Kyra. Kyra was outside the loop. She'd planned to take Kyra to the sea. A caravan. They'd have had a great time, and her mother would have been glad to see the back of her for a week.

She thought a lot about Kyra.

Otherwise she tried not to think of anything. She did word games in her head. Mental arithmetic. She was good at that. She had a smart brain. Wired up right, a teacher had said once. She did spelling backwards, very fast.

But when she slept she lost control and then she was back on the cliff ledge and the sea was waiting for her, leaping up now and then to try and get her, a tiger at the bars of a cage. It was green, like bile. The policeman on the ledge tried to push her into the water and in her dream she fought him, bit into his wrists until she drew blood, and then shoved him spinning down and down. He had made her mad, bloody superior git.

She hadn't meant to leave the girl. The girl was unfinished business and she couldn't stand that, it drove her mad, any of it left unfinished, hanging, not cut off. She liked to cut each one off, snip, finished. A clean end. She felt as if worms were writhing in her gut when she thought of it, not finished, not clean, not cut off. It was like an itch she couldn't scratch, one right inside where she couldn't reach, an itch in her liver or her gut. Nothing would stop it. That was his fault. Theirs. Men.

She woke up. The door banged open. Keys.

Man.

The tray went down on the table with a crash. Sausages smeared in orange beans. A doughnut. Water.

She stared at the man. At the keys.

She kicked the tray and it went over, orange beans swilling with water all over the floor. He cursed.

She was pleased. She didn't speak to them, none of them. Said her name, that was it. Didn't answer questions, didn't tell them what she was thinking. Kept quiet. She could do that for ever.

Good, she thought, when they gave up and left her alone. Good girl. She smacked her fist into the opposite palm. Good. It stopped the worms writhing in her gut. For a bit.

She wished she hadn't kicked the water over. She got thirsty. It was dry here, dry air, stale.

She began to kick her legs against the bench hard. It brought an image to her mind of the football one. He'd kicked. She'd had a bruise on her thigh for a week, purple and sulphurous where he'd kicked out. She'd even wondered for a moment if he was going to be the one who got the better of her, but he hadn't. She knew, really. None of them ever could. In the end, she was always stronger.

'Strong, Ed,' Dad had said, 'that's the girl. Go on, strong. Try and hurt me.'

She never had. He'd taught her. Before he was gone.

That was all she could remember.

'Strong, Ed. Go on, get on with it. That's the girl.'

It was enough. She went on kicking until they came, the grille banging open, the keys.

The woman, this time.

'Stop that, Sleightholme, pack it in. What do you want?'

'Water.'

'You should have thought of that, shouldn't you?'

But the water came. They daren't leave her without water. She drank half of it and threw the rest in the woman's face.

An hour later the door opened again and she had to go out, down the narrow passage, through swing doors, into another corridor. Into a room.

She knew these rooms now. No windows. No decoration. Table. Chair on one side, two on the other. Electricals for the tape machine. That was it. Bloody torture chambers.

She swung in behind them, eyes on the floor. They pushed her towards the chair and into it.

'All right, all right.'

They went. All but one. He stood by the door, behind her. She turned round. Looked into his face.

Him. She had a moment of terror, flashing back to the ledge, and then she thought she was going to fall again, her head spun, her ears buzzed, *she* was falling, not him. Not like in her dream.

Him.

He had another with him, face like a mushed-up turnip.

She stared at him. Then at Blondie.

'DCI Simon Serrailler, DS Nathan Coates. Interview with Edwina Sleightholme, time . . .'

The rigmarole. She had to be careful. She straightened herself up. She'd not had any time to prepare. Be careful.

She stared at him. But it was turnip face who spoke.

'What was your job, Edwina?'

121

'Ed.' NO. Don't say anything. Only she couldn't take it. Wina, she'd called herself when she was a kid. Couldn't say it, Wina. Mother called her bloody Weeny. Christ. But then she had decided. It was Ed and stayed Ed.

'Tell us what you did.'

She stared at him.

'You travelled.' He looked down at his paper. 'Fruit machines. You did something with fruit machines . . . one-armed bandits, that sort of stuff.'

She bit her tongue.

'Was it or wasn't it?'

She nodded.

'What?'

Nothing. Zip it.

'Did the Mondeo go with the job then? Company car, like?'

She smiled. Couldn't help it. Company car.

'Got you about the country, OK, didn't it? Not a bad car. Quite fast. Big boot.'

Silence.

She looked up at the ceiling. There was an odd stain. No cobwebs.

'How long did it take you to drive from here to Lafferton, Ed?' Blondie now. He had a nice voice.

'Where's Lafferton?'

'Lafferton's where you saw David Angus, waiting by his gate for the lift that would take him to school.'

She stared at the table. Her heart was thudding. They might look at the pulse in her neck, so she bent her head right forward. She had him in her mind's eye as clear as clear. The cap. School bag. The pillars on the gate. Felt the car slowing as she pulled into the kerb. A hand was squeezing her heart, like squeezing out a mop.

'What's the matter?'

Stare at the table. Stare at it. Don't look up.

'What did you say to him to make him get in? Or didn't you? Did you pull him in? Did he try and get away from you?'

No, he'd just come with her. Believed her. Got in. Not like the other. She saw his face clearly. Heard his voice. He'd talked a lot. All the bloody way, he'd talked, asked her stuff, whinged. She hated a whinger. Never whinge. She'd learned that damn quick. Zip it.

'Did you hit him? Did you gag him? Where did you take him, Ed?'

They were both asking now, playing ping-pong with her, one after the other. She wanted to laugh at them. It was easy, now that she realised they hadn't a clue. Easy. She was clever and you had to be, no use pretending they weren't clever too, that's where people went wrong. These people weren't stupid. Just that she was cleverer.

'Did you take David to the cave, Ed? Is that where you hid his body?'

Jesus. She felt the blood behind her eyes, pulsing. They'd got her, for a second; she hadn't thought they'd put two and two together and come out with it, bang, like that. It wasn't fair. They weren't playing fair.

'I want a solicitor.'

He smiled. Turnip head. She wanted to smash her hand into his ugly face.

'Why?' Blondie asked. 'Why now, all of a sudden?'

'Yeah, what brought that on, Ed? The cave, was it?'

She slumped down in her chair and shoved it back slightly, so that she could look at her own feet. Not see them. Not look into their faces. Their eyes.

She heard the cave in her head, the echoes, and the sound of the sea outside. She walked round it. She walked right to the back of it. She smelled the seaweed smell. Cold seaweed. Damp sand. She had loved the cave. All those caves. Years ago, it had started. She'd slept in one. She'd dared herself. She'd found them and they were hers. She was afraid of the sea but she'd worked out how the tide went. She'd slept in one.

A different one.

'Don't you think you should tell us where their bodies are, Ed? Think about their parents. Those boys. And others. Are there any others? How many did you take to the cave? David Angus . . . Scott Merriman . . .'

She could see Blondie's hands out of the corner of her eye. He was ticking the names off on his fingers. He said them again.

'David . . . Scott . . . you were taking Amy there too. How many others are there?'

How many?

She knew. They were in her head. You didn't forget. She was very, very careful. The thing was, now, that it was the end and yet it wasn't finished, the thread hung loose. The girl. It wasn't finished.

She smelled the green-sea smell of the cold cave.

They were lucky. No one would understand that but her. The cave was beautiful. She'd hidden there. She wouldn't mind ending there. What could be nicer? Quieter? Peaceful. They had each other. They were safe for ever there.

She felt very, very tired. She could hardly stop herself from putting her head down on the table in front of her.

'What about Kyra?' Blondie.

She sat up, angry, banged her hand down.

'What, Ed?'

'Kyra's . . . leave Kyra alone.'

'Kyra's what?'

Shut up, shut up, shut up, stupid. Only they wouldn't understand in a million years about Kyra and how they were going on holiday, her and Kyra, in a caravan, and how Kyra was different. Would always be different. How she loved Kyra.

'Take her back.'

He sounded disgusted. He looked into her eyes. Yes. Disgusted. He'd no time for her. She hated him for that.

'Get up.'

She thought afterwards, in her room, that she should have spat in his face. She should have done that.

The DCI beckoned Nathan away from the CID corridor. They went down the concrete stairs and out into the yard at the front of the police HQ.

'Let's walk,' Serrailler said. Not that he knew anywhere

decent to walk to. Just the straight main road, dusty now and smelling of tar from the heat of the day.

'I thought Ooop North was supposed to be great,' Nathan said, taking two steps to Serrailler's one stride, to keep up. 'Dales and that.'

'That's the other bit. Like the cliffs. The beaches.'

'This is rubbish. This is worse than Bevham.'

'Funny. It changes everything. No one in Lafferton can ever look at the Hill in the same way again . . . won't, for generations. I can't think of the coast . . . that stretch of cliff. The sea. It's some of the best coastline in the country . . . and it's blighted. It's stained. Nothing will shift it.'

'Do you reckon it's your cave where she took them?'

Simon shrugged.

'Forensics will go in.'

'Forensics. It's all we've got, Nathan. The house. The car. And the cave. If they don't find anything, we're empty-handed.'

'They've got to.' Nathan smacked his balled fist into the other palm.

'She won't talk.'

'Like an iron door, ent she? Gives nothing. Not a flicker. Only . . .'

'What?'

'Only she did it. She did them all.'

'Oh yes.'

'How long will she go down for as it is, do you reckon? Ten? More?'

'Ten minimum.'

'If we can get forensics . . .'

'Yup. Then it's fine.'

'If we don't . . .'

'I can't stand it. Loose ends. We know. She knows we know. But there'll be nothing She could have buried them in the sand. Thrown them into the sea.'

'Can a shrink get her to open up?'

'Doubt it. They don't win them all either. Only pretend to.'

'I get a smell off of her, you know, guv? That smell.'

'Guilt.'

'Badness. It smells.'

They reached a junction. The road went on for miles, shining and sticky in the sun.

'Come on.'

'We having another go?'

Simon was silent. Were they? They could leave it until the next day. Or press on, hope to grind her down, wear her out. It wouldn't work of course. She wasn't the sort to wear out. Ever. Yet he couldn't leave it, go back to Lafferton. Loose ends.

'I'll go in there without you this time. Take one of their team to sit in.'

'Guv.'

'No reflection on you, Nathan.'

'No, it's fine. I don't fancy looking at her any more today. I'm going to ring Em.'

'How is she?'

'Bloomin', thanks. Suits her. All, like, rosy with it, you know?'

Simon laughed. He remembered his sister, pregnant with her last. 'Rosy.'

It occurred to him that he would never know what it was like to have a wife, 'rosy' with his own children. He knew it instinctively in the same way that he knew Ed Sleightholme was guilty. You didn't ignore feelings like that, even if you were powerless over them.

'Be glad to get away from here, be glad to get home.'

A patrol car swerved, screaming, out of the station fore-court. Another.

'Where's the difference?' Simon said.

Twenty-one

They were to see Ed Sleightholme at ten. At half past nine, Serrailler sat in Jim Chapman's room with a plastic cup of sludge-grey coffee and DC Marion Coopey. Simon had asked for her. He wanted her take on Ed.

'You won't crack her,' she said now. 'She just stared me out and it's what she'll go on doing with you. How's your forensics team doing?'

'They've done the caves – the beaches, the cliff paths – nothing. They're in the house now. They've got the car and another lot are pulling that apart. We might be lucky. But I *want* her confession. I *need* her to talk.'

'She's got to you!'

'Well, of course she's got to me. Hasn't she got to you?'

The DC shrugged. She was wearing a cream T-shirt and short linen skirt. She looked cool. 'Not really. I try not to let them.'

'If I didn't get like this from time to time I wouldn't think the job was worth doing.'

'Shows you care?'

He swigged his coffee and ignored her. 'Do you think she's a psychopath?' he asked after a moment.

'Probably. On the other hand, she wants gratification. But that's the usual. It's like an itch . . . in the end, you have to scratch it. The urge is too great, and the satisfaction is great . . . for a bit. Until you start to itch again.'

'Why children? What makes a *woman* want to abduct children?'

'Why stress "woman"? What makes anyone want to abduct children?'

'It's a male crime, overwhelmingly. You know that.'

'I still don't see why the motives need to be different.'

He thought about it. 'Maybe . . . maybe they're not. But either the desire to abduct children and probably kill them is rare in women, or women suppress it more readily . . . something censors it very strongly.'

'So the censor is absent in this case?'

'Has to be. She has not only done it, she's done it again and again. Boys and girls. No conscience, no brakes . . . seize the moment. Gratify. Why?'

'It's sexual. Surely it always is.'

'In men.'

'Why not in women?' She was aggressive with him. She had him on the spot and knew it. 'Look, if you believe women have a tender side in relation to children, because they mother them, whereas men, who father them, don't – that's crap. And why shouldn't women's sexual feelings be as strong as men's?'

'No reason, if you're talking about normal sexual feelings, but these are not normal, are they?'

'Why does that signify?'

'There's a reason, somewhere . . . Why does she want to do this? Why does anyone need to commit this particular crime?'

'I know what the usual explanation is.'

'Emotional deprivation in childhood . . . abuse . . . possibly in care . . . lack of close and trusting relationships when growing up . . .'

'Blah de blah, de blah.'

'You don't buy it?'

'Dunno. It's trotted out as an explanation for most crimes. Makes me look for more.'

'I want Ed Sleightholme to *tell* us more.'

'She's not going to. You might as well get back down south.'

128

'Come on. Back in there.' He held the door open for her. DC Coopey went through with a contemptuous look.

Ed Sleightholme gave him no sort of look at all.

'Did you talk to the children?' Serailler asked. She was staring at the table and did not glance up but he thought he noticed a reaction, some sort of start or hesitation, some twitch in her body. She had registered. She had had to stop herself from responding to him.

'Or did you gag them? Knock them out? Or were they killed pretty soon after you got them into the car?'

Silence. Marion Coopey leaned back in her chair, one leg up over the other.

Simon plugged on. 'Are your parents alive, Edwina?'

'Ed.'

'Why?'

'Why what?'

'Why are you so bothered about it? I rather like the name Edwina.'

'Well, I hate it.'

'Why?'

No answer.

'Did your mother call you Ed?'

'No.'

'Edwina?'

'What's it to you?'

'I'm interested. Was it your father then? Who called you Ed?'

Silence.

'You love your parents, don't you?'

'What gave you that idea?'

'So you don't?'

'Don't know them. Never known them.'

'What, neither of them?'

She looked up straight at him. 'Fuck off.'

'Not yet. Were you adopted? In care?'

'None of your business.'

'Tell me about Kyra.'

That was it. He'd got it. Nothing else worked. She held back, or blocked him out, she was silent, or defiant. But with Kyra, he had got there. Twice now. Her eyes flashed and brightened, her skin took on the faintest flush. She leaned towards him.

'You shut up about Kyra, you hear me?'

'You're her friend, aren't you? She goes round to your house and spends time with you.'

She looked at him. He thought she was going to say something but, at the last minute, she did not.

'What did you do?'

'Made biscuits. Made toffee. Cut things out and stuck them in the scrapbooks. Coloured in. Did soap-and-water bubbles.'

'Fun.'

'Yeah. We had fun. She likes doing fun things.'

'Were they the sort of things you did when you were a kid?'

A flicker. What? A shadow across her face. Gone.

'When I was that age, we made peppermints on wet Saturday afternoons. With my mother. That was fun.'

She stared at him.

'What did you talk about?'

'Stuff. What we were doing. Anything. You know.'

'I don't know. Tell me.'

'No.'

'Kyra will.'

She blazed at him. 'Don't you talk to Kyra. Leave her alone. Leave her right out of all of this, OK? I don't want Kyra knowing . . .'

'Knowing what? About the other children?'

'Where I am. What . . .'

'What you've done . . . about Amy and David and Scott . . . and . . . how many others were there? Kyra may have to know.'

'If . . .'

Serrailler could almost see the tension in her, like an electric charge coming at him across the table. He felt excited. He was getting somewhere. Getting there.

130

'We have to talk to Kyra. She'll be asked about you . . . what you did together . . . how often she was with you . . . what you talked about . . . whether you ever did anything to her . . . tried to get her away.'

'We were going away. I was going to take Kyra on holiday. To a caravan.'

'Her mother didn't mention that. Did she know?'

'It was OK, she'd be fine.'

'Was the caravan in Scarborough, near the beach and the cliffs?'

'No.'

'I thought you'd have liked it there. With Kyra . . . she'd have loved it, along the sands, playing in the caves.'

There was a steel cable and it was stretching and stretching, thinning, growing tighter . . . He felt the pull on it. The room was hot and humid and the silence was extraordinary, an electric, quivering silence. It went on, as the cable tightened and stretched. He could feel Marion Coopey beside him, tense herself, hardly breathing. There was a faint smell of sweat.

Ed Sleightholme's hands were too still. She did not fidget with her fingers, did not move one hand on top of the other, did not scratch, did not pick her nails. Her hands were as still as wax hands, in front of her on the table. If hands could speak, perhaps they would tell most of all. They were ordinary hands, not large.

'Where were you going to take Kyra, Ed? You must have had a plan.'

'I said. Holiday. A caravan.'

'Is that what you told the others?'

'What?'

'Come on, we're going on a holiday, we're going to a caravan. Did you tell them their friends would be waiting there for them? Did you say, "It's fine, Mummy and Daddy are going to come on later"?'

She looked straight at him. Her eyes were steady. They hid nothing. Ordinary eyes. She was so ordinary.

It was what Serrailler had noticed every time he had been close to a murderer, unless they were high on drugs, or out

131

of their minds. The ordinariness. You wouldn't notice them in a crowd. Ed. Boyish. Not plain, not pretty. Not unpleasant. Not remarkable. Not memorable. Ordinary.

'How do you see yourself, Ed?'

She blinked. Then shook her head.

'Do you understand what I mean?'

'No.'

'I don't mean how you look, I mean what you are . . . how do you see yourself? As someone who would melt into the background? People wouldn't really be aware of you at all . . . If we said, "What did she look like?" they'd scarcely be able to remember. Insignificant, really. Is that how you see yourself?'

'No.'

'Then how?'

'I'm . . . Ed, that's what people see. Ed. Me. They know me. ME. Kyra . . . ask her . . . she thinks a lot of me, she's always wanting to come round. People think . . . they just think Ed.'

'Good Ed? Pretty Ed? Funny Ed?'

'How would I know?'

'But what do you think? Give me a word. Describe "Ed".'

The silence lasted minutes, not seconds. Ed was staring at her own hands, but the hands had still not moved. Dead hands.

Then Serrailler saw that she was crying. The tears were silent, and ran very slowly, individually, down her cheeks. He waited. She made no move to brush them away.

'Just tell me,' he said quietly. 'It's easy. Say their names. Then tell me what happened. Ed?'

Nothing. The silence went on and the waxen hands remained still and the tears came, one by one, and slid slowly down, and he waited. And there was nothing.

Twenty-two

'There's the men again.'

'Get away from that window, how many times do I have to tell you?'

'Yes, but they're going into Ed's house again, they've just opened the door. Ed wouldn't like that, I know she wouldn't. When she gets back I'm going to tell her. When is she getting back?'

'I said GET DOWN. Bloody hell, will you listen to me? I told you, you're not to talk about Ed, forget her. Forget she ever lived.'

Kyra turned round and stared.

'Go and put the telly on.'

'I don't want to put the telly on. I want Ed.'

'Jesus wept. You hear me, Kyra . . . if you say that name in this house ever again, *ever*, you hear me, so help me I'll beat the daylights out of you, I'll give you away for care, I'll send you in that panda car. You never say that name again, OK? Hear me.'

Slowly, silently, Kyra got down from the chair by the window and started to trail away out of the room.

'Kyra!'

She froze.

'You promise, right. "I will never say that name in this house again." Go on. Say it. SAY IT.'

Kyra had her back to Natalie. Her shoulders were stiff, her head rigid.

'Say it. "I will never . . ."' A pause. Natalie was shaking. '"I will never . . ."'

'I will never . . .'

She could hardly hear the child's voice. 'SAY IT LOUDER.'

'I will never . . .' It was still barely audible.

'"Say that name . . ."'

'Say . . . that name . . .'

'"In this house again."'

'In my house again.'

'"THIS house."'

'THIS house.'

'"I swear."'

'I swear.' Then, after a second, 'Amen,' Kyra said.

'Now bugger off. Get upstairs. Get anywhere. Go on.'

Kyra slipped from the room like a shadow off the wall.

Natalie shut the door and lit a cigarette. She had started again when it happened, after giving up for three years. It was the first thing she had needed. She stood back, so she couldn't be seen, watching the house next door, watching the police vans and the police in white spacesuits carrying stuff in and out. She'd watched and watched every day. She couldn't keep her eyes off it. She'd scarcely been out. She'd no idea what she might see, hadn't put her fears into shape, in case they came true. But somewhere at the back of her mind, the idea of bodies, things dug up in the garden, children, lingered like a gas, poisoning her.

She had scarcely slept since they had knocked on her door, barely an hour after she had seen the news on television. There had been three of them and she'd been waiting for them. Kyra was out, playing at a friend's house. They would want to talk to Kyra, they'd said, but not now, not yet.

The front door opened and two of them came out. One was carrying two black bin liners full of . . . of what? Natalie dragged on her cigarette. She wanted to go inside. She'd been once or twice, to fetch Kyra, but Ed had never asked her in properly. Besides, it had been just a house then, someone

134

else's living room and hall, someone else's interesting furniture. Now it looked different. Its shape seemed to have changed. It looked wrong, peculiar. She saw photographs of it, on the television, in the papers, Ed's house, the house next door, but not that house, somewhere else, with drawn curtains and police in white suits and vans outside. A murderer's house. One day it would be in a film or a Real Crime book, that house.

She needed to talk to Kyra again. The police hadn't been to do that and Natalie ought to get whatever it was out of her first. That there was something to get, she never doubted. There had to be. She went cold thinking of what had happened and, more, what could have – would have – happened any day, any week. Kyra.

She loved Kyra. It was difficult, on your own, and she had bad days. Kyra took it out of her, never stopping with questions and bouncing and wriggling about, never being still, not sleeping well. But she loved her. How could anyone even ask?

The white suits plodded back up the path and shut the door.

Natalie started to go after them in her mind. Into the hall. Turn left. Living room, same as this. Out again. Kitchen. Door to the back. The way Kyra sometimes went in. Used to. She saw the stairs, though she had never been up Ed's stairs. She wanted to now, wanted to stare and stare around every room, taking it in, peeling away the wallpaper and the curtains and the furniture with her eyes to get at what was beneath, or behind.

Several times a day, Natalie had got out the phone book and looked up the name.

Sleightholme, E.S., 14 Brimpton Lane.

It stood out from all the others on the page. The line wavered. Then it looked bigger, the ink blacker.

Sleightholme, E.S., 14 Brimpton Lane.

Already, it was more than a name, an address, a telephone number. It had a ring round it. It might have been . . .

Christie, J. R. H., 10 Rillington Place.

135

West, F., 25 Cromwell Street.

It had that look.

Only they were gone and this was real and she was looking at it, this red-brick house the same as her own red-brick house, a couple of yards away from her house in which she ate and slept and dressed and cooked. In which there was Kyra.

Natalie stubbed out her cigarette.

The house next door was quiet now. No one came or went. The vans were parked. That was all.

She'd been happy to let Kyra go there. More than happy. Ready. Any day. She didn't know what she felt about that. She didn't blame herself. How could she have known anything? Kyra had gone on and on, every morning, every night, every Saturday and Sunday. Ed. Ed. Ed. Ed.

Nothing bad could have happened, then, nothing so bad at all, if she had wanted to keep on going, every morning, every night. Could it? How could it? She'd never said anything. She wouldn't have wanted to go, if . . .

The police van shone white and square and odd in the sun. Natalie wondered what was in it.

From upstairs, there was no sound. No sound at all.

She lit another cigarette and smoked it to the end before going to talk to Kyra.

You could see Ed's house from her bedroom. As soon as she had been sent upstairs – which was always happening – Kyra had taken the little stool carefully over to the window, so that standing on it she could watch in case Ed came back. Every day, she hoped Ed would come back. Every day, she knew Ed would come back. She saw people going in and out of Ed's house and when Ed came back she would tell her about them. Ed might not know. She might not like it. Ed was proud of her house. She'd said so quite often.

'I'm house-proud.' 'Take off your shoes, Kyra, I don't want muddy marks, I'm house-proud.' 'Wash your hands after you've eaten that, Kyra, I don't want cake mixture on the furniture, I'm house-proud.'

It was beautiful inside Ed's house and she wouldn't want

136

the men messing it up. The floors were always shining and the carpets never had bits on them. Everything had a place, neat and careful, and the furniture smelled of polish. The mats were arranged just so and the cushions lined against the sofa back, just so, and when you put the mugs back on their hooks, you had to get the order right. Kyra did. She'd learned. Ed had taught her.

'If you're going to be here, you have to learn the rules, Kyra. The blue one, then the white one, then the green, the pink, the yellow and, at the end, the blue again.'

'Why do they go like that?'

'That's how I like them.'

'Yes, but why?'

'I just do. It's how I like them.'

'I like them that way as well, Ed.'

'Good,' Ed had said. 'Now wash your hands, you've been touching the plants.'

She loved the way it was. When she came home, Kyra wanted to arrange everything carefully. She tried to. But it never worked because their house was a tip. 'Kyra, stop bloody messing, stop fidgeting, will you?' But in her own room, Kyra could keep things the way she liked them. The way Ed liked them. She lined up things in her drawers – white socks, blue socks, white knicks, pink knicks, and her dolls and animals in a line on the shelf. She had learned.

'Gawd, what's wrong with you, Kyra, you're a funny kid, I don't know where you come from. Look at it, it's peculiar.'

'It's how I like it.'

'Yeah, right, well, let's wait till you're fourteen, it'll be a bleedin' pigsty, teenagers are.'

Kyra knew that it would not but she also knew better than to disagree.

She leaned forward. The back door of Ed's house had opened and two of the weird men had come out and taken bags to the wheelie bin, but they were not putting rubbish in, they were taking it out, emptying the wheelie bin over into the bags. Why would you do that?

Downstairs the phone rang. Kyra settled herself more

137

comfortably on the window ledge. Her mother would talk for ages.

When she had asked why the men and the vans were at Ed's house every day, Natalie had screamed at her. She was used to her mother screaming but this had been different, it had made her face twisted and frightening-looking so that Kyra had understood not to ask again.

'You listen to me. Ed's gone. OK? End. I don't want to hear about Ed, I don't want you asking anyone, I don't. Do you hear me, Kyra?'

Kyra had nodded, afraid to say anything at all, afraid to ask a question. Her head was so full of questions she wondered if it had grown bigger to accommodate them all, if people would notice. Questions buzzed all day, all night, like a hive of bees that were never still and the only way she could let them out of her head was through her mouth, by asking them, and she daren't do that, so they stayed inside, buzzing her mad.

Her mother had raised her voice now. Kyra turned slightly, to hear.

'What? When? When d'you hear that, Donna? Oh my God. Oh my GOD. It's a fuckin' nightmare, I'm living in one. Oh my God. No. Just the same, van and those white-suit people, you know, you see them on murder programmes . . . it'll be on the news, then. I gotta keep Kyra out, she's got ears out here, I don't want her hearing. I just said she'd gone and she wasn't coming back. Yeah, too right it's true . . . Oh my God.'

Kyra looked back out of the window. The questions were dancing up and down in her head now, making little hard taps every time. Where was Ed? Why had she gone? Why wasn't she ever coming back? What had she done? Why were the men in her house? What, why, why, when, who, what, why, why . . .

Kyra wanted Ed. Because no one else would be able to answer the questions properly, everyone else would shut her up, push the buzzing questions back inside her head and slam the door shut. But Ed always answered. Ed answered every question, though sometimes only to say, 'I can't tell you the answer to that one.' But somehow that was enough. That was an answer. Ed never said shut up, don't ask, stop mithering, it's none of your business, you're too young to ask, too young to know. Ed talked to her, and thought and listened. And answered. Ed told her things. Ed knew a lot. Ed. Ed. Ed. Ed.

But suddenly, she tried to see Ed in her mind, and there was nothing. No one. A blank space. She looked at the house from her window, stared and stared at it to try and conjure up the picture of Ed but it wouldn't come. Nothing came. She did not know what Ed looked like or sounded like. She couldn't find Ed at all.

She got down and went out of her room, terrified. This was what her mother must mean, that Ed had gone and would never come back. Ed had even gone from her head, her mind, what she looked like, her voice, her smell, her laugh. She started to go down the stairs, afraid as she had never been before of her empty room and being in it alone, needing to hear her mother, see her, even her swearing and her irritation.

Natalie was coming up. Kyra stopped and looked down.

'What you doing?'

Kyra was silent.

'Come on, I've gotta go to the shops, get some stuff. What's wrong with you, Kyra, for God's sake, you look like you've seen a bleedin' ghost.'

But she hadn't. That was what was wrong. She hadn't.

Very slowly, one at a time, Kyra came down the stairs.

There was always somebody outside now. Kids. Neighbours. People from the other side of the estate. They hung about, watching, talking to one another, waiting as the white suits came out, staring at what they carried, eyes following them back in. They knew better than to ask any questions. They just stood, waiting, hoping for something to happen, some excitement, and then television vans and men with furry microphones in their street.

Natalie dragged Kyra into the car and slammed the door so hard it made the windscreen rattle. Kyra did not look at Ed's house or the watchers, she kept her eyes down. She said nothing.

139

Natalie muttered something under her breath as she screeched the car in reverse, crashed the gears and then shot forward, making Kyra rock sharply to and fro in her seat belt.

Once, Ed had taught her a game where you closed your eyes and said the name of a colour and then tried really, really hard to see it in your mind and nothing else. Just pink. Just green. Nothing else. 'Even at the corners,' Ed had said. 'Black,' Kyra thought now, and made her closed eyes stare and stare until all they could see was black. She could do it. She'd learned. But for a few seconds she tried quickly to see Ed, before the black came down.

'Ed,' she said to herself. But there was no Ed, even at the corners.

They were out for an hour and when they got back, there was another car, black, outside their own door. The watchers were keeping an eye on it at the same time as they oversaw the activities of the white suits, swivelling round the moment Natalie's car turned the corner.

'There's someone at our house. There's a black car.'

'I've got bleedin' eyes, Kyra.'

'What's it there for?'

'Get out.' Natalie yanked the handbrake on and, as she left the car, put two fingers up to the watchers.

'What you done then, Nat?'

'Fuck off.' She pushed Kyra through the front door so hard she fell. Natalie hauled her up by one arm. 'Watch where you're putting your feet.'

The door banged.

There had been two people in the black car, they'd both seen that. Now, Natalie saw their shapes, on the other side of the front-door glass.

'Kyra, get upstairs.'

'I want –'

'Kyra . . .'

Kyra fled.

Natalie turned and waited for the doorbell to ring.

'DS Nathan Coates, DC Dawn Lavalle. Mrs Coombs?'

'No. Ms.'

'Sorry . . . Ms Natalie Coombs?'

'You bloody know I am.' She held the door open for them. In the sitting room, there was no chair which did not have something on it. Natalie shoved a few things at random on to the floor. 'I suppose it's about next door. You want a coffee?'

'Thanks, that'd be good. They keep us parched on this job.'

'Awww.' Natalie went to the kitchen. On the way, she glanced up the stairs. 'Kyra, what did I say?'

There was a slight shuffling sound, and the closing of Kyra's door.

When she got back, the ugly bloke was standing at the window looking across at next door.

The policewoman was examining a photograph of Kyra in burgundy taffeta as Natalie's sister's bridesmaid. 'How old was she in that one, Natalie?'

'I didn't say anything about Natalie.'

'Sorry . . . Ms Coombs.'

'Four. Sooo pretty.'

'Very. You must be proud of her.'

Natalie gave her a look. 'Right, get on with it. It's about next door – don't take a genius to work that one out.'

'It is. We've got some questions for you, but then we need to talk to Kyra.'

'Oh no, I ent having that, she's a kid.'

'And she went next door to see Miss Sleightholme quite regularly, I gather?'

'I wouldn't say regularly. I didn't let her.'

'Why not?'

'Well, you never know, do you? Someone on their own, having a little kid round all the time . . . not very normal, is it?'

'Did you think there was something not very normal about Edwina?'

'God, that's funny . . . never even knew she was called that. Ed, she was. Never anything but Ed.'

'And how did she seem to you – Ed?'

Natalie shrugged.

141

'But you did let Kyra go there on her own?'

Natalie shrugged again.

'How often, would you say? Once a week? Three times a week?'

'I said, just . . . sometimes.'

'Once a month?'

'Well, I didn't keep a fucking diary.'

'Was it just a casual thing, or did Ed invite her?'

Natalie sighed and lit a cigarette. She wondered what she'd have done without taking it up again.

'Kyra was always nagging to go round there and half the time I didn't let her.'

'Why?'

'Well, it's a nuisance, someone else's kid from next door always wanting to mither you, must be . . .'

'Did she ever go without asking you?'

'She's cunning is Kyra, she managed to slip out . . . made me mad.'

'Why?'

'Cos I don't like her being disobedient, that's why.'

'No other reason . . . to do with Ed?'

'Well, if I'd known about it then, bloody hell, of course she wouldn't have gone near, would she? What kind of mother do you take me for?'

'But you didn't know. Did you?'

'Of course I didn't bloody know!'

'Fine, you made your point, Natalie. What I'm getting at is . . . was there anything about Ed's behaviour that worried you . . . or did Kyra ever say anything . . . even just a hint?'

'No.'

'Nothing at all that you remember?'

'NO. I said NO. Is that it now?'

They got up. 'If you think of anything . . .' Ginger head.

'I won't.'

'OK, thanks for your time.'

'We'll want to talk to Kyra. Someone'll ring to make an appointment. I'll bring another officer with me, from the child protection unit . . .'

'She won't have anything to tell you. There's nothing to tell. At least I hope there bloody isn't.'

'Children pick up on things, that's all . . . and anything she can say about what she did there, what they talked about . . . it may help.'

'But she's arrested, isn't she? No way is she coming back here? You got her.'

They walked to the door.

'She's been arrested on one charge, yes. But we need a lot more information. That's why we want to talk to Kyra.'

Natalie closed the front door and paused. There was another soft noise.

'Kyra . . . get down here.'

Kyra got.

Twenty-three

'I'm out of here,' Simon Serrailler said. He threw a file on to the others beside his desk and switched off his laptop. 'Don't call me, don't expect me to call you.'

'Guv.' Nathan Coates followed the DCI out of his room. 'Not even if . . .'

Simon looked at him. 'Only a message,' he said. 'And only news. Not no news.'

'Understood. You off abroad?'

'No. London.'

'Seeing any shows or that?'

Simon smiled. 'You could say I am.' He ran fast down the stairs. 'Yes.' He waved his hand and dodged out to the car before anyone else could get after him.

He'd had enough. It had been exhilarating, interesting, draining by turns and he wouldn't have missed the last couple of weeks, but he needed to get away, from the station, police business, Lafferton. He had always thrived on cutting himself off and plunging into a different life, and as he drove towards the close, to get his things together before heading down the motorway, he was light-headed with pleasure. He was spending three days at the gallery supervising the setting up of his exhibition, after which there was the private view. Then he would see. Theatre, opera, good food, walking about London. He didn't care, he made no exact plans. It was the way he preferred to relax, surprising himself each day.

He had booked his usual, comfortable room in a hotel over-looking some quiet gardens in Chelsea. It was unfussy and as unlike a hotel as he could have found. It was also expensive. When he went abroad Simon travelled light and spent little; he was happy in Ernesto's modest flat in the Venice backwater or at a remote farmhouse bed and breakfast, a cheap parador. In London, he liked comfort and spent money.

As he joined the motorway and speeded up, he felt the usual shift, as if a switch had clicked within him. He left Ed Sleightholme, murdered children and kidnapped women behind, and his mind was cleared of them all. He was no longer DCI Serrailler, he was Simon Osler, with a solo exhibition of his drawings being staged at a Mayfair gallery. Many of the people who would come to look and to buy had no idea that he was a CID officer, and that was how he liked it. When he had had to deal with criminals who had led double lives he had usually understood and empathised. In itself, to lead two lives was not a crime; it depended on what you did in them. If he had been forced to choose between his two he would have found it difficult. They balanced one another; neither life was quite enough on its own.

Twice he heard his mobile ring but it was in his jacket on the back seat. He would check the messages when he stopped next. He had not left all of his involvement in current cases behind him.

Dennis Vindon from forensics got up from his hands and knees and went to the window. Outside, it was quiet. People had grown bored. There was nothing to see but white suits going out to the van from time to time, carrying things which they put inside before plodding back and closing the front door. The things were wrapped and no one could have any idea what they were. Dennis knew. They were sections of carpet. Cushions. Pieces of linoleum. The scrapings from the inside of cupboards. Bed sheets. Things bagged, tied and labelled.

No one spoke to the white suits and the white suits neither spoke to nor looked at the women hanging about the gate. It was always women, Dennis thought now, looking down at the sunlit street. Men – even unemployed men – didn't seem to have the ghoulish interest in watching a crime scene. If this was a crime scene. He had been at a good many and he had never known a neater, cleaner, more orderly house. And it was not a house that had been urgently scrubbed to erase traces, it was a house that was always tidy, clean and orderly. Nice house really. You had to say that. A few books. Some pretty china that looked like Victorian. Coloured cushions. It was a house someone had enjoyed putting together. He had a sense of things when he went to pull a place apart and his sense here was that there had been no crime committed; no one had been tortured or killed here. None of the missing children had been pushed into a cupboard under the stairs or their clothes taken out and burned in the garden incinerator. If Sleightholme was the abductor of the missing children, she had done nothing at home and brought nothing to it.

Jo Caper walked into the room and whistled.

They both stood at the window now, looking out.

'There isn't going to be anything there either,' Dennis said at last. The garden was tidy and well kept. A rectangle of lawn. Flower beds on either side, with rose bushes and a buddleia, a lilac tree at the bottom. A standard six-by-four shed which had been stripped already. A table with two plastic garden chairs upended on to it. 'Pity, that.'

Because, by the end of the week, they were going to have to dig it up. Waste of time, waste of effort especially in the sun; there would be nothing buried in the garden. He just knew.

'You?'

Jo shook her head. 'Nothing. Just finished bagging up her clothes. That's it then in the bedrooms.'

'Any news on the car?'

'I heard Luke say there might be. Tomorrow maybe.'

'That's where it'll be. If there's anything. It's always the car.'

'No it's not.'

'Yeah, yeah, but this time I just know it.'

146

'Ah, you've got your bent coat hanger out?'

'Stranger things have happened.'

'I heard.'

Dennis had once, just the once, doused a garden and found a well beneath a newly laid patio, and a body plus a lot of water.

'Right. Back to the underlay.'

'You want a Coke?'

'Nah, be lukewarm.'

'No, I put it in the fridge downstairs.'

'You shouldn't have done that.'

'Probably not,' Jo said, sailing out.

In her own house, Kyra sat in front of a *My Little Pony* video behind drawn curtains. Occasionally, she got up and pulled one back to peer at Ed's house but there was never anything to see.

My Little Pony had sickly voices and tinkly music and Kyra hated it, but she daren't switch the video off in case her mother heard and came in. Natalie was on the phone to Donna Campbell, her best friend.

Kyra sat back on the sofa and closed her eyes, but this time she didn't try to see a block of colour or black velvet; she went in her mind through Ed's front door and into each room of the house in turn, checking on things – the furniture, the books, the flowery cups and saucers, the two clown dolls dangling from the shelf. She tried to remember everything. Then she would know what the white suits had taken or moved around. She meant to get into Ed's house somehow – she had to get into it. She felt that Ed would want her to, would trust her and no one else to check on things.

Her mother woke her, raking the curtains open and shouting. The television had been switched off.

'Get up, I gotta take you out.'

'Where are we going?'

'See someone. Come on, Kyra, move, you need your hair brushing and a clean T-shirt, I'm not having people think I don't bother.'

'What sort of someone are we going to see?'

'You'll find out when we get there.'

'Where?'

'Oh, bloody hell, Kyra, you're one big blasted question mark, you.'

Natalie was furious. She and Donna had decided to take their kids to the supermarket where there was a supervised play area. They could shop a bit, have a coffee, talk, and not be mithered all afternoon by Kyra and Donna's kid. The fact that Kyra said she hated Danny Campbell was irrelevant to Natalie. When she had asked Kyra why she hated him, Kyra had said it was because he bit her when no one was looking. But the marks on Kyra's arm never looked like bites. More like pinches, and what kid didn't get pinched from time to time?

'Pinch him back,' Natalie had said, 'that'll teach him. Don't be a wimp, Kyra, you'll get nowhere in this world being a wimp.'

But when Natalie had put the phone down after making the arrangement, it had rung again and it was the police, saying she'd to take Kyra down now, there was a meeting arranged for them to talk to her. They wouldn't change it. It had to be now.

Natalie wrenched Kyra's head round to redo her ponytail. 'Bloody keep still, will you?'

'Where are we going?'

Natalie shook her head through a mouthful of pink nylon scrunchy.

As they went out two of the white suits were getting into the van, and as Natalie started the car another came out of Ed's front door, locked it and put the key in her white-suit pocket. Kyra stared at her hard, trying to memorise everything so that she could tell Ed.

Twenty-four

There were a dozen people kneeling in the Chapel of Christ the Healer. Cat Deerbon joined them at the back. The evening sun sifted through the side-aisle windows, so that the light was a dusty gold. She came to the healing service as often as possible and tonight two of her own patients were in the front pews.

Footsteps came across the chancel and as Cat looked round, she saw that it was Jane Fitzroy. There had been a paragraph in the local paper about her ordeal at the hands of Max Jameson, and Cat's mother, Meriel Serrailler, had mentioned that Jane was staying with the Precentor and his family for a few days. Cat glanced at her as she went by but could read nothing into her expression, though she seemed to hesitate slightly before going up the single step to the altar.

'In the name of the Father, and of the Son and of the Holy Spirit.'

'Amen.'

'Christ Jesus, who healed those brought to him in sickness of body and mind, hear our prayers this evening for those present and elsewhere who come to you in faith. Give the strength, comfort and assurance of your presence with us at the laying on of hands and look graciously on all who . . . on . . .'

Jane's voice faltered. For a moment, she was quiet and seemed to be gathering herself together to continue. Then, without warning, her body folded and crumpled as she fainted.

There was a murmur. Cat got up and went quickly over. She knelt beside her.

'Jane? Can you hear me? It's Dr Deerbon.' She took her wrist. The pulse was weak and Jane's face was chalk white, but her eyelids fluttered and she tried to move her arm. 'You're fine, you just fainted. Don't sit up for a moment.' Cat turned and looked at the anxious faces in front of her. 'Don't worry. She's fainted. I don't know why, but that's all it is.'

Jane was trying to sit up and there was a little colour in her cheeks. She looked upset and embarrassed.

Half an hour later, they were both in the sitting room of the Precentor's house. The French windows were open on to the garden and the smell of stocks came in from the terrace.

'I feel a complete idiot.'

'Yes, well, enough said.' Rhona Dow was pouring tea. 'I *did* tell her, Cat.'

'I'm sure you did.' Cat and Jane exchanged a quick glance.

'She had a frightful shock and she shouldn't be rushing to get back to normal . . . *and* to make a start in the very chapel where that man . . . Honestly, Jane.'

'I was sure I was OK. I can't sit about your house doing crossword puzzles for ever. I'm not a convalescent, I'm perfectly all right.'

'So why did you faint?' Rhona looked triumphant. 'Why did she, Cat?'

'No idea. But I'm not worried. Come and see me in the surgery though,' she said to Jane. 'We'll do a blood test for luck. I doubt if it will be anything other than absolutely normal but let's play safe.'

'And *I* will make the appointment,' Rhona Dow said decisively.

A telephone rang.

When she had swept out to answer it, Cat and Jane dared not meet one another's eye.

'Whatever,' Cat said, smiling into her tea. 'But do come and see me. I like to check new patients anyway.'

'I did register with you the week I arrived because . . .'

'Rhona told you to?'

'Hm.'

'Do you feel up to a walk round their garden? It's the nicest in the close.'

'I know. I live at the bottom of it, remember.'

Cat had. She wanted to see if Jane avoided her bungalow, which would give her an idea of what lasting impact her time there with Max had made on her.

Rhona's voice was still booming through the hall behind them.

'She has been a brick,' Jane said now, 'so kind, so good . . . so has Joseph. They've simply treated me as if I'd always lived there.'

'But you are now beginning to find it all a bit oppressive.'

'Isn't that shameful?'

They started to wander down the lawn.

'Understandable, I'd say. I can only take Rhona in small doses.'

'I'm so glad you were in the chapel. Thanks. I don't know what they thought, poor things.'

'They were concerned for you.'

'It's been quite a week or two. My mother was burgled and beaten up, I'd only just started to feel my way into Lafferton – it's a big job for me – then Max.'

'I don't wonder you fainted. I noticed you'd started straight in at Imogen House.'

'Yes. And I've had a lot of meetings at Bevham General, learning the ropes there.'

'We needed to meet – just not this way.'

They went through the trellis which divided the garden and turned right down a path between the fruit trees. The corner of Jane's bungalow was in sight. Cat felt her tense slightly, then stop.

'OK?'

Jane took a deep breath, then said, 'Will you come in with

151

me? Once I've been in it'll be all right.' For a split second, she hesitated again, but then went straight forward, round the corner of the bushes and up to her front door.

'Oh. They've changed the lock of course, they told me. I think someone up at the house has the new keys.'

'Never mind. Go to the window.'

Jane glanced at her, then moved up to the glass, cupped her hands round her eyes and peered in.

'All right?'

'Yes. It looks like someone else's house. I don't recognise that I've lived there at all. How odd. I feel I shouldn't be looking in.'

'But do you feel anxious?'

'No.' Jane turned. 'Detached from it really.'

'Fine. You're doing well. Next time, get the keys and go in. You'll have to sooner or later so make it sooner. I think you'll feel at home again.'

'Maybe. I'm not sure how much I've felt at home here anyway, even without Max. Not sure if I feel at home in Lafferton.'

Cat was silent. Jane might want to confide in her but now was not the time and after a few seconds they walked back into the garden, enjoying the first faint brush of evening cool.

The terrace was empty and there was no sound from the house.

'Can I ask you something?' Jane gestured to Cat to sit on the bench against the wall. The sun was touching the tips of the fruit trees ahead of them but the bench was in shadow. 'I feel I have to go and see Max. What do you think?'

'Why do you feel that?'

'He's in trouble. His wife's death affected him very badly. He wasn't trying to hurt me – as me – he was exploding with grief and anger and I got in the way. I think he needs help. Well, it's obvious he does.'

'You may well be right but are you the person to offer it?'

'Because I'm a priest?'

'No, because of what he did – there's no getting away from

152

that, is there? You haven't pressed charges against him but it was a pretty desperate way to behave and you've been in shock because of it, to put it mildly. Perhaps stand back a bit? Max is my patient – let me do it.'

'But that's medical help . . . maybe he does need that but I wanted to tell him it was all right.'

'And that you forgive him?'

'Exactly. I suppose you think that sounds too pious.'

'Not at all. Perhaps you could write to him if you think you need to say it?'

'Oh, I couldn't do that, it would be so cold.'

And you, Cat thought, looking at her, are quite the opposite – and perhaps too much so for your own good. She studied Jane Fitzroy's face now in profile, surrounded by the rich, springing Titian hair. She was not only beautiful but had a face with character – an unusual, thoughtful, intelligent face. Her skin was enviable, gardenia cream, her eyes green-flecked hazel, wide and direct. She would not fade into any background but there was a stillness and a depth to her, beneath the surface anxiety and tension.

'I have to get home,' Cat said, standing up. 'Look, do what you think is right but do it carefully. God, how patronising, of course you will. And make that appointment to come into surgery. This is your doctor speaking.'

Two hours later, after supper, Jane went to find Rhona Dow. She was cutting out a dress on the long table in what had once been the playroom at the top of the house; the Dows had three sons, all now away from home, one still at university, the other two both priests and both working abroad. Jane suspected that Rhona had been anxious to invite her to stay as much for her company and to muffle the emptiness of the big house as anything else. She was grateful. But she also knew that she had to move out.

'My dear, do sit down, shove all that stuff off the chair. I let this room get like a tip when I'm dressmaking, it seems to help.'

'I love the fabric . . . what is it?'

'Here.' Rhona pushed the cover of the dress pattern across. 'I need something smartish – there are garden parties and fêtes and weddings and teas with bishops from now until September and everything in the wardrobe has been about in public for too many years.'

'I can't thread a needle.'

'Well, you do other things. Have a square of chocolate.'

A large bar of Galaxy was open on the table beside the sewing machine. Rhona Dow was a heavy woman and after twenty-four hours with her Jane had understood why.

'I've come to tell you that I'm going back into the garden house tonight. You have been wonderful and it's made all the difference being here but I have to get back, Rhona. I know you'll understand.'

There flickered across Rhona's face an expression that Jane found all too easy to read. When she left, the house would be empty. Rhona busied herself as she could but Joseph was out a lot and it was clear that she was lonely.

'I won't start trying to persuade you to change your mind, my dear. Only if you aren't happy down there after that business, promise you'll come back. Even in the middle of the night. We shan't mind a bit.'

'I promise. Thank you.'

'Well, at the very least let me pack you up some things . . . you'll need bread and milk and –'

'No, I'll drive over to the supermarket. Honestly. I must get back to normal, Rhona.'

Rhona Dow sighed and broke off another square of chocolate.

The all-night supermarket on the Bevham Road was not a place Jane would ever have thought of as a haven but when she pulled into the car park, and saw the multicoloured blaze of lights and bright hoardings, she felt a lifting of her spirits. Inside it was warm and cheerful. She pushed a trolley round, exchanging words with other shoppers, picking out foods she would not normally buy as well as the dull essentials, eking out her time there. As long as she was surrounded by the cheerful hum everything else receded into the background and did not trouble her.

After the checkout she went to the café. She was hungry, she realised, queuing for her coffee, and added a plate of bacon, eggs and toast to her tray. She also bought a newspaper.

Supermarkets were good refuges, good for the lonely, those with empty lives, those needing a break and some company of the sort which committed you to nothing more than a few words and the price of a cup of tea. People who said they were soulless and that small shops were always best had not felt as she had, and been restored, even temporarily, by the wide aisles and bright clatter and activity. You couldn't linger in a small shop, taking advantage of warmth and company, for as long as you liked, and she had known plenty in London with brusque and unwelcoming staff.

God, she thought, the God I know, the God I believe in, the God of love and comfort, the God who sustains, is here as palpably tonight as in the Cathedral of St Michael.

The bacon and eggs were hot and surprisingly delicious, the local newspaper a carousel of gossip and titbits of information and the sort of photographs of amateur dramatic society productions, school sports and wedding pictures that delighted her.

As she was leaving the café a couple came up to talk, recognising her from the cathedral and wanting to ask about having all four of their children baptised together.

The streets were quiet as she drove back. The moon was a paring from a silver sixpence, over the Hill.

She slid her car up to the space on the cobbles beside the Precentor's house, which was in darkness. Joseph's car was back. She wondered how Rhona had got on with her dressmaking and how she managed to keep chocolate stains from the fabric. Now she had only to lug three carrier bags down through the garden to the bungalow, let herself in and put on all the lights to send any dark shadows and memories shrinking back into the walls.

155

The torch she kept on her keyring and which normally sent a thin, piercing beam some distance ahead was not working when she clicked the end, but she knew her way down the path by now. The bushes whispered as she caught against them, and out beyond the fruit trees she heard some creature scuttle away. In one of the gardens further along, a cat yowled, startling her. She edged her way up to the porch, touching a hand against the wall to help her get her bearings. Above her, the constellations of stars prickled against the sky. Key. It slid sweetly into the new lock. She pushed open the door. The house smelled of fear, her fear, the last time she had been inside it, trapped, held, caught claustrophobically inside with Max Jameson. She felt his arm round her throat and the chill edge of the knife blade and began to shiver. Her hand shook as she felt along the wall for the light switch and when the light came, for a second the place looked utterly strange, so that she was disorientated, half wondering if she had mistaken the house.

She went quickly round, turning on every light in kitchen, sitting room, study, bedroom, every lamp. She pulled her carrier bags of shopping inside, shut, locked and bolted the door, drew the kitchen blind and the curtains in each room. Only when she had done all of that did she take deep breaths to still herself. It was a while before her heart stopped thumping.

She made herself look about slowly. Everything was as it had been. Chairs, table, desk, pictures, television, books, all in their places, all familiar. There was the faintest smell of must. The garden house was damp in spite of the maintenance team's best efforts.

She went to the window in the sitting room. Stopped dead, hearing something. Some scrape or scratch outside, a stone kicked, a brick dislodged?

Of course she could not sleep with the windows open.

It was after midnight. She unpacked her shopping and put it away, switched on the kettle, took out a mug and tin of chocolate powder, milk, a spoon. Set them on the table. The slightest noise, of tin on table, plug into socket, sounded uncanny, loud and hollow, and when it was over, the silence was total, a nervous, taut, unfriendly silence.

She took her hot drink resolutely into the study, and picked up her prayer book from the desk.

'O Lord, support us all the day long of this troublous life, Until the shades lengthen and the evening comes.'

She spent some time over prayer, the reading of the office and then of her Bible, so that it was well after one before she went to bed. But the silence had taken on a different quality, become a quietness, pleasing and soothing rather than an anxious silence. She read A.S. Byatt's *Possession* for half an hour and then switched off the lamp. She felt a deep exhaustion that muffled her brain and made her limbs heavy. Sleep would come as a blessing.

She woke from a nightmare of slimy darkness, in which she was choking on some foul substance and her lungs were being pierced with blades, to sit up in a terror of sweat. In reaching for the lamp she sent it crashing to the floor. Jane cried out but then shook herself, got out of bed on the side away from the broken base and felt her way to the light switch beside the door. As she did so, she heard a sound in the garden.

No, she told herself, there is nothing in the garden, apart from cats and foxes, possibly an owl. Nothing. No one.

She fetched a dustpan and brush, cleared up the mess and put it in the kitchen bin. There was a spare lamp in her study, which she brought and set up, switched on and read by for another twenty minutes.

'O Lord, illuminate the darkness of this night with your celestial brightness, And from the children of light banish the deeds of darkness. Through Jesus Christ, Our Lord.'

The noise outside was a muffled bump as if someone had fallen.

There were several things she might do: ring the police; ring the Dows; look through the window; go outside . . . And she could do none of them, she was paralysed with fear, her mouth puckered and dry.

Through her head ran a film which she could not stop, of

157

Max Jameson pushing her down, holding her by the arms, staring into her face, holding the knife, laughing, crying in triumph, sitting opposite her, tormenting her with fear, and talking, talking, in a slow, peculiar whisper which susurrated in her ears.

She forced herself to climb out of bed, put on her slippers and dressing gown, and then to pull back the curtain. She had her hand on the latch, ready to open the window when she looked out into the night garden.

Max Jameson's face leered back at her. His body was in shadow, even his neck seemed wrapped so that his face, with its wild hair and mess of beard, was floating alone a few yards away. Jane would have shouted, banged the window, gestured to him to get away but she did nothing, only froze in terror at the window, looking out as he looked in.

The sight of the police torches flashing out across the garden, probing the darkness to reveal anything hidden was an inexpressible relief. They had arrived barely five minutes after she had called them. The patrol car had been in the area and the two young policemen were large, heavy-footed and reassuring as they probed bushes and roamed about behind trees, up and down the side paths, in and out of sheds. By then, the lights had come on in the Dows' house, and there were other voices in the garden.

Jane sat in the armchair, drinking a mug of tea. It was half past three. Another hour and it would be breaking light. She did not know what she had seen, could not tell now if the face of Max Jameson had been real or a trick of her anxious imagination. But if she closed her eyes, it was there, clear and fleshed not vapour, not ghostly. Max Jameson, staring at her from the blackness.

She started to shiver, and the mug of tea spilled. She reached out to put it on the table beside her but her hand would not do as she wanted it to and the mug smashed on to the floor, the hot tea splashing up, scalding her bare foot.

When Rhona Dow appeared in the room, dressed in a huge pink velour robe, hair on end, Jane burst into tears.

158

Twenty-five

DS Nathan Coates sat in the front seat of the car, concealed behind a broken run of wooden fencing, watching a vegetable warehouse. He and DC Brian Jennings had been watching the warehouse for the best part of two days, during which time a great deal was supposed to have happened and absolutely nothing had.

Nathan crunched hard down into an apple.

Jennings winced. 'Could you eat that a bit louder, Sarge?'

'You askin' or tellin'?'

'Only . . .'

'Only I have to put up with your roast chicken crisps every half-hour. You'd do a lot better getting your mouth round one of these.' Nathan buzzed down the window and threw the apple core on to the waste ground.

'People could take root here.'

'You have.'

'I think this is a fruit and veg warehouse. I don't think there's anything in there but fruit and veg. Nothing goes in but fruit and veg, nothing comes out but –'

'All right, you said it and said it.'

'I reckon the DI's got a dodgy informant.'

'We wouldn't be here –'

'One sergeant, one DC . . . and a load of bananas.'

'Hang on –'

'Oh look, Sarge, it's a fruit and veg lorry!'

Nathan picked up his binoculars and trained them on to the roll-up doors of the warehouse. The lorry pulled up and started to reverse slowly as the doors opened.

'I seen him before . . . that driver.'

'Yeah, driving a fruit –'

'Shut it. Get a take on the number plate, I want a shot of him.'

Nathan leaned behind to get his camera and angled it on to the cab of the lorry. 'Got him. That's Piggy Plater. I done him at a break-in on the industrial estate couple of years back, only he had a clever brief, he got off with a suspended, said he'd been forced into it by his brother. Well, well, Piggy Plater. So what's he doing here – and don't say driving a fruit and veg lorry. You on to that number . . .'

The DC was.

The man in Nathan Coates's sights had now jumped down from the cab and was talking into a mobile. At the back of the warehouse some shadowy figures were opening up the lorry. A dark blue BMW drove round the corner and glided up beside it. A man in a cream linen jacket got out of one door, a scruffier, heavy one from the other.

'Bloody hell, Frankie Nixon and his sidekick. This is *not* bananas.' Nathan clicked away for another dozen shots, before dropping the camera. 'We need to set up a twenty-four-hour on the place. Something'll be going up before long.'

His phone rang again.

'DS Coates . . .'

'Jenny McCreedy, Forensic Science Service. I've been trying to contact DCI Serrailler but I'm told he's on leave this week and to call you.'

Nathan sat up. His eyes were on the BMW. Frankie Nixon had climbed back in. His heavy was glancing around before sliding into the passenger seat. The car was out of the yard in one fast, sweeping acceleration. The lorry was inching back further into the dark maw of the warehouse and the roll-door had begun to close. But the scene took on the slightly distant quality of a film. Nathan had his head bent into the mobile receiver.

160

'You got something? Tell me there is a God.'

'We've got something.'

'From Sleightholme's house?'

'Nope, the house is clean. But from the car we have two hairs and a fragment of fingernail. Both hairs are from the same head and the DNA is that of the boy David Angus. The fingernail paring isn't, that hasn't been matched. Yet.'

'It's from the other boy then?'

'No. Nor from the little girl they found alive in the boot.'

'You telling me there was *another* kid?'

'Looks like it.'

'Dear God . . . Is that it?'

'No. They're not through. But as there was a definite match with your case I thought you'd want to know. When's your DCI back?'

'Don't worry, I've a number for him, he's not going to want to wait for this. Thanks a bunch.' Nathan punched the air.

The lorry had been swallowed up into the warehouse and the door was shut down. There was no one about. The afternoon sun made the waste ground around them look dusty. A finch swayed on a thistle head a few yards away.

'Let's get out of here.'

'What was all that about, Sarge?'

'David Angus.'

'They found him?'

'Sort of.' Nathan switched on the engine and ran the car hard back, making the tyres spin.

The DC leaned back. 'Tell us about this Frankie Nixon then.'

'I don't give a monkey's fuck,' Nathan said viciously, 'about Frankie Nixon.'

Twenty-six

'You don't look happy, Simon.'

'I think the group is too big . . . Can we try splitting off the two in the church? That would make a five and a two . . . over here?'

Simon walked backwards across the gallery and looked again. The hangers had done a near perfect job apart from this one group of Venice drawings. Several had dark spaces behind the faces of the old women and men he had seen praying in churches around the Zattere; grouped as they had been they cancelled one another out, separated altogether their impact was diluted.

It was always the way – most fell into place but the last few took ages to get right.

The gallery was small and had a low ceiling. Its proportions were perfect, its position in a prime corner of Mayfair ideal. He knew how lucky he was.

Now he leaned against the wall and glanced out of the window.

Diana was looking straight back at him from the sunlit street. Simon cursed under his breath. He did not like the past rearing up in front of him, especially past he had firmly banished.

But when he looked at her again, something changed inside him. He was delighted to be where he was, to be having this exhibition here, now, excited, proud, keyed up

– and strangely, the sight of Diana suddenly pleased him. He was glad to see her. She looked, as ever, beautiful, elegant, happy.

He remembered how it had always been – an ideal relationship, without commitment, with each suiting the other, each enjoying the other, each having a world and work to return to, neither wanting to pin the other down. It had been good. It had been fun. He had had some delightful days, evenings, nights in Diana's company. Her desperation, when she had pursued him at home the previous year, seemed a long way off. That must be over. Why could things not be as they had always been? Simon could see no reason at all.

He went out of the gallery door to greet her.

The last time they had been in London together they had seen *Eugene Onegin* at Covent Garden but tonight there was ballet which Simon could not take. Instead, they saw a new play, which was so bad, and so badly acted by a Hollywood star, that it became funny and they slipped out of their seats before the end.

It was a warm evening and still light and the pavements were busy. Simon took Diana's arm, leading her across the road towards a bar he knew. The outside tables were full but there was a circular verandah upstairs. He felt light-hearted, as so often in London, a different person, less inhibited, more spontaneous.

'Champagne cocktail,' he said, steering Diana to a seat.

'Perfect.'

Yes, he thought. This is good. Just this. Nothing more. Nothing heavier. This is exactly right.

Diana wore a pale green silk dress. She was the best-dressed woman in the room and the most beautiful. He touched her shoulder.

'Where would you like to eat?'

'You say. But I want to talk to you . . . talk and talk. How long is it since we did, Simon?'

'Too long. You go first. You sold the restaurants?'

'Months ago. And haven't decided what to do next, as that is your next question. Not another business which eats up

163

my life, I can tell you that. I bought a small house in Chelsea and put the rest of the money on deposit.'

'But you'll need a challenge. You thrive on them.'

'No.' She looked directly at him. She had tiny lines at the corners of her eyes, more on her neck. She was ten years older than him and sometimes he could see those years. It had never troubled him in the slightest. 'I want something absorbing and wholly peaceful. I had fifteen years of stress and a high mileage. Enough for anyone. Maybe I'll open a gallery?'

He laughed and began to talk about the exhibition. As always, he found it impossible to talk about his drawing, easy to tell stories about the room, the hanging, the buyers, the private view, the frames, the prices, who else was showing in London. Gossip. Unthreatening.

'And Lafferton?'

He shook his head. He preferred not to talk about that either, and his police work he never mentioned at all.

They had a second drink, then went out, to walk through the London dusk towards Piccadilly.

'In a couple of days, your private view will be over and every drawing sold,' Diana said. 'I hope I have an invitation.'

'Of course.'

They stopped by Fortnum's. 'Choices,' Simon said. 'Restaurant? My hotel?'

'Or my house.'

But she caught his hesitation.

'Right,' Diana said lightly, 'I'm hungry. I ate a tomato sandwich at twelve fifteen and I've just had two champagne cocktails. I might faint.'

Simon took her arm, laughing, and steered her down Duke Street towards Green's.

Twenty-seven

Natalie woke, heard the noise and pulled the pillow over her head. But the sound still came through so in the end she had to get up.

'Now what? Bloody hell, Kyra, it's two o'clock, what's up with you?'

Kyra was standing beside the window. Her curtains were open and she was staring across at next door.

'I said before, you let it alone. Come on, back in bed. Who was you talking to?'

Kyra pressed her lips together but let herself be led back and settled under her duvet.

'Kyra, you worry me. Talking to yourself, making them noises.'

Natalie sat on the edge of her daughter's bed. Her blonde hair was matted and she smoothed it with her fingertips. Funny, how kids were different at night, how you could love them more because they seemed smaller. Funny that.

'You want to tell me anything now?'

They hadn't let her come in the room when they'd talked to Kyra. There were two of them, both women, a young doctor they said was the psychiatrist only she didn't look old enough, and a woman family police officer.

It had taken over an hour. Natalie had started to fret in the end. She felt angry and she felt sick. There'd been stuff in the papers and on the telly. There'd been the posters everywhere,

165

when the little boy went missing first, and she'd talked about it, they all had and she'd been with them like any of the people in Brimpton Lane. Natalie had talked to a couple of the others in the past week and they'd said the same, how different they felt now. Their houses, their road, their neighbours, everything . . . their everyday lives. They felt different and they would never not feel different. They felt soiled and scarred, as if they needed to wash. A few had said they wanted to move. Someone had said they wanted to get up a petition for the council to change the name of Brimpton Lane when it was all over, only what would changing the name do to help, what difference could that make? They lived there, she'd lived there, the house was there. Only who'd have it now? Who would ever buy it and walk about in her rooms and sleep there and eat there and cut the grass and clean the windows? Knowing.

It was bad enough having to be next door. Bad enough going over and over it, remembering. Bad enough having doctors and police ask your kid questions for more than an hour.

'What did you tell them?' she'd asked Kyra as soon as they got into the car. But Kyra's mouth had firmed up, the way it did, and she hadn't spoken. Not at all, not once, not until after television and her tea and her bath and then it had been about a holiday she wanted. In a caravan.

'Where'd you hear about caravans?'

But Kyra hadn't answered.

'Did you tell them about what happened at Ed's?'

Nothing.

'About making cakes and that?'

After a long time, Kyra had nodded.

'Did they say it was all right, then? To make the cakes and stuff?'

Nothing.

'What else did you tell them? About when you went round there. What did they ask you? What'd they say?'

Nothing.

'Hell, Kyra, I'm trying to make it OK, I don't want them upsetting you, I'm trying to make sure it was all right.'

166

'It was all right.'

Natalie had given up.

Now, she stroked Kyra's thin fair hair, wispy as dandelion clocks over her ears. Kyra's eyelids drooped, and then snapped open again.

'You'd tell me, wouldn't you?'

'What?'

'Anything. Anything that happened.'

Kyra frowned.

'Did Ed . . . ?'

Kyra closed her eyes fast.

Natalie waited. Nothing.

Kyra's eyes stayed shut.

Natalie went downstairs and put the kettle on, lit a cigarette and sat at the breakfast bar. It was warm. A dog barked somewhere down the street. She wanted to be somewhere else. Maybe they could. She could work in a call centre in some city, go back to where her family were, try London even. Every day she woke up now, she felt bad, sour. Old. And she was twenty-six. She didn't deserve to end up in a house next door to a child murderer. No one deserved that.

For a moment, she thought she heard a sound upstairs, but when she went out into the hall it was quiet. For company, Natalie turned on the all-night radio and spent half an hour listening to the phone-ins, sad people needing to chat to strangers about being sad people at three in the morning.

When Kyra heard the voices coming faintly from the radio, she went back to her post at the window. Ed's house was lit by the street lamp. It looked sad.

They had asked her what she thought about Ed's house. When she had told them that she liked it more than being in her own house, and being with Ed more than being with her mother, they'd looked strangely at her. Asked her why and if she was sure and if she meant it and whether Ed had ever told her to say that, which seemed to Kyra the most stupid question of all. They'd asked her to tell them what Ed had said and whether Ed had taken her in her car anywhere or swimming or to shops or into the country and had she had any of Kyra's friends to the house, to do cooking and things, when Kyra was there or when she wasn't.

Questions. All about Ed. Weird questions, rude questions, stupid questions, but when she'd asked them questions they hadn't answered, not properly. She had wanted to know where Ed had gone and whether she knew about the people going in and out of her house and when she was coming back and if she could go and see her and they hadn't answered a single one of those questions. Not one.

Twenty-eight

'Why did you cry, Edwina?'
'ED. I keep telling you.'
'Ed.'
'Have you any idea why that was?'
Say nothing. Just like the police. Say nothing.
'It's just that you don't strike me as someone who cries easily.'
Nothing.
'Do you remember crying much as a child?'
Here we go. She knew what was coming. Bound to. Your childhood. That's all they wanted to ask about, all they blamed everything on, all they were going to pry into. OK, fine. Nothing to tell. And, even if there had been, say nothing.
It was a small room. Dark red tweed upholstered chair. Quite comfortable. The shrink sat in another the same, with a clipboard on her lap. She'd have expected any doctor to be behind a desk. Might have felt better if she had been, somehow. The other thing was her being a woman. Doctors were men. Should be men. Like nurses were women. Only not now. This was a woman. Young. Too young. How could she be so young and be here? Short, dark, shiny hair. Designer glasses. Oval rims. Blue T-shirt. Darker blue denim skirt. Flat pale blue shoes. Wedding ring. Another ring with a twisted bit in it and a tiny chip of diamond that caught the light. Necklace with big beads. Smiled. Looked straight at her. And smiled.

Say nothing. You say nothing, not to the police, not to the prison officers, not to the shrink. Nothing.

'Why do people cry at all?'

She seemed to want to know. Really to be asking her. Why do people cry?

She thought about it. Why do they? Your dog dies. Your cat gets run over. You shut your finger in the car door. She winced, remembering the pain that had made her feel faint and sick.

'What? Something you remembered?'

'Yeah, trapping my finger in the car door. Bloody hell.'

'Oh, yes, I did that once. It's agony. Worse than labour pains.'

'Wouldn't know.'

'That and having a hockey stick swung across my nose.'

'Ahh . . .'

'It was.'

Ed imagined it. Her eyes watered.

'So that's one thing.'

'What?'

'A reason to cry. Pain.'

Shit. They were talking, like normal people, like people talk, and she'd said things.

Say nothing.

There were a couple of plants on the window ledge and they looked neglected. Dusty. Yellowed leaves at the bottom no one had bothered to pull off. One of them wanted cutting back. She hated that. Why not have plastic plants if you couldn't be bothered to look after real ones?

The shrink's handbag was on the floor beside her chair, next to a plain black briefcase. The handbag had a photograph on the front. Scarlett and Rhett from the movie. She'd watched that half a dozen times. Scarlett had rhinestones stuck on for her necklace and there were rhinestones scattered on Rhett's shirt front. She couldn't get her head round a shrink having a handbag like that. She couldn't stop looking down at it. Scarlett and Rhett.

Ed didn't use handbags, she used her pockets and totes if she needed to carry bigger stuff.

'I think you cried because you remembered something.'

'No.'

'Right.'

Ed waited. The shrink was going to go down the list now. You cried because you remembered something when you were little. Your mother. Or your dad. Someone hitting you, someone shouting at you, someone pushing you into a dark cellar and shutting the door on you, someone telling you you smelled. Or because of something else.

She waited.

But Dr Gorley sat in silence, looking at Ed. Then glancing at her notepad again. Then back at Ed. But not in any hurry, not irritated. Not anything. Just patient. Relaxed. Just waiting.

Say nothing.

She knew why she had cried and she was bloody angry at herself but she hadn't been able to help it. The tears had just started. The policeman with the fair hair had been looking at her, asking his questions, looking, saying this, saying that. And then the picture had come into her head and with it had come the instant realisation of what would happen. And what would never happen.

She had seen herself in the caravan with Kyra. They had been coming down the steps, locking the door carefully and then walking off down the site towards where they could see the sea. Towards the beach, where they would go for the day. Kyra had a bucket and spade, Ed had a ball and the tote with their picnic in. But they'd buy drinks and ices down there. It was sunny. It was warm. They could hear other children's voices, people shouting and calling out and laughing from the beach. Kyra was bouncing along, holding Ed's hand, looking up at her now and then, excited. That week, that holiday, was going to be the best ever, best for Kyra, best for Ed. It formed a little see-through bubble in Ed's mind and the bubble was quite, quite separate from everything else. Everything.

And now without warning, it had burst. She had looked round the interview room. Looked at the cops. Looked at her own hands. And the bubble had burst and she had known

171

the truth, that the holiday would never happen and that she would never see Kyra again. No matter what she, Ed, said or did not say, no matter what else might happen. The bubble had burst.

Her eyes filled with tears.

'What is it?' Dr Gorley said. Her voice was soft, a nice, sweet sort of voice. She wanted to know because she cared and because she wanted to help and because she was a friend, not because she was a shrink, not because she was trying to probe and pry and then report back, not –

Shit.

The tears began to slide down Ed's cheeks.

Twenty-nine

Dougie Meelup was a kind man. Take this weekend. He had come home on Thursday with the coach tickets and the booking for the hotel, everything sorted, her treat. It wasn't her birthday or his or their anniversary.

'You could do with a bit of a break,' he'd said, 'and you like Devon.'

So here they were, walking along the seafront on a bright, blustery day, making for one of the benches in the sun. She had the afternoon off in any case and Dougie had taken a day of his holiday; the coach had left at half past one and now it was half past five, with two whole days to come.

'If we sit here, I can get us a cup of tea from that stall. You settle yourself.'

Eileen had been able to tell that he was a kind man the first night she had met him, when Noreen and Ken Kavanagh had dragged her out to the bowls club. Bowls was for old people, the women wore white hats, she'd thought, it just wouldn't be her sort of thing. But they hadn't taken no for an answer. The car had turned up and Ken had been at the door and that was that.

She'd been right about bowls. It might be something you could enjoy playing but watching it was like watching paint dry and she couldn't see herself there again. It had been Dougie who had made the difference.

Eileen had been widowed four years and by the time Cliff

Sleightholme had passed on, they had had precious little left to say to one another and that was how old age would be, she'd supposed. She had never imagined life without him and she had been shaken by how empty the house seemed, how she had taken his presence and the company for granted. They may not have said much to one another but there had not been loneliness. She had got the job on the checkouts within three months, partly because the money she was left to manage on was less than she'd expected, partly because she couldn't stand being on her own in the house day and night. It got her out and she had made friends with Noreen and a couple of the others, but once she was home she was still by herself there.

Dougie Meelup was kind. She knew no one at bowls apart from Noreen and Ken and he had got her a cup of tea and made a place for her on the bench at the front of the pavilion. He'd asked her about herself and when she found herself telling him, he had listened, listened properly, in the way people who are kind do listen. His own wife had gone off with someone else the previous year. 'Broke my heart,' he said, 'and I never saw it coming.'

But he had the boys. They were both married with a couple of children each, both living in the town.

'Campbell and Marie give me lunch every other Sunday,' he had said, after a few weeks of them seeing each other, going out to a meal, driving to the country one afternoon. 'So how about you coming along with me next time?'

'Don't be daft.'

'What?'

He had looked hurt. Eileen had felt a rush of guilt.

'I mean, they want to see you. They don't know me, why would they want me to be there? Of course they wouldn't.'

'They do. Marie said on the phone, bring your friend. She wouldn't say it off her own bat, she'd talked about it with Campbell.'

'How do they know about me?'

'Well, because I've told them, how d'you think?'

She had gone. It had been hard until Marie had opened

174

the front door smiling and after that everything had been good. Better than good. The next Sunday, it had been Keith and his Filipino wife Leah who had done the Sunday lunch, a barbecue that time, with Keith in charge because he was a chef and didn't think women could cook meat properly.

Marrying Dougie had been marrying his family. Their wedding had been all about them, the boys, the daughters-in-law, the grandchildren, a registry office full of them.

Eileen had cried because of happiness and because of Dougie's kindness, because of going from loneliness to a big family. And because neither Jan nor Weeny had been there.

'What do you mean, you're getting married again, what are you talking about, Mother?' Jan had said, her voice going up and up. 'What are you thinking? What about us? You can't just marry some strange man.'

Eileen had told her everything about Dougie in a five-page letter, and written the same letter to Weeny and sent photos, sheaves of them, Dougie, the boys, the children, the dogs, Campbell and Marie's caravan.

'He isn't some strange man. I told you all about him.'

'I don't know what you think you're doing, getting married again at your time of life.'

'I'm getting myself someone to look after me and keep me company in old age,' she had said, 'so you don't have to.'

Jan had shut up then. But she had not been at the wedding.

'It's too far to come all that way.'

'There's trains. You can even fly from Aberdeen. I'll pay your fares to fly, to get you here.'

She thought that had done the trick. Jan had agreed. Eileen had sent the money. Only at the last minute, one of the children had apparently gone down with something and Jan couldn't leave him.

'I don't believe her,' she had said to Dougie. 'I don't think Mark's gone down with anything at all. She just doesn't want to come. She'd no intention of coming.'

Jan had kept the air-fare money, though.

If she had hoped for one daughter at her wedding, she had known Weeny would not be there. Not after the note.

The card had primroses on it, and Weeny's writing was very neat. She said she was too busy 'Travelling' for her job as a 'representative'. Eileen had no idea what Weeny's job was. She wondered what she had done wrong – not now, in getting married to Dougie, but then, in the past, in their childhood. She couldn't think of anything. Cliff had been proud of Weeny. He had taught her to be tough, but the sisters had fought from the moment Weeny was born until Jan had left home to live with Neil. They had fought for attention, affection, pocket money, the biggest room, the first slice of pie and the last sweet in the packet. The house had been a battleground for twenty-two years and when they had both left, within a few months of one another, Eileen had felt that a long, long war had ended. But Cliff had minded. Cliff had ceased to have anything to say from the moment Weeny had gone.

Eileen sat in the sun, her coat collar turned up against the breeze, and looked out at the sparkling sea, creaming over on to the sand in little wavelets. A poem from schooldays came into her head. *They live on crispy pancakes / From the yellow tide foam.*

The gulls rode on the sunlit water.

'Here you are, hot and sweet.'

Nobody but Dougie Meelup would have got a tray out of them, with the two teas not in plastic beakers but china cups and saucers, and two slices of farmhouse fruit cake on a plate.

Eileen looked at him. He set it all carefully down on the bench beside her.

'What did I ever do to deserve you?' she asked. And meant it.

'Get on.' He settled back against the bench with a sigh. 'Lovely,' he said, looking out at the sea. 'Isn't that lovely? Glad you came?'

She looked with him to where the seagulls bobbed on the water. Years, she thought, years and years and years, you think that's it, that's the hand you were dealt, you have to make the best you can of it. But then, everything turns upside down and what have you done to deserve it? She didn't deserve Dougie.

'I just wish . . .'

He lowered his cup of tea. He knew what, from her tone of voice.

'It takes time,' he said, as he always did.

'But how much time? If they made an effort, came to meet you, it'd be all right then.'

He must be tired of it, always reassuring, always getting her to see the girls' point of view, look on the bright side, give it time.

'What do you want to do tomorrow? Go on a trip, stay here?'

'You –'

'No,' Eileen said. 'You. You always give me the choice, now it's your turn.'

He turned his head and looked out across the bay. Then he said, like a small boy wishing for a treat and fearing he would not get it, 'I tell you what, then.'

'Go on.'

'I'd give a lot to go out on a boat.'

Thirty

A bird was making an irritating noise just outside the window, not a song, a regular high-pitched sound, like no bird Serrailler knew.

He came awake with a shock to find a body beside him in the bed and his mobile beeping. The hotel's clock-radio read seven twenty.

'Serrailler.'

'Guv? I wasn't sure what time I could wake you . . .'

Simon sat up. Diana stirred and turned over. 'It's fine. What's up, Nathan?'

'I know you're on leave, only we got her. She's nailed.'

Simon whistled. 'Forensics?'

'Yep. Came through late yesterday, I tried to reach you –'

'What have we got?'

'David Angus.'

'Oh God.'

'Two hairs.'

'In the house?'

'Nope, in the car. Car boot.'

Simon blanked out the picture that came into his head. 'That it?'

'No. There's something else . . . fingernail . . . not David, not Scott, not the little girl . . . they haven't got a match yet.'

'So *another* child?'

'Looks that way.'

178

'Christ. Oh Christ. Has anyone been to see Marilyn Angus?'

'Not yet.'

'Then don't. This is mine.'

'Guv.'

'I'll be there in a couple of hours. No one else is to pick it up and go there, understood?'

'Got it.'

Simon sat forward, his knees up, head down. It was the best news. It was what they wanted. It was what they had all worked for and prayed for. It was Ed Sleightholme nailed. The rest would follow, it would only be a matter of time. However many there were.

But it was also the last faint flicker of hope snuffed out. For Marilyn Angus, for other parents, God knows how many, for everyone in the country who had watched and prayed, hopelessly yet always hopeful, that somehow, somewhere, David Angus and the other child, or children, would be found alive.

His throat felt dry.

'Darling?' Diana put out her hand and stroked his shoulder.

He did not respond and after a couple of seconds, pushed back the duvet. 'I have to get to Lafferton.'

'Why? You're on holiday for a week.'

'That was my sergeant.' He went into the bathroom, locked the door and turned the shower on hard.

Ten minutes later he was dressed, his hair roughly rubbed dry, and putting his things into his holdall.

Diana sat on the edge of the bed. 'Are you coming back to London tonight?'

'Shouldn't think so.'

'Tomorrow? How long is this going to take?'

He shrugged, packing his camera into the side pocket.

'Can I come with you?'

'No . . . sorry, but no, I might not be there long.'

'So . . .'

'Probably have to go to Yorkshire again.'

'Is this about the woman in the papers? The one with the little girl in the boot of her car?'

179

'Don't rush, order breakfast, take your time.'

'When will I see you?'

He did not want to look at her because he felt ashamed of himself and angry, angry with her. Angry. Her hand was outstretched to him. He looked at it but did not touch her.

'I see,' Diana said.

'This is what it's like. You know that by now.'

She did not reply.

'This is what police life is like.'

'No. This is what *you* are like.'

He picked up the holdall and went.

He was out of London and on to the motorway before he allowed himself to reflect on what had happened. What had he been thinking? Why had he taken Diana out to dinner? And above all why had he then slipped lazily into the temptation of letting her go back with him to the hotel and his bed? It had been the way things had once been and he had fought to break free of that way. He cursed himself and swore half a dozen times, picking up speed. Then he pushed Diana and everything that had happened in London out of his mind and began to think about Edwina Sleightholme.

An hour into the drive, he had to stop for petrol and went into the service station to check the papers and get a coffee. He was paying for it when his mobile rang.

'Darling?'

'Sorry, can I call you back?'

'I just wanted to hear your voice. I wish you could have stayed.'

Negotiating the narrow gap between tables with his cup, Simon dropped the phone and it skidded away. By the time he had retrieved it and sat down, the line had gone dead.

He rang in to the station, checked that Nathan had no updated news, and told him he would be off-line until he got back.

'Fair enough, guv, you are supposed to be on leave.'

'I want to think. There won't be anything that can't wait.'

The papers had nothing new to say. That suited him. He

flipped through the rest of the news and finished his coffee. In the car, he put in a call to the Yorkshire CID but Jim Chapman was out.

His mind was full of the case. There was a resolution. They had the killer and the evidence with which to charge her on at least two counts. He should have been pleased, but there was no pleasure in any of it, only a grim satisfaction that the small, dark-haired woman he had chased down the cliff path and crouched with on the narrow ledge above the sea was going to prison for life. But there had to be more. He had to understand why. What kind of a person was she, what had made her tick all her life? 'Mad' would be the word bandied about, but Ed Sleightholme had not seemed so to him. Simon had known the mad and felt sorry for them, while being unable to relate to them on any level either of them had understood. 'Mad' was an easy explanation and it was the wrong one. Yet what was *sane* about a woman like Ed?

He tried to unlock the puzzle, twisting and turning it inside out in his mind, for most of the way home. He concentrated on it. That way he avoided thinking about Diana.

The CID room was humming as he walked in to look for Nathan. The atmosphere was different. There was a sense of relief. They had a result.

'Nathan out?'

'Yes, guv, the DI wanted him on an op out at Starly . . . some weirdo been posting threatening notices up.'

'Up?'

'Yeah, on noticeboards, shop windows . . . quite nasty. Anyway, aren't you off this week, guv?'

'You haven't seen me.'

He went to his room. The team seemed to be focused on new cases, to have moved on. What had he expected? Why had he come back at all?

He sat at his desk and checked over the forensics report, then sat for several minutes staring out of the window. The faces of the murdered children as they had appeared on posters everywhere burned into his brain. Small bodies, small lives, snuffed out to gratify the urges of a woman who looked so normal, spoke like anyone else, would not stand out in any crowd, a woman who lived in a neat house and had neighbours, including a small girl who liked to go round and spend time with her. He had encountered psychopathic murderers often enough and he knew that at some place inside themselves they did not relate in any way to any other human being, were unrecognisable to other human beings, in the nature of their cravings and their lack of inhibition about gratifying them, in their focus and self-absorption, their cunning and deviousness, their lack of conscience, emotion, empathy, imagination. But the Ed Sleightholmes of this world were not mad, not in the sense that they could not function, could not hold down jobs and eat and sleep and drive cars and talk to people in shops and on buses. They did not hear voices urging them on or have fits of raving mania during which they behaved in the way people expected lunatics to do, raging in the middle of the street wearing nothing, singing and dancing crazily, their eyes unfocused, their brains a kaleidoscope of whirling, random fears.

Cold, calculating, unfeeling. Ed Sleightholme was all of those things and more but she was not, in the DCI's book, insane and unfit to plead. He knew that the psychiatric assessments would be under way and he was pretty sure that whoever did them would not be fooled, whatever tricks Sleightholme tried to pull.

He swung his chair round. He had to see Marilyn Angus. He had to go to the house now so that David's mother heard the news from him, privately, face to face.

His phone rang. He ignored it. On the way out to his car, the mobile rang too. He did not take it out of his pocket.

Just over an hour later, he was driving out of Lafferton and into the country. He had gone to see Marilyn Angus expecting to witness her raw grief and anguished tears again, as he had during the days and weeks immediately following David's disappearance and her husband's death by suicide. Instead, she had been controlled and calm, her mood neutral, as if, as

182

a solicitor, she were receiving news of one of her clients. She had been neatly dressed and made up, and by the time he had finished giving her the information about her son, he had felt that she was trying to comfort him rather than the other way about. Certainly she had thanked him, told him how sorry she was that he had had to bring the news to her, said that she was less distressed than he might have expected simply because, in her heart, she had accepted that David was dead long ago. 'I knew there would be something,' she had said, 'some sort of confirmation. But I didn't need it. The law needs it. That's all.'

Simon had felt there had been no contact between them. Marilyn Angus had built an invisible, impenetrable shell around her like a coat of varnish. He thought it would be there for the rest of her life. Perhaps her daughter Lucy was allowed in beyond it. Perhaps not.

In one way, she had made the visit easy for him, far easier than on those occasions soon after David's disappearance when she had made no attempt to conceal her angry, raging outbursts of grief. He wondered what she would do now, whether she would remain in Lafferton, in the same house, the same job, or change everything, go abroad, become a different person.

Lines came into his head. *O, call back yesterday, bid time return.*

People had the wrong image of policemen, he thought, imagining they did not, could not, let themselves be affected by the job, touched too deeply, stripped too near the bone by things they saw and heard and had to do. Much of the time that might be true, but only because the work was routine and there was nothing about it to upset anyone. But then a David Angus case came along and however experienced, however professional, you were shot to pieces by it and the cracks were only poorly mended. He knew how keenly his team had felt everything and that the rejoicing at the arrest was still tempered with distress. When it was all over, perhaps a year on, it would be the distress that would still be embedded in their psyches, never the triumph at a killer caught.

He pulled up in front of his sister's farmhouse. Cat was not yet working full-time and he had hoped to see her, maybe take her out for a pub lunch. But there were no cars in the drive, the windows were shut, doors locked. He wandered across to lean on the paddock fence. The grey pony looked up from grazing for a moment but did not make a move to come nearer. Chickens pecked about in the grass at its feet. It was very quiet. A bleak, depressed mood threatened him, like a cloud hovering at the edge of the bright sky. He was on leave. The station was buzzing along cheerfully without him. So was his family. He had behaved stupidly with Diana. The prospect of seeing her again at the private view was troubling.

Simon understood what made people disappear, take off for an airport or a ferry and simply go, wherever, leaving no trace. He could do it now. Africa. He had always wanted to go to Africa.

He shook his head to clear the thoughts. Such responsibilities as he did have were perfectly real and his conscience was better developed than his sister would believe.

He left the pony and the red-brown, pecking hens, and took the road that led to Hallam House and his parents. If anybody would welcome a good pub lunch and his company, it might be his mother.

Half an hour later, he was on the motorway back to London. There had been no one in at Hallam House either. Simon scanned through the radio stations in search of music, or comedy, or at least some good news.

Thirty-one

At half past seven Lynsey Williams put her gear into the sports holdall, covered the salmon salad with cling film and wrote a note saying '*Matt, food in fridge, xxxx*' and went out. Matt was at the floodlit five-a-side courts with the boys he trained out of school hours.

She wondered, as she walked down St Luke's Road, why some couples apparently found it so difficult to live together and be committed but also have individual lives. She and Matt hadn't found it a problem. Whatever people said, school holidays were quite long and she worked her own time off around Matt's, so they could go off together at least three times a year, skiing, diving, climbing, with one week doing nothing on a hot beach. In term, he was out from dawn till dusk teaching and then spent extra time coaching, travelling all over the place to matches, training. Lynsey crammed all her own work into Matt's term time. She was lucky, she could. Five years ago, she had bought her first semi-derelict property and done it up with a bit of help on the heavy work from Matt and her brother. Now, she was on to her twelfth house, selling some on quickly, letting others. She had hit the right time, the market had boomed. She was doing well.

The only problem was whether or not to expand, take on staff and double her turnover. She had played about with the figures for months, but it was not the money that worried her so much as taking the giant step up from being small and single-handed. She liked to do most of the work and all of the decision-making herself. Expansion? What was she thinking? But she knew she would go on brooding about it as she ploughed up and down the sports centre pool, doing her forty lengths, and it was pointless talking to Matt. 'Search me,' was his usual answer.

She turned the corner. Then, someone called her name. She looked round. The man was waving and calling again, running towards her up the road. Lynsey hesitated. She did not recognise him and he was still some way off but as she heard him shout her name urgently again, she waited. Perhaps he had looked round one of her houses, perhaps he was one of the tenants, though she did all the letting through an agency.

'Lynsey . . .' Was that what he said?

He was nearer now and the expression on his face was strange, as if he were astonished to see her and excited and somehow . . . the only word she could find was wild.

'Lizzie . . .'

He stopped dead, a yard or two from her.

'Hello?' Lynsey said. 'Sorry, were you meaning me?'

He was staring at her, his face contorted into something like anger, something like bewilderment – again, she could not read it. But she was nervous now and as she spoke, began to turn and move away quickly, towards the main road, towards passing cars and open shops and other people.

'No . . . don't go, don't. Stop. Please. Stand still. Stand STILL.'

She stood still. He came slowly nearer to her.

'Who are you?' he asked.

'Lynsey . . .' she managed.

'No. No, you're Lizzie. Turn round. Let me look at your hair.'

She froze.

'You're Lizzie. You have to be.'

'I'm Lynsey. I'm sorry, I have to go, someone . . . someone's waiting for me over there.'

He stood, staring, his eyes scanning her face desperately.

'Turn round.' Her hair was long, pulled into a cotton scrunchy. 'Please loosen your hair . . . I want to see your hair. I must, please . . .'

He did not come nearer but his voice was urgent, and his expression still so strange that she put down her sports bag, and obeyed, pulling the band off and shaking her head until her hair fell loose.

'Lizzie?'

'No. I said. I'm Lynsey . . . Lynsey Williams. Look, you've just mistaken me for someone else . . . please let me go, I'm late, I have to meet someone, I said.'

'Your hair's the wrong colour. It isn't Lizzie's hair.'

'No,' Lynsey said. 'Sorry. No.'

There was a low wall in front of the house beside them and the man suddenly reached out for it, as if he felt faint, then sat heavily down. Lynsey stood, watching, wanting his signal so that she could go, run, fast round the corner and out of his sight.

Then she saw that he was weeping, openly, silently, putting the back of his hand up to his face to wipe his eyes, which then filled and overflowed again. She felt embarrassed and awkward, unsure what to say, desperate to go. And in the end, because he took no more notice of her but sat on, wrapped in himself and his own distress, she simply did so, turning and walking away, slowly though. As she reached the corner, she looked back, upset at what she saw, wishing she knew how to help him – except that she did not know what had happened or what he needed or why.

It was not until she had swum a dozen slow lengths of the pool that she felt calmer, but for the rest of the evening, she had the image of the man in her head and could not wipe it away.

She took a different, longer route home and walked quickly, looking behind her time and again, listening in case she heard someone calling her name again.

No one did.

*

Matt was in the kitchen, the salmon salad eaten and the plates and cutlery washed and put away. Matt was a dream to live with, neat and tidy about everything, clean, organised, punctual. He was sitting at the kitchen table trying to finish the cryptic crossword.

'Hi, babe. Good swim?'

Lynsey dropped her bag.

'Lyns?'

'Something weird happened.'

He looked round. 'What? Are you OK?'

'I think so. Yes. Yes, I am. Only it was . . . a bit weird, that's all.'

She got a bottle of water from the fridge and wandered to the table, to the sink, back to the fridge. The man was still in her head, sitting on the wall in the street, crying.

Matt listened carefully. 'And he didn't do anything, didn't touch you?'

'No. I think . . . when I wasn't whoever he thought – this Lizzie, not Lynsey – he just crumpled up, you know? He didn't, sort of, notice me again.'

'Right, well, people do make mistakes, you see someone's back view, they turn round, it isn't whoever at all . . . but you don't ask them to take the band out of their hair. That's weird. That's what I don't like.'

'No.'

'What do you want to do?'

'How do you mean?'

'Go to the police? Now? Tomorrow?'

'What would I go to the police for? Don't be daft.'

'He could have been up to anything. You were on your own in a quiet street, he shouted after you . . . he could have been a rapist.'

'He wasn't. I don't know what it was all about but he wasn't going to attack me . . . it wasn't like that.'

'You can't be sure. We had a serial killer round here not that long ago, don't forget.'

'I haven't. No one has. Only, I said, this was . . . different. I wish I hadn't told you now.'

'*OK.*' Matt turned back to the crossword.

He was like that. He was hopeless to argue with because he never would, he just dropped a subject, forgot it, got on with something else. It drove her nuts sometimes but it made for a quiet life.

She went upstairs and ran a bath. The man was still there, in her head, still sitting on the wall, crying. She heard his voice, calling to her above the sound of the water gushing down from the taps, calling out her name, but not her name.

She wasn't frightened. But it troubled her.

Thirty-two

They had stayed in small B & Bs before, but on this trip Dougie had booked into a hotel, Sandybank, overlooking the bay. In the foyer was an advertisement for Turkey and Tinsel Weekends, from October. He nodded at it as they went in. 'You'd like that, wouldn't you?'

'You are joking, Dougie Meelup! Christmas is all very nice, I quite enjoy it when it comes, but it doesn't come until the last week in December. Some people want to get a life.'

He laughed. Dougie laughed a lot. It was one of the things she had liked about him from the start, his laughter and the way years of it had set his face in a laugh, so that even when he was asleep, he sometimes seemed to be smiling. They had a room at the front with a sea view, but the sun had gone in now and the sea was churning about inside itself under a threatening sky.

'What would you like to do? Drink in the bar here or wander along and find somewhere else you fancy for a glass of wine?'

'I think here looks very nice.'

The hotel was bright and clean and not too large, they had been welcomed as if they were wanted, not just customers, and she would be happy sitting looking out at the bay and the life on the seafront. Happy.

She was happy.

*

There was a handful of other people in the bar and in a small room next to it the television was on.

'I like that,' Eileen said, taking her glass of wine. 'I don't like places where the telly blares out at you whether you want it or not.' She looked behind her through the window. Most people had left the beach and the benches along the promenade now that the sun had gone. It was quiet. The tide was on the way out.

'I could live here,' she said.

Dougie raised his beer glass to her. But then he set it down again. 'Do you mean that?'

'Live here? Yes. By the sea. I would. It'd suit me very well.'

'Well, there's nothing to stop us. Eighteen months' time, I'll be a free man and I could always get a bit of a part-time job somewhere here. So could you, come to that.'

She took a sip of wine and tried to picture it.

'Oh, I don't know really. It'd be such an upheaval.'

'What's wrong with an upheaval? Keep you young.'

But she knew she would have to roll the idea about slowly in her mind, turn it over and over like a penny in her pocket, look at every bit of it, see the problems and drawbacks. She couldn't begin to take it all in now. It would be weeks. Pleasant weeks though. Whatever side she came down on, the thinking would be pleasant.

'I'll just go and have a look at the news,' she said. It was too exciting, that was the thing; she realised that the moment Dougie had suggested it, she had wanted to leap in then and there, say yes, yes, and move, be in a place like this, a house with the sea view beyond the windows, and it was a dream and you had to be careful with dreams. Very careful. She had had too many of them broken to be anything but wary by now.

She needed to calm down and have her mind taken off it. For now. Just for now.

The small TV lounge looked over the garden, with blue hydrangea bushes and a bird feeder swinging from the branch of a rowan tree. That was the sort of garden they could have, with bushes and trees and not too much weeding to do. So long as they had a view of the sea from it.

191

Dougie stayed in the bar. He took up the evening paper and ordered a second glass of beer. She glanced affectionately at him through the open door. He looked like anyone else. He was neither very tall nor too short, neither fat nor thin, bald nor with his youthful head of hair. No one would look at him twice, nor remember him, no one would stare at him, no one would envy her or feel sorry for her when they saw them together. No one could have known the goodness of him, the kindness and the way he had given her a new life.

The news was announced by the music Eileen always thought of as angry, but Katie Derham had an extremely nice navy blue suit on with white pipings.

'Good evening.'

Dougie Meelup went through the local evening paper quite thoroughly, always having believed that you learned more about life that way than from any national media. He had meant what he said about moving to somewhere like this, right on the sea, and after reading the news and sport he moved on to the property pages to get the measure of the house prices. They shocked him. Anything facing the sea or even with a fairly distant view of it looked out of their price range by miles, though there were some nice small new houses a short walk behind the promenade. But would Eileen like the view? He had seen the way she had looked out across the bay, from the bench and then from the bedroom window. He wondered how much money he might be able to raise and whether one of the boys might even be interested in coming in with them.

He took the pen he had won in a spot-the-ball competition years ago and which had been his only pen ever since and started to jot down figures in the margin of the *Gazette*. He was immersed in them, trying to juggle and massage them to make them look more promising, when he sensed Eileen standing near.

Dougie glanced up. She was in the doorway between the bar and the television lounge. Her face was so odd, so contorted somehow, in an expression he had never seen and could not interpret, that for a second he wondered if she had had a stroke. She was very pale but with two high spots of colour on her cheekbones and her mouth was twisted.

He put the pen down. 'All right, love?' But it was so clear that she was not that now the girl behind the bar looked at him and started to ask if there was anything she could do.

Eileen did not move. Her mouth opened and shut again but she did not move. Dougie went to her. Her eyes were huge and bewildered. He felt her shaking. But then, in a dreadful, surrealistic moment, she started to laugh, a weird, giggly laugh, not loud.

Another couple had come into the bar, they were standing staring, looking uncertain as to whether they wanted to sit down after all.

Between them, Dougie and the girl got her to the table and sitting down.

'Shall I fetch her a brandy?' the girl whispered.

'Maybe a glass of water.' He took her hand between his and chafed it. 'Eileen . . .' Her expression was still odd. It panicked him.

She fumbled for her bag and handkerchief and wiped her eyes and then her mouth in an aimless, unfocused way, looking at him, then away from him, and once or twice glancing round at the door to the television room, as if checking something.

'Do you feel ill? Shall I get them to ring a doctor? Can you just tell me what happened?' He kept her hand between his.

She smiled a wonky smile. She tried to lift the water but her hand shook, so Dougie held it up to her mouth as she took a few sips, before pushing it away.

'The thing is, it's all so stupid, it's not true, I mean, it isn't the right one, it's stupid, but it gave me a terrible shock. Well, of course it did.'

'What gave you a shock?'

'When they said her name.'

'Whose name?'

She glanced at the doorway again. Then she gave a deep, juddering sigh. 'It isn't as if it's such a common name, is it? Weeny's name. Edwina.'

'Not so common, no. No, I can't say I've known any other.'

'Only there it was. Edwina Sleightholme. Of course it isn't her, my Edwina that is, my Weeny, of course it couldn't be, but you can see how it gave me a shock, coming out of the television like that. The room went round.'

It took several more minutes for him to get the story fairly clear.

A young woman, the same name as Eileen's younger daughter, the same age, had been charged with the abduction and murder of two children, and the abduction, with intent to murder, of a third.

'It just seems unbelievable, that,' Dougie said. 'Just unbelievable. No wonder it gave you such a shock. Was it that little lad disappeared last year, that one?'

'Yes. And another boy and a little girl. It's terrible.'

'Of course it is. I suppose if they've got someone . . . it's . . . no, it's terrible.'

But there was something not right. There had to be.

'Where was this?'

'On the news. Katie Derham.'

'No, where was the . . . the one with the same name as your Weeny? Where was she?'

'That was the funny bit.'

'What was funny, Eileen?'

'The funny bit was not only her name and her age but where she lived. She lived there. Same as our Weeny. They even live in the same town!'

She started to laugh the terrible giggling laugh again, but her eyes were on his face and would not focus anywhere else, her eyes begged him to laugh with her, to see how funny it really was, that there should be two women of the same name and age, two Edwina Sleightholmes living in the same town, two . . .

Dougie Meelup's heart began pounding so hard he felt a pressure inside his chest, inside his ears, inside his head, an awful, pulsating pressure.

Thirty-three

'It's me.'

'Hi, you. How did it go?'

'Good. Great.'

'Many there?'

'Packed.'

'Sell any?'

'About half of them, straight off. At least half, I didn't count them properly.'

Simon sat in his car in a quiet street behind the gallery. It was just after nine o'clock and he had dodged away from the private view before everyone else, before Martin Lovat, the gallery owner, could buttonhole him to go out to dinner and, above all, before Diana realised that he had left.

'Si, I'm really, really pleased. I wish we could have been there. Did the folks turn up?'

'No. Ma sent a loving note.'

'Oh, honestly.'

'You know Dad wouldn't be seen dead in an art gallery and Ma wouldn't come without him. They've never been. I didn't expect them this time either.'

'Hang on, Si . . . I thought I heard Felix. Wait.' There was an acute few seconds of intent, listening silence before Cat said, 'No, false alarm. You going off to celebrate now then? Somewhere Mayfair and glam?'

'Nope. I'm driving back. I slightly wondered if I could come in.'

'What, tonight? You won't be back till gone eleven.'

'Sorry, not a good idea then.'

'Honestly not. His lordship is waking me two or three times a night at the moment and Sam keeps coming into our bed. I was just about to go up when you rang in fact.'

'OK.'

'You sound bleak. What's wrong?'

'Nothing. Did you see any news by the way?'

'Yes, it was all over the six o'clock. Hordes of screaming women racing after the police van taking her from court. Makes you shudder.'

'Ed Sleightholme would make you shudder.'

'Want to come tomorrow? I'll be home by four. Supper and stay.'

'Only if you mean it.'

'Oh bugger off, Simon,' Cat said cheerfully as she put the phone down.

Through his rear mirror, he saw a knot of people from the gallery coming up the street. He gunned the car away from the kerb and sped off.

He should have been on a high from the success of the private view. He had spoken to a couple of art critics from the national press, had watched the red circles being stuck on to the frames of his drawings, had heard the buzz of interest all around him. But he had felt both detached from it all, as if the drawings were nothing to do with him, and yet at moments when he caught sight of one, acutely aware of just how close they were to him and hating the way anyone and everyone was able to peer, comment, judge. What he loved was the work itself, the doing of it, silently, privately. The rest he could take or leave and some of the rest he resented. He shook his head ruefully at his own thoughts.

The news, such as it was, about Edwina Sleightholme's appearance in court, dominated every bulletin around the radio stations. She had pleaded not guilty on all counts and no application for bail had been made. Simon wondered how she had been in the dock, pictured her, small, slim, dark-haired, impassive. She had given nothing away to him or to any other officer and he guessed she would give nothing away to anyone else, not even the shrink. He had known other murderers. Apart from those who had killed in a blind moment of desperation, or alcohol- and drug-fuelled rage, they had shared Sleightholme's same opaqueness, the infuriating, almost arrogant refusal to participate in the normal intercourse between human beings. He thought of her beside him on the shelf halfway up the cliff, afraid, and angry with herself for being so. Defiant. Closed. Would anyone ever discover why she had done whatever unspeakable things she had, to God knew how many children? Could there be anything like a reason? Her face was fixed in his mind, until he realised that what he had wanted to do was draw her, capture that expression, pin the neat cap of dark hair and the impenetrable eyes on the paper for eternity. He did not often work from memory but he wondered if he might try to do so this time. Perhaps by analysing her face, feature by feature, by looking into the eyes as he remembered them, by studying the set of her mouth and head, by trying to capture her expression full on, perhaps he might find a way into her mind and motive. Perhaps.

'A thirty-eight-year-old woman, Edwina Sleightholme, appeared in . . .'

He doused the radio and picked up speed, wanting to put miles between himself and London quickly. He had steered away from Diana for the whole of the evening, apart from a hurried greeting. It had been easy, the room had been packed, people wanted to talk to him. Once or twice he caught sight of her trying to meet his eye, once he moved as she negotiated her way through people's backs to reach him.

A car pulled out without warning into the fast lane in front of him, giving him a fraction of a second to brake, missing a collision by centimetres. Simon flashed his lights and then, furious with himself, clicked on the hands-free phone and pressed one button.

'Lafferton Police.'

Simon read off the number of the car ahead of him. 'Can you alert motorway patrol please? We're approaching Junction 7 and I want him stopped.'

He dropped back slightly. Let the bugger reach ninety or a hundred just in time to be picked up.

Thirty-four

'Dad?'

'Hello?'

'Is that you?'

'I'm trying to be a bit quiet, lad, Eileen's just dropped off.'

'Bloody hell, Dad, is this true or what?'

'It's true.'

'Only Leah saw it on the news and said there was a name she thought she recognised and then when I went in . . . Jesus Christ. What's it all about?'

'I don't know, Keith, I just don't know. All I know is what it's been like here. She saw it on the telly as well, you see, and she said, wasn't that funny, someone with the same name, same age . . .'

'But it's the same bloody town. It's got to be her.'

'Yes, it is. It has got to be. Course. Only it was the shock.'

'So Eileen didn't know anything?'

'Of course she didn't know, how could she have known, what do you think?'

'Sorry, Dad, I meant, hadn't she heard from Edwina or . . . well, I dunno, the police or something?'

'Edwina . . . Weeny . . . she doesn't have anything to do with us, you know she doesn't. Not since we got married. Not her, not Janet, though Weeny sends a card at Christmas. I always thought I ought to do something, you know, go and see her, see them both, put things right. I don't want Eileen suffering because of me, losing her family because of me, only now . . .'

'Too bloody right, only now. Listen, I'm driving down tomorrow to fetch you. You won't want to be waiting around there and you definitely won't want to be going back on the coach. I'll be there around dinner time.'

'No, no –'

'Dougie?'

'Hang on . . . Keith, she's waking up . . . I'll talk to you later. Thanks, boy, thank you.'

'Dougie?'

'It's all right, love, that was only Keith.'

Eileen sat up, flushed in the face. 'What for? Is he all right, is it the children? What did he want?' She stared around her.

'He said he'd drive down tomorrow, take us back.'

She swung her legs slowly off the bed and then stood up gingerly as if unsure she could bear her own weight.

'Why would he do that?'

'He said you . . . we might not want to go back on the coach. With everyone.'

'I don't see.'

Dougie sighed. He did not know which way to turn, what to say or do that was not hopelessly wrong.

'It's just a mistake that's got to be sorted out, Dougie. I'll sort it out. Do you think I should ring them now?'

'Ring who, Eileen?'

'The police . . . the television. No, it won't be them.'

'You could maybe ring tomorrow. When we get home.'

'It wants sorting now, though. If it was one of your boys wouldn't you want to get to the bottom of it straight away?'

'Only, the thing is, it was her name, her . . . where she lives . . . you said –'

'Oh, I know it was her, I know it was our Weeny, not someone else, I know that now, well, of course I do, there wouldn't be two women with that name, same age, living in the same place, it's not like Ann Smith, is it?'

'No.'

'No, I mean, well, it wants sorting because of course she

201

couldn't have done anything like that, how could she? Well, to start with, it's men, that's what men do, it's always men.'

Rose West, Dougie thought. Myra Hindley.

'It's a terrible thing to make a mistake over, terrible. I have to go up there, Dougie.'

She stood looking out at the dark sea, and the fairy lights strung round the promenade. The road was quiet. In the end he went and stood beside her. After a minute, he put his arm round her.

'I'll ring Keith then,' he said.

'Yes. I think if he could fetch us, I'd feel better, it'd get us home quicker. I can start sorting it all out then.'

'I'll ring now.'

'What do you want to do about eating, Dougie?'

Eating. He did not know. The word did not have a meaning.

'They don't know anything, do they? Here. It's a mistake, but all the same, I'd rather it was like this, that they don't know. Meelup hasn't got anything to do with Sleightholme, has it?'

He felt tears prick, hot at the back of his eyes.

'Maybe we could just walk a bit.'

'Yes,' Dougie said. 'If that's what you'd like.'

'I don't know what I'd like,' Eileen Meelup said, turning back to the dark sea.

Going out of the hotel and away from the golden lights and warm voices into the street they instinctively reached for one another. They walked vaguely, not speaking, slowly up the promenade. There were a few people about with dogs, or just strolling, going into one of the pubs. The air smelled of seaweed and burned sugar from a candyfloss stall. At the top of the promenade, where the road began to slope away from the seafront, there was a small garden with gravel paths winding between shrubs. Eileen stopped beside a bench.

He did not suggest they sit, or walk on, he simply waited. He had no real sense of where he was or why and knew that it was the same with her. There was no room in their heads for anything but what she had heard and seen on the television screen and which, ever since, Dougie had tried to picture and hear for himself. It was impossible to understand. He wanted to be sure, as Eileen was sure, that it was a confusion and a mistake, a wrongful arrest, a muddle. What else was there to believe that was not the stuff of horror? He barely knew either of the girls and only felt unhappy that they had treated their mother thoughtlessly. She had been hurt and upset. He had been hurt and angry. But that was families. They'd come round. He had said it over and over. He had felt confident. Now he was treading water and any minute he would drown.

He felt Eileen's hand clutching at his arm as if she, too, were drowning and he was her last support.

It was some time before they went back to the hotel. They wandered around the town, staring into the lighted windows of closed shops, at shoes and jars of sweets and swimming costumes and necklaces on decapitated velvet necks. And each window they looked into reflected their own faces back and the faces were stark and grave and quite unfamiliar.

In the end, by some sort of silent signal between them, they turned and went back to the hotel and the buzz of gossip, the smell of smoke from the bar. In the doorway, Eileen hesitated.

'Be a good idea,' Dougie said. 'Maybe a brandy? I'll have a whisky. Be settling.'

A roar of laughter burst up from a group, and the laughter came rolling towards them and broke over their heads like a wave. Someone turned round and caught sight of them hesitating in the doorway. The woman glanced away.

It was enough. There was no question, after all, of going into the bar, of having a drink among the others, as if they were normal people and like them, as if none of it had happened, the television had not spoken, the day would rewind itself and begin again.

Neither of them slept.

Thirty-five

'I cannot *believe* what you just told me. I cannot believe what you did.'

'OK, spare me the sermon.'

'Why? Why the hell should I? It's about time someone preached to you, it's about time you got it full on.'

'And if not you then who?'

'Too bloody right.'

Cat dumped Felix in his playpen under the garden umbrella and stood over her brother, who was lying back in a deckchair with a glass of beer. It was hot. The air was thick and steamy, the midges jazzing in a series of small clouds over the garden.

'Listen, can we call truce? It's not the weather for an argument.'

'Oh, there is not going to be any argument, Si, none at all, because I am not going to argue, you are just going to bloody well listen. You are my brother and I adore you and you are a total and utter shit. You are a psychological mess and you are a menace. Whatever your problem is, you need to get yourself sorted because you are not a teenager, you are nearly forty. You have no excuse for treating women the way you've treated Diana. It was bad enough to string her along, enjoy everything she offered without commitment, but she was apparently doing the same. So OK. Then she fell for you which, let's face it, she was always going to do, at which point you backed off in a hurry. I didn't care for your way of going about it but I accept that by then Freya Graffham was on the scene and you imagined you had feelings for her.'

'Look –'

'Yes. Imagine is the word. It only got real for you once she was safely dead and don't interrupt to tell me that is a shitty thing to say because shitty or not it's true. You were in a mess and you dumped Diana in the most unkind and graceless and hurtful way. She still has feelings for you, still thinks there's hope, well, that's sad and the only thing to do, the *only* thing, Simon, is to be polite but distant. "Sorry, nothing's changed." She isn't a fool. She'd get the message.'

'Yes.'

'Yes. But what do you do? Not only take her out to dinner, which was stupid and thoughtless but not downright wrong –'

'But sleep with her. I know. Fuck it, Cat, I know, I *know*.'

'What were you thinking? You absolute and total bastard. You thoughtless, selfish, self-regarding, self-serving, mindless shit.'

Felix looked up at his mother's suddenly raised voice, his small face crumpling. 'Now look what you've done.' Cat picked her son up and took him on to her knee. He was sticky and radiating heat. Cat buried her face in his damp fair hair. She was shaking.

Simon sat in silence. She was right and he knew it and he was furious with her. The one person in the world by whom he had always felt unconditionally loved, the one person he trusted and to whom he had always been able to tell anything, had spun round and hit him hard in the face.

'I'm not sorry,' Cat said weakly. But she did not look at him.

'Clearly.'

'I don't know why I'm crying because I'm right and I'm glad I said it, it wanted saying, you're the one who should be crying.'

'Leave it.'

'Of course we can't leave it.'

The air was thunderous. They sat in silence, Felix

205

burrowing into Cat's shoulder and kicking his feet against her, fractious in the heat. Simon twisted his beer glass round and round. He wondered if he had better not simply go, now, let the air clear between them for a few days rather than stay on for supper and have a sour evening.

Cat set a reluctant Felix down on the grass. 'Come on, let's give the chickens their corn.'

She took his hand and they went slowly off, Felix waddling beside her towards the paddock. She did not look back. Simon sat on miserably. The last time he and Cat had fallen out it had taken the death and funeral of their sister to bring them together again.

He got up. Felix was standing on the paddock rails, held firmly round his waist, waving his arm imperiously at the chickens. Simon stood beside them.

'Why?' he said at last. 'I need to understand why and I don't. I can't.'

'Why do I harangue you? Why do you behave so badly to women?'

'Why am I like this?'

'Oh God.'

'Big question.'

'For a hot afternoon.'

'The thing is, I'm not unhappy. Inside my own skin.'

'Bully for you.'

'Cat . . .'

'Sorry. But listen to what you just said.'

'OK, I'm a selfish bastard.'

'Among other things. A whole lot of much better things.'

'Thanks.'

'Look, I'm not your psychiatrist, I'm your sister. The only thing I think you have to decide PDQ is what to do about Diana. Because you owe it to her. And don't say you don't know.'

'I don't know.'

'Are you in love with her?'

'Absolutely not.'

'Do you like her?'

206

'I enjoy her company.'

'Would that be enough for you?'

'Christ, Cat, I don't want to *marry* her.'

She looked at him. 'Here, take him.'

Simon took his nephew and sat him on his shoulders as they walked towards the shed to collect chicken feed. Felix drummed small feet into his chest, squealing with pleasure. The shed was cool and smelled sweetly of the dry corn and meal in galvanised bins against the wall. Cat lifted a lid and began to scoop some into a bucket and the dust rose in a pale golden cloud.

'OK,' Simon said, 'but what should I do?'

'Not for me to say.'

'That'll be a first then.'

'No, I mean it, Si. It isn't. You need to work it out. What do you want, who, where, when? I'd do most things for you but I can't do that.'

She scattered corn into the dry patches of soil around the hen run and the birds began fussing about, busying themselves among it. Felix drummed his heels again.

'Maybe I should just get right away, Cat? And don't tell me only I can decide.'

His sister linked her arm in his. 'OK, just say that again, but this time replacing the word "get" with the word "run". Think about it while I put sir down for his nap and fetch you another beer.'

Thirty-six

Lynsey was finishing her shower when the phone rang at ten past eight.

'Hi, it's Mel from Towers Rogers.'

'Hey. You're in early.'

'I know, but you'll like this. You know the fishing tackle place?'

'Behind Gas Street?'

'That's the one . . . there's the warehouse, the place they use for a shop which is actually the old lock-keeper's cottage.'

'You'd never know. It's a mess.'

'Someone – I can't say who – put in a plan for getting rid of the lot and replacing it with a block of flats but now they've gone bust. Since then local planning has tightened as you know and presumption is now not to knock down and have new build. The council wants the whole site restored in keeping for part housing, part small workshops for local people.'

Lynsey sat down at the kitchen table. 'You have my interest.'

'Thought I might. It'll go out from here tomorrow. You've got twenty-four hours to suss it out and decide.'

'That's not very long.'

'I'm not even supposed to be giving you that. If anyone finds out both our arses are bacon.'

'What ballpark figure would we be looking at?'

'It'll go to auction with a guide price of ninety as a come-on, expect to pay upwards of one thirty, maybe a hell of a lot more.'

'So if I'm interested, I could put in a pre-emptive of what?'

'I've given you the figures, Lyns. Up to you now. Have to go.'

Forty minutes later, Lynsey was parking her car in one of the side streets leading to the canal. She had a map of Lafferton on the passenger seat and knew roughly where she was headed but not how accessible the site would be, whether she was even allowed to be there.

In the car, she had run through figures in her head. Whether she had to put in a pre-emptive bid or risk attending the auction, she had to find a great deal of money. This would be the biggest project she had undertaken but Mel knew that she had been looking for something like this for over a year. To convert one of the last redundant buildings sympathetic-ally, to bring it back to its old glory and yet put it to new uses in the contemporary world, was a dream she had been keeping warm. Everything she had done as a property devel-oper up till now had been relatively small. She had no doubt at all about her abilities, about the people she could call on, about her taste and eye for detail and period, about how something like this could be turned into a major success. Whether she could – dared – raise so much money was another matter.

She got out of the car, folded the map and put it in her pocket. The street was quiet and shady. The forecast was for another hot day. She could see the towpath and the gleam of the canal.

'Lizzie! Oh God, Lizzie, please . . .'

She stopped.

'Lizzie, wait.'

He was a few yards from her, beside the entrance to the Old Ribbon Factory. He looked more unkempt and wild-eyed than she had remembered.

Lynsey touched the mobile phone in her pocket for safety.

209

'Wait.' He came towards her.

'I am not Lizzie,' she said firmly. 'Whoever Lizzie is, I am not her. You mistook me for her before. I'm sorry. I have to get on now, I'm meeting someone, I'm late for an appointment.'

'Why are you doing this to me?' He reached out a hand. Lynsey shrank back. 'Why did you come down here? Down this street?'

'I told you. I have an appointment.'

'You're doing it on purpose. Because you look like her.'

'I don't know you. If you don't leave me alone now, and let me get on without following me or shouting after me again, I'll have to call the police.'

'From behind you could be her. Everything. Not when you turn round, not when you talk, but from behind you're Lizzie.'

'No,' Lynsey said gently, 'I'm not Lizzie. You know that.'

She began to edge away from him, not turning her back completely, keeping her hand in her pocket, touching the phone. She wished someone would come out of one of the buildings but no one did. She wondered how long it would take to run away, how long before the police might come, whether he would follow her towards the canal. Perhaps it would be better to turn back. Someone might drive down this street any minute but once she was among the old buildings and if he came after her, anything could happen.

But he did not follow her. At the end of the street, she looked back. He was standing staring after her, an unfathomable expression on his face. She turned the corner, began to walk along the towpath in the direction of the semi-derelict buildings and sheds beside the lock-keeper's cottage.

A woman was coming the other way with a terrier on a lead. It saw Lynsey and began to bark and somehow the barking restored her nerve.

She stopped and took out her phone but then hesitated. She wanted to get on. She had to see the buildings before anyone else, and besides, what would she say? He had done

210

nothing. It was the second time and she felt threatened but, face it, he hadn't made any threats. The police would probably laugh.

The old warehouses were in a bad way but by no means as bad as she had feared. They were exciting. Lynsey wandered around, taking quick pictures, her brain calculating as she explored. It was cool and dim inside the main, large building with dust motes dancing in slants of sunlight coming through gaps in the boarded-up windows and down through holes in the roof. This section could be converted to perhaps four apartments. The lock-keeper's cottage ought to be turned back to its original state, as one house, but it was in a bad way. The sheds and outbuildings were easy. Small units for crafts-people could be quickly carved out of them at minimal cost.

The auction estimate was way lower than the lot would fetch. She would have to see the bank manager to find out if she could raise enough for the purchase and the work. In her head she knew it was unlikely but her head was also a business one and she had no doubt that, if she were to take the next big step up the ladder, the rung was here in front of her. Miss this and another such opportunity would be a long time coming.

The noise made her leap up from the old workbench she had sat down on to think. Someone was banging on the side of the building and she had no right to be here, she was trespassing and she could not use Mel's name for authority. She slipped the camera into her pocket as the side door gave way.

He stood, blinking into the dark space, the sun behind him, haloing his hair. Lynsey's skin prickled. He had neither touched nor threatened her but now she felt absolutely sure that he was about to do so and there would be no one driving or walking by down here. The chances of another dog owner coming along the towpath were probably minimal.

He came slowly inside and she realised that he had not actually seen her yet and that his eyes were still adjusting to the light.

'Lizzie? Where are you? I saw you come in here, I followed you. Why didn't you come home? Why did you come down here? Lizzie.'

Lynsey remained frozen, working out what to do. She was fit and a fast runner, she had the advantage of being able to see him and to see her exit behind him. She could wait and hope that as he came further into the building, away from the open door, her exit route would be clearer, or she could go for it now and risk his grabbing her as she fled past him.

She thought he must be able to hear her heart thudding. It seemed to her to be echoing round the empty space of the entire building.

'Lizzie?'

She remembered that the first time he had followed her he had started to cry. Now, his voice came through sobs again, hysterical, desperate.

She waited. It took a long time, but eventually, he did move, though not away from her to the other side of the warehouse, but towards her. In a moment, he was bound to see her. She had on a white shirt. He couldn't fail to see her.

'Lizzie,' he said very quietly now. 'What is it like?'

Lynsey opened her mouth to answer, then bit her lip hard.

'Being dead,' he said. 'Tell me. What's it like? I need to know. I need to picture you. Being dead.'

Lynsey made a single move, away from the bench and across the warehouse towards the oblong of bright light. She moved fast and with the purpose of an arrow and as she reached the sunlight, she skidded on something loose lying on the floor and crashed down.

As she fell, she screamed, louder than she knew it was possible to scream.

Thirty-seven

When it was bad you had just your thoughts to help you. Thoughts could take you anywhere.

It was hot. Her clothes stuck to her back and her neck and her hair felt sweaty all the time. The heat made everyone boil up. She could hear the racket, the shouting, swearing, banging, screaming, on and on into the night. It was like a lid on a boiling pan. She didn't see any of it. They kept her separate all the time, even on exercise, though when she did go out the others knew and started banging. It wasn't nice. It frightened her.

She ate her food alone, read, watched her television, went out, came back, walked through the corridors to see the shrink, walked back, and the heat was thick everywhere, you smelled it and breathed it.

But if she thought hard enough she could get away, for a bit.

The sea. Driving down the motorway. Her garden. Kyra. Those were the best. And when it got bad, there was always the other. She didn't tell herself that she went there sometimes. She kept away from that. But she did go. Usually it was at night when the banging started up and seemed to go right through her head, like someone driving nails. It was a secret, furtive journey, and it took her a long time. But then, it always had. Once she was there, she closed the doors behind her and locked them. She didn't know she was there then.

But they were there, sometimes together, sometimes one at a time. She went through it all again, step by step, from the moment she first saw them. Then, there had been a rush; now, there was none. She had recorded everything, her mind was a camera. She saw everything. She heard everything. She had photographs of their faces, close-up photographs. She had recordings of their voices. Every word they had spoken. The boy in the blazer. The boy with the sports bag. The girl on the bicycle. The girl with the shopping bag. The boy on the scooter. The one with the ice cream. Every face. Every word. Every detail. Every mile on every journey, every stop. Every last thing. Sometimes she stayed only for a short time, paid a brief visit then came out quickly, locking the door again and she never knew she had been gone, let alone where. Other times, when she felt safe or when it was hardest, she stayed for a long time.

But the shrink never found out. Sometimes she asked, but Ed never told her.

The place was like an oven. The banging went on. When the food came and it was hot, she had to let it go cold before she could eat it. The same with the coffee, same with the tea. Ice cream came but it was a sickly yellow puddle. Salad came and the lettuce was wet and the tomatoes lukewarm.

Once, she threw her food at the wall. They took her television away.

But it scarcely bothered her. She could think. She always had her own thoughts and her own pictures. Better than theirs. Far, far better.

Thirty-eight

'Right.' Dougie Meelup stood up and pushed back his chair from the table. 'I'm opening these doors. What's a garden for?'

Eileen watched him.

'I'll put the deckchair out there, you bring your book.'

'No, I'm better here.'

'Eileen, it is beautiful sunshine out there, I've put up the umbrella, you can be in the shade.'

'I can't sit out.'

'No one will see you. Next door are away.'

'I can't.'

'And no one knows anything else.'

'Of course they know. They know my other name and it's not like Smith, they all see the television, read the papers. They know I've two girls.'

'And what if they do? Whoever "they" may be? What if they do?'

'I don't blame you for losing patience with me.'

'I haven't. I just want you to hold your head up a bit. You can't skulk here for good, Eileen.'

'Hold my head up? Oh, I can do that. I can do that when I know it's a mistake and they've charged the wrong person and want to be sued. Will be sued. When it's all sorted. Only until it is, someone might believe it. Someone we know. Someone who'd see me.'

Someone already had, only Dougie had not told her. When he'd rung in to work to say she was sick, there'd been a pause first and then, 'Yeah. Right.' In a tone of voice you couldn't mistake.

It came in waves. But the waves were closer together now and higher. One day, Eileen thought, a wave would be so high and race in so fast it would break over her head and drown her and sweep her away and it was what she prayed for. Never to wake up. Pictures flickered on a screen behind her eyes. Weeny when she was three. Weeny on her way to school the first day. Weeny and Janet holding hands outside the gate.

In a box file on the shelf in the living room were the real pictures. She would get them out soon, because the pictures would tell the truth about how happy they had all been and what pretty little girls, about how they'd been such a close family. The truth was in the photographs. She knew that.

'Other thing is,' Dougie said, 'I'm going to ring and book that visit.'

She fiddled with the spoon in her saucer.

'I'll take you, we'll both go up there.'

The prison was Gedley Vale. The name had been given out on the news. Dougie had looked it up on the map. It was about ninety miles.

'I'll have to write everything down, what I want to say to her. I have to get it straight. She'll need to know I'm getting it together. Maybe I'd better find out what solicitors she's got, see them as well. Do you think?'

'I don't know what you're allowed to do.'

'How do you mean?'

'Well, solicitors and that. I've never had to sort anything like this out.'

She stared at him. 'You think I have?'

Dougie shook his head.

All the way home in Keith's car, she had fought out aloud, fought with the police and the papers and the television, fought for her daughter and the monstrous injustice of it all; fought down any particle of doubt. It had been a mistake. How a mistake could be this bad, get this far, she had no idea but it had and she had to stop it dead. Weeny had been charged with doing things too terrible to allow into your mind, things that only the most evil, wicked people could ever do and not so many of them. Weeny was not that sort of person. How could anyone think she was? How could it have happened?

Janet had been on the phone twice screaming and crying so that in the end Dougie had had to take the phone away from her and tell the girl to calm down.

'I've got kids,' Jan kept saying, 'I've got kids, you know.'

'But she hasn't done any of it, Jan, she hasn't done it.'

'What difference does that make? It's her name, all over the telly, all over everywhere, picture in the papers, everyone looking.'

'They won't look, they don't know she's your sister.'

'Of course they know and what they don't know they'll soon find out. I want to know what's going to happen to us, you've got to do something about that.'

Eileen got up and went to the sink, turned on both taps and watched the water swirl round and run away down the plughole. There were pots to be washed but she did not wash them.

'You'd best get back to work,' she said.

Dougie had taken two days off then asked to be allowed to come home at lunchtime, pleading that she was not well, couldn't be left alone too long. They didn't believe him of course but he thought they sounded sorry.

'No one's got any idea,' he told her.

Though they had. It wasn't difficult. Someone had asked him direct and he had turned and walked off which was all they needed. He'd cursed at himself.

His boys had taken it in and gone very quiet. Keith had said nothing on the drive home but he'd kissed Eileen and kept an arm round her for a minute and said he was there for her, Leah was there for her. It was a dreadful nightmare and a mess but it would be sorted. Of course it would be. But then it had gone quiet. The phone hadn't rung.

Dougie thought he'd go round to Keith's later, on his own. Once they had the visit to the prison sorted.

'I'm off then,' he said. 'Now you take your book and sit out. Make the most of the sunshine. You've no need to answer the phone or the bell and keep the front door locked. Just sit in the sun. I'll stop and get some eggs, bit of salad for later. Anything else we want?'

She was still watching the water run out of the taps into the sink.

Dougie came over and turned them off. He rested his hand on her shoulder for a moment.

'I don't know where to start,' Eileen said.

'You don't have to do anything. Best leave it to the professional people. They know the ropes, how it all works.'

'You think? They haven't done much of a job so far that I can see.'

'I know, love. That's how it looks, but they're the experts, aren't they?'

'No. I am. I'm her mother. What do they know better than me about her?'

He wondered if that was the truth but he had no answer.

He wished he could go up there himself, get a visit to her, stand in front of her and ask. Have it out. Get her to tell him how it had all come about. Get the truth out of her and he'd know what was the truth, and when he did, if it was an almighty mistake, he'd get behind her like nobody else. But he had to find out for himself.

And if there had not been any mistake? Oh, he would know that too. And then he would tell her what her mother was like, what it would do to her and what it would go on doing for the rest of her life, how it would break her and would go on breaking her, slowly, relentlessly, into smaller and smaller pieces which would be impossible ever to reassemble. If it was true he would want to get inside Edwina's head, split open her skull and peer in to see, to try and get at the root of it, get something, some explanation, some reason or else some flaw or illness or madness.

If it was all true, the something rotten that would be there ought to be got out and destroyed.

Rotten. He pictured it, a rotten, scabrous, festering area and then he pictured a razor blade and himself cutting the evil out. He could see the hole there would be left, the clean, gaping, open wound that would be left.

He realised what he was thinking.

He looked at Eileen's hair, brown going mostly grey, frizzled and dry. He could see a small patch of flaky skin on her scalp.

He pulled his hand away from her and went out, wanting the air and the sunlight and the normal world. Wanting to be on his own, and away from all of it, for a long time.

Thirty-nine

'You seem very determined to do everything alone. You don't want to accept help from anyone. You don't want to have any visitors at all. I'm just wondering if you can think why that should be.'

'I don't have to.'

'No, you don't.'

The shrink was wearing a pale blue T-shirt with a sparkly circle in the middle and a pair of smart black jeans. Smart, but it seemed wrong. She was a professional, a doctor, she was on duty. Jeans weren't the proper thing to be wearing.

Ed was sitting on her legs in the low chair. She was tucked in.

A fan in the corner sucked the warm air in, whirred it round and belched it out again.

'Your mother?'

'What about her?'

'I'm wondering why you said you had no next of kin. You've a mother, a sister, nephews.'

'So bloody what? They're nothing to do with me and nothing to do with you.'

'Why do you think that? They are your family, so they do have to do with you. That's just fact. Isn't it?'

Ed shrugged. 'That's all it is then.'

'I'm wondering why you feel like this about them.'

'Are you?'

Ed wanted to hit her. She never looked fazed, never looked mad, or upset or put out. She never looked anything other than relaxed and quite – pleasant, she supposed. Yes. Pleasant. Her face was pleasant. Her expression was pleasant. Polite. Pleasant.

She sat on her legs and waited. She knew what was coming. How did you get on with your mother? What was she like to you? What about your childhood, your sister, your dad, your dad dying, what's your earliest memory, did you have lots of friends, were people unkind to you, were you abused, did, didn't, was, wasn't, why, when, how, why, why, why.

'Have you ever thought of what it feels like to a child? To be safe and happy, everything normal, and then to be dragged into a car by a stranger and taken away from that safe, familiar world. Have you ever imagined the feelings?'

These were not the questions. This was not the way it was meant to go.

Ed was angry.

'Have you imagined what a parent feels like when their child is taken? Or a sister or brother? Neighbours and friends? Grandparents? Take a minute to imagine it.'

She wanted to stuff her fingers in her ears and scream. She wanted to run out of the room. She wanted to hurl herself at the young woman in the pale blue T-shirt with the sparkly circle and the black jeans and claw at her face and eyes and grip her round the throat.

The fan hummed.

The face was the same. Pleasant. She waited. She did not write or even look at her notepad. She looked at Ed and waited. Pleasantly.

'Are you thinking about it?'

'No.'

'Do you think you ought to?'

'No.'

'Do you think you can? Or would that be too difficult, take too much nerve? Would it be very threatening?'

'I don't know what you're talking about.'

'Have you ever felt threatened?'

221

'What?'

'Not physically. Or perhaps, yes, perhaps that. But I really meant have you felt a threat to you, to Ed, to who you actually are inside yourself?'

'Yadda yadda yadda.'

'I'd like to give you a word to think about for next time. I'm going to ask you to take it into yourself and really study it . . . look at it from all round. Think what the word can mean. To you. To other people. To your family, maybe. To a child. Write things down if it helps you. Focus on it. Not all the time, obviously. Give yourself a few minutes here and there to focus on it, let it sink in. OK?'

Ed shrugged.

'Good. Ed, here's the word then. "Love".'

Forty

The heat shimmered above the ground. Cat Deerbon drove down Gas Street in the vain search for shade in which to park, but the shady side of the street was bumper to bumper.

A police vehicle came crawling down as she got out into the Turkish bath that was the world outside an air-conditioned car. It made her think of Simon. She had rung him twice, left a message on his mobile. He had not responded. Part of her decided he should be left to digest the home truths she had dealt out to him. Most of her was ashamed of herself. It was almost six o'clock. This was her last visit of the day. When she had made it, she decided to go round and see if her brother was in his flat.

Number 8 of the Old Ribbon Factory was one floor above Max Jameson's apartment. She walked up the three flights of stairs and had to lean against the iron rail to get her breath, wondering why having three children and a job, a pony and a paddock full of chickens did not seem to have kept her fit.

The patient, a teenage boy with appendicitis, was swiftly dealt with and the ambulance called. Job done. Now for Si. She headed back down the stairs.

Max Jameson, unkempt, and looking spaced out, was coming out of his front door between two policemen.

'Max?'

He turned his head eagerly towards her.

'Afternoon, Doc.' The PC nodded to her.

'It's about Lizzie,' Max said.

'Lizzie?'

Cat looked from him to the policeman, who hesitated.

'Max . . .'

'I saw Lizzie and she ran away from me. That's all. I followed her.'

'OK, that's it, sorry, Doc.' They chivvied him between them down the stairs.

Cat watched in concern, then ran towards her own car.

Now she had an even more pressing reason to call on Simon.

The home-going traffic had eased and she had a clear run through town and into the Cathedral Close. Here, there was shade to park under the wide, spreading trees. The choirboys were walking in file from the Song School towards the side door and evensong, deep red cassocks beneath white surplices. She hoped Felix might be a chorister. Sam had set his face firmly against the whole idea. Chris was against it too. The routine was punishing, he said, early mornings, every Sunday eaten up, evening practice as well, holidays often interrupted by visits to other cathedrals at home and abroad. Nevertheless, hearing Felix raise his own voice in tuneful imitation when she herself sang a bar here and there before a St Michael's Singers practice encouraged Cat's private ambitions.

She watched the boys disappear through the door into the cathedral, hesitating whether to go in and hear evensong rather than tackle her brother, but as she stood, dithering, Simon's car came through the archway and flashed down the close towards the buildings at the end. She walked after him.

'Hi.'

Simon turned. 'Ahha. Come to smoke the pipe of peace? Not sure if I'm ready for that.'

'No. I just came from a patient in the Old Ribbon Factory in time to see Max Jameson being taken away by two policemen.'

'Don't know anything about that, sorry.'

'I do need to find out, Si. Obviously the PCs wouldn't tell me but he's in a bad way, I'm very concerned about him.'

'They'll be on to that. The sergeant will send for the FMO and he'll get the duty Psych if he thinks it necessary. You know how it works.'

'I ought to see him.'

Simon shook his head. 'I'll try and find out tomorrow.'

They stood in the shadow of the building, tension and anger still simmering between them with the stale heat of the day. Rows with Simon upset Cat more than anything else, perhaps even more than the very few she ever had with Chris, because Chris blew up, then forgot, Chris was reasonable, open, upfront. Simon was none of those things.

'He did commit a pretty serious offence when he held that young clergywoman captive.'

'She didn't press charges.'

'No, but so far as we're concerned it's been noted.'

'He was out of it just now. He said he'd seen his dead wife.'

'It's not in your hands. Just leave us to deal with it.'

'What's *wrong* with you? That didn't sound like the brother I know.'

He turned away. 'Perhaps because you don't know your brother.'

Cat watched him open the front door, go through and let it close behind him. He did not ask her up. He did not look round.

She walked slowly back to her car in tears and phoned home.

'Cat?'

'I'm on my way. Got sidetracked.'

'What's wrong?'

'Oh, nothing, I just had to call in on Simon to check something out.'

'Now what's your bloody brother said? I'm sick of him upsetting you.'

'I'm not upset.'

'If you say so.'

'You know what he's like.'

225

'Too bloody right I know. Just come home. We love you.'

'I'm worried about Max Jameson.'

'And you're off duty. Leave it. Hannah got a gold star for neatness.'

'Hey!'

'I cooked the salmon. Hannah's helping me do a potato salad.'

'Where's Felix?'

'Watching Wimbledon.'

'Chris, you know you shouldn't dump him in front of the television.'

'I didn't, Sam did. They're both in love with Miss Sharapova.'

Cat laughed.

'Good. Now come home to us.'

She took a detour via Gas Street and paused at the top. There was no sign of anything untoward. Max would be in custody. Perhaps, later tonight, he would be let out again. 'I saw Lizzie and she ran away from me. I followed her.' It was easy enough to hang a label on his state of mind. Deluded. Hallucinating. The human term was suffering. How many medical problems were human problems first?

But it was Simon she thought about for the rest of the way home. She hated the way he sometimes behaved, the cold side, the part of him that shrugged everyone off. The Simon who was arrogant. She remembered pouring a bottle of cologne over his head when they were sixteen or so and he had enraged her. He had smelled of cheap scent for days.

She smiled to herself. Maybe Diana Mason should do something similar.

Forty-one

Eileen Meelup remembered the reference section of the local library as having newspapers on poles hung against the walls, magazines on a stand, and shelves of dictionaries and encyclopaedias. There had been heavy wooden tables and chairs and your shoes had squeaked on the polished floors, making everyone look up. There had been a special sort of hush and a faintly musty smell. Like a church.

She walked in and stopped dead. Everything was different. They had painted the room white. The big books, the newspapers and magazines, the wooden tables and chairs had been replaced by a row of little tables on which stood computers, with swivel office chairs in front of them. The screens were bright and there was the soft click of keyboards.

She backed out again and went to the desk in the lending section. Newspapers? The girl muttered about there being a newsagent on the corner.

Eileen left. As well as the newsagent, there was a sandwich bar, takeaway but with a couple of high stools at a window counter. Eileen got a milky coffee and hauled herself up on to one of them.

Now that there were no newspapers she had to think again. At one time they had kept copies for the whole of the previous year, in a separate store. You asked for what you wanted and they had either got them out there and then, or you could go back. She had been relying on them, working

227

out in her mind how she would go through them in date order, last to first. It was all she had thought about for a week and it had kept her going. The newspapers would have had everything she needed, all the reports, the police appeals, the pictures, everything. Every case would have been there. She could have gone over them slowly, making sure she knew everything. And in one of them, somewhere, there would have been what she was looking for, however hidden, however small the detail, the proof that Weeny had had nothing to do with any of it, that there had been a gross mistake, a whole catalogue of mistakes. 'A miscarriage of justice.' All it would have taken would have been time and she had plenty of that now. She had handed in her notice at work so as to have all day and every day to do it. Now, she felt as if she had been set down in a place she had thought she knew but which turned out to be quite foreign to her. She could not find her way about, had no idea which route to take.

There had been no word from Weeny. Dougie had spent almost an hour on the phone trying to find out if it would be possible for her mother to visit her in prison. But no date had been fixed.

Weeny had always been funny about wanting to do things on her own. Cliff had taught her. Standing up for herself, not needing anyone. But now, faced with all of this, surely she would write, surely. Eileen scraped the coffee scum from the inside of her empty cup with the spoon. How could you get yourself into a mess like this, how could you face what was going wrong, without your family round you? Even Weeny couldn't do that.

When they were little, Janet had always cried, cried about anything and everything. Weeny never had. She had always been composed, always the same, not laughing a lot, not crying, not chattering away like Jan. Eileen had loved her for it, loved her quiet self-possession, loved to have her sit by her, reading, doing her scrapbook. She hadn't demanded fuss and attention like Jan. Jan had been her dad's little girl. Weeny had been hers.

Yet she had gone. Grown up and walked out and hardly been in touch since, still needing no one, still her own person.

Short of facing some dreadful last illness, there couldn't be anything worse than what was happening now. But still Weeny had not told them, not shared any of it, left them to find out via the television news.

What must it be like? To know you were charged with doing things so vile it was hard to let them into your head, to know you were being punished for what someone else had done, to know it was all wrong but to have to go through it just the same – it was unimaginable. Whatever she could do, she would, whoever she had to talk to, whatever she had to say to prove it, she would. Dougie would as well. Dougie knew it was a dreadful mistake as well as she herself did. They ought to be with Weeny. Surely to God Weeny ought to let them be there.

She paid for the coffee and walked back to the library.

The girl with the fingernails painted silver had gone and a plump woman was at the counter. Eileen waited for three people to check in their books.

'Good morning.'

'I came in before. I wanted to know about getting newspapers.'

'We –'

'I know, she said. You don't have newspapers now, so you wouldn't have the old ones in the store, like you used to?'

'I'm afraid not, they went some time ago. Was it old news cuttings you wanted to find?'

'Not very old. Just some things this year.'

'Have you tried online?'

Eileen stared.

'Newspapers have online archives. You can register and do a search.' She smiled. She had an encouraging smile. 'I take it you're not into computers yet?'

'Never touched one. No.'

'It's very easy. You can book half an hour on one and you can book tuition as well.'

'Oh no, I don't think I could manage it.'

'Of course you could. If you only want to look up some back news, you don't have to learn more than half a dozen steps. Why don't you book a session?'

Dougie was putting a new washer on the kitchen tap. Bits were spread all over the draining board.

'Now what do you want to get into all that for?'

'I need to find out, it's the only way, I've got to go into all of it, I've got to help her, I'm her mother.'

'I know. Only Keith could do it for you, couldn't he?'

'What's it got to do with Keith?'

Dougie looked hurt.

'I didn't mean it like that.'

'I meant on his computer. Save you.' He started to twist the tap round and round gripping the head of the pliers. 'Unless you want to. Get into all that. Computers.'

'I couldn't ask him.'

'Why not? He's family.'

'I have to do it myself, Dougie.'

'Suit yourself. Right, that's done, I'll get the water back on.'

She went to the window. It was gathering up for a storm, the sky like pencil lead. She hadn't meant to upset Dougie. But she couldn't ask Keith. Somewhere, like lightning far away on the horizon, she was aware of something flickering on and off in her mind, something she would not acknowledge but which was nevertheless enough to make her certain that she could not let anyone else, even if they were family, start the searching, the finding out, the questioning. It was a private thing. Private.

She turned on the tap to fill the kettle and the water sprayed out sideways, soaking her sleeve.

'Bugger.' Dougie stared at it.

Later, when he had taken the tap apart again and put it back and checked the water flow, he went into the front room. It was dark. The thunder was rumbling nearer and the rain began to hit the window in a series of slow single splashes. He did not turn the light on, just set down the tea and settled himself in his chair. After a moment, through the beating of the rain, he said, 'Maybe better just leave it, love.'

'How do you mean, leave it?'

'I just don't want you to get upset, get worried, trying to sort out what's beyond you. I don't want that.'

'How can you say that? She's my daughter, I can't sit back and watch it, I have to sort it out, of course I have to. If I can't do that for her . . . How can you say that?'

He let it go and started to drink his tea, watching the storm break and the rain hurl itself against the picture windows.

Forty-two

The receptionist put her head round the door.

'Can you see one more?'

Cat groaned. She had closed her computer and was checking through some notes. Morning surgery seemed to have lasted for five years.

'How many visits have I got?'

'Not too bad actually . . . Mr Wilkins has gone into hospital and Mrs Fabiani died this morning.'

'Go on then, but this is the last, Cathy.'

'I said you would. Only she has been waiting over an hour.'

The new receptionist was wonderful to work with, efficient, sympathetic, charming and organised. Her only problem was an inability to say no to patients.

Cat looked up as the door opened on Jane Fitzroy.

'I'm really sorry, I know you've had a long morning.'

'Sit down. I think I remember asking you to come and see me before now?'

Jane made a face. 'I didn't think I needed to and you know how it is . . .'

'Hm.'

'I'm surprised, really, I didn't expect all this to go on affecting me, it's over and done with. I ought to have put it behind me.'

'You had a frightening – no, a shocking experience. These things take longer than you might suppose. Tell me.'

232

'I just need something to help me sleep. If you can give me that, so I get a few decent nights, I'll be fine.'

'Let's see. I'll give you a quick check-over first.'

'No, honestly, don't waste your time, I'm a very healthy person. I just can't cope with not sleeping.'

'Are you having flashbacks?'

'Sometimes. Yes, when I go back into the house at the end of the day . . . especially if it's late. Yes. It's really stupid, I know.'

'Not at all. Really normal and understandable. Panic attacks?'

Jane hesitated. 'I'm . . . I get . . . I don't know.'

'You know what form they take, though? You're suddenly gripped by fear and panic out of the blue . . . you want to run away. Your heart pounds . . . sometimes you overbreathe, sometimes you start to shake. Some people feel nauseous or want to rush to the loo . . . some people feel giddy or faint. It does vary but the overwhelming feeling is one of fear. There's a sense of impending doom.'

'Yes.'

'How often do you get them?'

'Oh, it's only been a couple of times. Or so.'

'Or so?'

'A few.'

'Jane, you do not have to be ashamed of this. If I came to ask you to hear my confession I would expect to have to confess – everything. Now, I'm your doctor.'

Jane smiled. 'OK. It's getting worse. I seem to be having these attacks more often. Oughtn't they to be less by now? I'm not dealing with this very well, am I? The other morning, I had to leave the eleven o'clock service . . . I couldn't face it, I just froze. I had to get out. Everyone thought I was sick or something.'

'You were.'

'But how feeble can you get for goodness' sake?'

'This has nothing to do with being feeble. I could give it the correct medical term of post-traumatic stress. It might help you to understand that this is not a moral issue, and it has nothing to do with your lack of nerve, Jane. But you're right to think that being constantly short of sleep does not help the rest of it. I will prescribe you a short course of a sleeping tablet to break the pattern.'

'Oh, thank you, I –' Jane got up.

'That's not all though.'

'I don't want to take anything else . . . tranquillisers or whatever.'

'Not going to offer them. I think you'd benefit from a couple of sessions with a clinical psychologist. There are two excellent ones at Bevham General. You'd be able to talk everything through, and get some practical tips on coping with panic attacks and so on. It would really help you.'

'Not sure about that.'

'Really? Why, because you're a priest and shouldn't need it?'

Jane flushed.

'That's rubbish and you know it. Listen, this is not going to go away by itself and it will start interfering with your ability to do your work – which is stressful enough. You owe it to yourself and to the job to get this sorted.'

'I didn't think you were the kind to talk tough.'

'I am very, very good at that. You can take it.' Cat pulled the prescription pad towards her. 'Get these. And have a think for twenty-four hours.'

'Thank you.'

'Lecture over.' Cat got up. 'You're my last. Off on the rounds. But listen, I need to talk to you about Imogen House. There have been one or two issues there . . . you'll have come up against them by now.'

'Ah, Sister Doherty.'

'Sister Doherty indeed. Chris is out tonight at a meeting.'

They went out into the empty waiting room.

'Dr Deerbon, will you have a word with oncology at BG?' Cathy leaned over the reception desk.

'Yes. Jane – can you come to supper tonight? Potluck but in this weather it'll be yet another salad.'

Jane smiled. She is not beautiful, Cat thought, she just

misses that, but she has a face you have to look at and keep looking at. And her smile is something else.

'I would absolutely love to. I haven't been out much. It's just what I need.'

'Here . . .' Cat scribbled. 'We're easy to find. Fifteen minutes from the cathedral once the rush-hour traffic is over. Any time after seven.'

'Dr Deerbon, they are holding for you . . .'

'I'm there.'

She waved to Jane as she went to the phone, feeling pleased. An evening of surgery paperwork after she had put the children to bed had just metamorphosed into supper with a new friend.

Forty-three

'Nathan, have you got a minute?'

'On my way, guv.'

Simon swung his chair round to look at the heat shimmer over the tarmac of the station courtyard. The fan on his desk stirred hot air about and shifted the corners of the papers. But he was glad to be back. His week's leave had not been the best and he suppressed the knowledge that it was mainly his own fault.

Nathan Coates came in whistling.

'You're chirpy.'

'Morning, guv. Yeah, well, got some good news yesterday.'

'It's triplets.'

'Gawd, spare me that – be like living in a horror movie.'

'Oh, I'm sure my parents wouldn't agree with you.'

Nathan went red from the neck up. 'Aw, guv . . .'

'It's OK, I'm winding you up. Why should you remember I'm a triplet? So what is the news?'

'It is baby stuff though . . . me and Em went for a scan yesterday and it's a boy.'

'If that's what you both want, that's great.'

'Yeah, well, I wouldn't mind either way, honest to God, but Em's been dead set on a boy, she's chuffed as little apples. What's to do this morning then?'

'We're getting a temporary replacement for Gary Jones. DC called Joe Carmody. Coming from Exwood.'

DC Gary Jones had been involved in a hit-and-run incident the previous weekend when a getaway car had swerved into him. He was lucky to be alive.

'I'm sick and tired of drugs ops and it's escalating. The Dulcie is getting out of control. I'm going to a cross-border forces conference about the whole thing next week. I'd like you to show this new guy the ropes here. There's something for you to look at.' Serrailler got up and went to the map on his wall. 'Here . . . Nelson Road, Inkerman Street, Balaclava Street.'

'Battle Corner . . . Nice and quiet round there usually.'

'There's been some trouble . . . offensive graffiti, racist leaflets and posters, general nastiness.'

'Bit surprising.'

Battle Corner was home to Lafferton's small number of Asians, but they were second generation and had been absorbed into the community years ago without any trouble.

'It isn't only the Asians, this is anti-Semitic too. The synagogue is down there as you know but there have been one or two other nasty incidents around Sorrel Drive and Wayland Avenue. Jewish solicitor and a couple of business people have had their cars damaged and stuff shoved through the letter boxes. We've had patrols out but of course nothing ever happens while they're around. I'm a bit puzzled by it to be honest. So it's door knocking, talking to the people who've been targeted . . . generally sniffing around. When DC Carmody arrives, I want you to go after it for a couple of days, see what you can dig up.'

'Guv. Any leads?'

'Not really. Looks organised. I don't think it's kids.'

'Coming from outside Lafferton then, you reckon?'

'Could well be.'

Nathan went to the door. 'Any news on the kiddy killer?'

'Oh, yes, meant to say – heard this morning. Psychiatrist says she's not insane. Fit to go to trial.'

Nathan punched the air.

'I never doubted it.'

'Yeah, right, but you know what it's like, they're bloody clever, pull the wool over a shrink's eyes all right.'

'Not this time. Ed Sleightholme is as sane as you and me.'

'Jeez, though, guv. Bad not mad. Makes your flesh creep an' your blood run cold. Still, that's her down for life, no prob.'

He sailed out. Simon went to open up his emails, thinking of Ed. His worry was that although forensics had given them evidence of David Angus having been in the boot of her car, that did not prove he was dead or that Sleightholme had murdered him. They needed a body. Until they had one, all they could prove for certain was that the little girl Amy Sudden had been abducted. But Amy Sudden had been rescued alive.

Without something much stronger, any decent defence could drive a coach and horses through a murder charge, let alone any of multiple abduction and murder. Nathan's certainty that Ed Sleightholme would go down for life was by no means rock solid.

The day was desk-bound. He went to the Cypriot deli and got a takeaway sandwich and coffee, walked half a dozen blocks and went back to paperwork. It was not absorbing enough to blot out the occasional worrying thought of his sister and of Diana. He felt guilty about them both, though concerned only about Cat.

The phone put them from his mind.

'Simon? Jim Chapman.'

'News?'

'About Sleightholme? No. This is something else. Do you happen to know Colin Alumbo?'

'Chief in Northumbria? Only by repute.'

'First black Chief in our neck of the woods. Quite young. Very good. You could do worse for a Chief.'

'I couldn't do better than I've already got but carry on.'

'Had a drink with him before a long evening of Lord Mayors. He's looking for someone to head up a new task force. DCS.'

'What area?'

'Waking the Dead territory. Cold cases.'

'Erm . . .'

'I know what you're thinking. It's what they all think. Stone cold, dead end. Needn't be. I told him he needed someone like you.'

'I like action, Jim. I don't get enough of it as it is.'

'Hanging on to a cliff face by your fingernails, ay, I know. No reason why you wouldn't get it.'

'Sounds like a lot of hours trawling old paper files and a lot more in front of a screen.'

'There it is any road. Up to you. Nice up there.'

'Nice down here.'

'Thought you'd itchy feet?'

'Possibly.'

'Want me to keep my nose out of it and my gob shut then?'

Simon laughed. 'I'm flattered to be on your list, Jim. Don't rub my name off the whiteboard.'

But as he put the phone down, he knew that cold cases was the last area he wanted to work in. And contemplating a genuine job offer brought him back to reality. If he was to remain in the police force and make serious career progress, he would have to move from Lafferton. But he was not ready to be bounced into the wrong decision.

He got up and went down the corridor to the drinks machine. There were three or four people waiting to buy ice-cold cans. The heat was getting to everyone.

'You at nets tomorrow night, guv? Only we were pretty weak in the batting last Saturday. We handed them those first three wickets. Not enough regular nets practice.' Steve Philipot from the traffic-control room juggled with three cans of Coke as he spoke.

'I'll try.'

'Do better than that. Be there.'

Yes, he thought, wandering back to his office, he would. A bit of focusing on the way he returned yorkers would take his mind off just about everything else. But once back in his office, instead of returning to the file, he went on to the Police Review website and scrolled down the recruitment section,

239

to get a sense of what was out there. It was all pretty routine and nothing appealed.

He thought of his flat in the close. Where else would he find to equal that? Where else would he have his family round him? Where but Lafferton would he ever be able to call home?

Forty-four

They had left him at the entrance. Max Jameson stood and felt the heat rise up from the pavement and radiate from the brick walls of the Old Ribbon Factory. He felt disorientated and his head ached. He had been bailed and his solicitor had given him a lift back. Now all he had to do was go in and . . .

He had no idea what came next. He had the odd sensation that a bit of his mind had broken off and floated away, like a portion of an iceberg. He knew who he was and where, he knew where he had been and why. But he could not put the day, and his presence in it, into any context or proper order. He felt grubby and sticky and his clothes needed changing.

A pigeon flew down and began pecking about in the dust and debris of the gutter. Max watched it. Lizzie had hated pigeons. She had hated any bird larger than a sparrow, had had nightmares about big birds sometimes. She did not know why – probably some silly thing as a child.

He wondered if he should kill it for her. One less pigeon in the world to frighten her. One less big bird. He hated the thought of her being upset, being afraid. He was prepared to kill it but he knew that it would take off the moment he made a move and anyway, what would he kill it with?

He watched it. The feathers on its back were pearlised and beautifully, intricately folded.

'There's nothing to be afraid of,' he said. 'It's not even very big.'

The bird hopped a few feet further on down the street. He realised that he had spoken out loud. But there was only the pigeon to hear him.

He went inside. The darkness of the stairwell blinded him for a moment after the brilliant sunlight, he had to stop and wait for his eyes to adjust to it.

Is it bright? he thought suddenly. The place people believe you go to when you die. Is it bright? He remembered story-book pictures of heaven filled with rays from a setting sun and radiant faces. He did not believe in those and he did not believe in the place other people imagined was there. Where? Somewhere else. Waiting for you.

There had to be someone who could work it out for him. He should have asked the young priest when he had the chance. She might have told him. He cursed himself for forgetting to ask her everything he was desperate to know. He had wasted the time they had spent together. He could have got answers to the questions that tumbled round and round in his head like pebbles in a drum. He put his key in the lock and opened the door into the long, bright room.

'Lizzie?'

She was there, at the other end, always there, her hair back, her eyes looking away from him, her face grave.

He sat at the table. The silence filled his ears and pressed down inside his head like earth. He wanted to tell someone what had happened and then to explain what it felt like. Lizzie had died. Lizzie was dead. He knew that. He had watched her die. He had seen her dead body and he had watched her coffin slide through velvet curtains into the furnace beyond. Lizzie was dead. But he had seen her, seen her often, in the street, in the old warehouse, walking towards him, standing at the foot of his bed when he woke. He was not frightened of what he saw but he was confused. This was not a ghost Lizzie, not a picture of Lizzie, not a Lizzie in his mind, this was flesh-and-blood Lizzie, real Lizzie.

Lizzie was dead.

The only person who could help him was Jane Fitzroy. He could talk to her. There was a bond between them, though he could not put his finger on why or how it had come about.

He went to the cupboard, took out the whisky bottle and poured himself half a tumblerful, topping it with a inch of tap water. When he had drunk this, he would have courage to go and find her. It tasted of fire and salt and smoke. He sipped it at first, then gulped the rest and the fire snaked down into his chest and dropped to his belly, before the flames licked up through his veins into his head. He took a deep breath.

If he saw Lizzie in the street he would take her with him so that Jane would believe him. When she saw them coming to her together she would have to believe. For a second he remembered that he had been cautioned not to speak to Lizzie, not to approach her, not to acknowledge her existence, and that he had agreed to it all, signed his name to it. But he was not going to do her any harm. He wondered how they could imagine that he ever had or would, when Lizzie was his wife and he loved her. He had followed her, spoken to her, called her name, tried to get her to answer him, come to him, walk home with him so that everything would be normal again, but he would never hurt her. When she had tripped and fallen and screamed, he had been desperate to help her, look after her, take her away with him and nurse her here. He had tried to tell them that. They had appeared to listen but then they had turned on him, like a dog which snarls and bites your hand when you stroke it out of kindness.

He poured another tumbler of whisky and this time did not bother with the water. The water diluted the fire he needed to blaze up inside him and burn into his brain.

When he had swallowed it, he went out.

Forty-five

Nathan Coates pushed open the door of the CID room and looked round. Half a dozen people were at their desks.

'Anyone know if the new DC's in yet?'

'Carmody? Yeah, went to the Gents. You minding him?'

'Some racial stuff over Battle Corner. DCI wants me to take him with me once I've introduced him round.'

Jenny Osbrook made a face. 'I think you'll find he's done that for himself.'

'What's up?'

'You'll find out.' She nodded in the direction of the door. 'Cheers, chaps, I'm off to court.'

Nathan caught sight of the man who had just come in, letting the door go just as Jenny reached for it. If he had not been in the CID room, he would not have looked out of place in custody. He was not a particularly big man, no more than five foot nine or ten, but he was thickly muscled, and stocky, with a completely smooth, shining bald head. The back of it had a curious outcrop that jutted over his neck. He wore a navy blue T-shirt and no tie.

Nathan went across. 'Hi, I'm Nathan Coates.'

Carmody looked at him. 'Heard about you,' he said. 'The infant prodigy.'

Nathan felt himself flush and was furious about it. 'I ent that young.'

'Look it to me, sunshine.'

He ought to pick him up on it, correct him, make him say 'Sarge'. He couldn't. He hadn't been made to feel so small and stupid for a very long time.

Carmody swung himself into the Honda, pulled a flattened packet of gum out of his trouser pocket and unwrapped the last stick. He screwed the paper up and put it into the door pocket.

'Oi, you can take that out, thanks, my car ent a dustbin.'

Carmody rolled his eyes, picked it out with exaggerated care, and held it between two fingers. 'What would you like me to do with it?'

'Don't tempt me.'

The DC slid his legs forward into the well and folded his arms. 'Wake me when we get there.'

'You'd best be awake now, I got things to ask you.'

Carmody sighed.

'How long you been at Exwood?'

'Too bloody long.'

'Which is . . . ?'

'Twelve years, sunshine.'

'And stop callin' me sunshine.'

The DC laughed. 'Twelve years, seven months and four days. I told you, too bloody long.'

'In uniform there, was you?'

'Nope.'

'Where then?'

'Further south.'

'Why CID?'

'Why not?'

Nathan gave up.

The traffic round the railway station was snarled up as usual on Tuesday, when the cattle market was held to the east of it, next to the Lafferton football ground.

'What's this then, the local yokels?'

'Pretty old, the cattle market. Been here for centuries.'

'Time it went then. Can't be hygienic.'

'You're taking the piss.'

245

'Who, me? Think of how many houses they could get on there. Put the market out in the sticks, solve your traffic problem and your housing problem in one.'

'I wonder what you come here for at all.'

'A few days' peace.'

'Oh ha ha.'

'You on that serial-killer job, were you?'

Nathan used the sudden freeing of the traffic to avoid replying. He wasn't going to talk to the likes of Joe Carmody about what had happened, what it had been like. It was still there, still raw and it wouldn't ever really go, he knew that, Em knew that. Move on, people said. Well, you couldn't move on from some things because they moved with you. Wherever.

'Nasty that was. Wouldn't have minded being on it myself.'

'Now you *are* taking the piss.'

'Better than all this.'

'All what?'

'Bloody PC stuff. Bet you if it was my letter box they shoved turds through and my garage door they sprayed stuff on CID wouldn't be in any rush.'

'You got a problem with this job?'

'No problem at all, sunshine.'

'Don't . . .'

'Sorry. Nathe.'

'Sarge,' Nathan spat out before he could stop himself.

Carmody laughed. 'Get on with your DCI, do you?'

'Great, yeah. Top man, he is.'

'Heard a lot about him.'

'Right, well, unless it's all good, I don't want to know.'

'Don't worry, Nathe, I got no problem with gays. So long as they keep it to themselves.'

'The DCI ent gay. Where'd you get that idea?'

'Come on.'

'I said, where'd you get that idea?'

'All right, all right, what's the big deal?'

'Because he's not.'

'If you say so.'

Nathan slewed the car round against the kerb to put paid

246

to the conversation. 'Right, this is Inkerman Street. We'll walk down from here. Corner shop, couple of houses round about. Knock on a door or three. You all right with that?'

Carmody shrugged and swung in beside him. They walked in silence. The streets were quiet in the morning sun. A woman pushed a pram with a toddler in a seat on the front. An elderly man in a turban shuffled along, tapping a white stick. The houses were uniform terraces, with bow windows at the front above and below and doors straight on to the street. The shop was on the corner of Trafalgar Street. They went into the usual densely packed mini-market-cum-video rental store that smelled of musty spices and floral air freshener.

'Mr Patel? I'm DS Coates, this is DC Carmody, Lafferton CID. I gather you've had a bit of trouble?'

The usual questions, the usual story: graffiti sprayed on the windows and walls; offensive, crude, racist abuse; excrement pushed through several letter boxes. Leaflets. Nathan asked to see one. Joe Carmody was wandering round the shop peering at shelves and into freezers.

The leaflet was printed, an A5 bill. It was a crude denunciation of 'immigrants and asylum seekers', claimed to speak for the Alliance of True Brits and all with a Birthright to Belong. A paragraph in smaller print ranted against 'alien parasites', with a mention of Muslims and Jews in passing.

'Very nasty,' Nathan said. 'They all like this, were they?'

They were. Several hundred of them spread round the network of streets. Swastikas had also been sprayed on the walls of the synagogue, on a couple of front doors and several strips of pavement, along with trails of dripped red paint.

The shopkeeper seemed relatively unworried, putting it all down to a few 'yobs and vandals'. They had never had any trouble like this, never been bothered in any way. It would blow over. But a couple of people had complained because some of the older residents were frightened and the children had started to ask questions.

'You did the right thing. We ent having this. We'll slap down on it hard, stop them before they've got going. Thanks for your help.'

Out in the sunshine, Joe Carmody unwrapped another piece of chewing gum and dropped the paper on to the pavement. Nathan turned on him.

'What's your problem? You want someone to drop that on your doorstep, do you?'

Carmody rolled his eyes.

'Pick it up and stop messing with me.'

The DC kicked the paper into the gutter and went on kicking until it reached a drain. He pushed it down one of the slats with his toe. Nathan watched him. He was annoyed, but he was also uncertain how to deal with the man. It seemed easiest, at least for the moment, to ignore everything but the job in hand.

'OK, you take those two houses – 14 and 16, I'll take 21 and 23.'

'What for?'

'We're asking if they've had any leaflets, stuff through the letter boxes, and we want to know if they've seen anyone, heard anything . . . the usual.'

'They won't have if they've got any sense.'

'What's that mean?'

'Right, 14 and 16. Let's hope they speak English.'

Carmody wandered across the road. Nathan watched him, not wanting to turn his back. Not that the DC wasn't right. No one would have seen anything and if they had, they wouldn't say. You couldn't blame them. They weren't dealing with a handful of little scrotes from the Dulcie estate bunking off school and looking for trouble. Little scrotes didn't get leaflets printed.

Carmody moved away from number 14, gesturing across that there had been no reply. He hammered on the next door.

They got nowhere much. One woman produced a leaflet. The old man had reached his house and stood outside as they approached him. He shook his head at the questions.

'Told you,' Carmody said. 'What can you do?'

'Keep on asking.'

The synagogue was closed but the caretaker lived in an adjoining house and was at home. He was also voluble. He

248

had taken digital photographs of the graffiti, had collected as many leaflets as he could find, had spent time watching the street, had his own fully formed opinions as to who was responsible.

Neo-Nazis. Thugs from Bevham, a local offshoot of a national organisation, well trained, cunning, good at planning. A worldwide problem, a worldwide hatred of Jews, an internationally organised alliance of anti-Semitic and racist forces.

'Gordon Bennett,' Carmody said as they walked back to the car. 'Thought we'd be there till dinner time. Got a bee in his bonnet.'

'Wouldn't you have?'

'I bet you make them very proud, Sarge.'

'I don't know what you're on about half the time. I need a coffee.'

'You toe the line, see? Goody-two-shoes. You'll go a long way, Nathe, a long, long way. You know which side your bread's buttered. Me? I come in, do the job, put away some criminals, make a few people sleep easier in their beds at night and bugger the rest. Call me old-fashioned.'

'I ent calling you anything. Get in.'

'Waste of a morning.'

'Not. Plenty to go on.'

'That caretaker was right. All of this – it's national. Lafferton's nothing. Dot on the map. They'll be miles away.' He slid down in the passenger seat again and folded his arms. 'Your DCI,' he said.

'Leave him out of it.'

'Why, fancy him, do you?'

Nathan felt his right hand itch. But all he hit with his fist was the steering wheel.

Joe Carmody laughed. 'You fall for it,' he said, 'every time. Makes it fun.' He reached over and pinched Nathan's cheek. 'Sarge.'

Forty-six

He didn't think he knew her. She was maybe thirty, maybe less or more, he always found it hard to tell with young women. She had nice hair, straight and brown and clipped back at either side, showing her face off. Nice face. Heart-shaped. Lovely eyes. Dark blue. She smiled. Nice smile. A bit – shy? Nervous? Made him warm to her. She had a big bag over her shoulder. Green. Bright green. Funny that. Handbags used to be brown or black or navy and now they were pink and had jewels on. Or bright green.

All of that in the split second after he opened the door. She wasn't trying to sell him anything, he could just tell that. She was nicer than that.

'Hello. I'm sorry to trouble you but I'm trying to find Mrs Meelup – Mrs Eileen Meelup. I asked round here and someone said this was the house? If it isn't I'm really sorry to bother you.'

He smiled. She brought a breath of fresh air with her and, whatever she wanted, he was grateful for that. Fresh air. Ray of sunshine. There hadn't been much of that lately.

'It's no bother at all, my dear, this is the right house.'

'Thank goodness for that. I hate it if I've barged in on someone and they're busy and they'd come downstairs and then it isn't the place after all . . .' She looked relieved and worried and pleased and nervous all at once. He liked her.

'Don't you worry. Now, it was the wife you wanted you said? Eileen? I'm Dougie Meelup.'

She put her hand out, trying to stop the big bright green bag from falling off her shoulder and pushing it back and laughing nervously and then her hair came unclipped at one side.

'Here, you'd better step in, sort yourself out by the look of it. Come on, come on in.'

She hesitated. Seemed not to want to intrude. She looked nervous again. A bit worried.

'Come on, lass. Eileen's in the back.'

'Well, if . . . thank you, thank you so much. I only want a quick word, but if it isn't convenient, if she's busy, I can come back, it really doesn't matter.'

'She's just doing something on the computer. Tell you the truth . . .' he drew her back a bit and lowered his voice, 'I'll be glad of an excuse to get her off it. Visitor and that, she'll stop. It's new, you see, and a bit complicated. I dare say you know all about them, the young ones all do, my sons, they do and their boys, only it's all a bit much for Eileen to take in. She would do it though, said she had to . . . anyway. You come in the back.'

The computer was on a card table by the window. Keith had got it for her and set it up; the wires trailed a bit, the screen was too big and the whole thing, which was an old model, too cumbersome, but it worked, did the job, as he had said, and Eileen had watched, twitching to start, twitching to use it to find out everything she had to about those children, where, when, what, so she could find the mistake they had made with Weeny.

Two lessons at the library had shown her enough. She had said she wanted to check things about her family. Family trees. 'Oh, everybody's into genealogy now,' the woman had said, 'we get dozens in here. Mind you, nothing will take the place of getting out there and looking up public records, church records, all of that. You won't find everything on the Internet and in my view it won't be half so exciting. The detective work's best done on foot, you know.' But she had said it was a start. That was what they'd agreed on. How to make a start. It was easier than she had expected.

She was clicking on the mouse as they walked in.

'Here, there's a visitor for you, love. Can you drag yourself away from that for a minute? It's . . .'

The young woman introduced herself quickly.

'Lucy,' she said. 'It's Lucy Groves.'

'Lucy Groves,' Dougie repeated. He looked foolish. Hadn't he asked her name at the door? Now he said, 'I'll put the kettle on.'

Eileen had found a newspaper report about one of the abducted children and it was in the middle of the screen. She swung round on her chair and then swung back again in confusion, wanting to get rid of it and not knowing how.

'Mrs Meelup?'

A nice-looking girl. Pretty. Nice hair. Smiling. She held out her hand. Eileen hesitated. She had no idea who she was or why she was here and Dougie had his back to them, busy with the kettle. Eileen glanced round again at the screen, hoping the picture might have vanished of its own accord, but it had not. The headline bored into her brain. 'Just a moment . . . I have to just do this. If you'd wait a minute . . .'

She swung her chair round again. It was an old typing chair. Keith had got that too, from a friend whose office had closed down. The screen was full of print that she did not want anyone else to see. She fiddled with the mouse under her palm, clicking it this way and that. The printing moved sideways and back again but that was all.

'Can I help?'

The girl was at her shoulder, looking at the screen. 'It's a nightmare at first, isn't it? Your husband said you were just learning. You'll be an expert in two ticks, honestly, but if you want me to do anything . . .'

Eileen felt her neck prickle. The girl was too close and she seemed to be both looking at the screen and looking at her, in an odd way. She smelled of something like sweet apples.

'No.' Eileen pressed the knob on the front of the screen and the picture shrank to a pinpoint of light and went out.

'Ah . . . don't know if they told you, but it's probably not a good idea to do that. It's really better to close down first – just switching it off can mean you lose data.'

Eileen backed away and got off the chair. 'It doesn't matter.'

'I'm so sorry, you must wonder what on earth is going on, some total stranger walking in and trying to teach you how to work your computer. I do apologise.'

Eileen said nothing. The girl put her bag on the sofa. Bright green. Big. A big bag.

'I'm Lucy Groves.'

'You said.'

'I'm so sorry to barge in . . .' She looked confused. A bit pink. She pulled the grip out of her hair at one side, fiddled with it and put it back. Eileen felt suddenly sorry for her. 'I wanted to talk to you, if it's possible. I really won't take up much of your time but it is quite important.'

Dougie was mashing the tea.

She was from the police. It was obvious. A plain-clothes policewoman. It was the only thing she could be and it was all right. In a way, Eileen felt a huge sense of relief that someone had come who knew about it, so that she didn't have to skulk and didn't have to pretend. It would be good to talk to her. A nice young woman. Her eyes were the most wonderful deep blue. Eileen had never seen such a deep but bright blue in anyone's eyes before.

'Sit down,' she said, 'please. Dougie'll get us a cup of tea.' She jumped up and went to the cupboard for the tin of biscuits. Empty. She'd been lax, not bothering with things, not stocking up. She saw everything at once, as if the young woman had shown it all to her. How she'd neglected things.

'Dougie . . .' She beckoned him out of the room into the hall. The young woman sat, fiddling with her hairgrip again. 'Can you pop to Mitchell's, get one of their malt loaves and something . . . Swiss roll or a Battenberg, whatever they've got?'

'But the tea's mashed.'

'Doesn't matter, we can have another pot, only it seems rude, I've got nothing in, I'm ashamed of it.'

'You don't –'

'I do.'

He looked round for his jacket.

'Police,' Eileen whispered.

'What is?'

She jerked her thumb. 'You can tell.'

'Oh.' He hadn't been able to.

'Plain clothes. She'll be a help now, she'll be able to give me a better idea what to do, how to go about getting it sorted out. You got enough money?'

'Of course I've got enough money.'

At the door, he glanced back. Yes. Policewoman. Now she'd said so, it was obvious, of course it was. And it was always going to be a policewoman. It was always going to come.

He went out to the car.

'What a lovely man,' the girl, Lucy Groves, said. She leaned forward slightly, smiling. She had her hand on her bright green bag. 'But perhaps you'll feel more comfortable talking to me now we're on our own.'

'Dougie and I don't have secrets.'

'No, no, I'm sure you don't. But isn't it true that sometimes it's difficult to say some very personal things?'

Eileen was silent.

'Mrs Meelup, you're probably wondering who on earth I am and why I'm here. I should explain everything carefully. There's nothing at all to be alarmed about . . . absolutely not. Quite the contrary. I'm here to protect you, if anything. You can talk to me. I can reassure you. I know you will want to talk, people in your sort of situation always do. You need to talk and I do understand that it isn't always easy to talk to those closest to us. You'll want to protect your close family . . . that's so natural. It's perfectly OK.'

She spoke quite softly, but quickly, so that Eileen had to

lean forward to catch everything she said, and the girl leaned further forward in her turn, so that they seemed almost to be putting their heads together, to be forming an intimacy with scarcely a space separating them.

'I don't know what terms you use,' Eileen said. 'I mean, are you a constable, or a detective policewoman or what? Seems funny not to know how it works.'

Lucy Groves smiled but moved back slightly, widening the space between them again. She reached up and took out her hair clip, fiddled with it and pushed it back. 'Please don't worry, please. I can understand how frightening it is.'

'Not frightening. Only you didn't say.'

'It is alarming when the police arrive, you feel threatened, don't you, wondering what you should say or dare say even, what they might make you confess to?'

'Confess to?'

'It's normal. It's natural. People do feel like that. Nothing that has happened is your fault, nothing at all, yet you will feel it is. Goodness, that's understandable.'

'I don't follow you.'

'Maybe the best thing would be for you to start telling me how exactly you do feel? I don't want to put words into your mouth. I want you to tell me the story as you see it. As it affects you. How you feel now, whether you're bewildered or angry or ashamed. Have you seen Edwina yet?'

There was something awry, like a picture that wasn't straight or a voice that was odd. Eileen fumbled around in her mind, trying to work out what it was. Have you seen Edwina yet? 'I thought you'd know that sort of thing. I thought it would all . . .'

The girl was leaning forward again. 'Mrs Meelup, can I just ask you if you would let me . . . ?' She had her hand on the bright green bag. Eileen looked at it. Smoke. She was going to ask to smoke, which surprised her. She didn't think police did, on duty. Like drinking. Maybe it was different when they didn't wear a uniform. Only she didn't care for smoking in her house.

'I'll understand if you say no, of course, and it is absolutely up to you, completely. It's just that it would make it easier for me. To remember.'

'Remember?'

'I want to be sure that everything you say, every word, is accurate. I'm here to help you tell the truth, to put your side of things, your story. I'm not in the business of putting words into your mouth, you know. You do understand?'

She didn't. She was understanding less and less as the young woman said more and more.

'So would it be all right?' She reached into the bright green bag and took out a small silvery box. She held it up. 'To use this?'

'I thought you were going to ask to smoke a cigarette,' Eileen said.

Lucy Groves laughed, a loud, high little laugh. 'Oh help! No. God, no, I don't smoke, haven't for about ten years, not since we smoked walking home from school, you know, thought it was soooo sophisticated. God, how funny.'

'What's that?'

They both looked at the small silvery box which Lucy Groves had set down on the table.

'State of the art. I promise you. No whirring, no clicking, no interruptions, you'll forget it's there in ten seconds.'

'*What is it?*'

'A recorder.'

'Tape recorder?'

'Yup. Digital. Everything you say, everything you whisper, will come up clear as crystal. It won't miss a thing.'

'I didn't know you used tape machines.'

Lucy Groves smiled. 'I promise. It looks after itself. Don't worry.'

'I'm not –'

The front door opened.

'Reinforcements,' Dougie Meelup called.

'Dougie?'

Something was wrong. Eileen's voice told him that but he couldn't quite tell how badly wrong. The young woman

256

started up, and he noticed that the shyness had got hidden, that she seemed a slightly different person now, not fiddling with the hair clips, not looking down at her lap.

'Mrs Meelup, what I would like you to consider very carefully is this. You will get other people coming to see you. If we can find you, so can the rest of the others, and not everyone will play fair, I warn you. Now, I have a very, very good offer for you. Not everyone will offer you anything at all. I'm glad I got here first because we aren't in the business of deceiving and cheating. You have a story to tell, we need your story. Your daughter Edwina Sleightholme stands accused on some very serious charges. Whatever the small details, those are the facts as everyone knows them and is talking about. They are talking about them, you can be quite sure . . . well, of course they are. You would, wouldn't you? Now, what we want is to hear everything from you . . . about Edwina as a child, her growing up, school, friends and all of that, how she got on with you, with her sister and her father . . . the full story. If it's interesting we would run it over at least a couple of weeks, maybe more and it could even be a book, so of course you'd stand to make even more. But our initial offer is just for the story. Exclusive to us. Now, clearly nothing can be printed until after the trial, it's all *sub judice*, but the moment everything is over, we'd run with it . . . no one else would have it, and you can tell the truth, the whole truth . . .' She laughed a short little laugh.

Eileen sat staring at her. Dougie saw the confusion on his wife's face, the shock and bewilderment, the uncertainty about what to say or how. He took a step forward so that he was in front of Lucy Groves.

'I think I'll speak now if you don't mind.'

'Oh, Mr Meelup, the man with the cakes! But the trouble is, you see, you're not really anything to do with all of this, are you? It really is your wife's story, the story of Mrs Sleightholme, not of Mrs Meelup. If . . .'

'I said I would speak now and I'd be glad if you would let me do it.'

She fluttered her eyelashes in mock surprise. 'Well, please do.'

257

'Thank you. Now, young woman, when you came in here, I very foolishly didn't ask you your business. You oiled your way inside and my wife took you for a policewoman, as well she might. Instead of which it turns out you're a newspaperwoman. *A newspaperwoman*. Well, I thank you, but we don't want you. I'll ask you to put your things together and leave and I'll ask you not to come back, not to dare to show your face anywhere near.'

He was shaking. Lucy Groves hesitated. He could see her, working it out, trying to see a way past him or round him or through him to Eileen but there was no way. He didn't move. And then Eileen found her voice.

'You pretended to be the police,' she said softly.

'Mrs Meelup, I did no such thing.'

'You sat in my house and you took my trust.'

'I'm really sorry you see it like that. I'm here to try and look after you. Because, believe me, you are going to need it. You are going to need all the help you can get. It's only a matter of time. And you'll find, when you think back, that I didn't mention the police.'

'What do you mean, I'll need help?'

'I should have thought it was pretty obvious. Mrs Meelup, listen to me . . . I'm trying to help you here. OK, yes, we get something out of it, of course we do, but only if you run with us and trust us. Then we look after you when the going gets tough. Which is when people find out who you are . . . those that don't know already. I'm amazed, frankly, that you haven't had anything nasty happen so far.'

'I think you'd better go now,' Dougie said.

She ignored him. 'You do know what I mean, don't you, Mrs Meelup?'

'You took me in.'

Lucy Groves shook her head. She was putting the recorder away.

'The thing is, it's all a big mistake. She's done nothing, nothing wrong at all, and never these terrible things, not in a million years. Of course she hasn't, you've only to know her. Of course she hasn't.' Eileen stood up, summoning

258

reserves of dignity and strength. 'I know what the truth is. The truth is that there's a dreadful wrong being done. Someone who took and harmed and killed little children is out there wandering the world waiting to do it all over again while Wee– while my daughter is under wrongful arrest. That's the truth, and when it's all sorted maybe I'll tell it. Only not to you. Not to you.'

She turned as her courage drained away and her face seemed to fold in on itself. Dougie picked up the big bright green bag and stood holding it out to Lucy Groves, and in the end, she took it without saying anything else at all, got up and walked from the room with him close behind her. He thought if he hadn't kept his arms folded he might have pushed her out of the door.

Forty-seven

The house was always shady. Only the kitchen got the sun for much of the day. The study was the coolest room in the house, so Magda had spent the hot days there. She had tried to work but it didn't amount to much. Her usually clear, concise thoughts seemed to have gone through a shredder and she was appalled by the feebleness of what she had written.

Now, she lay on the couch half reading, half dozing. The window was open on to her small garden and a blackbird was hopping about on the mossy paving stone. The garden was in shadow from the high wall, apart from a wedge of brightness at the far end.

She closed her eyes. She felt weak and when she'd woken that morning she had been tearful. In hospital she had felt safe and had company, not so much people to talk to as to watch and think about. She had also been fed and nursed and now she realised that she had come to depend on that, which was why she had wept earlier. Daily life had become a slow and tedious struggle. In half an hour she would like a cup of tea but the effort of getting to the kitchen to make it would probably defeat her.

I am not like this, she thought. I have become a stranger to myself and it frightens me.

She had been in control all her life, an achiever, a strong, vigorous woman, independent in mind and body. Now, someone else lay on her couch and dozed and was lonely and dreaded the dark.

The blackbird came closer. She had never noticed birds. The garden was a secluded green space but she had never cared about flowers or plants. Animals took from you and gave nothing in return, she had always said. As a child, Jane had wanted hamsters and rabbits, a cat, a dog. 'Animals are not equal companions for intelligent human beings.'

Now she watched the blackbird with fascination. Its whole life was a quest for food, without guarantee that food would be found. Perhaps it had come upon a reassuring supply here. She had no idea what blackbirds ate. Other people put out breadcrumbs and nuts for birds, a thing it had never occurred to her to do. But she felt a sudden surge of feeling for the blackbird. She had a few bits of food in the pantry and the fridge and she was never very hungry, but when supplies ran out she would somehow have to get more. Did grocers still deliver? Who could she ring and ask to shop for her? What had always been straightforward was now an impossibly complex challenge. Everything was a challenge, going from room to room, dressing, undressing, washing, bathing, sorting out clean clothes. She was a pathetic old woman and it angered her.

But the deep green shade of the garden was soothing to look out on. She closed her eyes and opened them again at a slight sound. The blackbird had gone.

The movement in the room was quick and soft so that by the time she had registered what had happened, he was standing beside the couch. Magda started to shift about, trying to pull herself up.

'Hello then, Miss,' he said quietly. 'I'm hoping you remember me.'

She stared, trying to place him. He was very tall and he wore jeans and a T-shirt with Atlanta Olympic Games 1996 stamped but barely still visible on the front. Something about him, something . . . she managed to sit almost upright. But not enough.

'Come on, come on, Miss, you have to remember me.' His

261

voice was both threatening and pleading. 'It's no good telling me you forgotten, Miss.'

'How did you get in?'

'Ah, that's our secret. Only if you don't remember me, which is a sad thing and all, you'll remember my mate Jiggy, he come here not long ago, Miss.'

'The one who broke in and took things and hit me, is that your mate Jiggy?'

'Sounds like you do remember him then, so you try and remember me. I think I'm sitting down a bit here.' He did so, in the chair opposite her, but he pulled it across the room first, so that he was closer. 'Now you look into my face, Miss, and tell me you remember? That'd be something.'

She found that she had to look into his face. She could do nothing else.

'Remember now, come on, Miss.'

'Why are you calling me Miss? I don't remember you, not at all.'

'OK, OK then, Doctor. Doctor. Doctor. Doctor. Now you'll remember me.'

She put her hand to her eyes and closed them, blotting him out. He had huge teeth, wide-spaced, with a broken one at the side. Huge hands.

'Doctor.'

'If you've come to take things, take them . . . whatever Jiggy left. Just take and go.'

'No, no, no. I'm not taking anything. No, no.' He laughed. He had his knees apart and his huge hands resting on them. 'That's not my idea. No.'

'What is your idea? What are you doing here? Please go. I want you to go. I'm not well and I need to sleep. Please, just leave that way.'

'I know the way. The way in, the way out. Only I'm for staying here. Till you remember me, which you should, which you'd better.'

'Why should I remember you? I've never seen you before.'

'Oh yes, oh yes, Miss Doctor, Miss Doctor, you've seen me, you've seen me a dozen times, maybe more, in your room,

262

in your office, where you wore glasses. No glasses today. No glasses.' He laughed.

She looked into the tiny pupils in his egg-white eyes. 'You were a patient? You came to my clinic?'

'Hey, yes, now then, you see? Hey. Good. Now we're getting along fine, a lot better. OK.'

'I don't remember you.'

His face tightened and he suddenly slapped his fist on to his knee. 'You better tell me you do.'

'It must have been years ago.'

'Many, many years. Many years. I was six or seven . . . or eight years old. You see, now I don't remember. Remembering is hard, isn't it, Miss Doctor? A little boy then. But I remember everything else. I remember you talking and talking and talking and I remember the writing you did, writing and writing, and the questions and questions and questions. I remember. I didn't know the answers all the time, I just heard the questions and the talking and saw the writing. Then I was sent away. You remember now maybe?'

'Sent away?'

'Nobody forgets being sent away.'

'But I didn't send you away.'

'You did so. You asked questions and wrote stuff and wrote stuff and I kept being back in your room and then one time I got sent away. I don't forget that.'

'What's your name?'

'You pretending you don't remember that now?'

'No, I don't remember. What is your name?'

'Mikey.'

'I didn't send you away. I couldn't. I didn't have the authority to send children away.'

'Maybe you told someone else then. Maybe that. I only know what happened. I remember that OK . . . that's why.'

'Why?'

He got up and came to stand over her so that she shrank back. He smelled of something sweet, but it was not a sweetness she recognised.

'Where I went, Miss, I remember that. I remember everything. You remember nothing. That's too bad. I know what *I* remember and who made it happen and that is you, Miss, you, Doctor Doctor, and I've waited to come and help you remember and here I am.'

He was speaking more and more quickly, the words running together. Once or twice she felt his spittle on her hand and then on her cheek.

And suddenly, she saw him, a stick-thin boy with huge hands and scabs on his head, bruises round his neck and on his arms. He was sitting on a straight chair in her room looking at the floor, touching his ear or his leg now and again in a gesture that was more than random, that was as someone touches a talisman. He was shocked into silence, malnourished, angry with a confused, hurt, pent-up anger, too frightened to release even a whisper to her. She saw him time after time and, once, only once, she heard him speak, but she could not catch what he was saying. A word she had never caught.

'I remember,' Magda said. 'Mikey.' His smile was triumphant, wide, gap-toothed, a mouth of a smile which opened into a roar of what she thought was delighted laughter, a second before she recognised it as rage.

In that second, she lifted up her arms to shield her face before he came down upon her savagely, roaring still, as the light shrank to a pinpoint behind her eyes and then went out.

Forty-eight

He had thought he would wait until it was dark but he felt in pain with the frustration of waiting, of the heat, of being able to do nothing else, of having it bang against the inside of his head. He rinsed his head under the cold tap in the kitchen and went out just before seven. The pavements radiated the heat of the day back up and the tarmac was melting at the sides of the road. He turned to take the canal path. It was a longer route but shady, pleasanter. No one was about except one old man on a broken bench, whispering to himself.

They had come here a few times to walk, in winter, in spring. Lizzie had longed to see a kingfisher and someone had told her kingfishers occasionally flashed blue from bank to bank of the canal and nested under the willows, but she had died and the kingfisher remained unseen. Now he stood staring at the willows, still in the early-evening heat. Nothing.

He passed the lock-keeper's cottage and the warehouses. Lizzie had come there for him but when he had reached out to her she had run away, tripped, fallen, cried and sent for the police. It had been a confusion and a misunderstanding but he had not been able to explain adequately, they had seemed obtuse. But then, he had always believed that policemen were obtuse, overtrained and undereducated, without subtlety or fastidious intelligence.

The cathedral bells rang the hour.

Lizzie's death was someone's fault. Whoever had once fed

her contaminated meat. Doctors who had diagnosed her disease too late. Doctors who had failed to treat her. Doctors who had stood by watching her symptoms crawl into her brain and eat it away. Nurses in the hospice. People whose prayers were useless. God. God. God and God's priests.

He crossed the canal at the narrow iron bridge on to the town side. Here, the backs of terraced houses overlooked it; people might look out of their bedrooms on to the green-black surface of the water, on to the cardboard carton bobbing against the base of the bridge, on to the supermarket trolley embedded in the undergrowth, on to the peeing dogs and the narrow boats and the willows and the secret kingfishers.

He pushed his way through a patch of nettles and briers, through a broken-down gate and up a long tube of a garden without grass. No one saw him. No one came. A dog barked somewhere.

He was sweating. He smelled of sweat.

The house was in a mess, a honeycomb of let-rooms with dirty curtains. The house on his left was the same, but on his right, someone had a garden. He went across and looked through the broken fence panels. Marigolds. A wooden archway with trellis and a rose climbing up it, peachy-coloured. The path was lined with tiles like hoops. There was a bed of vegetables – onion tops, potato tops, a cane bean-wigwam. A couple of nut holders swung from a laburnum tree. There was a tiny pond. At the far end, behind a privy, he could just see a birdcage set against the brick wall and a flash of canary yellow. He tried to push his way through the fencing but it would not give. He wanted to be in the garden, beside the tiny pond, near the birds, among the potato tops and marigolds.

Abruptly, Max began to weep, resting his head against the broken fence, and his weeping turned to a torrent of anger, making him shake the wood panels violently until someone shouted from a house. No one came. Just the shouting, then silence again.

His hand had blood on it from a piece of broken wood which had punctured the pad below his thumb.

And then he saw her. She was sitting with her back to him on a bench near the archway. Her hair was fairer, as if she had been in the sun for a long time. He pulled at the fencing slats and this time a half-rotten one snapped and when he kicked at the space it opened enough for him to crawl through. He stood still, amazed that he was inside the garden as close to Lizzie as breathing. She was there. She had not stirred or turned. She might be waiting, though he wondered why it should be here, where he had found her quite by chance.

He wiped the back of his wet hand across his face. The cut had stopped hurting but still bled. She would know what to do.

'Lizzie,' he said.

It was very quiet. He waited.

'Lizzie.' She did not move and so he went forward a step or two, reaching out his hand to her, to touch the slightly fairer hair.

'Lizzie.' He realised that he had been saying her name but silently, saying it in his heart and in his head but not out loud. Now he spoke it clearly into the still garden.

'Lizzie.'

She turned round then and screamed and the screams were like knives tumbling and falling through his brain and he lunged forward, desperate to reach her and stop her, to show her who he was and that she did not need to scream, but when he felt her body and looked into her face and the open, screaming mouth, Lizzie had gone. It was not Lizzie and his brain caught fire.

Forty-nine

The small hands were slightly damp. Like a clammy sort of sea anemone on her arm.

'Bloody hell, Kyra!'

Natalie woke up completely and leaned across Kyra to switch on the lamp.

'What you done?' She sounded weary. She was weary. This was the fourth night in two weeks. 'You wet your bed again or what?'

The small hands were pulled away.

'You bloody have. Honest to God, Kyra, how old are you? Wetting the bed is what babies do, little kids, you're six years old, nearly seven. OK, tomorrow morning, we go to the doctor, first off, and you don't go to Barbara's till you're sorted.'

Kyra curled up on the farthest side of her mother's bed. She didn't mind about not going to Barbara's. In the holidays she was there eight till six. She only minded about the doctor.

'Shut up, it's me should be crying, you're wet at both ends these days, you. Come on, get out of there, you want a clean nightie, I'm not having you make this bed wet and all. I'll sort yours tomorrow. And if you stop in here you stop still, right?'

It only took five minutes but then of course she couldn't get back to sleep. Kyra slept. In the morning, she'd barely remember any of it.

Natalie lay on her back, arms behind her head. She knew why she wasn't sleeping and it wasn't only that Kyra kept waking her, if not because she'd wet the bed then because of bad dreams. There was something wrong and Natalie knew it, only Kyra was like a bloody oyster, clammed up tight. She hadn't said anything at school, she wouldn't say anything to Barbara, and Natalie had given up. She'd tried talking, tried asking questions, tried pleading, screaming, shutting her in her room, giving her treats, confiscating her toys, forbidding television, taking her out, making her stay in. Nothing. All Kyra said was, 'I want to see Ed,' and sometimes, 'Where *is* Ed?'

But she wouldn't talk about Ed, except to say the old stuff. I like Ed. I like going to Ed's house. We made buns. We made toffee. We read stories. We did the garden.

'Did Ed ever do anything to you?' Silence.

'Did Ed ever tell you about other children she knew?' Silence.

'Did Ed tell you where she worked? Did Ed ever ask you to go in her car? Did Ed ever tell you off?' Silence. Silence. Silence.

Natalie was more worried than she found it easy to admit even to herself. She wondered what she ought to do now, whether she ought to ask the doctor if Kyra needed to see someone else. Or maybe she ought to get her away, take a holiday, go to Butlins or Center Parcs or camping in France like Davina at work. Ha bloody ha. She hadn't got camping money or Center Parcs money or even, probably, Butlins money. Everything went on the rent and keeping them going, even the bit of extra benefit she got. That and the bloody car wanted mending. And then there was the business she hoped to start. The one she had had planned in her head for as long as she could remember. Dream on, Natalie.

She wasn't going to start weeping or whingeing to anyone, because she wasn't the weeping or whingeing sort. She was tough. She was independent and she was bringing up Kyra to be the same. Only sometimes, like now for instance, in the middle of the night, the toughness got cracks in it.

Kyra mumbled and murmured like someone with a mouth full of pebbles. Natalie had strained to hear any words, anything that made sense, but there never was anything. Just pebble mumbling.

She turned on her side and tried to sleep but her brain was shot through with brilliant light and jazzy pictures and she didn't finally drop off until after dawn. Kyra had not stirred from her place, rolled up on the very edge of the bed.

The surgery was overflowing and one of the doctors had been called out. Kyra sat on the bench swinging her legs. Every time she swung them back they banged against the wall and a woman opposite glared. If she hadn't, Natalie would have told Kyra to stop swinging and banging, but because of the woman, she let her go on doing it. They were seen nearly an hour after their appointment time and were in the room for three minutes. He had looked at his computer all the time and not at either of them and asked how old Kyra was twice.

'OK,' Natalie had said, 'so you think it's just normal, then, her suddenly wetting the bed. Fair enough.' She couldn't be bothered. He hadn't even asked if Kyra had had any upsets, hadn't seemed to know a lot about anything.

'Stop scraping your shoe like that, Kyra, I gotta get back to work.'

'Can I have an ice cream?'

'No, you bloody can't.'

'Why not?'

'No money, no time and they rot your teeth.'

'Not just one?'

'Oh Gawd, all right. But only . . .' Natalie stopped. She took hold of Kyra's hand tightly, 'only if you tell me.'

Kyra stared at the pavement.

'Kyra?'

'What?'

'What happened with Ed?'

Silence.

'OK, that's it then. No talk, no eat. Come on. And stop scraping your bloody shoe, will you?'

'When's Ed coming back to her house?'

'Never,' Natalie said, feeling suddenly vicious.

She waited for Kyra to cry but there was no crying. Nothing. Just the silence.

She'd taken the morning off, so she might as well have it. Kyra went to Barbara's. Natalie went to Top Shop and bought herself a pair of shorts. There was time for a wander about and a milk shake.

And then it came to her, like a bubble popping inside her head and letting out an idea like a gas. She sat for a long time, thinking it through, having a Coke after the milk shake, which wasn't the best idea because the two seemed to froth up in her stomach for the rest of the day. But the idea was a good one. By the end of the afternoon she'd worked it out quite carefully, how much she might possibly get, how she'd use it.

She didn't go back to work. She had too much to think about. It was very hot and she took her thinking, and three different newspapers, into the garden. Ed's house was odd, like a ghost house, a hollow shell sitting next door, not just a house where they were out at work or even away on holiday. Different.

It wasn't just about getting money. It was about telling someone. She began to go through the papers. There were articles with the names of the people who had written them at the top and she wrote one or two down, but only women. She couldn't have explained why, but she knew it had to be a woman.

Melanie Epstein. Anna Patterson. Selina Wynn Jones. She liked that name. There was a postage-stamp photograph at the top of the article, which was about women sex addicts. Selina Wynn Jones had straight blonde hair to just below her ears and what looked like quite a big nose, which was re-assuring, somehow. She wanted to have someone called Selina Wynn Jones as a friend. Friend. Natalie was struck by the word because she supposed she had thought of Ed as a friend, because of Kyra. Ed had had patience with Kyra, more than she herself usually had. They'd cooked things, started tomatoes off in pots and sunflower seeds in the garden, Ed had read books to her, and if you'd asked, Natalie knew she would have said that Ed was a friend. She didn't have many. She was a bit like Ed, private, not always in and out of other people's houses, other people's lives, and that had meant they suited each other as neighbours. She remembered hearing them over the fence in the garden, Kyra rabbiting on in her scratchy little high voice, Ed saying the odd thing, but mainly being quiet, letting Kyra talk. Once, Ed had come in for a cup of tea. Once, Natalie had taken her post round when it got misdelivered. They'd said Hi. Was that being a friend?

Jesus Christ. She stood up as if a wasp had stung her, remembering what had happened, what Ed had done. If she had. Maybe there was a mistake. They did make mistakes, even big ones. Papers were full of them, people standing on the steps of a court, weeping, waving, arms round their mothers and sisters and wives, innocent after twenty years, the something Four, the somewhere Seven. Whatever.

Ed?

Natalie went indoors, got a half-finished bottle of lager from the fridge, drank it, threw the bottle in the bin and went to the telephone. She got the number of the newspaper in ten seconds and wrote it down. That was the easy bit. Then she went upstairs.

Kyra's room was neat. Kyra was neat. Sometimes Natalie told her the fairies had swapped her for someone else's kid she was so neat. Tidy. Her picture books were edge to edge and her soft toys arranged big to small down the shelf. Bloody hell. It was like Ed's house when Natalie had been into it the odd time, clean, tidy, neat. What was that all about?

She looked out of Kyra's bedroom window. The walls were there, the roof, the garden, the gate, the fence panels. It was there. The same. Ed's house. She wondered what the men in white suits had found. She wondered what it felt like in the house, whether by standing in one of the rooms you would know. Just know.

272

She ran down the stairs fast and took the portable phone into the kitchen.

'I want to speak to Selina Wynn Jones.'

'Thank you.'

She hadn't expected just that. Just 'Thank you', and the tinned music, Whitney Houston; she didn't know what she'd expected and it had taken three seconds.

'Selina Wynn Jones.'

Natalie's mouth went funny, as if she'd sucked on a lemon. She thought she couldn't speak.

'Hello? Can I help you?'

'Yeah. I think . . . well, can I ask you something? That's it really.'

'Who is this?'

'Natalie . . . Miss Natalie Coombs.'

'From?'

'What?'

'Sorry, are you an agency or what?'

'No. I just . . . I read you in the paper. I've got something to say.'

'About?'

'My neighbour . . . and my daughter. About Kyra.'

'You've lost me.'

'OK.' Natalie took a slow breath. 'Right. Sorry. My name's Natalie Coombs and I live next door to a woman murderer. I live next to Ed Sleightholme? The one with the missing children – the little boy who was murdered and that. She's in prison, she's been charged. I live next door to her.'

'Right. I know the case you mean but I'm not sure you're talking to the right person.'

'Oh.'

'I'm not crime. I'm not news at all. I'm features.'

'Oh.'

'You really need the news desk.'

'Do I?'

'I'd think so.'

'I want to talk to someone . . . to tell them my story.'

'Oh, right, got you. Ah . . . hang on . . . give me your number, will you? It's Lucy Groves. Yes, Lucy Groves will call you back.'

She never would. Natalie knew enough to know she'd been fobbed off.

She'd have to fetch Kyra in ten minutes. She looked in the fridge but there'd only been the one bottle of lager and what was she doing drinking lager in the day? She didn't even like it much.

She got a glass down for some water and the phone ringing made her jump and smash the glass on to the floor.

Fifty

Early that evening a spectacular thunderstorm ripped open the bubble of hot, clear weather. Simon watched a sudden whirlwind swirl rubbish out of the gutter and high into the air beyond his office window and then the rain came sluicing down. Lights went on around the building.

'Guv? Can I have a word?'

'Come in, Nathan. Did you get anywhere with our graffiti merchants?'

'Not really.'

'I know they're usually dead-end jobs, but this sort of thing has a habit of spreading like hogweed if we don't get on top of it from the start. It'll be yobs, but go after it.'

'It ent the job . . . well, it is, only it is and it isn't.'

'Come in, sit down, make yourself clear.'

'Thanks, guv.'

Nathan sat rubbing his hand about in his yard-broom hair. Simon knew the sign.

'What's up?'

'This new DC, guv. We got a problem.'

'Go on.'

Nathan hesitated. 'I don't like telling tales out of school, I ent one to come running, I can look after things –'

'Nathan, I said go on.'

'Right then, he's a bad apple, guv. You know anything about him?'

275

'Not much. It was a case of beggars not being choosers – we're two down, Exwood let us have him for a couple of weeks . . . What's the problem?'

Nathan told him. Carmody was a racist, a bully, a skiver, he looked slovenly, was offhand to members of the public. 'And he kept calling me sunshine.'

Simon kept a face as straight as a bat. 'Was this in private or in front of the public?'

'Bit of both. Don't get me wrong, guv, I can take a word, only it was the other stuff I didn't go for, nasty little comments, you know, about the synagogue, about the Asian bloke at the shop . . . it was everything.'

'He's not with us for good and he's not ours, we can't go in heavy. You're his senior officer, sort it with him.'

'I don't like the bloke.'

'I don't like everyone I work with here.'

'OK.' Nathan always wore his heart on his sleeve. Now, he went disconsolately to the door, head down.

'Nathan?'

He glanced round.

'Snap out of it.'

'Guv.'

The rain had stopped but the thunder was still grumbling around. Simon half thought of taking a wander into the CID room and a look at DC Carmody, thought better of it and reached for his jacket. He went out of the building and walked the half-mile into the town centre through the subsiding storm. The florist's where he had bought Martha her last bright flowers and balloon was just closing, galvanised tins empty on the pavement. Simon tapped on the door.

'Hello, Inspector. I'm closed really but if you see anything you want, take it quick.'

He had been a customer for a long time, buying all the flowers for his mother and sisters, for birthdays and christenings.

'Last minute, I suppose?'

'Peace offering, Molly. Can you put something really special together?'

'Go on then. Come back in ten minutes.'

He went from the florist's to the bookshop and scooped up half a dozen paperbacks for Cat's children and then a bottle of champagne. He knew perfectly well what his sister's comment would be.

The flowers were waiting.

'Best I can do. Told you it was the end of the day.' Deep blue delphiniums and white agapanthus in a huge tied bunch.

It began to pour again as he was carrying everything to the car. The lightning was livid, red-rimmed, the sky sulphurous. He remembered the crash of the waves below him as he stood with Ed Sleightholme on the cliff ledge. Excitement. It had been excitement. He craved more of it. Cold cases might be many things but they rarely held out the hope of much excitement. QED.

'Uncle Simon, Uncle Simon, this is Jane, she's brought us two books, I've got a new Lemony Snicket and Sam's got –'

'No you haven't, it isn't just for you, Lemony Snicket is for me as well, so –'

'Sam . . .'

'Well, I read Lemony Snicket first, I found out about it and now Hannah's pretending she likes it best.'

'And the other book is called *The Fantora Family Files*, have you read that?'

Felix started to wail. Mephisto the cat leapt off the kitchen sofa and fled out between Simon's legs and up the stairs. Simon stood in the doorway, besieged by the children, his arms full of presents. Cat was at the table but was now reaching down to haul the wailing Felix on to her lap. Beside her sat the young woman priest who had been kept prisoner in her house by Max Jameson. She wore a pale pink T-shirt and no dog collar.

Cat gave a single sharp look at the stuff he was carrying. 'Ah. Guilt offerings.'

'God, I knew you'd say that.'

'Well, it's true. Come on then, hand over. Lovely, lovely booze, oh, Si, what fantastic delphiniums.'

'I'm afraid one of the books seems to be redundant.' He took the Lemony Snicket volume out of its paper bag.

Sam came over and held out his hand. 'Thanks,' he said, 'one each. I can read mine to myself. Hannah has to have it read to her.'

'Sam . . .'

'Oi, I'll have you carpeted, DC Deerbon, that's no way to talk to your DCI.'

'Sorry, guv.'

Simon dumped the bottle on the table and went to the cupboard to look for a vase to put the flowers in, Hannah beside him, clinging on to his arm, Sam following, trying to push his sister out of the way.

'Jane and I were planning on a nice quiet girls' night in.'

'OK, fine, I know where the fish-and-chip shop is.'

'It's fish and chips here . . . well, haddock and a potato-and-parsley bake.'

'So much more delicious.'

He filled the vase with water, stripped off the paper and cut the stems from the flowers. Jane Fitzroy was watching him.

'Oh, yes, he's quite handy,' Cat said, seeing her.

'Uncle Simon, there was lightning with blue in it.'

'In Lafferton it had a red lining.'

'Scar-y.'

'Lightning is caused by –' Sam began.

A mobile phone rang. The room was a picture in a frame, the children silenced.

'Oh, help, it's mine, sorry, sorry. Where is it?' Jane got up and looked round the kitchen.

A denim bag was hanging on the chair handle beside Simon. He looked down at the blue light flashing on the mobile in its depths. 'Seems to be here.'

'Help . . . sorry, how stupid. I hope it isn't anything, I'm enjoying myself too much.'

'That's because of us,' Sam Deerbon said airily, plonking himself on the sofa and opening his own copy of Lemony Snicket.

Jane went out of the room, holding the phone to her ear, still apologising.

'Sorry,' Simon said to Cat, watching Jane.

'OK. Thanks for the guilt offerings.'

'Not sure it was my shout.'

'*What*?'

He held up his hands.

Cat subsided. Felix reached out and grabbed the pepper-mill, which crashed on to the floor.

'I don't mind going. If you've got things to talk about.'

'We'd finished the business meeting. Hospice politics.'

'Problems?'

'Yes. You don't want to know. Stay.'

'I'd like to.' He glanced at the door through which Jane had vanished.

'No, Si,' Cat said. 'Absolutely not.'

'I didn't see it at first. She's beautiful.'

'Yes, she is. And no!' But then Cat looked up. 'Jane? What's the matter?'

Jane's face was pale as a candle as she stood just inside the doorway, staring at her phone.

'Jane?'

It seemed a long time before she could speak. 'That was the police. About my mother.'

'Isn't she back at home?'

'Yes. Apparently someone broke in.'

'Oh no, Jane, not again . . . have they taken a lot?'

'They . . . he didn't say. About anything being taken. Just that they'd beaten her unconscious. She's very ill.' She looked around her as if not understanding where she was. 'I have to go,' she said. 'I have to go to London.'

Simon put down the wine glass he had been holding. 'Let me have your phone. For the number. I'll call them back.'

'I have to go.'

'I know,' he said, holding out his hand. Jane handed him her mobile. 'You just get ready,' he said, leaving the kitchen to make the call outside. 'I'll drive you there.'

*

279

Ten minutes later Simon closed the car door, glanced back and saw Cat beckoning. He hesitated, then waved, and swung the car towards the gate, without looking back.

Five minutes later, his own phone rang. He clicked it on to hands-free.

'Guv?'

'Hi, Nathan, anything? I'm just setting off for London.'

'Oh. Right. Only we've got a body.'

'Hold on.' He slowed and glanced at Jane. 'Sorry, I'll have to take this.'

'Don't be silly, it's your job. It's fine.'

'Sure?'

She smiled. 'Just do it.'

'Nathan?'

'OK, guv, young woman, Hayley Twiston, single mother, one boy, living in a couple of rooms in Sanctus Road.'

'Behind the canal.'

'That's it . . . neighbours heard her baby crying for a long time. Went round eventually. Baby was on its own in a cot, quite distressed, seemed to have been there for a bit. They found the mother in the garden. She'd been hit over the head, probably a brick or a stone from the garden path. Someone had smashed down part of the fence. There's blood marks on it, whoever it was cut themselves getting through.'

'The girl?'

'Doc says dead from one of two blows on the head.'

Jane drew in a sharp breath.

'Right. Forensics there?'

'Guv.'

'You take over now, Nathan, find out what you can, put people on to the neighbours, all the rest. I want everyone in the area questioned, anyone who might have seen someone on the canal path this afternoon. Relatives?'

'A brother in Bevham. Someone's on to that.'

'The baby?'

'Social services are dealing.'

'Good work. I don't know when I'll be back, I'm driving

a friend – her mother's been taken to hospital. Keep me posted.'

'Guv.'

'You're probably having second thoughts about Lafferton,' Simon said.

'No. I didn't want a retirement village.'

'All the same. You were taken prisoner in your own house. Not good.'

'You live in the close, don't you?'

He nodded.

'The peaceful life?'

'At the end of the day's work among the violent and disaffected, yes.'

'It isn't where I live or what happened which makes me wonder if I've come to the right place.'

'Do you wonder that?'

'Yes.'

He accelerated down the slip road and on to the motorway. The traffic was heavy.

'But everything's connected, I suppose. The moment I arrived, my mother was burgled and I had to be back in London.'

'Is that where you were before Lafferton?'

'Yes. Assistant priest at a big north London church. Before that I was in Cambridge. That was where I trained.'

'Why did you move?'

'The cathedral. And I wanted to move into hospital chaplaincy . . . the job came up. That's what happens. People don't always realise it.'

'Like the police. You look for a particular job. Apply for it. Move.'

'Will you?'

'Move?' He shrugged.

'Sorry.'

Simon zipped into the fast lane and picked up speed. 'Police driver,' he said, 'so hang on.'

She did not speak again until they had left the first motorway and joined the next, which was quieter, now that the home-going traffic had eased. Then she said, 'Poor girl. How will they start looking for whoever it was?'

'Probably straightforward. Usually is. It'll be a relationship thing, boyfriend, some score to settle. Could well be sorted by the time I get back.'

'Just like that.'

'Hm.'

'Not like my mother.'

'Is there anyone who might have it in for her?'

'Only the thugs who came last time.'

'The Met's pretty hot. They'll have them.'

'But that won't help her, will it? She can't stay there. I'll have to bring her to Lafferton, somehow.'

'Do you have room?'

'I'd have to find room.'

'Would she want to come?'

'To live with me? No. My mother's an independent woman. And she finds it pretty embarrassing having a priest for a daughter.'

'Ah. My father finds it embarrassing having a policeman for a son.'

'Why on earth –'

'Serraillers are doctors. Hadn't you noticed?'

'Like Fitzroys are Jews. My mother's a child psychiatrist. A Hampstead intellectual atheist.'

'You'd fight?'

'Yes. But there's no other solution.'

Simon had spoken on Jane's mobile to the London police, so he knew that her mother's condition was more serious than she realised. Lavatory paper had been pushed into her mouth, she had been tied to the sofa leg with wire, and then beaten.

Now he said calmly, 'Take it bit by bit.'

'It would make it even more difficult for me to move.'

'So Lafferton was one big mistake?'

'I don't know, Simon. It feels like it some days . . . nothing is working. I don't like the bungalow; but is that because I was attacked there? I don't find my colleagues in the cathedral easy; but is that because I'm so much younger than them and the only woman? I'm not getting on that well at Bevham hospital because not many people want a chaplain and a lot of those who do are Catholics or Muslim, which leaves me a bit of a spare part. I love the time I spend at the hospice but there's a problem there . . . that's what Cat and I were talking about this evening.'

'So you'll run away.'

She was silent.

'I'm sorry. I don't know how I could have said that.'

'Perhaps because you're right. I was feeling sorry for myself. People who feel sorry for themselves quite often run away. It's been a bit of a turbulent few weeks. Your sister has been a big help.'

'That's Cat.'

'You're close?'

'Usually.'

The phone rang.

'Nathan?'

'I'm at BG, guv. Just talked to the girl's brother. He's here to identify. Nobody on the scene – child's father's a Greek, holiday fling. Never been in the country. No other boyfriend so far as he knows. Doesn't look like your open-and-shut. They're getting DNA on the blood. No one saw or heard anything – no one much around in the afternoons there any road. You in London yet?'

'Another half-hour or so.' The call ended and Simon sighed.

'Worrying,' Jane said.

'DNA's a wonderful thing.'

'Maybe.'

'They'll go over your mother's house for it, don't worry. There's an awful lot can be done nowadays.'

'How do you cope? You have to have a coping strategy, we all do.'

'I switch off.'

'How?'

He hesitated.

'I'm sorry. Not prying. But it's interesting. Cat and I were talking about it, oddly enough. She has her family.'

'You have God.'

'Do you?'

'Not sure. I draw.'

'Draw?'

Simon negotiated the roundabout between the motorway and the stretch of dual carriageway into London. It was raining now. A stream of dipped headlights crossed theirs, heading in the opposite direction.

'As in pencil,' he said. 'It was a toss-up between that and the police. Maybe still is.'

'So you're good?'

He shrugged.

'With me, it was swimming.'

'Water or God, then?'

'Not mutually exclusive.'

'There's a good pool in Bevham.'

'I stopped. In sport, there's a point when you either go for it, to the top – or quit. I wasn't going to the top. And even if I had, in the end swimming wasn't enough.'

'Why not?'

'I'm not competitive enough. And you have to be. Aggressively competitive. I'm not.'

'Lafferton should suit you. Not a very striving, achieving sort of place. Nor, I guess, is the Church of England.'

'Oh, you'd be surprised. But I didn't come to Lafferton for the quiet life.'

'But you did come to get away from London.'

'Not really. I came to get away from my mother.' She put her hands to her face. 'Oh God.'

'It's OK,' Simon said quietly.

Under an hour later, he stood just outside the main entrance to the hospital talking to the Met's DI Alex Goldman. He looked younger than Nathan Coates.

'She's in a bad way. Docs aren't hopeful.'

284

'This isn't the first time.'

'Might be unconnected. This time, nothing was taken, nothing disturbed. Forensics are all over everything. We'll get them. You a relative?'

'No.'

The DI gave him a sharp look. 'Right.'

'Just no.'

'We'll need to talk to the Reverend at some point.'

Simon's phone rang.

'Nathan.'

'Nothing new, guv. I'm for home. Be in first thing. Get on top of it then. You OK?'

Simon hesitated. He wanted to tell Nathan where he was and why, and the need to do so puzzled him. 'Fine. Just sorting something out for a friend. I'll see you in the morning.'

'Cheers, guv.'

Two women, a hundred or so miles apart, one young, battered to death in her garden, one old, battered almost to death in her house. No obvious suspects, no obvious motives, no robberies, no trace of anyone or anything. They were unconnected and yet, to Serrailler, they seemed linked in some dreadful intangible way, part of a pattern, part of a connection with him and with his work and his life. He was angry at the apparently pointless, random violence, but there seemed more behind both incidents than there would be behind a couple of street muggings or burglaries which had got out of hand.

He was putting his phone away and heading towards the entrance doors when he saw Jane Fitzroy walking slowly down the corridor. He watched her. She looked small, distracted, pale. Vulnerable. Her hair was like curling copper wire, glinting in the artificial light. He wanted to freeze her image until he had caught it with pencil on paper.

He went through the doors towards her.

'She didn't come round.' She was shaking. Simon took her arm and led her to a bench against the wall.

'She didn't know I was there.'

'But you were. And you know you can never be sure . . . people often do sense someone with them.'

'I've said that. I've tried to make people feel better. But she didn't, Simon. She was miles away and she just went further and further . . . like someone drifting out to sea. I couldn't reach her and then she was gone. She looked . . . terrible. She didn't look like herself. Whoever did this to her . . .'

She fell silent. Out of the corner of his eye Simon saw DI Goldman and waved him away.

'What am I going to do?'

'Do you want to go to the house?'

'Must I?'

'Absolutely not. There won't be anything else for you to do tonight. I'll take you back.'

'Where?'

'Back to Lafferton.'

'Yes. Is that home? I suppose it is.'

'I'll ring my sister. You shouldn't be on your own and her spare room is always ready for someone.'

'It'll be too late, I couldn't . . .'

'Jane. It's fine.'

'I feel hopeless. I ought not to be like this.'

'Oh? And why is that?'

She smiled weakly.

'So, policemen and doctors and what DI Goldman calls reverends are superhuman – whatever.'

He stood up and held out his hand and, after a moment, she took it. As they reached Simon's car, she began to cry.

Fifty-one

He was wet. He was near water. He put his hands up to his hair and it was wet. His head ached and his left hand burned with pain. The sky growled. Lizzie. He fumbled about in the dark cavities of his memory to find out what had happened to her. Lizzie. She had been sitting in a garden with her back to him and there had been something wrong, something different.

Max realised that he was bending forwards, as if he had been trying to vomit on to the ground but there was no vomit. He sat up. It was almost dark. He stood up. The canal smelled of rotting vegetation churned up by the storm. No one was near. Not Lizzie. Not . . .

He stumbled away, along the path, slipping on the mud. Something was wrong, something buzzed in his head like a warning, but he had no sense of what it could be. He had been drinking whisky but the bottle was no longer in his pocket. It had been hot and humid and he had seen Lizzie in a garden but something had been different. His hand hurt.

It was like having a broken dish with the pieces scattered randomly about the floor and some of the large, important sections missing altogether. He kept shaking his head as he made his way back down the towpath to the gap, through it and into the street. There was no one about and he wanted there to be someone, anyone that he could speak to, anyone who would reassure him that he was still a man, who existed, who had a name and a home, who was . . . There was no one. He needed warmth and a drink, dry clothes. Lizzie. Anyone. If he did not see someone he might somehow lose all sense of himself, lose his grasp on where he was as well as who, lose everything that he had left.

He went slowly up the stairs to the apartment. Someone might be there now, Lizzie might have come back before him. He thought he could smell her, the slightly sharp, lemon scent she always wore.

There was no one, of course. No Lizzie. No anyone. The flat always brought Max back to himself.

His clothes seemed to be drying. He took out a fresh bottle of whisky, poured himself a tumbler, and switched on the radio beside the sink.

Ten minutes later, he was running, the whisky burning in his mouth and the pit of his stomach, the flat door left open, the radio still on. He ran through the streets like a deranged animal, chased by the voices, slipped on the wet pavement and almost fell, crossed the road and was almost struck by a motorbike, ran through a knot of people, ran round a couple, skirted a bus shelter, took a wrong turn and came down a cul-de-sac and had to retreat, still running, running, running, and now the rain came again, soaking him for the second time and somehow helping him, clearing his head and washing everything out of him and down into the gutters.

Running, running, running, away from the voices and towards the place of safety.

Fifty-two

'Whatever I may have said, whatever impression I gave, my childhood was good. By comparison with most of the people I deal with every day, it was a paradise. The same probably goes for you, so let's set aside the fucked-up childhood . . . begging your pardon, Reverend.'

'If you call me Reverend once more, I walk.'

'Walk home?'

'Right.'

Simon looked at her across the table. 'I bet you would too.'

He had pulled off the motorway for petrol, and for food and coffee. The place was almost deserted. The all-day breakfast was surprisingly good, the coffee foul. Jane put a piece of bacon on the end of her fork, stared at it, then set it down again.

'Eat.'

'I have.'

'Half a piece of tomato. Uh-huh, Reverend.'

But he saw that the joke was over. All jokes were over. There was no joke about where they had been and why.

'You're right of course. My mother was difficult, but my father was wonderful, we had a comfortable home, I liked my school, I had swimming. Nothing to whinge about. Will they want me back there tomorrow?'

'No. It'll wait a few days. They'll focus on finding whoever it was.'

'Why would they come back again and then take nothing? Why?'

'For the record, I don't think they did. I think this was someone else.'

Jane shook her head.

'I'll be on to them in the morning. Nothing for you to do.'

'I'm at Bevham General all day. That'll keep my mind occupied.'

'Sure you should? It isn't business as usual. Your mother was murdered, Jane.'

'Thank you. I know what happened.'

As they went to the door, a car pulled up and unloaded a pile of young men, in various stages of abusive drunkenness. Two of them barged through into the café, the third was violently sick all over his own feet. A fourth swayed towards Simon and Jane.

'What you fuckin' starin' at?'

'That's enough,' Simon said quietly.

'Oh yeah? Enough, enough . . .' He spat hard.

Simon glanced back into the café. He could see the drunks, leaning over the counter, shouting, grabbing trays and food. There were a couple of women behind the counter, a teenage girl clearing tables.

'Take the keys, lock yourself into the car. I'll call a patrol. Go.'

Jane ran. Two of the men were still on the forecourt. Simon backed away, so that he could keep his eye on them while he used his phone. But now the driver of the car had parked and was walking towards him.

'Stay where you are, I'm a police officer. Stand still.'

'So fuck yourself, Blondie, who you telling to stand still, I ain't done anything, what've I fuckin' supposed to have done?'

'Driven a car while under the influence, for starters. I said, stay where you are.'

There was a scream from the café, then another. Simon swung round and in through the doors. One man was standing on a table, holding a chair up in the air, the other was leaning over the counter, gripping the wrist of the server. The only thing in Simon's favour was that they were drunk and all over the place and he was focused, but he was outnumbered, and the others would be inside at any moment.

He pressed the button on his mobile again, and issued another, urgent request, keeping his eye on the two men, barring the door to the others as best he could. The women were screaming and in the split second it took him to glance at the girl who was being held, the man with the chair jumped down and hurled it at Simon's head. He ducked but by now the man himself was lunging forward, fists going for Simon's face, foot up ready to kick into him.

There had been no one else in the café, but, as he warded off a blow with his arm, Simon saw a figure come forward in a rugby tackle and bring his attacker crashing down and yelping with pain as he hit the floor, his arm bent under him.

Seconds later, the forecourt was full of screeching tyres and spinning blue lights and the café full of uniform.

The man who had brought Simon's assailant down was brushing his coat sleeves. He was in his fifties with the build of a tank.

'Came from the Gents and heard the screaming. You OK?'

'I'm bloody glad you did. Thanks. You'll be needed as a witness. I'm a police officer by the way – not with this force. I was having a pit stop when it all kicked off. They'll take your details.'

Simon shook the man's hand. How rare, he thought, how almost unheard of for a member of the public to wade in instead of making a run for it. He deserved a commendation. Press recognition. A medal.

Jane was in his car, the doors locked, white as chalk. She let Simon in.

'I think I've had enough,' she said.

The roads were quiet and Simon drove fast. He had called

ahead to Cat and the spare room was ready. For half an hour, Jane slept. The phone woke her.

'Serrailler.'

It was the duty sergeant processing the drunken young men.

'Gentleman who stopped your attacker, sir – you get his name by any chance?'

'No. Didn't ask. Your mob showed up so I left everything to them.'

'Right.'

'Go on, don't tell me.'

'Well, apparently there was mayhem, and the bloke didn't wait. We got his car on the forecourt CCTV though.'

'Well, trace him through that.'

'We did. Car's registered to a Bishop Waterman.'

'Didn't look like a bishop.'

'He wasn't, that's the thing. Car was reported stolen *from* the Bishop a couple of days ago.'

'No wonder he didn't give me his name.'

'Some hero!'

'Look, Sergeant, I don't care if he's nicked a bus. So far as I'm concerned he stopped a fist before it hit my face.'

'We'll need a statement.'

'Goodnight, Sergeant.'

'When I was younger,' Jane said, 'my mother had a saying: kindness never pays. I hated it then and I hate it now – as if you do a kindness in order to be paid. Only the trouble is, and it's very, very annoying, it so often turns out to be true.'

'Do a good deed and it turns round and bites you?'

'Something does.'

'Right. We call it police work.'

'You drive very fast.'

'Sorry.' He eased his foot off the accelerator.

'I suppose you have automatic immunity.'

'No, not when I'm not on duty.'

'Will you take me home? I can't land on your sister.'

'She likes it.'

292

'I feel I'm losing myself in all of this.'

'No. You've had a series of appalling things happen. Let other people take the strain. What's wrong with that?'

'I do the strain-taking. I should.'

'Oh, for God's sake.'

'Yes.'

'I'm not sure about God. You'd better know that.'

'Why?'

'Not sure. Cat always has been – she says she couldn't do her job otherwise.'

'Not: why not God? Why had I better know it?'

He did not reply.

'I meet more people who are not sure about God than who are. I often meet them at the point where they start asking the question.'

'I'm not asking the question.'

'Fine. But I didn't become a priest to preach to the converted, though I suppose I do that most of the time.'

'You prefer being at the hospital to being in the cathedral?'

Jane leaned her head back wearily. 'I don't know, Simon. I honestly don't know if any of it is working out. I used to think I'd become a nun.'

'God Almighty.'

'Indeed.'

'I'm glad you changed your mind.'

'I don't know that I did.'

'You can't mean that?'

They were on the Lafferton bypass making for the Deerbons' farmhouse. Simon was aware that he had been driving too long. He thought he would make sure Jane was settled and then sleep on the sofa in the kitchen. He was too tired for another twenty-minute drive back into Lafferton.

'I go on retreat to a monastery twice a year. Sometimes I think I'll stay.'

He had nothing to say. The idea appalled him but too much had happened for him to feel safe to ask why. He turned into the farmhouse gateway. Lights were on upstairs and down. It was after two o'clock.

293

Chris was in the kitchen waiting for some milk to heat and upstairs Felix was crying.

'Hi. Bad night?'

'Bad night,' Simon said.

'You're Jane, I'm Chris. I've just come in.'

Ten minutes later Jane was upstairs talking to Cat who had resettled Felix. Chris had taken hot chocolate to them both.

'Whisky,' he said, coming back into the kitchen.

'Now you're talking. I'll kip on here if it's OK, I can't drive home.'

'Sure. Her mother died?'

'Surprised she made it to hospital, the injuries she sustained. I saw the DI on the case.'

'What's going on, Si? Patient of mine was murdered in her own garden and I was called out to the hospice tonight to a body in theirs. Bloke slit his wrists out there. Some poor woman whose husband had just died went out to get some air and found him.' Chris slumped on to the sofa. 'I've had it up to here.'

'Have a weekend off. Ma'll have the children.'

'She can't cope with Felix. Not sure she can cope with the others now, to be honest. We've been a bit concerned about her.'

'I need to go over there. I get so caught up. Bloody stupid. What's wrong?'

'Not sure. Cat wanted her to go for tests but she won't of course. I feel like heading off, Si.'

'Thought you were heading back into hospital life. You're just tired of being a GP.'

'Tired, period.'

There it came again, the threat Simon tried to ward off, that the new start would mean Australia. That and Jane Fitzroy's threat –

'You could have the camp bed in Sam's room,' Chris said getting up. 'Or I could put it in Cat's office.'

'I'm too tall for the camp bed and Sam wakes up at half past five.'

'See you then.'

Simon fetched the blanket and pillow from the playroom. He liked the kitchen. It was warm and it gave off a faint, comforting hum. The red light glowed from the dishwasher. After a couple of minutes, he heard the bump of the cat flap and felt Mephisto leap on to the sofa, curl into the small of his back, and settle down to purr.

Fifty-three

The noise was the worst thing. She wasn't bothered by the rest of it, only by the noise. Banging, rattling, shouting, clanging. Everything here was made of metal, everything made a racket. Plates and doors and staircases and corridors and keys. Nobody walked about without their footsteps sounding through your head, nobody spoke without their voice echoing round the iron stairwells. In the day it was bad but the nights were worse. Someone started shouting, another followed, someone else screamed, someone began to bang on a door. Then the footsteps and the keys and the shouting again. Ed had put her pillow over her head but it made no difference. She screwed toilet paper into plugs and stuffed them in her ears but the noises were still there, only hollow, like noises heard at the bottom of a well. Still heard though. Her breakfast had come. She'd eaten the toast and drunk the tea. Everything else was filth. Slime and filth and grease. But the toast was OK. More or less cold but OK.

Then the footsteps and the key.

'Morning, Ed.'

That was one thing. They'd asked what she wanted to be called and she'd said Ed and that had been that.

This one's name was Yvonne and she was like a sparrow, not much bigger than Ed. Her hair had a red streak down the side where she'd tried out a colour, she said, only thank God she had just done the one streak. 'What was I thinking?'

296

'How are you?'

Ed shrugged.

'Right, there's been a contact through the Prison Location Service. Your mother sent in a visitor's request.'

'I don't want to see her. I don't have to.'

'No. You don't have to, you have that right. Only – think about it, Ed. How's she feeling?'

'Haven't a clue.'

'Do you not get on with your mother?'

Ed shrugged again.

'Fell out?'

'Not exactly.'

'She's your mother though, and you've just got the one. She'd be a support, wouldn't she?'

'I don't need a support.'

'You sure about that?'

'What do you keep asking me things like that for?'

'Because most people in your situation need support . . . they need all the support they can get, ask me.'

'She isn't involved.'

'Looks like she wants to be.'

'Well, I've said, I don't want her. So I don't want to see her. Anyway, she's got other fish to fry.'

'You got sisters and brothers?'

'Nothing to do with you.'

Yvonne sighed. 'Gawd, you make life difficult.'

Silence.

'Not difficult for me, Ed, difficult for yourself. What are you so proud for?'

'The sausages are disgusting. Tell them I said so.'

'Right. I mean, right, your mother will be told via the PLS that you don't want contact, not right I'll put your complaint to the kitchens. You should be so lucky. Thing is though, Ed, she can write to you. She can't come and see you without your agreement, but wouldn't it be good to get a letter?'

'No.'

'Think about her.'

'You've said that once.'

'She'll have things she wants to say. Questions maybe.'

'She won't get answers. I told you, she's got other stuff . . . she got married again. Leave it there.'

'You don't get on with your stepfather then? Well, that's nothing unusual. Matter of fact, I don't much go for mine but he's made my mum happy. Think about it, Ed.'

'Can I go to the library?'

'Sure. Open at ten. I'll fetch you.'

'What do you have to fetch me for? Let me go on my own, for God's sake. What do you have to nanny me for? Bloody hell.'

Yvonne leaned against the wall and looked Ed full in the face for some moments, in silence.

She's OK, Ed thought. She's not soft, she's not clever, but she's OK. I could do worse for a minder.

The cleaning stuff was dropped in three times a week, mop and bucket, broom, duster and polish. She looked forward to it. She liked cleaning, liked making the place as good as she could get it, though never as good as her own house.

She didn't want to think of her own house but a picture was in her mind straight away and she couldn't get rid of it. In the end, she gave up trying and went round, room by room, looked at the furniture, the wallpaper, the cupboards, what was in the cupboards, the windows, the front path, the back garden, looked and looked until she thought she'd go mad.

She'd go back there of course. When they got her off, which they would because she knew and they knew and her brief more or less knew, that there wasn't the evidence. Not much evidence at all, except for taking the girl. She couldn't get out of that one and she wouldn't try. No point. 'Pleading guilty,' she'd said at the first interview. One kidnapping. But they had nothing else. Just a few specks in the car. But no bodies to link them with.

Ed closed her eyes so she could see her house more clearly. The garden was looking nice but the edges wanted straightening. She had a little cutter on the end of a long handle to do them. It made a really neat job. Kyra liked watching her do that, though she would never ever let Kyra have a go. Too dangerous.

'I can do it, Ed, I can, go on, let me do it, I've watched you lots of times, I can do it.'

But she might slice off her toe or anything, it wasn't safe. She wasn't going to take any chances with Kyra. Kyra was special. Precious. She would do anything at all to make sure nothing ever hurt Kyra. Nothing. Ever.

She didn't want to see anyone, not her mother, not Jan, not anyone. But if she could see Kyra, she'd jump at that. Would they let Kyra come with her mother? Ed didn't see why not. People had their kids to visit, Ed had heard them enough times on visiting afternoons. Why couldn't she ask to see Kyra? Natalie would have to bring her, that was why, and she wouldn't see Natalie. There wasn't anything wrong with Natalie, apart from being a sloppy mother, not good enough for Kyra. Natalie wasn't bad. But Ed wouldn't see her. Just Kyra.

She opened her eyes.

Of course they wouldn't let Kyra come.

The noise began again, buckets being dropped off outside every door, clang, clang, clang, then the brushes, against every door, bang, bang, bang. They went all the way along one side of the corridor, then all the way back down the other, before Ed's door was unlocked, and the fat woman shoved the bucket and mop and broom inside, without glancing in Ed's direction.

Bloody cheek. She was a remand prisoner, she wasn't someone they could treat like that, by ignoring her, by pretending she didn't exist. Yvonne wasn't like that. Yvonne knew her place OK. Ed thought she might have a word. They ought to speak to her, ought to be polite. She was on remand not convicted. She'd a right to be spoken to.

Later, she'd definitely complain about it. Definitely.

Fifty-four

Last time round, frothy coffee had come in shallow see-through cups and tasted of nothing. Now it came in a tall glass with a tall spoon and tasted strong. Dougie Meelup sat at a table towards the back of the café with the tall glass and the newspapers. Three newspapers. He had read one and a half from cover to cover, aside from Business, and all the sport, apart from golf, and if he stayed another half-hour or so he'd finish them all. Then he might get another paper and come back for a bit.

In the past couple of weeks he had spent as much time in the café as he had at home, during the day at least. Eileen had barely noticed. He was worried about it and it was driving him mad, both together. At first, she had spent every hour there was on the computer, learning how to work it and then beginning to look everything up, every word that had been written, it seemed, first about Weeny's case, then about the missing children. She had got Keith to buy her a printer and set it up, so then the printing-out had started, all day and into the night, chug chug churn churn, until the kitchen table was a white sea of paper and there were boxes of stuff printed out from the Internet all over the house.

'I have to do it, I have to find out and I have to under-stand, if I don't do that then I can't help sort it, Dougie.'

Then the papers had to be filed in the box files she had gone into town to buy. Then it had gone quiet while she had

300

read them through, painstakingly, every single one, occasionally making him listen to some of it out loud, asking him
what he thought. He found it hard to answer.

'I don't know, Eileen, it sounds too legal, it's all police talk,
I don't know.'

'You get used to it,' she had said, 'legal things and the
police talk. You get to see through it after a bit.'

Then she had started on the names and addresses, sheets
of them. And then the letters had begun. She was writing a
letter about Weeny to half the country, he thought, asking
Lord this and Sir that and Mr Justice whoever. He'd looked
at a few when she was in the bath. They were all the same,
asking for help with the case, asking for letters to be written,
asking how it could have happened that Weeny could have
been arrested for dreadful, terrible crimes she could not have
committed, asking for more names and addresses, more
people who would join her campaign, asking, asking, asking.
After a bit, the replies had started to come. Then she had
begun to telephone people, newspapers, police stations, MPs,
judges. Half the country. Half the world.

He got his own meals. She ate a banana or a packet of
biscuits or cut a chunk of cheese, and made tea. There were
tea mugs on every shelf, every window ledge. The sink was
full of empty tea mugs. He washed them up and put them
away and tidied the kitchen and went to the supermarket
and cooked and tried to get her to come to the table for a
meal and in the end gave up and sat down on his own. But
after a bit, he had taken to coming into the café and drinking
the tall glasses of frothy coffee, stirring three spoons of sugar
in each one with the tall spoons. He read the papers, tried
the crosswords, marked the racing columns, learned how to
do Word Wheels so that his score moved up from Fair to
Good and, once, Very Good.

His life had been turned upside down and he couldn't get
a purchase on what to do about it, how to get it back upright
again, how to help, how to bring Eileen to her senses. How.
How. He knew one thing. He wouldn't have said it aloud,
not to Eileen, not to anyone at all. But he knew. They didn't

301

arrest a person for terrible things like this without being sure. It wasn't like shoplifting, say, or pinching a purse. They didn't take someone in and have it official if it was a maybe, a look-alike, an educated guess.

He didn't know Weeny. She had been to see them once, called in, on her route, she'd said, brought a bunch of garage flowers, stopped for a cup of tea and a biscuit. A slip of a thing, dark hair, dark jacket, dark jeans. When she had gone, he had had the strange feeling that nobody had been there, no one he could pin down or remember, a nothing sort of person, a small, dark, fleeting shadow. She hadn't said a lot to him but what she had was perfectly nice, perfectly pleasant. But he didn't remember much of it. It was as though even her words hadn't been there, hadn't left any trace on the air, just breath which had evaporated, leaving no mark in his memory.

He looked down at the paper. Musselburgh 3.30. It was a choice between *Empire Gold* and *Miljahh*. Nothing to split the two. Perhaps he'd Dutch them, a fiver each. That would be around seven-pound profit whichever won. Was it worth walking to the bookies and standing in a queue for seven pounds, always assuming he was right and one of the two did win? The café was quiet. They had the back door behind the counter open on to the yard whch let in some air as well as the smell of dustbins.

The bookies would smell of sweat and smoke.

Eileen would be printing-out or click-clicking, her face close to the screen.

He felt a sudden drop down into despair. He wanted to ask someone what he could do, what he could say, how he could help, how he could support Eileen and at the same time get her out of this cage she was in, the cage of trying to prove what was unprovable, that Weeny's arrest was all a terrible error. It wasn't an error and he could never say that. She asked him over and over again what he thought, if he would write letters, and his tongue seemed to swell in his mouth because he could never answer, the right words were not there and the truth could not be spoken. He wished she hadn't

302

given up her job. She had said she needed all her time on what she had started to call her campaign. But he thought she might be afraid, too, afraid of someone knowing, pointing, whispering, telling, spreading words. He wandered out into the sunshine. The town was busy. He thought he would go to the bookies, place his bets, and then buy something for her, though he didn't know what, or even if she would notice.

The price on *Miljahh* was a lot better than he'd expected, 100–30 instead of 7–4, so he had ten pounds instead of five and watched it win by a length on the bridle which ought to have cheered him but somehow didn't. He went out and sat on a bollard in the sun and wondered what to buy Eileen. Flowers. Chocolates, which she'd always liked. But he knew she'd ignore the flowers and leave the chocolates unopened.

He went back to the car and began to drive towards the roundabout and home, but instead he took the first exit, almost without knowing he was doing it.

Leah was in the garden, rearranging the little lights she had planted, on the path, up the rockery, in the trees. Dougie had sometimes wondered if the lights were something to do with her religion but never liked to ask. She clambered down from rehanging one when she heard the gate.

Dougie Meelup would never have said he was a prejudiced man, never one so much as to notice the colour of anyone's skin. Human was human, even if it wasn't always easy to get on with everyone. But when Keith had said he was marrying a Filipino girl, he'd been concerned. Everything was different, wasn't it, not just the colour of your skin, everything, the way she'd been brought up, her education, her family, her religion, food, weather, clothes, customs. Everything. 'How's she going to like it? That's what worries me. It's everything new, everything different, and a husband as well. What if she isn't happy? You couldn't blame her, but what would you do? Burning her boats, coming to live here, it's a big step, and if it goes wrong, what will you do?'

But it hadn't gone wrong. It had gone right from day one. Leah had never been away from her country but her English would do and soon got better and nothing else had seemed to matter. It was as if she'd been born to come here, Dougie thought, even though she had Filipino friends and met up with them quite a lot and emailed everyone at home now. He'd never asked Keith how they had met but Keith had always been a wanderer, always off with a backpack some- where or other, so he'd supposed they'd met in a bar or on a beach or even an aeroplane.

'Internet,' Keith had said, laughing his head off. 'Internet dating agency for English blokes to find Filipino girls.' And gone on laughing at the look on Dougie's face.

'Hey, you here, that's great, Dougie, I'll make a cold drink or you want tea as usual?'

Always the same, he thought, always offering something, a drink or food and the best chair the minute anyone arrived. Like now, she was whipping into the shed, pulling out the deckchair, setting it up in the shade, brushing it down with the corner of her skirt.

'Hey, this is so nice, you sit here now, Dougie, tell me what drink you want.'

It had been the right thing to do. The right place.

'Keith is out, you know of course, you don't expect to see him this time of day, but that's all fine, if you want just to see me.'

Dougie sat down. He had to sit down. If he didn't, he would offend her.

'You want cold drink or tea now?'

'A cup of tea would be just the ticket. Thanks, Leah.'

'No problem, only few minutes.'

And she was off, quick as a flash, into the kitchen.

The garden was like the house, bright and tidy as a new pin. Leah had never before had any such thing as a garden and she had taken to it with spirit, filling the beds and the hanging baskets and the windowboxes with flowers in as many vivid colours as she could and the rest of it with the little lanterns. Every evening from spring until autumn when it wasn't raining, she went round lighting the candles inside the lamps.

Dougie closed his eyes. He had to say it, all of it, had to tell the whole story and think aloud about what to do and Leah would listen and not speak, not judge, not admonish.

The tea came on a tray with the best cups and a fresh cake. He knew better now than to offer to help her with anything.

'This is really, really nice, you know?' she said, smiling, handing him the tea. But her eyes were questioning.

Dougie took a bite of sponge cake, ate it slowly so that she saw him savouring it, drinking the tea before he set down his cup and said, 'It's Eileen. Something dreadful is happening, Leah. I don't know what to do. I'm about at the end of trying to work it out.'

Fifty-five

'Hi.'

Ed didn't look up.

'I'm Kath. I get called Reddy.'

The woman sat down next to her on the bench.

There was a badminton game going on. Ed had thought about asking to play, but in the end it saved the hassle to sit on the bench watching. It was the second time she'd been out among some of the others. Presumably they'd decided she wasn't going to run amok.

'I know who you are.'

Ed moved along the bench a bit. The woman moved after her.

'We get to see the telly, get to see the papers. No probs. Edwina Sleightholme.'

'Ed,' she said. It was automatic.

'You're shit paper.'

Ed stood up.

'Come on, Linda, slam it at her, slam it at her.'

Ed began to slide along the wall at the back of the sports hall. She hadn't wanted to mix, she'd said so, she preferred being on her own.

'Yaay.' A cheer went up.

Ed slid nearer to the door. She would go back and read.

There was a push for the doors as the game was over. The woman called Reddy was there first, up against Ed. 'Scum.'

Ed felt the pressure of something bullet hard in her lower back. The push to get out of the doors was getting worse and the pressure became a sudden excruciating pain that made her giddy.

The push freed like a cork out of a bottle as everyone burst out into the corridor.

'All right, all right, stop pushing and shoving, what's the matter with you? Haven't you heard about queues? Let's have some order or someone will get hurt.'

Ed turned round but everyone was scattering. She couldn't even see Reddy's back. She made it halfway up the iron stairs in the midst of the clatter, then passed out.

Ed was never sick and she wasn't going to start now.

'I'm not seeing a doctor. I was hot.'

'Really? Can you walk there?'

'I don't need to see the bloody doctor.'

'Ed, you don't have any choice here. You fainted, you see the MO. It's not like out there, it's the rules. You OK to walk?'

She didn't say no, that the pain in her back was still a molten poker stuck in her. Walking made the poker twist about. She clenched her fists and made herself stand upright.

She wasn't bothered about being with other people. She'd rather be on her own, but she did want to be able to go about, outside, to the sports hall and the library, not be stuck in her room twenty-four/seven.

'You sure you're all right?'

'I said.'

The poker was twisting the other way now but she wasn't going to say. Provided the doctor didn't want to strip her and go over every inch, she was all right, she'd get some painkillers for an invented headache, they'd do.

The walk along the last corridor to the end was the worst she'd ever taken. The poker was being pushed forward, twisted one way, twisted the other, pulled out and pushed in again. She made it because she made herself make it but it was close.

*

307

The MO had the sort of spectacles Ed hated, rimless and oval, and when she looked up she failed to smile. Ed wanted to scream at her. I'm remand, I'm not banged up, you smile at me.

'Good evening.'

Ed said nothing. Why should she?

'I hear you fainted just now.'

'Sort of.'

'Well, they had to pick you up.'

'It was hot.'

'Is that something you're usually affected by – being hot?'

Ed shrugged.

'When did you last eat?'

'Tea.'

'When did you last see your GP?'

'Never. I'm never ill.'

'Right. Periods normal?'

'Yes.'

'Have you a period now?'

'No.'

'Your medical on admission was all normal by the looks of things. You're not on any medication. Right, we'd better take a look at you.'

'I've had a headache all day. I need something for that, then I'll be fine.'

'I'll examine you first. Bad headache?'

Ed shrugged.

'Do you get many headaches?'

'No. I said, it was hot.'

'Fine. Go behind the screen and strip to your bra and pants please.'

'I said, I'm OK, I didn't need to come here.'

'Are you refusing to strip?'

'Yes.'

The woman sighed. 'All right, but I need to take your blood pressure. Low BP can cause you to faint. Would that be acceptable to you? If so, I'd like you to roll up your sleeve please.'

While she was pumping up the cuff on Ed's arm, the doctor looked away from her and out of the window.

'That's fine. Perfectly normal. Put your head back, I want to look into your eyes.' The light probed. The pain in her lower back was steady and still and red-hot. But at least the poker wasn't twisting now.

She clicked off the torch. 'Fine. I can't find anything wrong.'

'I said. It was hot.'

'Yes. I'll prescribe you some paracetamol for the headache. Drink plenty of water. If you get dehydrated that won't help the headache or the faintness. If it happens again I'll do a blood test.'

She pressed the button on her desk for the warder. At least she'd waited outside the door. Ed followed her out.

'Good evening,' the doctor said. It was sarcastic. Ed didn't bother to reply.

Walking back was a nightmare again. The poker started to twist and dig the minute she moved. The doctor had given her four paracetamol tablets, two now, two in four hours if she needed them. Four bloody tablets. She needed forty for a pain like this.

'You want to watch the film? It's *Notting Hill*.'

'No.'

'Great film. I've seen it three times.'

More fool you, Ed thought. It wasn't her sort of film.

A memory slipped through a side door into her head, of sitting on the sofa with Kyra watching *James and the Giant Peach*. They'd loved it. Kyra had wanted it to go round again but it wasn't a video so of course it hadn't. Everything was there, in detail, in colour, the room, her plants on the window ledge, the ornaments, the leather of the sofa, the curtains, carpet, wallpaper. Kyra.

'Here are your tablets, take two, get a drink of water with them. Have a lie-down, why don't you?'

Ed swallowed the white pills and drank two glasses of water. She was sweating now with the pain, and as soon as she had swallowed the tablets she felt sick. The pain was worse. Even lying down, it made her feel as if she was fainting. After half an hour the edge of it was only blurred so she took a third tablet and after that she slept until someone started banging at one in the morning, banging something hard and heavy on a door, which went through her skull and down her spine into her back and banged there.

She took the fourth tablet but they slid the grille back every hour to check on her, so that every hour she was woken. It was only around dawn that the pain finally dulled.

Fifty-six

'Sam, stop it. How many times have I told you . . . don't wind her up. You just make everything worse. Go and see if there are any eggs.'

'I went and there weren't.'

'Go and read.'

'I've read all my books.'

'Well, read one of them again.'

Sam gave her a pitying look and trailed outside, scraping his feet as he went.

'Do they have to make such a noise? I'm trying to read the paper,' Chris said.

'Bully for you.'

'Sorry, but you weren't up half the night.'

'Actually, I *was* up half the night, with Felix.'

'Not the same.'

'Well, don't worry, any minute now you won't be on night call ever again. When the new system comes into operation, you can sleep – I'd say like a baby, only I never knew a baby that slept – you can sleep and if you think that's fine and dandy, fine and dandy.'

Chris lowered the paper. 'I don't want to have a boring political row about health directives. It's Saturday afternoon, it's warm and sunny and I am trying to forget about anything to do with medicine, the NHS, night calls, day calls, patients, surgeries –'

'You think I do want a row about all of that? You think it's my favourite way of spending a fun weekend?'

'Mummy, Sam's thrown my Rapunzel Barbie into the hen muck.'

Cat closed her eyes. 'You think I don't understand but I do. I honestly do.'

'Right.'

'God, you're so bloody male. Listen, it's not you, it's the system. You know how it used to be. When Mum and Dad were practising, doctors could start in hospital, go into general practice, then slide back into some sort of part-time hospital consultancy – it made for better doctors. It certainly made for more all-round doctors. But it just isn't possible now. Or rather, it is but –'

'I'm too old. I've been told that quite a lot lately.'

'If you want to do it, I've said, I'll back you.'

'Forget it.'

Chris was angry, his pride was hurt, he was frustrated. Cat knew it, and minded. She also minded his reaction. He wanted to leave general practice and retrain so that he could work in hospital psychiatry and he had found out that the only way he could do it would be to start over as an SHO, on roughly a quarter of his present salary, and try to move up. He was forty-one. Ten years?

'I hate you being unhappy. No one ought to feel like this. Just because I don't, doesn't mean I can't sympathise.'

'So you keep saying.'

'Mummy . . .' Hannah came roaring across the grass towards them, furious tears streaming down her face, her hands filthy.

Cat got up. 'OK, if he really did throw Barbie in the hen muck, he's for a roasting. But if it was because of something you did to him or said to him, Hannah, you're for frying. Come on.'

Chris watched them march off, his wife, his daughter, Cat feisty, straight, fair-minded, Hannah less so. Hannah was what Sam called a wimp. He turned back to the paper, then thought better and went into the house. Ten minutes later,

Sam and Hannah were both in their rooms, banned from re-emerging for half an hour, and Chris had made a jug of iced coffee and brought it out to the garden, where Cat had taken over the paper.

'What are we thinking?' she said, looking up.

'Why?'

'Max Jameson.'

'Yes.'

The inquest had been opened and adjourned for further reports but it was clear that the verdict would be suicide. There were no suspicious circumstances. Max had lain down on a bench in the garden of the hospice and slit his wrists and his body had eventually rolled off, on to the grass. The police report was incomplete. Cat had given a statement and might be called on by the coroner. She sat staring down at the newspaper, at the photograph of Max, her eyes full of tears.

Chris put out his hand to her.

'We mustn't quarrel. Anything can happen. I'll tell the kids they can come down.'

'Oh no. They were both being brats, they can cool off.'

'Thanks for making this. And I do mean it – about work.'

'I know. But it would put too big a burden on you, and if I failed, it would be very hard to get back into general practice. Forget it. Only . . .' She knew what he was going to say. 'Would you think about taking three months off? Paying someone to take over for the whole of that time?'

'Australia?'

'The children are still young enough to have that time out of school but this will be the last year we can do it. They'd have the trip of a lifetime and we'd recharge our batteries.'

'Six would be better.'

'Six?'

'Months. If we're going to do it at all. They could go to school in Oz, come to that.'

'Do you mean this?'

Cat poured more coffee and sat back, thinking. Six months away from everything was not the point for her, but it was

313

for Chris. But six months travelling, living in Sydney, giving the children a taste of a different world; six months. If the farmhouse went with the practice, it might be easier to get people to take it over. House, car, pony, chickens.

'Simon,' she said aloud.

Chris groaned.

'Mum and Dad.'

'There's always going to be someone.'

'Six months is nothing in terms of anyone except them.'

'How long does it take to fly home from Australia?'

'I know. You're right. Of course you're right.'

'Try harder.'

Cat laughed. 'OK,' she said. 'Deal. Start looking.'

'Oh, I already have.' He got up and ran.

Fifty-seven

The sands were almost empty. In the far distance, a family played a late game of beach cricket. Beside the railings on the south shore, two young men were stacking up the last of the deckchairs. The sea was far out, the sand at the edge flat and shining. It had been hot again, too hot. This was the best part of the day. Soon the foreshore lights would come on.

Gordon Prior walked along the beach, away from the town. He often went three or four miles in this direction. It was always deserted, he saw no one. It wouldn't be dark yet.

His black-and-white sheepdog scurried along the edge of the water, skirting the ripples of the waves, making a line of pockmarks which vanished behind him as he ran. Then he stopped and waited. Gordon teased him with the ball, feigning a throw this way, then that, once into the sea, once back the way they had just come. Buddy waited. He knew.

'Go for it!' The ball sailed into the air. Buddy ran, sending up a little flurry of water.

Five seconds and he was back. The ball lay at Gordon's feet. Buddy waited, quivering. This time there was no tease, Gordon threw, hard and far. Buddy raced away.

Gordon stood and looked out to sea. A tanker was on the horizon, a painted ship on a painted ocean, seeming absolutely still. He had lived here all his life and had never had the chance to enjoy it as he did now, morning and evening, bringing the dog down here, had never appreciated what was under his nose because he had not had the time to look. He was sixty-six. He hoped he had another twenty years of it.

He looked round. Buddy was nowhere. Gordon whistled. Back towards the town, far away and out of sight, the game of cricket would be over. The deckchairs would be stacked and covered. He began to walk away from the sea towards the rocks and the caves and the cliff, whistling all the time.

It happened. The ball would be lodged in a crevice or a rock pool too deep for Buddy to retrieve it. After a few minutes, Gordon heard the dog bark. At first, it was difficult to place where the sound came from. Gordon reached the rocks and threaded his way in and out of them, calling and whistling, taking care not to slip on the drapes of vivid green seaweed.

The barking grew more demanding and eventually he traced it to one of the caves that went back into the cliff. He stood at the mouth of it calling but the dog didn't emerge. Sighing, Gordon went in. It was dark, probably too dark to find the ball, wherever it was stuck. He waited a moment to let his eyes get used to it, then went further in to where the dog was crouched, looking up and barking furiously. The ball had somehow bounced up, then, and was on a ledge in the rock at the back of the cave. Gordon hesitated. If he could not reach it by stretching, he was not about to start climbing up there on his own over slippery rocks in the semi-dark. They would go home without the blasted ball. He pulled Buddy's lead out of his pocket.

But the ledge was just within reach. Gordon stretched up and felt about with the flat of his hand for the ball. At his feet, Buddy went frantic, leaping and barking.

'All right, calm down, how did the flaming ball get up here anyway? Buddy, shut up.' Each bark hit the roof and walls of the cave and bounced back double. 'For goodness' sake, Buddy.'

He felt about again and then his hand touched something. Not the ball. Gordon shuffled it forward to the edge. He could barely see. Only feel. He closed his finger and thumb over something cold and hard and pencil-thin. A stick or a twig. He edged his finger and thumb higher, to the top, where the straightness gave way to roundness and the thinness to a smooth knob. Gordon stopped moving his finger and thumb and let them rest. Buddy had stopped barking now and began to whimper.

It took half an hour to get back to the foreshore road where he'd parked the car. He ran but not as fast as he wanted to run. The dog was on the lead but kept dragging back, wanting to return, alternately barking and whimpering.

It was almost dark. The beach was empty but the cafés and arcades along the foreshore were open and busy, the smell of fish and chips and beer and hot candyfloss steaming out of the neon-lit doorways under the strings of lights.

At the entrance to an amusement arcade a waxwork clown opened its mouth and cackled with loud artificial laughter.

Gordon got to the car, pushed the dog on to the passenger seat and drove, away from the beach and the lights and the foreshore, faster than he ever usually drove, in search of someone to tell, someone who would know what to do and take the whole thing away from him.

Fifty-eight

'Waste of time,' DC Joe Carmody said, banging his way out of the Gents.

'Forensics'll get something.'

'Don't make me laugh. Flamin' wild-goose chase, same as usual. Only one answer.'

'Which you can keep to yourself.'

'Make it legal.'

'I said shut it. Not in here.'

They walked through the small department store towards the manager's office at the back of the ground-floor showroom. The man had been almost hysterical when phoning to say traces of cocaine had been found on a shelf in the Gents. Nathan had gone in with the aim of calming him down by taking the find seriously, in spite of knowing that coke was sniffed in any number of toilets, in stores and other public buildings all over the district. Joe Carmody's attitude in front of the man had been openly cynical.

'You're not chucking a load of bull at this, Nathe? Tell me you're takin' the piss.'

Nathan dodged round a stand of duvets and turned. 'I said shut it. We take this as serious as we take any other reported case of drugs – coke, spliff, whatever . . . every needle find and every little speck of white powder. We have zero tolerance, right? There's kids in this town deserve better than scum selling stuff to them before they're into secondary school, so you do your job and keep your opinions to yourself.'

'Whatever.'

'And no bright ideas in the bloke's office, he's aerated enough.'

'He wants to get out more.'

They had reached the door when Nathan's mobile rang.

'OK, you wait here.'

'I can sort him, don't need my hand holding.'

'That's exactly what you bloody need. I said wait.'

Walking quickly out to the street where he could get a signal, Nathan cursed Joe Carmody. In spite of his reports to the DCI, Carmody had been taken on at Lafferton for a further six months. 'Very nice,' Carmody had said with a grin. 'Feet under the table or what?' To him it seemed an easy berth. Nathan knew he would be proved wrong but his own frustration was growing, and in the past few days he had realised that it wasn't basically to do with Joe Carmody. Carmody was a flea.

He reached the street and dialled back. 'Guv?'

'Where are you, Nathan?'

'Outside Toddy's . . .'

'You short of work or what?'

'I wasn't sending DC Carmody on his own, guv, he ent safe.'

'Oh, grow up, Nathan. Get over it. And get back here. We're going to Yorkshire.'

Fifty-nine

'Come in, Jane.' Geoffrey Peach came round his desk and took her hand in both of his. He had got back from his holiday in Sweden, where his wife came from, late the previous night. Now it was just after eight thirty, Jane was the first person in his study. 'My dear, I can't begin to tell you how sorry I am. It is absolutely appalling. To have a parent die is always hard but to have this . . . Is there any news from the police?'

'Not yet.'

'And what about you, Jane? I'm concerned.'

She leaned her head back in the armchair and looked around the comfortable room. Books. Papers. Pictures. A small table with a cross and a kneeler in front of it. Photographs, of children and grandchildren, of weddings and christenings, of Swedish lakes and mountains, of small dogs and large horses. In its quiet and peaceful atmosphere, its sense of love and prayer, the room seemed to be an extension of the cathedral itself. It would be easy to lie back and absorb it all, let it wash over her and seep into her and bring its own steady healing. Easy.

'Whatever you want – whatever seems the right thing to do. Tell me.'

She looked at Geoffrey. Tall. Rather awkwardly tall. Angular. Bony features. Deep-set eyes. She respected him and liked him. She had wanted to be here, to work with this Dean, above anything else. Now?

320

'Too much has happened to you in so short a time. You need to step back.'

'More than that,' Jane said. 'Geoffrey, I don't think I can stay here. I don't think this is the right place for me.'

He shook his head. 'That's how you feel now. But it would be a decision made in haste and out of shock. A reactive decision. They're never the best, as I'm sure you know.'

'I do. But this is not because of everything that's happened . . . Max Jameson, my mother . . . I thought this was the place I should come to. I wanted it to be. But it isn't. I am not right for the cathedral, for Lafferton – and they're not right for me. That would be true even if none of the other things had happened. I'm sorry. I am so sorry, Geoffrey.'

There was a long silence. Somewhere, a door closed. Another. Silence again.

'I won't insult you by asking if you have thought about this carefully, and prayed about it. Clearly you have. I wouldn't expect anything else. But if you feel Lafferton is not right for you, then what are you thinking of doing? What *would* seem to be the right place? It's easy to go – it's where to that takes some working out.'

He was right and Jane knew it.

'Can I ask your advice?'

'If I can help you, of course I will. I may be able to see things with a small amount of detachment. But it is small, Jane – I want you here, I value you and I don't want you to leave us. I don't think you should leave us. So don't expect an impartial judgement.'

'That means a lot. Thank you.'

'It is sincerely meant, as I hope you understand.'

'Yes. Maybe someone else in my shoes would run away – I mean a long way away. Try to work in the Third World or something. I wish I could be that sort of person but I don't think I am. And anyway, the Third World deserves the best, not our rejects.'

'You are most certainly not a reject.'

'I think I'm rejecting myself.'

'Dangerous.'

'There are two things I'm drawn to. You know I've spent some time on retreat in a monastery – St Joseph's nuns prefer to call it that rather than a convent. But OK, monastery, convent, whichever. I would like to go back for longer. If they'd have me.'

Geoffrey Peach frowned. 'And the other idea?'

'To go back to academic work for a year or two. I loved doing my theology degree, I loved doing the master's. I miss that very much and I'd like to find a way of going back and doing a doctorate. There are areas I want to investigate in more depth. I'd have to combine it with a job, I know . . . a part-time curacy, something like that?'

'Forgive me, Jane – but you don't seem to me to have worked this through yet. Possibly a retreat into conventual life, possibly a higher degree, possibly combined with something or other . . . You are not convincing me.'

'I'm not sure I'm convincing myself yet. It isn't clear.'

'No.'

'Are you thinking I might be jumping out of the frying pan?'

'I hesitate to think of the Cathedral Church of St Michael as a frying pan . . . You need more time. Rushing into anything is usually a mistake. Except perhaps marriage. I rushed into that after knowing Inga for three weeks. Take six months off and have a complete career break. Don't do anything or go anywhere, apart from a holiday maybe. But you'll need to be in London some of the time presumably, while the police sort out your mother's affairs. Could you find a bolt-hole somewhere and use the time to read and think and pray? And just recover, Jane. You need to recover.'

'I don't know. I suppose there'll be some money from my mother's estate and then the house. But that could take a long time.'

'There are ways and means. Let me investigate. I am very serious in advising you not to make any life-changing decision at the moment.' He stood up. 'I know there'll be some coffee brewing. We'll go and find it after we've said a prayer together. Relax and be quiet for a moment.'

322

Jane closed her eyes. Let go, she thought. Trust. All will be well.

'Lord, bring peace and calm of mind to Your servant Jane. Pour down on her Your healing grace and love . . .'

She tried to focus on the voice of the Dean and on his prayer to steer her out of her darkness and confusion, which seemed to have gathered and deepened until it was shrouding her and keeping out everything that was clear and hopeful.

Sixty

Simon.

I am not going to try to speak to you, to see you or even to leave messages on your various machines. It is much the best for me if I write this and if it is not best for you, then forgive me, but I don't intend to take that into account. However, it would be churlish not to tell you what is happening after the good times we had together, churlish and unkind. Whether it will even be of interest to you is not for me to know, and whether you respond or not is up to you.

As you know, I sold the restaurants and have been casting about for a new investment. Casting about for a future, too, as I had for a long time hoped there would be one for me with you. But I'm pretty clear now that you at least never intended any such thing.

Through a company in the City I met someone who has properties in France and through him I have bought a pair of hotels in a hilltop area beyond Moissac. One is inside the walls of a medieval village, one in a wonderful situation nearby. They are run-down and need a lot of investment as well as time and loving attention. I have bought a cottage between them, in a small market town, from where I will organise the complete refurbishment of both hotels over the course of the next year. The plan is to open the one in the walled village first, and the second in the following season.

I have sold the flat. I have burned my boats, Simon.

The friend through whom I found the hotels, Robert Cairns, will come with me and will take over some of the business side of the venture. At present that is all he is – a friend. I like him, I enjoy his company. So who knows? But he is a good deal older than me and, besides, I am not ready for anyone else yet and will not be for some time. It is all too raw. For that I blame you. I blame you for a lot of things but I hope I can come to stop blaming you in time and to remember the pleasure and the fun and none of the pain.

I am determined to make this venture work and I am very excited about it. I know the hotels will be a success. I am good at my job. It is a completely fresh start. Please wish me well. There is no reason for you not to. There's every reason why I should wish you ill but that would be petty and small-minded and so I do the very opposite.

All love, still,

Diana

When I am settled, cards with addresses etc. will wing their way to you.

Sixty-one

The sun hit the surface of the sea and broke it into a million gold splinters. The beach shone like glass. It was seven o'clock.

The teams clambered out of three police Land-Rovers which had driven up as near to the cliff as they could get. Serrailler and Nathan Coates were in the front with Jim Chapman. The third vehicle had brought the forensics team.

'Right – this is some distance from where you followed Sleightholme, Simon . . . couple of miles. The cliffs all along this bit of the coast are riddled with caves and we've concentrated on those nearer to the scene of the arrest. But the plan has always been a painstaking search of as many as possible, though some are so inaccessible there would be no point – if we can't reach them, she couldn't – and of course we're hampered by access being only at low tide.'

The area of the caves for half a mile along the cliff was cordoned off with black-and-yellow tape. Chapman turned and began to walk steadily towards one on the left, the others following. Behind them, the forensics team were putting on what Simon always thought of as the suits of death.

At the entrance, Chapman stopped. 'Prior, the man walking his dog, had chucked the ball hard and it must have bounced several times off the rocks into here and then again up on to the ledge. Blind chance. The dog scuttled in after it, tried to jump up and started whining and fussing

. . . not sure whether it was because of the lost ball or because of what else it was sensing. By the time a local team got down here it was getting dark and the tide had turned, but we managed to get lights in and the cordon, and take a quick look. Today we've got scaffolding and platforms so forensics can work until the tide gets too close. Then they have to retreat and wait. It's frustrating but they'll need to scour this place and it could take days. Longer. Depends. Right, let's get in.'

They had flashlights and the team would set up a generator and cables but, because the sea half filled the cave twice in every twenty-four hours, equipment had to be hauled above the water level and would take some time to be up and running. For now, they had to rely on half a dozen high-powered beams carried by hand.

Jim Chapman went to the back of the cave, ducking his head. He flashed his torch along the wall for a second or two, then held it steady.

'There. The dog was crouching just where you're standing, Simon.'

'I'll climb up,' Serrailler said.

'Thought you might. We'll light you.'

The cave had filled up with the forensics and their gear, but now they stood watching the DCI as he hauled himself up on to the wooden platform wedged into the scaffolding. There was a muffled echo round the dank walls every time anyone moved or spoke.

The cold and seaweed smell came off the rock into his face as he edged his way, bent almost double, along the ledge. To his surprise he found that it went quite far back. He pulled his flashlight out of his belt and switched it on. The hollow black mouth flared in front of him.

'There's the space of half a room going back into the cliff,' he shouted down. 'Not sure I can get into it though, I'm too tall.'

'Sleightholme's not tall,' Chapman said.

It was not only the smell of the salt seaweed and the cold that came into Simon's face now. The sense of what had happened here overcame him in a wave. Anger. Nausea. An immense sadness.

He moved along towards the mouth of the cave at the back, until he could let the beam from his torch light up the interior.

There were four on the ledge, and more, he was sure, further back in the hollow in the rock, the cave within the cave. Four small skeletons, four silent, pale groups of bones. He closed his eyes for a moment. He was not like his sister. He didn't feel moved to pray every time he came upon a dead body, someone murdered, someone who had suffered an appalling end. But now, the only response he had was some sort of prayer.

'Four here that I can see,' he called down. 'I think there'll be others further back. No, hang on . . . there's another ledge . . . just suspended above this one. I'm going to climb up a bit further, see if I can see.'

No one told him to be careful. No one said anything. His light wavered and swerved against the black rock as he got a foothold and then hauled himself a few feet higher. He moved the torch. Reached out his hand and felt forward carefully.

'Dear God,' he said. 'This is a deep ledge. Goes way back.'

He saw more skeletons, lying close together. The arms of one were folded, the arms of another up over the face.

His lamp went out suddenly, leaving him staring into blackness.

They came out into the brilliant sunlight and blue skies of a perfect morning and stood in silence, looking at the sea. Then, after a moment, they began to walk away from the cave and the blackness and the heaps of small bones, towards the waterline at the far end of the flat, shining sand. Simon took deep breaths of air as if he were pumping life itself into his lungs and veins, along with the oxygen. Behind, the men in the death suits were taking in equipment. They had a few hours in which to work before they had to abandon the caves to the tide again.

'The stench of evil,' Jim Chapman said.

Simon nodded, remembering the last time he had been in a confined space with it, when he and Nathan Coates had broken into the unit used as a morgue by the Lafferton serial killer. He had had the same desperate need to get out, into the air, into the light, and the world of normality.

They reached the tideline. The sea was very calm, tiny wavelets folding over and over back upon themselves, frilled with cream foam. The sky was silver at the horizon.

'How many don't we know about?' Chapman said at last. 'God Almighty. Who's interviewing her this time? Me? You? Half the forces in the country?'

'She won't talk.'

'Happen.' He looked round. 'Haven't had a peep out of you, DS Coates.'

'Sir.'

'Upsetting.'

'Right. We're having a baby. Me and Em. Brought it home, this has.'

'No good telling you not to let it get to you. Things like this – they get to you. Have to or you'd not stay human.'

'Sleightholme ent bloody human. Not any human I recognise.'

'*If* it is her. *If* they're connected. Let's not run off with t'ball.'

They weren't fooled. He had to say it, and they had to think it, and it meant nothing.

A woman was coming towards them with a pair of Labradors, all three of them splashing through the water. Simon bent down and picked up a piece of driftwood. When the dogs got nearer he threw it. They raced, plunging into the calm sea, mouths open and barking with excitement. The woman hesitated.

'What's going on?' She pointed towards the cars and the tape.

Chapman's ID card was ready. 'Best go back from here,' he said, 'you'll get turned round anyway.'

'But what is it, what's happened? Has there been some sort of accident?'

Serrailler and Nathan left him to it, and began to walk away from the sea, back towards the cars.

329

'You all right?'

'Guv. Just makes you think. Bloody hell.' He shook his head. 'What'd you want to come for, guv?'

'Our case.'

'Only one of them. Only one of them was our case.'

They reached the Land-Rover and stood waiting for Chapman.

'Thought it was, like, a courtesy. Did he *expect* you to come up?'

'He did.'

He had. 'You'll want to be here,' Jim Chapman had said. 'You'll want to go in.' The courtesy – if that's what it was, to the DCI from another investigating force – would always have been extended, but this was more. For Serrailler, from the day David Angus had disappeared, this had been personal. He had needed to be in on the end of it. Was this the end? Ed Sleightholme would be interviewed again, by him, by Jim Chapman. She might even be brought here. Were there other places? Hiding places? Burial sites? He knew he would have to leave most of it to others. All he wanted was to have final identification of David Angus and to see Sleightholme go down for that. It would take a long time and he would be involved in different cases. But until it happened he would not be able to close this particular case, in his own mind.

Later, driving back down the motorway, Nathan said, 'There's a job going.'

'With Chapman?'

'Only he'll be retired come Christmas. There'll be a big reshuffle. Vacancy for a DI. Moors area.'

'And?'

'Wondered what you thought, guv.'

'If you want to move up you'll have to move on. Long way of course.'

'Tell the truth, guv, I've had it for now where I am.'

'DC Carmody? Come on, Nathan.'

'Nah, I can sort him before breakfast. Only, Em and me've wanted to get into the country more. This'd be a chance.'

'Think you've got enough experience as a sergeant under your belt?'

'Dunno. Reckon Chapman wouldn't have mentioned it though. Does that mean you wouldn't back me, guv?'

'No. It's up to you. If you think you're ready and it's where you'd like to be, go for it and I'll back you.'

'Yessss,' Nathan said quietly, thumping his fist into the other open palm. 'Thanks.'

'Good luck.'

He meant it. He knew Nathan ought to move. He was going up the ladder and he was going to do well. He deserved to and anybody who turned him down would live to regret it. He told himself all of it as he drove down the last stretch of motorway towards home. But he felt a sudden pang of regret, not only for the young detective he had nursed and promoted and with whom he had gone through some tough days. He regretted something else, something of his younger self that he saw going away together with Nathan Coates.

He felt old. Today had not helped. The small piles of bones lying on the cold rock shelves had not been out of his mind since the morning. Perhaps they never would be.

He felt things begin to slide away from under him, like the tide going out and leaving him on the beach.

Sixty-two

It was years since anyone had delivered newspapers to Hallam House. Instead, the post office in the village a mile away received a consignment every morning and it was then up to people with regular orders to collect their own. Since his retirement Richard Serrailler's life had been carefully and clearly structured and the walk to the post office in all weathers was a fixed part of his routine. He set off at nine after his bath and breakfast. He had seen too many of his colleagues retire into a cloudy sky of vague, drifting days without point or purpose, the only exercise they took being on the golf course before and after too much lunchtime gin.

He went to the drawing-room windows which were open on to the garden. A branch of the rose New Dawn which climbed up the side wall had bent forwards under its own weight, come away from its supporting wires, and was blocking the path. Meriel was working in the long border, clearing out and dead-heading.

'I'm going for the papers. Don't try and shift that branch on your own.'

She waved.

'Do you hear me?'

'Perfectly, thank you.'

'I'll get the axe to it later.'

'Good.'

He watched her long back, as she bent down to pull up

some groundsel. She was still wearing her cotton housecoat over the usual green wellington boots. She had never been especially interested in the garden during her years at the hospital and when the children were young – it was there as a background, a place for them to play and her to sit occasionally, the grass mowed and the edges cut by someone from the village. But with retirement had come a sudden passion, first to have the garden redesigned and planted, then to spend what seemed to be every waking moment fiddling with it, no matter what the season. Since Martha's death she had been out there even more.

They did not speak about Martha nor about the confession Meriel had made about their daughter's death. There was nothing to say. But the truth, once told, had opened up a fault between them which neither had been able to close.

He watched her working for a moment before going out, taking the walking stick made on the Isle of Skye, which he had inherited from his father and which had accompanied both of them for miles on foot over fifty-odd years.

It was already warm, the sky cloudless, and he did not hurry. He liked to think. The previous night Cat had telephoned to say she wanted to bring the children to tea. There was some news. They had not heard from Simon for over a week. Meriel fretted. Richard did not. But he wished Simon would settle, marry, produce a family, move up his career ladder. He also wondered if he should try once more to get him to allow his name to go forward as a Freemason. The following year Richard would be Worshipful Master of his lodge. It would give him satisfaction to have his son beside him. He would phone later and offer lunch.

If he had planned to go on turning the matter over on his way home, what he saw in both newspapers took his attention away from it.

The discovery of the skeletal bodies of children in caves off the North Yorkshire coast made all the front pages. Richard stood in the village shop scanning the reports, seeing Simon's name, recalling the disappearance of the Lafferton schoolboy

333

David Angus, son of one of his own former hospital colleagues.

What kind of person did such things? Unusually, what kind of woman? A psychopath? Certainly. A damaged soul? An abused child growing up into a warped adult?

He knew the considered view, the opinion the professionals would put forward. But for him, there was no excuse, no rationale, no justification. This was a child murderer hard-wired as evil, unredeemable from birth. That such individuals existed he had never doubted. Someone, somewhere, would be concocting a case against the woman's parents, siblings, carers, minders, schoolteachers, God knew who else, all of whom would suffer the torments of guilt and self-blame for the rest of their lives. But why should they? This was no one's doing. This was the Devil stalking the earth, seeking whom to devour. Richard Serrailler was not a religious man but he had had a childhood and upbringing steeped in the Bible. And it was at times like these, he thought, still reading about the piles of small bones as he walked up the drive of Hallam House, that the Bible stood him in good stead.

He opened the front door. The percolator would be on. They might take it, with the papers, into the garden.

But to his surprise, there was no smell of coffee and the kitchen was empty.

Richard went to the window.

At first, he thought that she had tripped over the rose branch and as he hurried out he cursed himself for not dealing with it before he went to fetch the papers. But in fact she was lying a foot or so away. She had not moved the branch.

He bent down and touched her hand, then felt for the pulse in her neck. After a few seconds, he turned her over gently. Her blue eyes were open. He stroked her face with his finger. The skin was soft as chamois, and cool.

For several moments, Richard Serrailler did not leave her, only sat on the path, holding her hand. Once he said, 'Oh my darling.' The garden was hot and still around them. The secateurs lay on the path beside her, next to the trug full of weeds,

dry stalks, spent flowers. A wood pigeon made its monoton-
ous cooing sound from deep inside the holly tree.

In the end, he went inside to call Ian McKay, their GP for
thirty years. After that he rang Cat. She was taking a surgery.
No, he said to Kathy, he would not interrupt her but she must
call him straight back.

Simon was not at the station. He left a message and another,
into the middle of the Australian night, for Ivo. Then, method-
ically, he spooned coffee into the percolator, filled it with water
and put it on, before collecting a thin quilt from the airing
cupboard, and taking it outside, to lay carefully over his dead
wife. He closed her eyes and brought the quilt up to her neck,
not covering her face, so that she lay in the sun like someone
peacefully sleeping.

Sixty-three

'Jesus wept.'

Natalie read the whole of the newspaper article again more slowly. She couldn't get her head round it, couldn't take it in at all. What else were they going to find? How many more, for Christ's sake?

Kyra had gone to a theme park for the day with the Jugglers Holiday Club. The coach had left at seven and they wouldn't be back until late.

Bloody good job. Bloody . . .

It was one of the hottest days of the year and Natalie felt cold. There were goose pimples on her arms. After a minute she went upstairs. Kyra's room was still and silent and neat and clean. She looked out of the window, on to the house next door. Then she looked at the garden.

Fred West. They'd dug up the patio first, then the whole garden, then dug under the cellar. She couldn't remember how many they'd found.

Ed's flower beds were overgrown with weeds and the grass hadn't been cut. The police in white suits had poked about a bit and then gone. No one had been near. It looked a mess. Kyra kept wanting to go next door and do stuff, get the grass mown, weed the flower beds, kept saying how Ed would mind it being untidy, Ed would be pleased if they did it, Ed wouldn't like coming home and seeing it like it was. She couldn't shut her up.

336

The heat haze shimmered over the concrete path. Over the long grass.

Right.

She ran down the stairs, found the scrap of paper she'd scribbled on and rang the journalist, Lucy Groves.

'Not at my desk. Please leave a message. I'll get straight back to you.'

'It's Natalie Coombs. I've changed my mind. I said I wouldn't but I will. I'll do it.'

Natalie went out. She had to go out. Staying in and thinking about the house and garden next door was more than anyone could stand.

There was a knot of people by the gate of Ed's house. Natalie didn't recognise any of them. Gawpers. Made her shudder. She went to open her car door and they turned to gawp at her.

'Bugger off,' she shouted. 'Leave us alone, this ain't a bloody peep show, people have to live here.'

As she headed down the road, a television van was turning in. She hoped it wouldn't still be there when Kyra got back or there'd be more questions, more fretting.

She drove across town to Donna's. Donna had a new baby and no car so was mostly in.

She'd been to school with Donna and in those days they'd had plans, plans for getting out of here, plans for going abroad, plans for making a lot of money, plans for doing what you wanted not what everyone told you to, plans for getting a name in the world. Then Natalie had had Kyra and Donna, stupid cow, had taken no notice of anything she saw or Natalie said, but gone ahead and done the same, had Danny first, and now Milo who Kyra called Lilo.

Natalie had wanted to shake her, still did, except that she knew it was herself she wanted to shake. How had they got like this, when you looked back and remembered everything they'd said, planned, promised, agreed? 'No way.' They had gone through the list often enough. Men. Dead-end jobs. Drugs. Smoking. Being a slag. Babies. No way.

The only one they'd both stuck to was the drugs. No way. But sometimes Natalie thought they might as well have done drugs.

Donna was in. The front door was open and Danny was standing in the hall wearing only a T-shirt and peeing on to the stairs. Milo was screaming somewhere. Natalie knew better than to try and make herself heard by knocking or shouting out. She walked straight in to where Donna sat at the kitchen table, crying.

It took twenty minutes to change Milo, clean up Danny and the stairs and set him in front of a *Rugrats* video, make tea and listen to some of Donna's misery.

'Right,' Natalie said, 'now shut up. It's my turn. You remember all that stuff we used to say about getting out, going somewhere else and making something of ourselves, all that.'

'Yeah, right. Stuff.'

'We're gonna do it.'

Donna got up and went to the freezer drawer of the fridge and took out a tub of ice cream.

'No,' Natalie said, 'you put that right back. What good will that do? What you just been moaning about? That you're fat and spotty, right, well, why are you fat and spotty, Don? You never used to be fat and spotty – well, OK, we were all a bit spotty but not fat. You eat that all day, what do you expect? Put it down the sink. Now listen. I got plans for us, girl.'

'Plans,' Donna Campbell said, sitting down again heavily. 'Ha.'

'We're getting out of here. Going to somewhere by the sea . . . maybe North Wales, or maybe Devon, I haven't quite made up my mind, only we're going. We get there, Kyra'll be at school, yours can go somewhere two or three days, a nursery or maybe a minder, and we'll start up. In the end, we'll do proper catering, dinners and functions, but not first off, we –'

Donna put her hand up. 'Please, Miss –'

'I know.'

'You don't.'

'I'm psychic. Pick a card, any card. Word you was going to say is "Money".'

'Too right I was and that don't take a bloody crystal ball.'

'Not a problem.'

'Now you *have* taken something.'

'I am getting money. I'm getting five grand any day now, and when it's all sorted, another, wait for it, forty-five grand. Makes fifty. Fifty grand.'

Donna stared at her. She didn't argue. Natalie hadn't taken anything. Natalie didn't say things she didn't mean. She wasn't any kind of a dreamer. Donna waited.

'Next door.'

'Ed, you mean? If that's why you want to move, I'm not surprised.'

'It is and it isn't. I'm sick to death of having people knock on the door and peer through the windows and hang around outside. I'm sick of looking into that garden and –'

'– wondering what's buried.'

'T'ain't a joke, Donna. You heard the news last night?'

'I know. Couldn't get my head round it. That could have been your Kyra. Could have been Danny. Bloody hell. What's it got to do with money anyway?'

'I rang up a paper. I had a reporter come.'

'Christ, Nat.'

'I know. It's my story. "I lived next door to Ed Sleightholme." Mine and Kyra's. She's coming again Thursday. I've started off but we're going to have to see each other a few more times. She takes it all down on tape.'

'I thought they couldn't print things when there hasn't been a trial and that?'

'They can't. Only it'll all be open and shut and they pay me some money now after I've signed the contract – I have to say I won't talk to another lot – and then when the trial's over, they print the whole thing and I get the rest.'

'Fifty thousand pounds.'

'It's a lorra lorra money, Donna.'

'Jeezz.'

'And the point is, I get five thousand soon as it's signed, up front. That's enough for us to move on. How much notice do you have to give the council?'

'Month.'

'Right, same with my landlord. By the time we've done that, I've got the money and we're off. We need to sort out where, find a place to rent – we'll have to share to start with, no point in wasting money.'

'Hang on. What was the idea? You said you knew how we'd start.'

'Right. You know sandwiches? You get rubbish in most sandwiches and you buy a sandwich from a garage, more than rubbish. They're disgusting. OK, we suss out a place which has four or five garages with shops . . . and we sell them sandwiches. Good sandwiches. Sandwiches women would want to buy, lady reps and that, not truckers, they only want grease. Nice salads, good bread, organic maybe, and done up nice, little cardboard plate, napkin . . . and home-made cakes in slices . . . cost, what, about three quid a cake to make, less, sell them for one fifty a slice. They get petrol on their credit cards, they look round, grab all sorts of stuff, drinks, crisps . . . well, they'd grab our sandwiches, our cakes . . . What?'

'Just thinking what you said. "Lady reps".'

'Oh Christ.'

'Seems kind of . . .'

'Appropriate.'

Donna poured herself more tea. Her face was sad. Natalie wanted to shake her.

'Big step, Nat. I mean, it all sounds great, only –'

'Listen, you get a chance. One. This is ours. If you're not on, I'm still doing it, Don. Just rather have a mate to do it with.'

'Right.'

'Oh, for God's sake, what? What?'

'Nothing.' Donna looked at her. 'I was just imagining it. Living by the sea.'

340

They looked at one another.

From the living room came the sound of Danny singing to the *Rugrats* music and of Milo working up to a scream.

Sixty-four

It was what heaven would be. Once they had given her drugs to take the pain away for hours at a time, it was what heaven would be. No one else was in the hospital wing for three of the four days she was in there. The walls were white and there was a window through which the sun shone, on to the white walls and the white bedcover and the white pillow.

No one bothered her. She could lie for hours listening to the quiet and looking at the sun on the white walls.

She had said nothing about how she got hurt. There had been a load of questions.

'Don't know.' 'Don't know.' 'Don't know.'

So in the end they'd given up.

But this morning heaven had gone. There was no sun. Another woman had come into the wing and made retching noises half the night.

She ate breakfast. Saw the doctor. Got dressed.

Then it hit her. It hadn't hit her until now, until she was putting her feet into her shoes. The wall was grey not white and the woman was being sick again and it hit her that this was it. It. For however many years. Life. What did life mean? Life. It wasn't temporary, it wasn't a few weeks or a misunderstanding. She knew that now. They knew it, she knew it. Nothing was said. Nothing might ever be said. Didn't need to be.

Things would happen of course. People. Journeys. Questions.

Courts. However long it took, it would all happen, but at the end of it, that would be that.

Ed picked up her cup and hurled it at the wall, and when it smashed, the dregs of tea dribbled down the greyness. She watched the drips. It was hours before they stopped her from watching them and made her leave and then it all started up, more of them talking at her, more questions, the doctor, the shrink, the Governor.

The sun came out and went in again. She saw it now and again through windows or reflecting on different walls.

Once she heard a noise. She was being taken down a corridor, to see someone else, and the noise started, a hissing noise that grew and seemed to be coming at her from all sides, as if someone were spraying the sound out of a hose. They'd seen her then. They knew. Someone shouted. The hissing stopped.

She was moved. Not just out of the hospital wing. Moved to another section of the prison. She seemed to have spent the entire day walking about.

'My back's bloody killing me.'

'Not time for your painkillers yet.'

'Jesus. Where's this?'

She stood in the doorway of the new room. It was smaller. Different. There was a glass panel in the wall. An outer lobby with a chair.

'What's this for?'

'You've been moved.'

'I liked where I was.' The woman shrugged. She had two hairs on a mole under her chin. Ed wanted to pull them out. 'Where's Yvonne?'

'Who's Yvonne?'

'I want to know what's going on.'

'I said, you've been moved. You're on special watch.'

She had said nothing, answered none of the questions, but it was if they'd got a tin-opener to her brain and taken out what they wanted.

'What for?'

'Your own protection.'

It had been decided then. They knew what she'd done, so now she was on her own, no socialising, no work, no library, no gym, no canteen. Exercise in a patch on her own, in her own separate time. And watched through the glass panel twenty-four/seven.

She sat on the bed. The red-hot poker was screwing round again deep in her lower back. She lay down carefully.

It hit her again, a wall of water crashing on top of her. This was it. This room or another like it, with the glass panel. This.

She'd rather be rammed in the kidneys and made to suffer agony for it than this.

This.

The walls were beige and the window was too high for the sun to touch them. It.

Ed brought her knees up and pressed her back into the low bed against the pain.

Sixty-five

Once there had been bands playing on Sunday afternoons. The bandstand was still there, paint peeling a bit, rust showing through, but it could easily be spruced up again, Dougie Meelup thought, stopping to look. People still played in bands, didn't they? Why had it been let go?

It was hot but the park was quiet. A couple of boys threw a frisbee, a few mothers and prams were gathered on a bench.

He wandered down to the pond. The ducks had been invaded by Canada geese, which made a disgusting mess. The council had tried to round them up and get rid of them, but there'd been an outcry from some daft activists, and anyway, it would only have been temporary. Canada geese would always be back. Mothers didn't let their toddlers near to feed the ducks now, the geese were so big and pushy.

He sat on a bench some distance away and set his plastic cup of coffee down, peeled off the lid and opened his paper.

Ten minutes later, the paper rested in his hand and the coffee was going cold.

From the beginning, ever since they had been in the Devon hotel and Eileen had seen about the arrest on television, there had been a niggling voice in the back of Dougie Meelup's mind. It had been whisper-quiet then, but as the weeks had gone by and details had emerged one by one it had grown louder. He had known really. Not suspected. Known. He could never have said a word to Eileen, of course he couldn't,

345

he had said nothing at all, just tried to keep things ticking over.

He looked down at the paper in his hand. There were photographs, of the entrance to the caves, the cliffs, the police vans. The paper had made yellow and white dotted lines and arrows to mark the routes, the cave mouth. Seven, it said. So far they'd found seven.

He couldn't take it in. But he knew.

It wasn't as if it had been some vagrant, some lone man with a beaten-up car seen here, seen there, someone under suspicion, someone in the area with a record of crimes that seemed to fit. That was when you might question it, that was when anyone might doubt. Too often they seemed to pick the obvious suspect because it was easy, and then you did wonder.

Not now. How could they make this kind of mistake? How could they arrest and charge a young woman with a job and her own house and car, a neat-looking young woman with short dark hair who lived miles away from any of it, who had a respectable family and had never been in any kind of trouble. They didn't just pick a name out of the phone book.

How could they be wrong?

They couldn't.

He sipped the cooling coffee. The Canada geese had waddled off in a bunch to a muddy patch beneath the willows, leaving the mallards free for a while to circle round and round the pond.

He had come out to fetch a few bits from the shops and to buy more stamps for Eileen. Money didn't seem to be spent on anything else now except on paper and envelopes and stamps and new cartridges for the printer. He had never counted how many letters she sent out. Sometimes he looked at the names and addresses if he went out to post them for her. MP this and Lord that, bishops, actors, chief constables. There had even been one to the Queen. He had hesitated about posting it. What was the chance of the Queen reading a letter from Eileen Meelup, let alone being interested and

346

getting involved? No chance. But he thought maybe the letter would get opened by someone and that they'd be polite enough to do a printed acknowledgement. Eileen would wait. She had a chart and ticked off every reply. None of them said anything much, no one supported what she called The Fight. Why would they? He knew that if they'd read anything at all about Weeny, they would know, as he knew, that there had been no mistake. Couldn't have been.

The house was a permanent mess which he tried desperately to sort out. He shopped and cooked the meals – which Eileen only picked at – and hoovered round, but he was no good at coping with the washing and ironing, making beds, all of that. It depressed him but he felt desperately sorry for her, so that he could not have said a word against what she was doing or complained about the effect it had. Weeny was her daughter, charged with snatching and murdering little children. What could he say?

He had no heart to read the rest of the paper and even less to carry it about with him. He couldn't take it home. Eileen no longer watched or listened to the news, believing that it was all biased, all fed with false information. She need never know.

Dougie took his empty cup and the paper and buried them in the nearest litter bin. A wasp sailed out and circled his hand.

He couldn't go home. Not yet, not while it was all swirling round his head. He felt a revulsion against it and not just the news, or just Weeny, against Eileen and even his own house. He wanted to run away, catch a train to Scotland or a plane to South America. Or just walk. Walk and walk the dust and filth and horror of it off his shoes.

But after an hour he got in the car and drove home, back to Eileen and the next pile of letters begging for help in the Fight to Free Edwina, the next effort to clear up a bit, make lunch and try to get her to eat it, the next thing he could do, because he was really all she had, even though he did not believe there had been a mistake, even though, locked inside himself, was what he was certain of, what he knew.

347

Sixty-six

Richard Serrailler watched the last cars go out through the gate and away. It was still hot, the air heavy.

'Dad.' Cat came up and took his arm. 'Come with me while I feed the pony.'

'No. I would like to get back home.'

'You can't go home by yourself. Not tonight. Stay here. You'll feel better in the morning.'

'Why would I do that?'

Cat sighed. Why was it that he had always, always to be like this, always confrontational, always asking for the exact, the rational explanation behind a vague remark? He had never had small talk, never been able to ease himself into a conversation or a friendship. She wondered how her mother had sustained over forty years of marriage to someone so . . . Simon would say pig-headed.

'I don't like to think of you going back to Hallam House on your own tonight.'

'I have been there every night on my own since your mother died. I see no difference.'

'OK. You know best.'

He smiled slightly. 'Thank you for preparing the funeral baked meats. I never understand why they are provided but you provided them admirably.' He looked at the gate as if expecting a car to drive in. 'A great many people came,' he said. 'I suppose some out of curiosity. There are professional funeral-goers.'

'No, Dad. People came who knew and respected and liked and admired her. People came who wanted to say goodbye. Their feelings were genuine. Why must you be so cynical?'

She turned away, choking on her own tears. The funeral, conducted by the Dean, with Jane Fitzroy assisting, and the full cathedral choir, had overwhelmed her. The music, the words, the presence of so many people who had worked with Meriel through her professional life, and who represented the charities she had given her retirement to, the pale, awed faces of Sam and Hannah.

Simon had wept and Sam, standing beside him, had reached out and taken his hand.

And throughout it all, through his own Bible reading, through the committal at the cemetery afterwards, through greeting the dozens who had come back to the farmhouse, their father had been silent, straight-backed, tight-lipped. Unfathomable.

Cat wanted to beat him with her fists, to scream at him, to ask if he had loved her, if he was distressed, how much he missed her, whether the future frightened him, but could say none of it.

'Just come with me while I do the animals.'

He shrugged slightly, but after a long moment turned and walked with her to the paddock gate.

'The children behaved well.'

'Of course they did. They know how to. Besides, the whole thing overwhelmed them.'

She unbolted the feed store. Somehow, she had to tell him about Australia. But Australia today meant Ivo, who had not flown over for the funeral. Cat could barely bring herself to think about it. She did not think she could possibly begin to talk about their going out to the same country as her brother. Richard had shrugged off Ivo's absence with barely a word. Simon had raged and blamed. Cat knew Ivo's absence had nothing to do with Meriel. It had to do with distancing himself from his entire family, physically since the age of twenty but in every other sense since early adolescence, for complex reasons of his own and because of quarrels he himself had always instigated.

Meriel had been the one who had kept him in the family loop, with letters, phone calls, and then emails and several visits out to see him on her own. Cat and Chris had been a couple of times, Simon once.

Simon did not know about Australia either.

She scooped stud-mix into a bucket, worrying. How could she tell either of them, today, that they were leaving Lafferton for half a year? But if not today, when? There was never going to be a good day.

'Let me carry that.'

'I'm fine.'

'Just stubborn.'

'And I wonder where I get that from?'

They smiled at one another quickly and then Meriel stood between them, Cat felt her presence as strongly as if she could see her. Tell me what to do, she asked. Help me out here, Ma.

The grey pony was waiting. Cat unlatched the gate and pushed him gently away to let her pour the food into the metal holder. The hens scratched round his feet waiting for any grains that fell, though few ever did.

'Why you saddle yourself with all this I'll never know. As if a husband and three children and half a general practice were not enough.'

'As if.'

She handed him the empty bucket and bolted the gate. Then she said, 'There's something else.'

He waited in silence, giving her no help. From the farmhouse she heard Felix let out a long wail, of rage rather than distress.

'Well?'

'We're going to Australia. We've found a couple who will take over the practice and Derek will do locum. We're going for six months. It −'

Richard Serrailler began to walk away from the gate so that she had to scurry to catch up with him.

'Dad?'

'Catherine?'

She felt six years old again.

'Say something, for God's sake, tell me what you think.'

'I think your children will run wild.'

'You know what I mean.'

Silence.

'If it's too soon . . . if you'd rather we didn't go, of course we wouldn't dream of it. Or maybe you could come with us.'

'I think not. I will have a busy winter. The journal continues. There will be a great deal of work for the lodge.'

'But you'll be on your own. Of course you'll be busy, of course you have friends, but you won't have Mother or us. Family.'

'Oh, come,' he said, glancing at her slyly. 'I shall have Simon.'

Sixty-seven

'Guv? The pub's the Flaxen Maid, it's on the Golby Road. Victim is male, twenty-two years old, stab wounds to the neck and chest. Ambulance on way. Uniform got here in ten, only they'd made off, natch – someone took the car reg though.'

'Be nicked. Is the place clear?'

'Yeah, everyone scarpered when it started up. Landlord is Terry Hutton. Says it was pretty quiet tonight.'

'Does he have any take on it?'

'Nah. Or if he has, he's watching his back. My guess is it was someone who knew the bloke was in here, knew it was quiet, came in, picked a fight, got him to come outside . . . that was it.'

'The usual. Check up, see if this Hutton knew who was drinking in his pub, whether they were local. House to house then. Witnesses outside? Forensics might get something if he was in a hurry. We'll talk to the dead man's family and friends in the morning. Have they been informed?'

'Yes, and they're taking his mother and brother to the hospital now.'

'Make sure there's a trace on the car and pump the landlord again. Try and get some names. If he was a regular then who did he talk to, who did he drink with. We'll pull anyone in tomorrow.'

'Guv.'

Simon put the phone down. Another young man dead.

Another fight over drugs or money or just possibly a woman and knives out. It was routine. Patient detective work would turn up the likely suspects, routine inquiries and a bit of luck would track them down and, between them, questioning and forensics might possibly score a hit. No, make that probably. It looked like that sort of case. One of police life's less interesting. So what was 'interesting'? he thought, clearing up a couple of mugs and a plate and taking them into the kitchen. The Ed Sleightholme case. Seven children, if not more than seven, abducted and murdered and their small bodies hidden on stone ledges at the back of caves. Interesting?

He loaded the china into the dishwasher.

An hour earlier, he had left his sister's farmhouse, driving too fast, shaken at her news and unable to cope with it in the aftermath of the funeral.

'You're making more of a song and dance than Dad did.'

'That figures.'

'For God's sake, Si, it's six months, we're not emigrating. Get over it.'

Cat had been angry because she had been upset. It had come out in a rush and he had been too appalled to react calmly. He didn't want to stay in alone. The stabbing at the Flaxen Maid pub didn't warrant the overtime attention of a DCI even if he had wanted to work. Yet an absorbing job was the thing he needed.

His father came to his mind, dark suit, black tie, grey hair brushed back, basilisk-faced, cool and polite in his greetings to those who had gone back to the farmhouse. What had he felt and thought as he had stood next to his wife's coffin with its single small circlet of white flowers?

Simon had scarcely been able to bear the sight of it. He had loved his mother more than anyone apart from his sisters, the living Cat, the dead Martha. He had never fully understood Meriel but he had admired her unreservedly, enjoyed her company, laughed at her, teased her. She had driven him mad and irritated him; he had felt sorry for her, wanted to defend her, and after an hour or two, had usually needed to get away from her. But his love had never faltered or been in question. And she had loved him. He often thought no one else ever had or ever would love him so absolutely, though her love had not been uncritical.

He had thought that she was immortal.

His drawing of her was on the wall. Others were in his bedroom, and more in portfolios in the chest. He had loved to draw her elegant, but at the same time, gentle beauty. He wished he could have drawn her as a young woman. Photographs had never done her justice, and in any case, she had hated the camera.

He looked at her. She was serene and calm, her head slightly to one side. He had drawn it the previous year as she had sat in the kitchen one winter afternoon bringing her garden diary up to date, with the low sun filtering in through the window. When he closed his eyes, he was there. He could smell the faintly scented China tea in the cup at her elbow.

His eyes pricked with sudden tears.

He felt like going out and getting drunk. But he was not a man who had mates to call on for that sort of expedition. His brother-in-law would be busy at the farmhouse, Nathan either still working or back home with his pregnant wife. Drinking alone was not Serrailler's idea of fun.

And then he knew what he wanted to do; the idea dropping cleanly, satisfyingly into his mind. He was surprised by it.

Sixty-eight

'I confess I feel unequal to any more funerals,' Jane Fitzroy said, holding open the door of the fridge. 'Max Jameson, which was desperate – six people were there and two of them were your sister because she was his GP and me. My mother, for which she left explicit instructions – no religious service, no prayer, no readings, no music. Have you any idea how bleak that sort of thing is in a crematorium? Your mother's today which was triumphant but draining. I haven't any more emotion left. I do have eggs, cheese, some rather nice home-baked ham from the farmers' market and the makings of a salad. And a decent bottle of wine.'

Simon looked at her. How could she be a priest, a clergy-woman – whatever she liked to be called? She wore pale blue jeans and a white shirt with a frill down the front. Her hair was longer than when he had first seen her. Earlier, during the funeral, it had been tied tightly back and then coiled into a black silk scarf. Now it was loose and brilliant in the light through the kitchen window. She wore no make-up and looked twenty.

'Jane, I came to take you out, not to have you cook.'

She looked at him for a slow moment, as if working out the meaning of what he had said. 'I know. And I told you, I couldn't face it. I was going to watch *Ocean's Eleven*.'

'Great film.'

'The best. Brad Pitt eating pretzels.'

'Brad Pitt answering the little acrobat guy's Chinese speech – only in English.'

'Have you seen *Ocean's Twelve*?'

'Saving it up.'

'Don't bother.'

'Ah.'

She was piling things on to the table of the tiny kitchen, bowls, forks, eggs, tomatoes, avocado, the ham.

'I wish I'd known your mother better. I think we might have been friends. Maybe that's presumptuous.'

'No. Ma liked making new friends. She was good at it. It made up for my father.'

She did not ask, did not look at him, just took a bottle of Sauvignon out of the fridge.

'Dad doesn't like them. Friends.'

'Just not a people person then,' Jane said with equanimity.

'Just a bloody Freemason.'

She gave one swift glance and started to laugh. 'And you?'

'God, no.'

'I'm sorry, I shouldn't, but the whole thing just cracks me up. It's the little suitcases and the aprons and the funny hand-shakes. Honestly, boys.' She handed him a chopping board, a knife and a pile of tomatoes. 'Thin slices.'

No one, Simon thought, there has been no one in my life like this. What is it? Funny. Irreverent. Straight. Honest. Sensible. Light-hearted. All of those things. More than those. He had never imagined that a life such as Cat and Chris had would be his, a life of children and a warm kitchen, a Cat, a garden, a . . . there had been Freya. He might have had those things with Freya. Would. Might. Who knew now? He had never found out.

But after Freya, he had doubted that those were the things he even wanted.

He sliced the tomatoes wafer-thin. Jane put a glass of wine by his left hand.

'Did I tell you, they've gone back through my mother's patients? It's been so painstaking . . . they've pulled out the name of anyone they thought might have clashed with her –

356

mind you, where my mother was concerned that would be most people. But they've found three they think may have been serious about getting at her. The Inspector rang me yesterday. He's going through the files, he's talking to the other staff there. I can't really help him. She didn't talk about her patients of course. She talked about her theoretical work. The academic stuff, never the children.'

'They'll get there.'

'Ah, CID solidarity.'

'Most of it's down to trawling through the detail.'

'Is that what got you Edwina Sleightholme?'

'Oh no. Luck. Big lucky break. You need them. Do you believe in the Devil? I suppose you have to.'

'I believe in evil. The force of evil. Pure evil and evil person-ified. If that is what you meant.'

'Not sure. I'm not a theologian.'

'Nor am I. Those look OK.' She took the plate of tomatoes. 'Thanks.'

'I felt it. Evil. Looking at her. But it wasn't what I expected. It was impenetrable and pointless. Cold. Locked away. Shut up inside itself.'

'Despairing?'

'Yes. I suppose you could say that. Odd. I felt I had no point of human contact with this person, not a single spark of recognition that we belonged on the same planet.'

'Would she have gone on?'

'Yes. So long as she was alive and fit and went undetected she would have gone on. People like that can't stop. But she isn't mad.'

'Sure?'

'Absolutely and completely sure. Whatever evil is, yes, whatever mad is, no.'

He was glad they had not gone out. Out would have been different, other people, noise, interruptions. It was best like this, talking quietly, the food simple and good, coffee in an Emma Bridgewater mug on the low table beside him. He thought of Cat. When he got home he would ring her. He had

357

left the farmhouse in a bad mood and his mood was now entirely changed. Everything. Entirely. Changed. He could not stop looking at Jane.

'I've been wondering how sorry I really will be to leave,' she said.

The room went cold.

'Ah, you didn't know. Well, why would you?'

'You've only just come. Why? Is this to do with your mother?'

'No, no. I just made the wrong decision. It happens. Even to priests. I don't know why.'

'How can it be wrong? What is wrong?'

'Me. What happened in this house when Max attacked me. Plus I don't fit into the cathedral hierarchy . . . the Dean is fine, he was the one who wanted me here and pressed on until they let me in. But they don't want a woman, they're not ready for a woman, you know, and that really isn't a battle I'm going to fight. I've other things to do.'

'I thought it was a battle won.'

'Yes, you'd imagine so, wouldn't you?' She poured herself another half-glass of wine.

'Too many battlegrounds. The hospital, Imogen House . . . I'm not a fighter, Simon, I just want to get on with my work, there are more important things. I can't play politics.'

'Oh come on, why let them win?'

'That isn't a language I speak. Not in this context anyway.'

He looked at her in dismay, thinking only that he had somehow to produce enough reasons – not arguments, he sensed those would fail – to make her change her mind. He had no doubt that he would succeed. He had the best of all reasons. But he did not yet know how to put it before her.

'What about you? Lafferton for life?'

'No, this is about you. You.'

'Me?'

'What makes you think it will be different anywhere else? There are always battles. Didn't you have them before you came here?'

'Every day. And most of my growing up. My battle to go

358

to church, be baptised, read theology, go for ordination. My battles in the last parish with recalcitrant PCC and a very difficult bishop. I know all about bloody battles, thank you. I'm leaving the field.'

'What, not be a priest any longer?'

'I'll still be a priest. I'm going into a monastery for a year. After that, either I'll want to stay, or I'll go back into the academic world. I feel a Ph.D. coming on.'

He sat silent, appalled. The room was dark. Jane reached out and switched on a lamp and sat in the circle of the light. He was transfixed by her beauty, the calm way she sat not on a chair but on the floor beside him, leg bent, arms clasped round it.

'Jane . . .'

'People have quite the wrong idea,' she said, 'about convents.'

'I don't have any idea about them, I only know you can't incarcerate yourself in one.'

'See what I mean?'

'Christ, you'd be . . . walling yourself up. For what? To do what?'

'If I say "to pray", I don't expect much of a response. Leave it.'

'I can't leave it.'

'Why? Why is this something that always gets people so worked up? I don't want to argue, I don't want a battle. Please.'

'Go and do your Ph.D., if that's what you want you should do that.'

'Later. Maybe. Maybe not. The other first.'

For a long time there was a silence so complete, so absolute, that he did not know if he could ever breach it, ever utter again, ever be able to say another word to her for the rest of his life. The silence was a distance and a time span as well as the absence of sound. It was a space he did not think he had the nerve or the skill through which to travel.

He said, 'I don't want you to do this.'

She looked puzzled.

'Please don't.'

'It is rather rude when people say "What has it to do with you?", but all the same –'

'It *has* to do with me.'

'How? You don't even come to the cathedral.' She sounded bewildered too, at a loss to follow him.

'It's got nothing to do with the cathedral.'

'Or anything. I'm not a police chaplain, I'm –'

'Christ. No. Not the jobs . . . you.'

He stood up and walked to the window. He remembered standing on the other side talking to Max Jameson. The bushes had been cut back so that he could see the lights of the Precentor's house, shining out on to the garden.

'I want to see you. I want you to stay here.'

She laughed. It was a light laugh, not unkind, not mocking. But she laughed before she spoke. 'Simon, you don't know me. You've hardly met me.'

'I want to know you. I came to take you out because of that. This is better, to be here. But the next time we'll go out.'

'No. No next time. Thank you. I'm flattered and I have really enjoyed your company. It wasn't an evening for either of us to be alone. But that has to be all.' She got up. She came to the window to stand beside him, and touched his arm. 'Simon, we could have been good friends, we might have worked together. Any of that. I'm very glad you came this evening. But now you should go.'

The blood did not seem to be moving through his veins. It was a warm night and he felt cold.

'Simon?'

'Why is it such an appalling idea – for us to see more of each other?'

'Because I'm the wrong person. You have to take my word for that.'

'I can't, I need to know why.'

'I don't want anyone. I never have. I have – other things.'

'For God's sake, Jane, don't waste yourself, how can you think of it?'

'I wasn't thinking of it. I'm not staying in Lafferton, for all the reasons you heard, none of them to do with you. How could they be to do with you, you're virtually a stranger. I'm not staying here, there wouldn't be any point. I don't want to deceive you, Simon. That would be wrong. You're a nice man.'

'Why does that sound like something I don't want to be?'

She smiled. 'You deserve the right person and that can't be me. It just can't and I'm not prepared to try to explain any further.'

When he left to walk up through the garden back into the Cathedral Close it was almost as warm as it had been in the middle of the day. The air was quite still. Simon turned not left towards his own end of the close but right and out of the gate into the warren of cobbled streets leading to the square. People were about, sitting on benches, piling out of the pubs, eating late in a couple of Chinese and Thai restaurants. He watched two young men and a woman swaying about in the middle of the road, the worse for drink but at the moment causing no trouble. A family strolled with a toddler high on its father's shoulders and a boy bouncing about at his feet. He remembered those nights, when it was too hot to sleep and he had leaned out of his window for hours, smelling the night smells, talking to his brother in whispers. No one would ever have suggested bringing them out to enjoy the late-night town. He smiled at the thought and remembered his mother with a sense of pure anguish at the loss of her. Loss. He felt as if he had never won. He knew he was being maudlin and could not have cared less, let alone help himself out of the pit of misery into which Jane Fitzroy's response had tipped him. He was angry too but not with her, only with himself for being a fool.

He reached a corner where the town, the shops and pubs and cafés, started to give way to residential streets. The Old Town. The grid called the Apostles. Beyond here lay the Hill. Beyond the Hill, the broad avenues of the more prosperous Lafferton suburbs. Sorrel Drive. And so on, to the bypass and the Bevham Road, other ways to the country, to his sister's village, to that of his parents – father, he checked, just father now. East and you eventually came to Starly Tor and then Starly, home to a fat cluster of New Age therapists and ley lines.

He turned back. He had always loved this place. He knew it better than he knew himself. But it was changing. A gang of teenage girls was sitting in the gutter. One was trying to take off her clothes. One was being sick. Two were wielding disposable cameras and shrieking. He skirted round them. Obscenities drifted after him. Even five years ago the girls would not have been there. He met the family with the small children, piling into a car, both boys asleep like felled logs.

What did he want? Jane. Love. Children. A life like his sister's. Jane?

Yes. Her image was fixed in his mind as she sat on the floor beneath the lamp, her leg bent up, arms round it, hair like an angel's.

He had been on the brink of falling in love with Freya Graffham and if she had lived would almost certainly have fallen out of it. Diana he had been fond of. Never loved. There had been other women but none for whom he had had any serious feeling. Some had loved him. Perhaps a lot of them. He had taken care not to know.

Jane.

He could not think of her in some ghastly habit immured in a convent – call it a monastery, call it whatever, it was a lot of women cooped up with their frustrations and hysteria together. The thought made him sick. At least if she had wanted to go back into university life there was some hope for her. No, not for her. He meant, hope for him. He would have been able to contact her, write to her, see her, pursue her, persuade her. How in God's name could he follow her into a bloody nunnery?

He reached the archway leading to the close. The cathedral stone was bathed soft silver in the floodlights. Simon hesitated. He would go back. Make her listen to him. He had never wanted anything so much.

He stood. He could not go near her again.

362

'Oh, for fuck's sake,' he said aloud.

He went quickly down the avenue, unlocked his car and got in.

Ten minutes later, he was spinning on to the forecourt of the station. No one would be about much. There was always paperwork to kill off fast while it was quiet and he was not likely to be interrupted. There was always work.

'Guv? Anything up?' The duty sergeant looked from his computer to the DCI in surprise.

'Nope,' Simon said, heading for the stairs. 'Not a thing.'

'Glad to hear it.' The sergeant bent his head and resumed his soft tapping at the keyboard.

'Not a thing.'

He worked until almost two o'clock. He cleared his desk. On his way out, one of the police vans was unloading three of the girls he had seen earlier. One had dried blood down the side of her face.

'Who you fuckin' lookin' at? I'll fuckin' have you for fuckin' harassment, fuckin' men.'

There were two messages on his home answerphone, one from the Chief Constable.

'Simon. Paula Devenish. I'd like to run something past you. Is there any chance you can come over to headquarters tomorrow morning around eleven?'

The other was from his father.

'I was hoping to find you in. I wondered if we might have lunch at some point. Would you be so good as to call me?'

Simon poured himself a whisky. The flat was hot. He opened all three of the tall windows to let the night air drift in.

The Chief. The previous occasions on which she had asked to see him and it had not been about an ongoing case had been to suggest he might like to head up the new drug squad and next if he were interested in something similar in the area of Internet paedophile crime. Perhaps this time it would be traffic management. Jesus. But he would have to go across to HQ, just as he would have to call his father first thing in the

363

morning and arrange to have lunch and another bout of pressure to become a Freemason.

But there had been the faintest trace of something in Richard Serrailler's tone, which Simon hesitated to label 'need' but which was certainly a plea.

There was no one to answer it but himself.

Sixty-nine

The Chief had said she would like to see him around eleven o'clock but there was no 'around' about her appointments. Her door opened to him as his watch hands touched the hour.

'Two things, Simon . . . the child abduction cases. If North Riding forensics eventually come up with a positive identification of David Angus's remains, it occurred to me that his mother might want to go up there. It sometimes helps. What would be your take on that?'

The picture of the beach and the soaring cliffs above it came into his mind and then the dark, dank cave with its high shelf on which he had touched the piles of small bones. He shook his head. 'It isn't like the pleasant grass verge beside an RTA scene after everything's been cleaned up.'

'I know. All the same.'

'Do you want me to get in touch with her?'

'Wait till we have the results. Then go and see her. Give her the opportunity. If she wants you to go up there with her, you should.'

The door opened. Her secretary brought in a tray of coffee and biscuits. I'm being softened up, Serailler thought. Traffic management.

'I have been in some ACPO meetings with the Home Office,' Paula Devenish said. 'There's a new initiative.'

'And it would be cynical of me to say "What – another?"'

She smiled. 'This one is a runner. One or two of us were asked to put forward special candidates.'

If this had come out of the Association of Chief Police Officers in conjunction with government at least it wasn't likely to be traffic management.

'Essentially it's this. There will be a special team – an Exceptional Crimes Special Task Force – consisting of five or six senior CID officers hand-picked from different forces. You are the only name I want to put forward from this force, Simon. Tell me what you think?'

'What would you be putting my name forward as, precisely? May I ask?'

'Of course. To head it up.'

'I don't have the rank.'

'The rank of Detective Superintendent would come with the job. That would almost certainly become DCS within the first year.'

'This new force would be based where?'

'Each member would remain as they are with secondment to the task force when called. But in fact I'd want you to come here to HQ.'

'As?'

'DS.'

'And "Exceptional Crimes" to mean?'

'That's a bit of a compromise word. More than "Serious". We argue that we take all crime seriously but clearly there's major and there's minor. Exceptional is something else.'

'The murdered children.'

'Oh yes. Harold Shipman would be another example. It excludes organised crime and as you know for the most part that means drugs, or anything dealt with by Immigration, Special Branch and so on. I think it's a case of recognising something as Exceptional when it turns up.'

Simon finished his coffee. 'Take your first reaction seriously' had been a motto of his for a long time, in work especially. It was a variation on 'obey your instincts'. His first reaction to this had been a gut one. Excitement. Promise. Yessss. After that would have to come the deliberation, the weighing up.

But he knew that the Chief appreciated a direct and immediate response, whether or not it was what she wanted to hear.

'First reaction?' she pre-empted him.

'Is – yes. Certainly yes to having my name put forward. That may be as far as it gets of course.'

'There'll be competition, that goes without saying. Whether it'll be what I'd call Good or Stiff competition . . .' She shrugged. 'I'm backing you, Simon. I have a meeting at the HO on Friday.'

He raised an eyebrow. But Paula Devenish stood up. 'I knew you'd be up for this.'

'Thank you, ma'am.'

'Simon. Sorry we're losing young Nathan Coates by the way.'

'So am I. But he needs to spread his wings and he'll love it up there. Jim Chapman had him in his sights from the start.'

'I rather feared he might have you in them as well. That was another reason for me to move on this task force. And let me know what Mrs Angus wants to do.'

A reminder, as he left. Not that Marilyn Angus would slip his mind when the confirmation came that her son's body had been one of those in the cave.

He got into his car and put in a call to Cat. She had just finished surgery.

'You going home?'

'Hi, bro. Good God, what do you think GPs' lives are like?'

'You're part-time.'

'Ha.'

'Time for lunch?'

'What's happened?'

'Stuff, as Sam would say.'

'You can have half a sandwich here.'

'Take an hour off . . . meet me at the Horse and Groom at half twelve.'

He switched off before she could argue.

*

367

The pub, celebrated for miles for its good food, was already filling up when he got there at twelve fifteen. He bagged a table and sat with his beer beside the open door leading into the small garden. Sunlight flooded in. There was a tree laden with early plums. Simon felt suddenly optimistic. He wanted the new job. He was surprised at how much he wanted it. Perhaps the Chief could work miracles. He did not let his mind dwell on Jane Fitzroy or on the previous evening. He felt the raw smart of rejection, though she had been gentle and generous; he thought she had not been snubbing him personally so much as turning away from any close relationship, for her own particular reasons. If he allowed himself to mull over what had happened he knew that he would have begun to feel more guilty about how he himself had behaved towards Diana.

The pub was buzzing when Cat blew in just before one. 'You look unravelled.'

'Tell me. God, I'm hungry, I haven't had a decent lunch in ages, unless it was cooked by me.' The menu blackboard hung on the wall opposite. 'I'm having the lot. I've got a clinic this afternoon and I'm doing an evening locum for Derek Wix. God knows when I'll eat again.'

'And this is the woman who was having half a sandwich. Make the most of it.'

'Right . . . crab and avocado salad, then the sea bream. And a ginger beer.'

Simon looked across at his sister from the bar as he waited to order. Unravelled was about right but Cat looked happy. She had lost the last of the weight she had found so hard to shift after the birth of her third baby, she was tanned, she looked younger.

'It's the prospect of Australia,' he said, setting down her drink. 'Given you a sparkle.'

'Thanks. Cheers, Si. Do you know, I am really, really looking forward to it now. You're dead right. I didn't want to go, I resisted like mad, but now it's all sorted, I am so longing for a new life for a bit. Lots of sun and sea and surfing and that lovely laid-back Oz attitude.'

368

'Don't get too keen.'

'No. We'll be back, never fret. Apart from anything, there's Dad.'

'He left me a message last night. Wants to lunch.'

'Bring him here.'

'It'll be about bloody Freemasons.'

'You've fought that one off before. He'll be lonely, Si. They were married a long time.'

'Hm.'

'I know. Ma had a tough row to hoe but I think things got better, you know. Something happened between them in the last year or so. I don't know what. But something. Things were better.'

'I was dreading it. You going off, having to field Dad on my own.'

'But?'

'The Chief sent for me this morning.'

Cat's salad and his fresh sardines arrived. She ate and listened while he told her about the task force.

'I daren't think about it because I may well not get it. It'll be tough competition. Paula has a good standing among our masters but her colleagues will fight dirty for their own candidates over this one.'

'You want it.'

He squeezed lemon over his fish. The smell of them, mingling with the sharp citrus, was pungent and delicious. 'I really, really want it,' he said.

'I'd better put you high up on the prayer list then.'

'Shouldn't think a job for me would get top priority.'

He watched her pile the last few creamy flakes of crab on to her fork. He wanted to tell her about Jane. They had become friends, he knew, though they did not see a great deal of each other. But Cat might ask, might put in a word, might . . .

No.

If he told her what had happened on the previous evening he knew precisely what his sister would say. 'Serve you bloody well right. The shoe's on the other foot, so how does it feel?'

He was not going to be humiliated by Cat and he could not face either the brisk talking to or the sympathy. He was taken aback by the feelings Jane had stirred in him. They were new, keen and wholly unexpected, and they had been trodden on. It was too private. He had never kept very much from his sister but he was keeping this.

'Did I tell you about the house in Sydney? Two storeys, big garden all round, balcony, right on the sea, twenty minutes from the surgery – which is new and purpose-built for three medical practices. The schools . . .'

He listened. She was raring to go. He hoped to God they would, as she promised, also want to come back.

They lingered over puddings and coffees. 'This has to do you,' Cat said. 'Till next May.'

'I'll miss you all but it will fly by, especially if this job comes off – don't hold your breath – and you'll be back. Ma won't.'

'It didn't sink in until last night, you know. Not really. It was something Hannah said about Hallam House . . . that the garden would be sad, because Grandpa wouldn't know how to do it properly.'

'She's right there. It'll be mow, chop, done. He can't stay there. He'll rattle. He'll be desperately lonely.'

'Don't think of telling him that.'

'As if.'

They wandered out to the cars. 'Thought you were in a rush.'

'So did I. Been good.' She stopped and looked at him. 'What is it? Just Ma?'

'Sure.'

'Liar.'

'I can't talk about it.'

That was as much as he could bear to say. Cat put her arm through his. 'Go easy on yourself.'

His mobile rang. Nathan Coates. Simon listened to the brief sentence.

'What?'

'I have to go from here to call on Marilyn Angus. To tell her forensics have reported on their findings in the cave.'

'David?'

He nodded. Cat reached out, hugged him, then waved as she drove away.

Simon stood for a few seconds in the sun. They had been among the last to leave. It was quiet. A party of newly-fledged swallows swooped and dived high above his head. Tears came into his eyes, and the bright face of David Angus as it had appeared on posters and in the media day after day.

He zapped the locks on his car and opened the door but then stood a moment longer, watching the swallows, looking up at the sky.

Seventy

'It is so pointless,' Marilyn Angus said. 'Perhaps that's the hardest thing. The thought that it is all pointless.'

There was drizzle and low mist though the air was mild. Serrailler wondered if that were better, if a glorious sunlit day on a golden beach would have made the thing more painful or whether that was simply irrelevant.

He had driven them up during the night. She had wanted to be there at dawn, she said, but would not stay anywhere, so that they had travelled, for the most part in silence, up the network of motorways among the long-distance container lorries, and he had had no words of comfort, nor did she and Lucy expect any. But 'I want *you* to be there,' she had said, 'only you. No strangers. No one else. Please.'

They parked on the hard sand a couple of hundred yards away. The tide was going out. It was a little after five.

From here they could see the fluttering black-and-yellow police tape. They walked slowly and in silence, Lucy Angus keeping herself a few feet apart, quite separate, her eyes down. Once or twice she stopped to look at a coil of sand-worms or a starfish caught in a tiny pool between low rocks but she did not speak and Marilyn Angus walked on, looking straight ahead, as if her daughter were not there.

The wind blew off the sea, bearing a salt spray. Gulls flapped in the sky and settled in droves on the cliffs, making their ugly, rawking cry.

A couple of yards from the cordoned-off area they stopped. There was no police presence here this morning, at Marilyn Angus's request, and the forensics team would not arrive for another few hours.

'Will you stay here now please?'

'I need to show you –'

'No. We've got the torches. I can manage.'

'All right. Go to the back of the cave and – the ledge is above your head. Be very careful on the scaffolding. The flashlight is pretty powerful.'

Marilyn hesitated. Lucy stood, silent and separate, half turned to look out to the sea.

'Lucy?' Simon said. 'If you don't want to go in, stay with me here.'

But without a word she detached herself from them and walked under the tape and into the cave mouth without hesitating or glancing back. After a moment, Marilyn Angus followed her, though at the entrance she stopped, so that Simon thought she was unable to face it and would retreat.

He waited.

The gulls called, rose up and wheeled round.

Marilyn went slowly forward, holding the torch up and ahead of her, into the cave.

He strode along the beach. After two or three miles, he saw the path leading from the clifftop and the ledge on which he had crouched with Ed Sleightholme, waiting for the rescue helicopter. He stared up at it. From here, he saw that it was sheer, the path narrow and crumbling away at the sides, the ledge barely wide enough to hold them. Simon shivered. He walked slowly now, thinking, but having to steer his thoughts quickly away from so many things that preoccupied him, from his mother, from Jane, from Cat and her family going to the other side of the world, from his father's inevitable vulnerability. From the children whose lives had ended on a ledge in a dank, cold cave burrowed back into a cliff. From the possibility that he might not get the job he increasingly wanted.

He wondered if he could ever return here on a clearer day and draw the cliffs with their extraordinary outcrops and shadows, draw the gulls perched on the ledges and wheeling about the sky.

He walked away from the cliffs towards the sea. More gulls rode the waves, bobbing like corks. If he had simply been here by himself he would have begun to enjoy himself, in spite of the greyness and the drizzle. The sense of space and emptiness refreshed him so that he stopped going over things in his mind, anticipating the months to come, fretting, and simply let himself revel in the freedom. He picked up a couple of stones and tried to skim them without success, walked nearer to the water's edge so that he could hear the waves pulling back into themselves, rolling over and falling, rolling and falling.

He realised that he had been out there on his own for a long time. He had seen no one. He glanced at his watch. They had been in the cave for almost an hour. Simon began to run.

Marilyn Angus was sitting on the wet sand at the very back of the cave, her hand up to touch the slippery rock face, her head bent to rest on her arm. She was silent, not crying, scarcely seeming to breathe. Feet away from her, face averted, staring out to the open world, the sky, the grey sea, Lucy stood, still as stone. It was like some terrible tableau into which the two were locked, unable to move together or to break free, unable to do anything but stay, trapped in their own thoughts, their own separate and unreachable grief.

Simon edged back, away from them, out of the cold, seaweed-smelling darkness and stood, his jacket collar pulled up against the rain, staring at the distant water. Waiting.